RIVER

FAWCETT COLUMBINE • NEW YORK

RIVER

A
Novel of
The Green
River Killings

RODERICK THORP

River is a work of fiction. While based upon the public record of a series of murders committed in the Pacific Northwest during the early 1980s, the story, the characters, and their thoughts and actions are products of the author's imagination. Any resemblance to real living people is not intended and should not be inferred.

A Fawcett Columbine Book
Published by Ballantine Books

LIBRARY OF CONGRESS CATALOGING-IN-PUBLICATION DATA
Thorp, Roderick.
River / Rod Thorp.
p.   cm.
ISBN 0–449–90704–X
1. Serial murders—Washington (State)—Green River Region—Fiction. 2. Police—Washington (State)—Green River Region—Fiction. 3. Green River Region (Wash.)—Fiction. I. Title.
PS3570.H67R58   1995
813'.54—dc20   94–27631   CIP

Manufactured in the United States of America

First Edition: July 1995

10 9 8 7 6 5 4 3 2 1

For Claudia
AND
for Our Granddaughters,
Carolyn, Lucy, Stacey, and Valerie

The author wishes to express his gratitude
to Alicia Agos and Daniel Holster.

The paradox is that evil comes from man's urge to heroic victory over evil.

—ERNEST BECKER, *ESCAPE FROM EVIL*

I always knew it was him.

—A MEMBER OF THE GREEN RIVER TASK FORCE

TRIGGER

August 1982

The interior of the Ford roared under the hammering of the hard steady rain. Boudreau switched the ignition key off and sat still, bracing himself for the soaking to come. Beyond the end of the dirt track a necklace of boiling red, white, and blue lights looped a hundred yards down a gloomy slope of waist-high weeds. In the distance figures in black-and-yellow slickers moved with seeming aimlessness, like grazing cattle, in the reeds and cattails at the river's edge. Boudreau checked the vehicles. Cops from three jurisdictions. No, four, because the federals were here. On the crest, held at bay by another black-slickered officer, a cluster of people watched the activity below with the twitchy intensity of fight fans. The media, fifteen or sixteen reporters and camera operators. The radio call that had fetched Boudreau had been the tip that this was a Big Deal.

"Boudreau, get back to me on the landline ASAP, will you? We need your help on something."

And then, a few minutes later, over the telephone: *"Boudreau, they got a dead kid floating in the Green River. It might be one of your girls. Run down there and check her out, will you?"*

Sure, but why the rush? One of his girls rarely got such attention in life, and afterward he was never called until she was tagged UNIDENTIFIED on a stainless-steel table. Boudreau turned up the collar of his raincoat, pulled his hat down over his brow, and stepped out of the car. The rain hit him hard, not the usual heavy mist that drifted out of Puget Sound, but a true summer storm in from the mid-Pacific. The people on the crest saw him slogging along the track, but their attention returned quickly to the main action at the water's edge, where a couple of detectives were erecting a screen as high as an upright piano. No film at eleven, someone had decided. That was fine with Boudreau, who had a cop's distaste for television news.

Three years ago he had spent a week touring the Pike and Pioneer Square, Seattle's most notorious districts, with a young KIRO-TV reporter who showed up for ride-alongs wearing three-hundred-dollar dresses and real pearls to complement her bouncy, perfect, blond pageboy 'do. Haughty, ambitious, a twenty-three-year-old know-it-all who contemptuously pumped him for sexual scandal among the local pols—who but a vice detective would know the city's most spectacular gossip? He had shined her on, sensing that confiding in her would only lead to trouble. A month later she was on the air telling Seattle that his first name was Felix. Actually, it was Philippe. *Phil*, for those who couldn't handle French. For weeks both his fellow cops and the street people sang the "Felix the Cat" theme song when they saw him coming. He never bothered to phone in a correction to the television station. Last year the young lady moved on to Chicago, where she was now a weekend anchor with a reputation for being hard-assed and street-smart.

Boudreau made his way down the hill in the rain past cars from King County and the suburban city of Kent, the unmarked federal cars, and three or four Seattle cars. The Emerald City had something at stake here. And federal presence so early in the game always meant they had been invited. Why? Boudreau took another quick glance around as he tried to get his brain up to speed. A King County detective he knew tapped another on the shoulder. The second man turned around.

Ronald Beale, newly appointed captain of King County Major Crimes. Beale was fifty, gaining weight, his stubbly gray crew cut receding from his temples. Even with the rain dripping from his heavy brows, Beale had the fish-eyed, baleful stare of a career law-enforcement bureaucrat. Beale especially disliked Boudreau. Beale was an elder in his church and he was sure that a New York–born, nonreligious Seattle vice cop who disliked him back was helping himself to samples. Fundamentalists like Beale always amused Boudreau. He guessed Beale was hatless today because he wanted to show that even a driving rain couldn't cramp his safe-in-the-arms-of-the-Lord, macho asshole style. Everyone else was puffy with the humidity.

"Boudreau," Beale said, glancing at the other cops, "we just want you to take a look at this and tell us if you know her. You might want to take it easy on yourself. You vice guys don't see many stiffs, especially in this condition. She's been in the water awhile."

Was the needling necessary? Boudreau would have thought that Beale wouldn't bother to try to impress the federal suits in the crowd. Boudreau was having trouble figuring out who had called them. Back east twenty years ago, when Boudreau's father had been a detective on the NYPD, the locals and federals had despised each other. Q: Why were they buddy-buddy now over what looked like a simple murder? A: Appearances were deceiving. An inch or two shorter than most of the men here, Boudreau nodded to those he knew as he followed Beale to the water's edge. Umbrellas opened as Boudreau stepped around the screen and found himself standing over the body of a teenage girl.

The heavy, swollen body had been dragged onto the shore less than a foot from the swiftly moving water. The body was wrapped loosely in black plastic, the work of the killer. Men wearing hospital greens under their slickers stepped back to give him a better view. The medical examiner's troop. Nobody seemed to be in a hurry—had they waited for him? After Boudreau had gotten the call, he had taken nearly an hour to drive here. He didn't get down this way much, and never to the Green River. The city of Kent wasn't much more than a suburban slum, cheap crackerbox houses fenced off from garbage-strewn empty lots. Now Boudreau could see that the river was the town's appropriate waterway, a churning yellow broth carrying away the area's household and industrial detritus. One of the ME's people reached down to move the black plastic away from the torso. Disturbing the plastic released a stifling whiff of the stench of death. Boudreau forced himself to focus on the dead kid.

"Terrible," he said aloud, his eyes involuntarily rolling up to the fouled riverside, the flat sky, the drenching rain. Suddenly it was an awful day, the worst.

"What did you say?"

Boudreau didn't recognize the voice. He had no answer he wanted to utter aloud. What the hell was he doing here? He forced himself to look again. This body was a long way from having been a human being. Fifteen or sixteen years old, so badly bloated and chewed on, covered with the river's waste and insect larvae, that even her age was only a shot in the dark. Eyes gone. Naked except for her brassiere tied tightly around her discolored neck. Her cheeks bulged. What was left of her tongue, blackened and the diameter of a banana, protruded from her mouth. The body looked as if it could burst. Dirty-blond hair? Boudreau had to imagine her with some kind of light and movement in her eyes. A pretty kid? No. Malnourished, more likely, a drug user, even an addict. Maybe as old as seventeen, if she had been small for her age. A picture was beginning to dance before Boudreau's eyes. Did he know her after all or was his mind playing desperate tricks? Now he saw a tattoo on the inside of her thigh, a tiny dagger. He knew her. The realization hit him so hard he winced. He heard the rain again. A real face appeared, came alive, smiled. A face and a name, a street name. He turned around and spoke without hesitation.

"Yeah, I know her. Called herself Hot Lily, the way street kids do. I have her real name in my monicker file."

"How do you get that?" Beale asked, his eyes narrowed. "Look again, there's something else we want you to see. What do you get from that bruise on her neck?"

Boudreau had not known he was looking at a bruise. He saw it now, almost on the side of her neck, under the brassiere strap, a dark, straight mark more than an inch wide and four or five inches long. He shook his head. Moving closer, Beale said, "Would you mind telling us how you make her from a tattoo on the inside of her thigh?"

Boudreau was looking at the body again. He drew a breath and said, "Last year she was living with a pimp named Uhuru. Big sweaty black guy with a ring through his nipple. A great American. I went up to his place to ask him about something. Another case. The kid here was naked. Stayed that way. She paraded it around in front of me." Boudreau eyed Beale. He remembered the something he had gone to talk to Uhuru about, a report about a missing girl, a hooker, but what he was seeing here, all this authority focused at this moment on him, made him want to be dead-slow cautious about volunteering anything.

"What do you mean, she paraded it?"

Boudreau recognized the voice as the one that had asked what he had said a moment ago. He looked the guy over. Black hair and blue eyes. An Irishman? The FBI liked Irishmen. Boudreau took a breath and answered, "They like to flaunt it. You should work my beat sometime. I see pussy the way a dentist sees cavities."

"All right, that's enough," the guy said. With a dead child at their feet, he worried about dirtymouth. Boudreau asked, "How long has she been in the water?"

"Maybe a week," Beale said. "Can you find this guy Uhuru?"

"I don't know. Sometimes he's on the circuit—"

"Circuit?" parroted the FBI.

"Vancouver, Portland, Reno. It's how they flee prosecution."

"You've got a strange beat, Boudreau," the FBI said.

He was like a seventh-grader looking for a fight in a schoolyard, Boudreau decided. He kept his eyes averted.

"Aren't you going to answer me?"

"What for?"

"I asked you a question."

"No, you made a statement. You want to ask me a question, start it with who, what, where, or whatever."

The guy bared his teeth. Maybe he was trying to grin. "All right, don't you think you have a strange beat?"

"I might think it was strange, if I was a guilt-ridden, anal-retentive, Irish-Catholic asshole like you."

"Watch your mouth!"

"Fuck you."

The guy moved forward, just like a kid in a schoolyard, until his training or age took over and forced him to restrain himself. Beale stepped between them, turning to the ME's people. "Open her legs."

Hot Lily's legs were spread and lifted as she would have done herself in life for sexual intercourse. Nested in her pubic hair was something metallic, small. Brass. "What is that?" Boudreau asked.

"Looks like a bullet," Beale said, watching him.

Boudreau saw another bullet behind the first. Her vagina could be full of bullets. He faced Beale again, keeping his eyes away from the FBI. "You want me to ask around about a guy who puts bullets in it?"

"Those are thirty-eight-caliber hollow points, the same as I have in my revolver, and all the other guys here who aren't carrying nine-millimeters. I don't want you to ask anybody anything about this until you hear from us again, do you understand? Keep your mouth shut." Beale tilted his head toward the group on the side of the hill. "And in particular don't talk to *them*. Don't talk to *anybody*. This is not your case. And we want your monicker file."

Over Beale's shoulder Boudreau spotted a city of Kent patrolman who was riveted to every word. A young guy, twenty-five or so, with blond hair, blue eyes, thin lips, and a heavy jaw. He was paying such close attention he looked afraid to blink. Beale wasn't asking what kind of a piece Boudreau was carrying. Maybe he knew it was a thirty-eight. Beale had the clout to pull Boudreau's file. "I'll copy Hot Lily's sheet for you," Boudreau said, trying to ignore the young patrolman's darting eyeballs.

"You weren't listening," Beale said. "I want the whole file. Everything you have."

Boudreau pulled himself up and drew another breath. No matter: just that quickly, he was wrestling with an anger as strong and slippery as an octopus. "You know better than that. You'll get a copy. A copy of the whole damned monicker file, if that's what you want."

"That's exactly what I want."

Not exactly what he had said, but Boudreau decided against telling him—and against asking if Beale wanted him to canvass the girls on the Pike about a guy who was posing as a cop. The thought had not even faded when the face of an asshole who got off on pretending to be a cop flashed into memory and was gone again. Boudreau blinked, dizzy suddenly. For a moment the face wanted to elude him, but years of practice with remembering faces let Boudreau draw it up once more. A face with a name and a whole long story to go with it. Boudreau knew him. A woman-hater, completely crazy. *Yes! He was the one! He was a perfect fit!*

Suddenly Boudreau was fixing the guy's name, trying not to hyperventilate. He wanted to check his watch. How much time had he passed here? Not five minutes. Two? Cracked the case! *CRACKED THE FUCKING CASE!* For a moment he thought he was going to black out. "And you want that immediately, eh?"

"You got it. And keep your mouth shut."

"I understand. Where do you want me to send the file? The copy." The crowd parted again to let him through.

"To me," Beale said. "Send it to my office."

Boudreau started away, his heart thumping in his chest. His stomach fluttered, and his skin prickled with nervous sweat. He could feel the FBI idiot's eyes on him all the way. When he was fifteen feet from the group he heard a heavy movement. The young Kent patrolman was falling in step behind him. A tail? No, it was too blatant to be a tail. The kid wasn't concerned with being seen, apparently, but Boudreau didn't know enough about what was going on here to decide if that was a good thing or bad. If the kid didn't understand the seriousness of the situation, he was the last guy Boudreau wanted for a new friend. Boudreau kept going, pacing himself, trying to get a grip on his emotions. You could never tell what a screwball like Beale was up to, but the FBI? That FBI idiot? He and Beale were a lethal combination. Now the press started yelling.

"Detective Boudreau! Were you able to identify the victim?"

"How old is she?"

"Who is she?"

Boudreau didn't recognize the guy who had called him by name, but he knew a few of the others by sight—their television images. A woman shoved a microphone at him.

"What were the objects found in the girl's vagina?"

Beale wanted secrecy? The young woman had an unpleasant, whiny way of pronouncing *vagina*. Boudreau shook his head and tried to move on.

"Phil, did you know the girl?"

A voice he knew. He stopped to look at a guy from the *P-I*, the Seattle *Post-Intelligencer,* whom he had known for almost a decade. Boudreau gestured to the crime scene behind him. "You'll get it from them."

The microphone was thrust up again. "Tell us about the objects in the *vagyynuh*, detective. What are the objects in the *vagyynuh*?"

Boudreau locked her eyes for a moment. The kid from Kent was right beside him. Boudreau gave a shuddering sigh. "Rocks," he heard himself mutter, and turned away. He had meant to add, *Like the ones in your head.* He knew he had made a big mistake even before he heard three people repeat the word. *Rocks?*

More than a big mistake. No end of trouble.

The Kent kid stayed behind him until they were up on the dirt track, and then Boudreau heard faintly the jangle of keys that meant the kid had reached his own car. At the head of the line, which made sense. A city of Kent car would have been first on scene. Boudreau knew he was not calming down. He continued to his car, thinking as he got in that the kid wasn't in any hurry here, either, or maybe he was only adding to his notes now that he was out of the rain.

No. The kid's cruiser swung out behind Boudreau's plainwrap Ford as it started rolling and stayed a short, not-discreet distance back. Boudreau watched the cruiser in the rearview mirror as he reached the two lane highway and threw on a directional signal. The kid signaled he was going the same way, away from downtown Kent and its police headquarters. A quarter mile to the four-lane north. Another signal, another response in the mirror. Around the corner, Boudreau pulled onto the gravel shoulder and turned on his four-way emergency lights.

The kid pulled up behind him, touched the siren once for a *WHOOP!*, and lit up the rack on the roof. Boudreau unlocked the passenger-side door and turned the wipers off. As the kid got in a stream of water poured from the rain gutter onto the floor.

"Mine does the same fucking thing," the kid said agitatedly. "You'd think they could build them so they don't piss on you every time." He stuck out a thick, hardened mitt. "Wayne Spencer. How're ya doin'?"

"Phil Boudreau." He shook the hand. "Spencer? You look like a Norwegian to me."

"I take after my mother. Most people can't even identify Scandinavians when they see them. You know the differences?"

"Nah. I could smell the *lutefiske* on your breath."

Spencer laughed. In addition to his fair coloring and heavy jaw, he had the sloping shoulders and big, square head of some Norwegian types. When Boudreau had arrived in the Pacific Northwest ten years ago, he'd realized quickly that these people were more unlike New Yorkers than the French. For that matter, they were more unlike New Yorkers than the only other people in the world Boudreau knew well, the Panamanians.

"You fucked up back there," Spencer said. "Enough of them *journalistos* heard you. I'll tell Beale she got on your case and you were trying to get rid of her, but that's the best I can do."

"Yeah, whatever you say. I appreciate it. But I think I'll survive."

"And I saw your face when you were looking at the shit floating in the river. Don't judge the river by what you see down here. It's real pretty up in the gorge."

"I'll remember that when I want to go camping with my kid. 'Let me show you where we found the murdered girl, Paulie.' Now, what's on your mind? You don't get anything out of me until I know exactly why you want it."

Spencer's eyes grew round. He swallowed.

Boudreau said, "You were behind me all the way from the river's edge. Nobody missed it. You want it *badly*."

"Well, that won't be *your* problem. Look, you were called to ID her, right? I was first on scene. The law says it's my case. If those guys decide to fuck it up, they can put it all on me, as much as they want."

A big rig roaring past rocked the car in its roiling gray wake. "Keep good notes," Boudreau said.

"You're not going to help me? You're not going to tell me who she is?"

"You saw the body. They called Seattle vice for the ID. My notes will confirm your notes." Boudreau grinned. "But don't worry, I'll give you what I have."

Spencer bit his lip. "You're a prick. I should have figured as much. It was like they were waiting for it. Somebody was listening to the radio transmits."

"Who found the body?"

Spencer blinked. "I'm not completely stupid. You gotta tell me who the victim is."

"I told you not to worry. You have the deal—but you gotta go first. Who called it in?"

"An old guy who patrols the river for junk he can sell. He called it in."

"In this weather?"

"Rain or shine. Everyone in town knows him, even the chief. She was up against a bent bicycle frame. There's no telling how far she floated, and I don't think they're going to find much evidence along the riverbank in this weather."

Boudreau told Spencer the name by which he knew the dead girl. Spencer looked unhappy. Boudreau said, "When I have her real name, I'll pass it on to you." He wasn't going to create more problems for himself with Beale. But with so many representatives of the media so interested in the case, her name wasn't going to stay secret long. "Tell me what makes you think they were expecting it."

"No, I said *like* they were waiting for it." Spencer removed his hat and wiped his brow. "They were here very fast. The FBI in force after one call from the King County guys. Something really important got said on that call. Hot Lily. That's so goddamned dumb!" Spencer's chest heaved. "Are you going to get back to me fast? We've got the holiday this weekend—"

Boudreau laughed. "Sure. I was just twisting your horns."

"You're a prick, all right." Spencer reached for the door handle. Cold water dumped onto the young officer's lap again. "Shit!" He slammed the door behind him.

Boudreau's laughter ended quickly as he realized it would be smart to take care of the kid. He got the Ford up to traffic speed on the shoulder before pulling into the right lane, asking himself if they knew about his connection to the man whose face flashed before him. No secret—it was a matter of public record, in fact. This case wasn't two hours old and already glowed with the heat it generated. What was going on? And Beale did not like Boudreau: most important, in the American law-enforcement bureaucracy, when you had any doubt whatsoever, you played the game by the book. Exactly.

Boudreau had the name. No doubt at all. As soon as he had the monicker file copied and on its way, Boudreau was going to dig up what he had on the guy, going back to—when? More than two years?

Boudreau remembered him perfectly. Everything he had on him would be on its way to Ron Beale ASAP.

Garrett Richard Lockman.

September 1982

Ten days later, a thousand miles to the east, in Kearney, Nebraska, Garrett Richard Lockman quietly let himself out of his room on the third floor of the Marriott Hotel and stepped with increasing confidence past the door of the room where his aunt and uncle were loudly snoring.

The two old people and the young man had driven west this afternoon from Gary, Indiana, Lockman behind the wheel for every sunbroiled mile, the aunt and uncle, who had also been his foster parents way back when, bickering and nattering over everything from the car's air-conditioner setting to the natural color of Lucille Ball's hair. Al and Hazel were tiny people, under five feet two, and they bounced around in the backseat of the big Buick Electra like preschoolers. Al liked to tease Hazel about mildly off-color matters, such as the real hair color of movie stars, to provoke her rage. Hazel was a frozen old prude, and Al had a little boy's sense of humor, probing and merciless. Now in their late sixties, Hazel and Al were beyond the possibility of change, and so when they went at each other, as they had today, Garrett Richard Lockman simply stopped listening. He had spent the day quietly contemplating the content of tonight's adventure.

He had his camera, a gizmo-laden Japanese thirty-five-millimeter, a pocketful of boxes of film, and an assortment of business cards. Lockman was his uncle Al's sister's son, but he was tall, six feet three, lean, and he moved in gawky undulations, like a teenager who had just come into his growth. Lockman was twenty-eight years old. He had a long, bony face, slightly bulging round brown eyes, and a small mouth with round, puffy lips. His hair was kinky, sticking out from his skull; usually he kept it in place with spray. Tonight, to create a certain effect, he had left it uncombed. Some people, including Hazel, thought it made him look Jewish, which was what he wanted. Hazel and Al were anti-Semites, Hazel worse than Al, and it tickled Lockman to think of the elder Lockmans' pride and joy so "disguised" and on the particular errand he was running. What the hell, if Aunt Hazel ever learned what her favorite nephew really was, she would drop dead on the spot.

Lockman could see Hazel landing with a crash on the pavement, and it made him almost giggle out loud.

In the dimly lit lounge downstairs, as he had seen advertised on the hotel's roadside marquee this afternoon, a trio was playing, guitar, bass and drums, and as Lockman had anticipated, the music had drawn a youngish crowd. Lockman considered himself an expert on America's nightlife. Wearing a jacket, he was almost overdressed for the place, the other men in shirtsleeves, short shirtsleeves, mostly. His clothing fit his purpose, too, like his wild hair. The women were dressed well, as they always were in places like this. A few couples were dancing in front of the bandstand. Now the three performers leaned into their microphones and shouted the lyrics of "California Dreamin'." Everything was exactly as Lockman had thought it would be. Originally Kearney, Nebraska, had been Fort Kearney, of the U.S. Cavalry, back in the days of the Indian wars. The excitement of the frontier had run out of the area like water from a tub decades ago, and today people were bored shitless, looking anywhere for excitement. Garrett Richard Lockman maneuvered himself up to the bar next to a petite blonde in a black dress that showed a shadow of perky cleavage. She was a lot like a girl in Harrisburg with whom he had just shared an adventure, tiny and delicately formed. She seemed to be alone, no male hovering over her, no half-empty glass on the bar indicating he had gone to the crapper. Lockman put the camera on the bar, where she could see it. The bartender, a big, burly guy with a handlebar mustache, came up to take his order.

"You leave that there, it's going to get wet," the bartender said.

"No problem," Lockman said. "It's watertight." The blonde looked from the bartender to Lockman. Excellent. Blue eyes, smooth skin. He could almost feel her small tit cupped in his hand. "I'll have a Budweiser." Lockman offered her a smile. "I found out how good this camera was in Hong Kong. I had these great pictures of Bruce Lee on the set of his last movie, and I dropped the camera in the harbor, plop! I would have been very upset if I'd lost those pictures, because they turned out to be worth a lot of money. Lee died the very next week, and I was able to sell the pictures all over Europe."

"Gee. That's interesting."

She reached for her cigarettes, Virginia Slims. A real femme. The best. *Thank you, God.* The bartender brought the beer. Lockman took out his flash roll, fifteen twenties wrapped with a couple of hundreds, and let her see it as he peeled off the top hundred.

"Got anything smaller?" the bartender asked.

"No, I'm sorry."

The bartender grabbed the bill and headed to the cash register. Lockman took a swig and set the bottle down. "I'm Sid Zimmerman," he said to the blonde. "This is my first time in Nebraska. Been here a week, working on a picture book for Time-Life. American heartland stuff. You've all been very, very kind to me. Lovely people." He removed from his breast pocket a card that identified him as Sidney Zimmerman of Time-Life, Avenue of the Americas, New York City, and held the card in front of her until she took it. So exciting: he could feel his blood coursing into the tips of his fingers. "I spent the day taking pictures of cows. Now my editor wants to know what kind of cows."

"These parts, they're probably Holsteins," the blonde said.

The bartender returned with the change, his eyes on Lockman's. Lockman waited, watching the bartender move away. "Enough about cows. I came down here to take some pictures of people. What's your name?"

"Oh, I don't want my picture taken."

Lockman smiled. "Oh, I wouldn't do anything without your permission. But actually, you'd be perfect as the star of a sidebar about what young single people do at night in the prairie states. Wouldn't take any time, and nothing would be printed until you saw it and signed a release. Usually there's a small payment that goes through when you sign. Want to try a few?"

"No, I don't want to."

Lockman picked up the camera and aimed it at her. She was too close to be brought into focus. It didn't matter.

"Hey, I said no!"

But he had already depressed the shutter release. The camera flashed in her eyes.

"Charlie!"

The bartender reappeared. "What, babe?"

Frowning, she tried to look at Lockman. Her expression was almost funny. As if she realized it, she quickly looked away, even more annoyed. "I want to be left alone. He just shot that camera off in my eyes. I can't see a thing."

"You heard her, bro."

She thrust Lockman's Zimmerman card at the bartender. "He says he's a photographer for Time-Life taking pictures for a book."

The bartender suddenly wrested the beer out of Lockman's hand. "Beat it," he said.

"What? I want the manager. Get the manager."

"You're going to get my foot up your ass if you're not out of here. I saw you check in this afternoon with those two old people. The girl at the desk put your registration card where I could see it. All three of you had the same last name. I don't remember what it was, but it sure as shit wasn't Zimmerman. You're up to something. Now get the hell out of here before I twist your geeky head right off your skinny neck." He poured the beer into the sink. When his eyes came up again, they were hooded with menace. The blonde looked from him to Lockman and back again, her lips curling in a small smile. Other people were turning around, beginning to pay attention. Lockman backed off the bar stool and, head down, clutching the camera to his chest with both hands, pushed through the crowd. At the door he looked back. The blonde was giving the bartender an enthusiastic high five. Immediately Lockman saw himself cutting her tits off.

He hurried across the garish lobby and out into the heavy summer air. He fought the urge to yell, to let out his rage and pain in a primitive animal shriek. Would the bartender call the police? Suddenly that seemed like a real possibility. And just that quickly, Lockman had a solution to the problem. He would watch from across the street for half an hour. If the police came, he would have to leave Hazel and Al where they were. They would have to drive themselves home. They would understand. Especially if the police questioned them.

The gas station at the entrance to the interstate had an outdoor telephone booth near the curb. A few hundred yards beyond, the I-80 roared. He called Seattle collect. This was going to be great. The operator announced his presence and the male voice on the other end of the line responded tiredly: "Yeah, okay, I'll accept the charges."

Lockman didn't wait for the operator to tell him it was all right to talk.

While she was still on the line he said, "Hello, homo, do you want to lick my dick again?"

With a gasp, the operator clicked off.

"She heard you!"

"Oh, be quiet. This is Oscar calling."

"I am not going to play *Odd Couple* with you. I am not going to play that game."

"Oh, Tonto, you're in a snit! I called to say hello. I want to tell you about an amazing adventure."

"I'll bet you do," the distant voice said. "How are Hazel and Al?"

"Still aboard the *Enterprise*. I beamed down, but I can still see it in orbit." Lockman was looking back at the Marriott. "Let me tell you what happened on the planet Harrisburg, on my way back from the eastern galaxy."

"You're boring the shit out of me, Lockman. Why did you call? Collect, at that, I should say, in addition to all the other money you owe me."

"Oooh, we are in a snit." Lockman was holding his crotch. "You Pawnee faggot! I did it! I did it in Harrisburg, P-A!"

"I am not a Pawnee," said Lockman's best friend, Martin Jones, who was, in fact, a fully qualified member of the Sioux nation even if he knew nothing about Indians. Twenty-five percent Sioux, thanks to his maternal grandmother. "If you're going to try to play your little games, I suppose I'm better off hearing about your Gettysburg escapade. Drone on." His voice was flat. Lockman knew how to perk him up. A pink '58 Buick Roadmaster went by, fresh paint gleaming under the gas-station fluorescent lights.

"Harrisburg. Yes, you have to listen. The camera scam worked. I'll never have a thrill like it again. She went the whole way. It was absolutely wonderful."

"I thought the object of the experiment was to humiliate the subject."

"I wasn't always crazy, I told you that. I had a moment of crystalline lucidity." He continued to fondle himself, mildly aroused and invigorated.

"Did you have sex with her?" Now Martin Jones sounded alarmed. As impressive as his voice was, Martin Jones was, as Garrett Richard Lockman had told him once, the least savage redskin ever to run loose in North America. He was shaped like Jabba the Hut and had the muscles of tapioca pudding. Martin Jones was five feet eight and weighed two hundred and seventy pounds.

"We had our fun," Lockman said carefully, listening for the effect.

"You're a liar," Martin Jones said. His voice rose. "You're making it up about Gettysburg or wherever, just as you've made up everything else. I told you not to take your aunt and uncle on that trip and you did it anyway. I told you to call me and you deliberately let three weeks go by without so much as a word! I'll tell you the truth, Lockman, I'm not afraid of your anger anymore! Three weeks! You're lying about this just as you've always lied about what happened the night I got drunk!"

The central issue between them. What was making him bring it up this time? He sounded different. Distant. Lockman grinned anyway. He could always control Martin Jones. "No lie. I told you, just before you passed out, you got down on your knees and lip-locked Mister Jim."

"Stop it! Stop it!"

Lockman cackled. "Can I help it if I have a big, tasty dick?"

"It never happened! Nothing happened in Harrisburg, either. You did not pick up a girl and talk her into taking her clothes off in your room. Not an amateur. A pro, always, for the money, but not an amateur. But I'll tell you what is true. Did you see the papers last week?"

Lockman laughed out loud. At least he said Harrisburg: Jones liked to fight such little skirmishes to express his seeming independence. "The papers? Little Beaver, Red Rider is in Kearney fucking Nebraska!"

"I did it. I avenged myself against you. I told you not to go on that trip with Hazel and Al, but you did! I told you to call me, but you didn't! You'll know how you've upset me. I'll show you." He was gasping in a way Lockman had never heard before. "The police are looking for you for murder, or they will be soon. I did it—executed our plan as you were never willing to do."

Lockman hesitated, alarmed. What was the little monkey up to now? "You're full of shit."

"Oh, no. Oh, no. Listen: I put on my uniform, the one we got last month? I took your car out and got a girl. She got in the car just as I always said. I always told you it would be easy, and it was. You said it was going to be difficult. That's because you're a gutless, worthless piece of shit. I did her with the chloroform, put her in the trunk, and took her down to Portland to your place. To the secret room. *Your secret fucking room, man!* I made a *snuff* tape!" He swallowed. "Audio. You can play it, if you like. You can find the tape with those bullets you bought for that lousy revolver of yours, the thirty-eight hollow points."

Lockman was frozen. "*What did you do?*"

"I'm telling you," Jones said. "I did the bullets thing to her, what you're always talking about? What you're always going to do to the I-5 hookers? Remember? One thing you don't remember is how many people you talked to about it, because you're the one who can't control his drinking. Am I right? Who's been telling people all over town for years what he was going to do to one of those hookers? Pack her snapper full of bullets? If the police know anything about their jobs—you're the one who's always talking about how smart they are—"

"Within limits, I always say."

"You bore!" Jones shrieked. "They're going to trace the bullets to you!"

"Even if they could, which they can't, you Neanderthal queen, *I don't believe you!* You're trying to do to me what you always accuse me of doing. And you're doing it badly. Very badly. In addition to all your other inadequacies, you can't even run a good scam."

"I called Ron Beale," Martin Jones said evenly.

"When did you call Beale?" Lockman asked. "You don't know Beale."

"The Sunday morning after I snuffed Hot Lily. I got his number out of your desk. You're the guy who has to have everybody's home phone number. What do you ever do with them?"

"Are you trying to tell me you snuffed *Hot Lily*? You're going to have Uhuru after you. You want that? You want his big black dick up your ass? I'll bet you do. What did you tell Beale, Running Sore? This better be good. You didn't make the call from my number, did you?"

"No," Martin Jones said calmly. "I waited until I was back in Seattle. I called from a booth on Fifth Avenue. It was a Sunday, I told you. The Sunday before last. There wasn't any traffic."

Suddenly Lockman felt an icy, delicious release of tension. This was too rich! His faithful Indian guide wanted him to believe he had killed a girl and phoned it in to the police? Brilliant! "Tell me what you said to Ron Beale." He could hardly suppress his laughter.

"I wrote it down and read it to him. Wait a minute, I'll get it." Lockman heard the telephone being put down. If he really didn't believe any of this, why was he being overtaken by this strange gust of terror? His penis was shriveling into his abdomen. He had heard new power in Jones's voice. Lockman had always thought Jones capable of a desperate act—it was what Lockman liked about him. But Jones was in love with Lockman, which was an interesting sensation for the love object, as he told Jones whenever he wanted to stir his interest. Jones insisted he was not a homosexual. More important, he was not a man who could kill: Lockman was absolutely certain of that. He heard the phone being picked up again. "Are you listening?"

"Yes."

"Louder! I want to know you're paying attention!"

"I'm listening!" He could never let Martin Jones think he was afraid of him. Nothing between them would ever work again. "Read the fucking thing already!"

"I'll fix you," Martin Jones muttered. "Here goes. 'The girl's killer wants to be like you, only he's too wild. When you find the bullets, look for the strangest cop of all.' What do you think of that?"

Out on the interstate, a truck's air horn blasted. "I think you're full of shit."

"I liked it, Garrett. I liked it a lot. Now I'm as crazy as you are. Read the papers if you dare. Oh, yes, you big pile of shit, read them before you come home!"

"Give yourself a break, Martin. Take some aspirin. You're not going to get me to believe that you committed a murder you read about in the papers—"

Suddenly the handset on the other end clattered again. Lockman heard someone's heavy breathing. "Listen," a female voice hissed urgently, "I don't know who you are or where, but call the Seattle police! Please, in the name of God, call the police! I'll do anything! Call the police!"

The phone moved again. There was silence for a moment. Martin Jones said, "I had to get the sock back in her mouth without her biting me. It's absolutely wild, Garrett. This has given me a new respect for you. I'm going to put your bullets in this one's cunt, too. The story going around is that they found rocks in Hot Lily, but they didn't print it in the papers. It's supposed to be a secret, and they have it wrong. You're right, the cops are pretty clever. Hafta run. Even using your newfangled technique, it took me twenty minutes to strangle Hot Lily. I want to see if the practice has enhanced my skill." The telephone went dead.

Lockman stood there holding the handset next to his head until he noticed that his mouth was literally hanging open. His bullets found in Hot Lily's vagina? How did Jones know that the police didn't have a way of tracing ammunition? Lockman was thankful no other physical evidence could be traced to him. Getting rid of the gun and the bullets would be no problem once he got home.

How had this happened? Had Jones snapped because Lockman had manipulated him once too often? Or had Martin Jones simply decided to turn the tables? He could have hired the girl Lockman had just heard. *In the name of God.* That didn't sound like a joke—or the language of a street girl, either, for that matter. It would be just Martin Jones's luck to have grabbed a *real* person.

Lockman realized that he was looking at a police cruiser parked in front of the hotel. He had not seen it pull up. How long had it been there?

A single officer emerged from the hotel and got in. He cranked the starter and drove away. No pausing for making notes or getting on the radio. What did it mean? Garrett Richard Lockman realized something else.

He had urinated in his pants, and now it was getting cold. He did not remember doing it. A blank spot rose up in his memory. How could he have wet his pants and not known it? Murder! Was Martin Jones murdering another woman at this very moment? The police car had rolled up and Lockman had wet himself and he couldn't remember either one. He had a hole in his memory now, he knew, even as it rolled out of view over the bloody gray horizon of his one-of-a-kind brain. A yellow 1953 Mercury sedan rolled past, a gum-chewing woman in the passenger seat slowly raking him with a desultory gaze. A decal bearing the word PRIDE next to an American flag was affixed to the right rear vent window. Was Nebraska the secret capital of flashy old American cars? Lockman removed his jacket and tied the arms around his waist so the back of the jacket could cover his wetness. At least he would be able to get into the hotel. He wouldn't even have to go past the entrance to the lounge to get to the elevator to his room. He wanted to pick up the telephone again. No! Not if Jones was trying to kill some woman. Lockman knew he had to see it in a newspaper first, had to restrain himself until he had confirmation.

September 1982

The morning after the discovery of the second body, Ron Beale's freshly minted second-in-command, Dan Cheong, called to ask Phil Boudreau if he could stop by. Cheong was trying to make it sound casual, so Boudreau played dumb, and sure enough, Cheong stumbled into the tip-off phrase:

"It's important."

Cops never expected to have their own tricks played on them, and the result was that the tricks always worked.

Cheong was in his early thirties, and like so many third- and fourth-generation Chinese Americans on the West Coast, a relatively big man, almost six feet tall. He worked out and was powerfully built. And like so many West Coast cops, he liked to buy his clothes at the Jack Webb Thrift Shop, sport jackets, sharply creased trousers, white or blue dress shirts, and muted striped ties. He arrived with the black-haired, blue-eyed FBI guy who had paid such close attention to Boudreau over Hot Lily's body. Kevin Donovan. Special Agent Donovan. You were supposed to remember to say that. They were all special agents, so they were exactly the opposite, with nothing special about them. No business card. Boudreau was supposed to remember his name, and then not be able to reach out for him later. It was all attitude. Today was another rainy day and Donovan was another macho macho man who didn't want to dress for it, and so his clothes smelled. He stood over Boudreau's desk, staring at him, as Cheong ran through a statement he had apparently prepared on his way over. Boudreau decided to keep his eyes on Cheong. The Young King of the G-men could go fuck himself.

"We had a hell of a time with the press after you opened your mouth, Boudreau," Cheong said evenly. "If you've been reading the papers, you noticed that they decided to cooperate with us and print nothing about objects found in the first victim."

"They knew half of it already—"

"Let me finish. The kid who was first on scene has bailed you out. But you were told specifically not to run your mouth. Are you going to tell us why you did?"

"If the kid bailed me out, then he told you that the reporter got to me. I don't get a lot of that kind of attention."

"Why so touchy?" Donovan asked.

Now Boudreau turned to him. "I'd just been looking at the body of a murdered child."

"You identified her as a prostitute."

"What's your point?"

"Why do you call her a child?"

"That's what she was."

"Seventeen?"

"The law says a child. And it says the crimes committed against her by her johns are a lot worse than prostitution."

"Give me a break."

"You gotta go by the law."

"You do, eh?"

"You think I don't? What are you doing on this case? The FBI?"

"None of your business," Donovan said.

"How did you recognize her?" Cheong asked quickly. "Will you go through that for us again?"

Boudreau thought he would be enjoying this if he knew what it was really about. "Ron Beale saw. The tattoo of the dagger on her thigh. I told him how I knew."

"We're just trying to get it straight, Boudreau," Donovan said.

Boudreau almost said "*Detective* Boudreau," but Donovan was the kind of prick who was only going to ride a guy harder if he saw he was having success at it.

"When was the last time you saw her?" Cheong asked.

Boudreau had spent part of the night after the trip to the Green River going through his notebooks, trying to remember all his contacts with her. In Pioneer Square. Along the Pike? Once she had run away from him. He had almost caught her—at what? "Taking a date," was what the girls called accepting the propositions of the married-with-children suburban perverts who cruised downtown and the Sea-Tac Strip shopping for blow jobs. Who were the criminals in this so-called victimless crime? "Probably on Pike Street around Second Avenue," he said to Cheong.

"Pike Street," Donovan interrupted. "That's what the kids call 'the Pike'?"

"That's right," Boudreau said. "And probably in the late spring."

"How do you get to that?"

"It's a guess. When I was looking at her, I thought that I hadn't seen her in a while. That's how I get May or June. She lived on my beat, remember."

Donovan said, "It sounds like you have some kind of feeling for her."

Feeling had come out as if Donovan thought it disgusting. That made him dumb enough to be really dangerous. Boudreau said, "I liked her, if that's what you mean. She was a kid with the kind of problems she might have outgrown."

"You knew her pretty well."

"I tried."

"Anything else you can think of?"

"It's all in the package I sent to Beale that afternoon."

They looked at each other. Donovan said, "You were supposed to send the monicker file."

"A copy. I did."

Donovan and Cheong exchanged glances again. Maybe they couldn't figure out how to ask the next question without telling him they didn't know what else had been in that package. Beale was keeping the name of Garrett Richard Lockman from his own people? Was Beale not playing straight with his own team? No, he and Cheong had been partners for years. If anything, the two of them were not playing straight with the FBI. Boudreau saw he could not conduct himself in a way that would let him look like *anybody's* accomplice, or coconspirator. He kept quiet. Boudreau's father's advice about police politics: *Don't trust anybody, even out there,* meaning Seattle. The Old Man, whom Boudreau had once called *Papa,* in French, had given him the best advice a cop could ever get. After domestic disputes and traffic stops, the most sudden trouble came from other cops, because you never knew what they were up to. Cheong and Donovan got to their feet.

"One more thing," Donovan said. "You made a crack out there. At the river. I don't know why you made it."

Boudreau wasn't sure what the guy was talking about. "What crack was that?"

"About seeing a lot of pussy."

"But I do. You know that."

"No, I don't know that. Why did you say it, if you were all shook up about her being dead?"

"I don't think I said I was all shook up."

"You haven't answered the question."

Boudreau shrugged, determined not to let the guy get under his skin. "I'm a New Yorker. I don't think like these guys. The ones who don't know that sometimes have trouble with me."

"You don't have a partner? You're on some kind of special assignment?"

"Not really. Stan Pfeiffer, the Seattle chief of detectives, wanted to try something different. We see eye to eye on street vice." They figured he was withholding something? They moved toward the door without saying thank you or good-bye. If there had been so much as a nod, Boudreau had missed it. He was willing to believe they had wanted to tell him not to leave town.

He remembered Beale's eyes on him at the river—and now this FBI yutz staring at him all the while he had been watching Dan Cheong?

Jesus! Boudreau almost said it aloud.

A *suspect?*

———

THE DISCOVERY OF the second body allowed the press to trot out Ted Bundy, and that made the behavior of Beale and his team a bit more comprehensible, if not completely rational. Washington State law enforcement still had not recovered from its failure to arrest Ted Bundy, who had terrorized Seattle and the surrounding area for most of the 1970s. Utah and Colorado hayseeds had run Bundy down, and now Florida crackers were getting ready to finish him off. Seattle and King County had had Bundy under surveillance and had not been able to make a charge. Thirty victims here? More? You could not script a law enforcement humiliation more abject. A Pacific Northwest officer could not go to a national or regional convention or professional meeting without being badgered with questions about the Inside Story. There was no Inside Story. Bundy had outsmarted thousands of people in the service of an impulse to rape, sodomize, brutalize, and finally kill pretty young women who resembled his former girlfriend, or more likely, the longtime girl of his dreams.

What was lost was the real Seattle Inside Story, the end of Seattle's status as a one-company town and its emergence as a major American city. Boeing was the one company, still America's number one exporter, doing bigger business abroad than all of Hollywood, which was second, or any other industry. Seattle was a day's sail closer than other West Coast ports to America's new trading partners on the other side of the Pacific Rim, passing on a huge savings in fuel and inventory maintenance. On Seattle's docks Toyota sometimes stacked its little trucks six stories high. Instead people wanted to talk about the most flamboyant sexual killer since Jack the Ripper.

Boudreau had seen the Bundy victim photographs. By comparison, Wendy Harrison, a.k.a. Hot Lily, the perfect victim, had died easily. But these guys always got worse, and this new one could have been in the area in the seventies, watching Bundy work. This one might be a lot smarter than Bundy at picking his victims. Bundy had liked college girls, knockouts whose absence everybody noticed at once. Beale suspected a cop? Victim number two of the Green River killer, as he was already being called by the media, was a fifteen-year-old prostitute and methamphetamine user named Cindy Lou Dorcak. Miss Dorcak's body was relatively fresh, no more than four days old when pulled from the water. Boudreau knew nothing else about the condition of the body, if it had been tattooed, if objects had been placed in her vagina. He had not been called this time for the purpose of identification. He did not even learn there had been another killing until he heard about it on his car radio. If there was any scuttlebutt inside law enforcement about the killings and who was a suspect, Phil Boudreau was not hearing it. He was out of the loop.

And since he was only a Seattle vice cop, not a hotshot King County Major Crimes detective, that was as it should be. All he had to do was go about his business. And keep his mouth shut.

That was the way things worked, and even the young first-on-scene City of Kent officer knew as much.

———

PHIL BOUDREAU WAS a divorced father with court-ordered child-support payments and weekly visitation rights. He made the former and exercised the latter with perfect faithfulness. Boudreau's son, Paul, who was six years old, knew every inch of the Kingdome, Seattle Center, and most of the ferries that plied Puget Sound. His parents' marriage had ended when the kid was still in diapers: father was now three girlfriends away from mother, who was a whole second marriage and divorce away from father. Paulie didn't know anything about his father's family, his grandparents half a decade dead now, and the uncles, aunts, and distant cousins in France who still exchanged Christmas cards with his father—people Boudreau had never seen. Paulie was living a life his father would not have wished on an enemy, in an anonymous, prisonlike garden apartment where the Chinese-American landlord prohibited pets and scowled at pictures hanging on his precious cardboard walls. The apartment complex was only blocks from the university, where Paul's mother worked. Adrienne was a U admissions counselor who routinely altered lives with the computer equivalent of a rubber stamp, yes or no, up or down, in or out. She could afford a better apartment, but would not let herself spend the money. Occasionally Paul visited his maternal grandparents in their mobile home outside Bellingham. His whole life could blow away in a storm—not that Boudreau's own was much different. Only the people in his triplex knew Boudreau was a police detective, and nobody else in Queen Anne, his neighborhood, save a few storekeepers, knew him at all.

Cindy Lou Dorcak had been tagged and bagged for five days when Boudreau went around to pick up Paulie for dinner and a movie down the hill. Friday night on the town, ending up with the kid getting to play his video games while his old man had a latte and rested his dogs. And thought about the Green River case. Beale should have called him about Lockman by now, if only to cover his ass. What had happened after Lockman had been released from jail? The release should have happened in the last six months. Boudreau's covering note to Beale indicated he had thought of Lockman when he returned to the office that first afternoon. It was impossible to prove otherwise. The record was made that he had thought of a suspect, and had sent over what he had with all possible speed. Only when Boudreau thought that perhaps he had covered his own ass too well did he decide he was slipping into paranoia.

Boudreau's ex-family's apartment was on the second floor of one of the two off-street buildings in the tiny, wood-frame complex. He was about to ring the bell a second time when Adrienne opened the door a crack. She was a slender, brown-haired woman with small bones and a thin nose. No makeup tonight: she was staying at home.

"Oh, Jesus," she said. "I forgot about you."

"What's the matter?" Boudreau asked. "Isn't he ready?"

The door opened only a little more. "He's got the mumps. I tried to call you, but I can't get used to that damned answer machine."

She had just said she had forgotten about him. There was no response that wouldn't lead to an argument. He had bought the answering machine to make communication between them easier: sometimes she did not want to talk to him, and he never knew when those times would be.

"I had to take him out of school yesterday." Suddenly she gave him a crooked smile. "Have you had the mumps?"

"Oh, yeah. Can I see him?"

"He's in bed."

"Let me just say hello to him. He must have heard the bell."

"All right, but make it quick. And don't get him excited."

She led him across the apartment, the curve of her spine showing the weight of her disappointment with life, this same person who had just enjoyed the possibility of exposing an adult male for the first time to mumps. Boudreau could barely stand the sight of her. The apartment smelled sour and stale—now he caught himself: with a sick kid in it, how was the place supposed to smell? Boudreau stuck his head inside Paulie's room. Sitting up in the bed was someone who looked like a child until Boudreau focused on his jowls, where he looked sixty. Even with a heart full of pity, Boudreau had to stifle a laugh. "How ya doin'?"

"Oh, okay," came a reedy squawk.

"Sore throat? Running a temperature?"

He nodded. "Think so."

"Next time, pepperoni-and-sausage pizza."

The little old man in the center of the bed made a weak thumbs-up sign. Boudreau said, "I'll get you stuff to read."

"The Hulk. Get me the Hulk. Superheroes, stuff like that."

"Don't indulge him," Adrienne said.

"He's sick!"

"*Don't start!*"

They moved back toward the living room. "Tell me when I can drop off the reading material."

"I can't yet. You can see that. The doctor said he may get worse before he gets better. You'll have to call me. Don't ever expect me to talk to that goddamned machine."

Boudreau sighed. Adrienne maintained that she had been the one to terminate her second marriage, but he had serious doubts. Childbirth had caused her to lose interest in sex, she had "confessed" to him on one of their own last and worst nights, telling him she had been faking orgasms, even interest, for almost two years. The marriage had already died; she didn't see that a timelier disclosure of her difficulty might have saved them. That same night she claimed to have lower expectations of life than he did, that he was an incorrigible dreamer who needed to preserve romantic illusions about the world. Whatever; after their first rush of sexual curiosity, their minds had never seemed to mesh. In the end, he had had to hold on to his sense of himself and say adios to her. He stopped in the hall.

"Do you want anything from the store?"

"No. Let me go." Suddenly she closed the door in his face and he heard her turn the lock. Just that abruptly he had the peephole two inches from the end of his nose. She had done this to him before and now he knew enough to ride out her rudeness, hostility, rage—maybe all of them put together. She would deny she felt those things anyway, act innocent, maybe even smile, tell him he was imagining things. He turned and went down the wooden stairs, knowing not to hesitate, to hurry, to shed his emotions behind him as he went. Projecting motivation into her behavior was pointless. She was what she was, which, from his point of view, was the reason why court orders enforced his right to see his child and have some influence on what became of him.

Whether she liked it or not, he would telephone tomorrow, ready with Paulie's comic books. This was Boudreau's old neighborhood. In the seventies he had patrolled here, caught his first homicide, and later had taken courses in criminal justice and psychology. The University District. Friday night. Eight o'clock. He parked the car on a side street and crossed the avenue to a bar where he had stopped regularly for years.

The joint had changed hands; it was now a sports bar crowded with locals and graduate students watching television sets mounted high on the walls. The place was loud, but not because of the television sets, all turned soundlessly to the same baseball game, Phillies at Atlanta. The conversational volume had reached such a pitch that people were yelling to be heard, whether they knew it or not. HENRY'S ON TAP, said a sign behind the bar, and with a wave of the hand Boudreau directed the bartender's attention toward it. The bartender had a familiar face. "I remember you," he shouted as he pulled the tap. "Want to see a menu?"

"This place used to have great burgers."

"Still does. Salmon burgers, veggie burgers, turkey burgers. You can have sprouts instead of fries, if you like the taste of dirt. Want a designer pizza all the way from Los Angle-eeze, California?"

"Buffalo chicken wings?"

"Now you're talking. Hot, real hot, or real, real hot?"

"Real, real."

The bartender put the beer in front of him. The head was an inch thick. "You were a cop. What happened to you, get a divorce?"

Boudreau couldn't help laughing. "How did you know I was a cop?"

"Quiet, keep to yourself, shifty eyes that always worked the room. You still got 'em. My first take on you was either a cop or a crook, and you eliminated the second choice when you didn't put the hustle on somebody, as a crook always, always does. Okay?"

"You ought to take the test, we could use you. How do you figure a divorce?"

"A guy like you disappears, that's usually the reason. You get all knotted up on shame, guilt—I'm just a pissant bartender, what do I know about being a gunslinging macho asshole like you?" Grinning at Boudreau, he waved a waitress over. "Super-hot wings for my man here." An eyebrow arched. "Want the double?"

"The single will hold him," the waitress said.

"Get the double," said another woman, standing behind her. Boudreau didn't recognize the voice, and when the waitress stepped aside, he didn't recognize the young woman, either—dark-haired, very dark-eyed, not tall, full-figured, even a little plump. She was wearing a white blouse and tight, faded blue jeans. No jewelry. Little makeup. She had a half-filled mug of beer in her left hand, a purse under the arm. "I'm going to join you." She squeezed her right hand into the hip pocket of her jeans, pulled out a crumpled twenty-dollar bill, and tossed it on the bar. "I'll buy the next round."

Boudreau grinned. "I'm easy. Do I know you?"

She said, "Criminology class. Four years ago? Professor Rogers. You sat by the door." She looked over her shoulder to a table where three women her age were laughing so hard they were hiding their faces with their hands. "They're goofing on me."

He moved closer to hear her over the din of the bar, and got a hint of her perfume. "If you say so, but I still can't place you."

"I know," she said. "I'm embarrassing the crap out of myself. Your name is Boudreau. Rogers didn't use first names."

"That was him, a primo dickhead."

"But then I saw you on television, on the news," she said. "Your first name is Felix."

"It's Phil. The news was wrong."

Her eyes grew wide. She blushed. Boudreau looked away for a moment to let her get control of herself again. He sipped his beer.

"This is knocking the hell out of your girlfriends."

"It would." She tossed her head back. "Betty. My name is Betty Antonelli. I turned in my master's thesis today. I'm celebrating and I'm a little loaded, but not from this." She drank from her mug. "I love guys with hairy bodies."

He laughed, thinking she was a long way from loaded. He saw *loaded* on the streets, sleeping in doorways. This was *tipsy*. "Hairy bodies?"

"Sometimes you'd wear a T-shirt. When you said in class you were a cop, it was like I almost passed out."

"You like cops?"

"A lot of women do. Trust me."

He didn't have to. Almost any cop could fill a book with his adventures with the most unlikely women, control freaks in business suits, angry feminists, Goody Two-shoes with tiny angelic smiles. Alone with a cop in good shape, they howled like coyotes. Boudreau raised his mug in a toast. "To you, Betty Antonelli. You get big points for style."

"Good. Let me tell you how major this was. My friends over there? After I heard it on television, I had to tell them I thought your name was cute." She angled her head toward the table where the three women were still racked with laughter. "They sang that cartoon song to me. Now here they are at my thesis delivery party. I told them an hour ago I intended to have a big night tonight. And then you came in. I don't have any brains at all: I told them who you are. And in fact years ago you never noticed me. Fabulous."

Boudreau picked up her twenty and waggled it at the bartender, who, grinning to himself, dug in the ice for fresh mugs. For all he and Boudreau knew, Betty was winning a bet. When Boudreau turned back to her, her eyes were locked on his. He leaned over and brushed his lips against her ear, breathing in her perfume deeply. A pause. "Did you hear what I said?"

She tilted her head back, offering her neck to him. "Oh, yes," she whispered, through the applause and cheers from her table. "Loud and clear." She had smooth skin. And she smelled wonderfully fresh. Her hand came up and gently held the back of his head as she kissed him on the mouth.

The bartender said, "Do you want those chicken wings to go?"

They laughed out loud. And ate at the bar. It didn't take Boudreau long to see that under her easy chatter was a loneliness made more bleak by her lack of awareness of how easily it showed. He liked her, but wondered how intense his feeling would have been if he had not been subjected to Adrienne's burst of venomousness just minutes before. It was a good question for Phil Boudreau to ask himself, because he had not been so self-critical when he had met Adrienne in Panama. Back then, he had wanted to end his own loneliness so badly that he had lied to himself about what he had felt for her. The bartender had been right about why he had stayed away from here. Shame. And all the guilt in the world over fathering Paulie only to seem to abandon him.

After the wings, another round of beer, and two chocolate cappuccinos, it took them five minutes to get to his place in Queen Anne. His tiny, two-bedroom apartment was on the third floor of the building, and if you sat on the arm of the sofa, close to the living room's gabled window, you had a view of the Space Needle, the downtown skyline, Elliott Bay, and when you consulted the schedule, the ferry churning north to Victoria. Tonight a sliver of moon cast a milky sparkle on the water. The apartment was furnished in Garage Sale Moderne—the table in the miniature kitchen, for example, was from the thirties, made of brightly trimmed brown-enameled metal, and accommodated only two. Boudreau liked color, and lots of it. When he returned to the living room with his bottle of White Label and two glasses, Betty was taking a deep pull on a joint. He stopped. After seeing his eyes, she put it out in the room's only ashtray.

"Sorry," she said.

"I took an oath."

"Thanks for not busting me. I guess." She looked around. "The second bedroom is for your little boy?"

He nodded. She had listened. He had listened, too: her parents had come to the Pacific Northwest from New Jersey after the Korean War. She said she was one of the rare members of her generation who was one hundred percent Italian, as far back as anyone in her family could re-member. Italians weren't all that rare in this part of the world, but she had gone through grammar and high school without ever meeting another. She had a wonderful smile that showed a bit of a gold crown on her first lower right molar. The perfect flaw. *Cinderella.* A streetwise scullery maid putting the best face on no expectations of a prince. In the car on the way here Boudreau had asked himself what the hell were his own expecta-tions. He wanted to like her. He had been in a penalty box of his own long enough.

"I didn't mean to be rough on you," he said.

"Fear of intimacy."

"You think so?"

"I heard an edge. You're afraid of something." Betty turned to him, close, as he brought his lips to hers. Her mouth opened. He held her, breathed her in, tasted her under the taste of the scotch. Amused, she watched him unbutton her blouse, and then began to undo the buttons on his shirt. Boudreau looked over her shoulder toward his bedroom, where the small table lamp was lit. Her eyes followed his.

"The scene of the crime?"

"What?"

"Where you take all your victims. Like me."

"The truth is that I've been saving myself for my next marriage. I didn't plan it that way, but that's how it's working out."

"Bullshitter." She let him lead her into the bedroom. Boudreau slipped his hand into her blouse and over her breast, which was heavier and firmer than he had ever experienced. His pleasure and surprise showed— he could see her taking delight in him. He kissed her again, their arms going around each other in their first true lovingly passionate moment together. She sighed, looking again into his eyes, as if thinking, as he was, that they might be venturing into something more than they could handle. But that was the very point of it all. They kissed again deeply as he pulled her blouse out of her jeans, slipped it off her shoulders, unclasped her bra. He angled back to look at her as she swayed in his arms, astonishingly limber.

"A human lollipop."

"Shhh." Her eyes closed. "This is my fantasy." She rubbed her face against his chest, dropping to her knees, unzipping his pants. "Jesus. What planet are you from?"

"I'm not circumcised."

"Oh. Well. There's a first time for everything."

She was loving and skillful, continuing to undress him. He stroked her head, gently thrusting his hips as his penis swelled in her mouth.

"I want to return the compliment."

She stood up, stepping out of her jeans. "Too late." Laughing, she grasped his erect penis snugly and towed him to the bed. As she lay back he tried to position himself to perform oral sex on her, but she pulled his body on top of hers. "No, you don't have to."

"You don't know how much I want to do it."

"It's not necessary." She guided him into her.

"I love your body. You're so beautiful."

Suddenly she arched her back and again they were eye to eye. "Would you please shut up?"

———

HE AWAKENED SLOWLY, alone, foggy-headed until he remembered Betty. The apartment was dark, not as they had left it when they had come into the bedroom. They had made love twice—or rather, one of them had made love to the other. In the middle of the night, with the two of them ready to get busy a second time, he had tried again to perform oral sex on her, and just as she was beginning to respond, she had pushed him away and squirmed out of reach. *No. Don't.*

Later, when it finally dawned on him that she had not reached an orgasm at any point, he said so. She said he was right, but by the way she remained drawn away from him, alert and full of energy, it was clear that she was not going to allow herself to find out if there had been any recent changes in her appetites and capacities. It was the way she had always been, she said. There was no point in even trying to touch her. A little time and the right kind of attention might allow her to let down her guard, if that's what it was. He saw a wonderful sweetness in her.

Stepping out of the bedroom, he found her standing at the little window, looking downtown to the darkened high-rises. He took her by the shoulders, kissed her neck. She pulled away, extricating herself as if at her front door with someone she didn't want to kiss good night.

"No. I'm done." She turned and looked into his eyes. "I don't want to do any more."

"What?"

"I mean it. I want to see you again, but let me just have this my way now, okay? Maybe I went too fast and got carried away by my own giddiness."

"Whatever you say, but to let you know, that's the part I liked."

"That's because you're an animal."

"I'm trying to say that I won't hold this against you, if that's what you're worried about."

"I don't think you're that kind of guy. I was kidding with the animal crack. I want to see you, I just didn't think it was going to get so complicated. I have my own fears of intimacy."

"I know."

She kissed his cheek, an instantly identifiable consolation prize. "I was going to get back into bed and sleep until daylight, if you hadn't gotten up. Let me stay until daylight?"

Boudreau had been around too long not to see that if she got home too soon, she would have nothing to tell her friends about her evening. There was no guessing what she was willing to do to evade the experience, but she needed the right to brag about having had it. How old was she? There was no point for him in going back to bed. He was going to be wide-awake for hours. But he said, "Sure, let me hold you. You have to go to work, you said."

"Nordstrom's, nine o'clock. But I want to go back to my place first. Just call me a cab."

"No, I'll take you home—"

"Cab it is. I'd rather. Don't worry about anything. You were—are— wonderful. It's just—look, you've given me enough to think about."

"I was thinking we could have dinner next week someplace nice, like Shuckers."

"In the hotel downtown? That's expensive for a cop with child-support payments."

"It would be my first date in months. What better time for you to stop living like a grad student?"

She was headed back to the bedroom. "I like the way you think. Come hold me."

He did, although in a few minutes he was ready for more lovemaking. For a while she ignored it, or him. She looked around at him. "Do you want me to take care of that?"

Which answer failed the test? "Are you offering a rain check?"

"Only if you want one."

Who was testing whom? He laughed and rolled her onto her back again, and this time he felt her excitement, if not satisfaction. He could not help dozing off. He awakened as she got up without ceremony and went into the bathroom. Daylight. Had she slept at all? Happily he started coffee and called a taxi, and wrote down his address and telephone number for Betty to take with her. She came out of the bathroom and did a little pirouette.

"You look great."

"I'll be fine if I don't sneeze." She threw her arms around his neck. Peppermint breath. "I'm going to be very sore today. A perfect celebration. Thank you."

He gave her the piece of paper he had prepared and a ten-dollar bill. "For the cab. You've been a very cheap date. Maybe the cheapest ever," he added.

"Smart-ass." She took the ten and scribbled an address and telephone number on the top sheet of the pad on the counter. Eighteenth Avenue, walking distance from the U. In the street, a horn blew. She pressed her lips to his lips, gave him a flick of her tongue. "Don't walk me down. You're old and I want you to get your beauty sleep. And take your vitamins."

Grinning, Boudreau kissed her good-bye and closed the door behind her. Hearing her on the wooden stairs, he put the coffeepot under the tap. He went to the window. Outside, the sky was still dark enough for the taxi to have its lights on. It started away. Boudreau had missed her coming out of the building and crossing the sidewalk.

On the other side of the intersection, a Chevy Caprice four-door pulled out from the curb and followed the cab. No lights. Boudreau pressed his face against the glass so he could see to the farther corner. The cab turned. The Chevy turned.

Somebody was following her?

Boudreau wasn't even sure she had gotten in the cab. He pulled on his pants and hurried down the stairs. The door to the first-floor apartment opened a crack. The Gunters. Boudreau kept going. The hall to the street was empty. Betty was gone. As he turned back the Gunters' door started to close.

"Wait! It's Phil Boudreau!"

The door opened again. Mrs. Gunter, who was about sixty-five, wearing a housecoat, stood in front of her husband, a bony little guy in a T-shirt and cotton pants.

"The young lady," Boudreau said. "Did you hear her go out?"

Mr. Gunter smirked. "We heard a whole bunch, all night long," he sang.

"Shut up, you pig," his wife snapped. "He watched her get in the cab," she told Boudreau. "He had to have a look."

"Then she definitely got in the cab," Boudreau said.

Mrs. Gunter glanced over her shoulder. "Well? Did she?"

"Yeah," the old man growled. "She got in the cab."

"Did you see the Chevy that followed the cab? Did you see who was driving?"

"I don't want to get involved," he muttered.

"Tell him, you son of a bitch!" Mrs. Gunter cried. "You know damned well he's a cop."

"Two guys," the old man said, and walked into the other room.

"Thanks," Boudreau said to Mrs. Gunter. He turned for the stairs again.

Mrs. Gunter said, "You know they found another girl's body in the Green River. That makes three."

He froze. "When?"

"Yesterday afternoon. It was on the six o'clock news."

"Yeah," the old man called. "They think a cop is doing it!"

Mrs. Gunter shook her head. "I'm going to kick his ass. What was on TV was that the *TNT* printed a quote from one of the cops down there."

The *TNT* was the Tacoma *News-Tribune*. There had been the same story when Bundy was loose. Cops nattered like back-fence biddies. Seattle to Tacoma. They thought it might be a cop? And the one who knew the victims best was the one being kept out of the case? "Thanks," he said to Mrs. Gunter, and headed upstairs.

He dialed the number Betty had given him. The telephone rang seven times before it was picked up.

"Hello?" A sleepy female voice.

"Is this Betty Antonelli's residence?"

"Yes, it is, but I don't think she's here. Hold on, I'll check." The handset clattered too quickly for him to stop her. He heard her call: *"Betty!"* Knocking on a door. *"Betty?"*

Who were the guys in the Chevy? *Come on!*

The telephone was picked up again. "Hey, look, she's not here now—"

"I know, she was with me. She left here just minutes ago. Ask her to call me as soon as she gets in. If she doesn't get there in the next five minutes, *you* call me. Will you take my number?"

"Wait a minute, she was with you?"

He sighed. "If you were in that sports bar last night, I'm the guy you saw—"

"Oh, right! Wait a minute, I see a cab pulling up outside. Hang on."

Another clatter. The cab was Betty's, he was sure. It made sense. At this hour there was no traffic and few cops on the streets and the driver could go as fast as he liked.

He heard a distant sliding sound—a window being opened?—and then the roommate's voice: "Your friend is on the phone! Him! Yeah, *Felix!*"

Boudreau leaned back against the refrigerator and let a shudder of relief rattle through him like an earthquake. He heard the telephone being picked up.

"Hello, Felix? Hello?"

"I'm here. What is it?"

"Another car just pulled up and two guys got out."

"Call her! Tell her to get inside!"

"Just a minute." She dropped the telephone again. "Betty?" Another long silence, then: "Hello, Felix? Look, I gotta run."

And the line went dead.

October 1982

Garrett Richard Lockman did not return to the Pacific Northwest until a week after the third girl's body was fished from the Green River. Janet Freeman, fifteen years old, a runaway with a record of streetwalking and drug offenses. Naked. Strangled. The newspapers and television accounts did not mention mutilations or objects being found in her body openings. In Cheyenne, Wyoming, on his way home with Hazel and Al, Lockman had found an old public-library copy of the Seattle *Times* reporting the discovery of the first girl's body, just as Martin Jones had told him. Whatever the truth about who had done the killing, Lockman was left in a state of intense agitation, sleeplessness, and distraction. The reports he found in Boise of the second killing said nothing about bullets, either, although Lockman was sure that if Martin Jones had done these killings, he had done them exactly as he had said, inserting Lockman's hollow points in the victims' vaginas. Lockman was beginning to see that he had in fact pushed Martin Jones too far, allowing him to tap into an energy and courage neither had known he had. Lockman could only believe that

Jones would subside from this peak experience, as people always did, to his everyday drab self. Lockman was going to maintain control of the relationship. He could not imagine living enslaved to the whims of another person, especially a little geek like Martin Jones.

But just as important to Lockman, the second victim was another teenager, not a woman whose voice could match the one Lockman had heard over the telephone from Kearney, Nebraska. Had that woman been in on some wacky gag cooked up by Jones? Not funny—and dangerous, under the circumstances. Jones wasn't the one with the police record. The police didn't know Martin Jones was alive, much less the author of some doggerel about a strange policeman.

But the woman's voice! Lockman couldn't believe he had been the victim of a hoax Jones had arranged with a coworker when bodies were being found. Not only too risky and elaborate for Jones, but beyond the level of his social skills—to wit, he didn't know any women.

What did Ron Beale think of Jones's telephone call, if in fact Jones had called him? The strangest cop·of all? That pointed to a *cop*, not someone in Lockman's position. And Beale was such a strange duck himself there was no telling what, or who, he thought was normal.

Lockman weighed all these things in Coeur d'Alene, where Al and Hazel wanted to spend the night before the final short drive to the elder Lockmans' home, in Spokane, Washington. A very bad, sleepless night, Lockman plagued by visions of devil worshipers running armed and naked through the woods. The area around Coeur d'Alene was that kind of crazy place. Human sacrifice out in the woods, infants conceived for the purpose. Everybody knew it. People chanting and dancing around altars. If you saw them, if they caught you spying on them, you would never be heard from again.

In Spokane Lockman decided he wasn't going to call Jones right away. He was staying clear even if he wasn't completely convinced that Jones was guilty of anything more than a trick. But Lockman couldn't help wondering about that woman's voice. Who? How? Jones had never been able to get a woman to do anything, even for money.

Lockman had things to do in Spokane anyway. He had several caches of souvenirs, records and documentation around town. The caches were on Al's rental properties, a garage here, an attic there, spaces Lockman had talked the old guy into giving him, padlocked to keep the tenants out. Of course Al thought the stuff was shit and wanted Lockman to get rid of it. Lockman never answered when Al mentioned the subject—just stared, silent, until the old goof backed down. While Lockman intended to dispose of nothing, he had to be sure he wasn't holding anything that could connect him to Martin Jones's present alleged activities or, for that matter, whatever Lockman may have discussed with Jones in times past.

Who could remember? Jones had been right about Lockman drinking to excess and blacking out. Hell, Lockman *loved* to drink and black out. And while he had no taste for the tedium of searching his files and records for anything incriminating, he felt himself caught in crazy, dangerous times. *Wonderful!* Lockman loved the whirl of conspiracy, waltzing with danger, almost as much as he feared the growing sense that events were proceeding without him.

Lockman hated Spokatropolis, as he called it. His mother, Al's sister, had lived and died in Medford, Oregon, which was the biggest city between San Francisco and Portland, just as Spokane was the biggest city between Seattle and Minneapolis, Minnesota. Originally nineteenth-century fur traders' outposts, the two cities—and dozens of others in the Pacific Northwest—had eventually evolved into railroad towns, the original tank towns. *Jerkwater* towns. The old perjoratives had meanings in history: the old steam-powered locomotives had stopped under large water tanks where the engineers jerked open spigots to fill the engine boilers. These parts, the cattle were probably Holstein, too. These parts constituted the end of the Oregon Trail, the last great destination for the covered-wagon pioneers. America's last great exuberant dream. These days, the tallest building in Medford, the city's only high-rise, was an old people's home planted in a hillside like a gigantic tombstone.

Spokane was bisected by the narrow Spokane River, with old Protestant money locked into dark, heavily gingerbreaded Victorian houses on the high land on the south side. Working-class Catholics were packed in nine-hundred-square-foot bungalows on the low-level north, where the neighborhoods were known by the names of the Catholic parishes. As beautiful as it must have been when it belonged to the Indians, Spokane was now a grimy, gloomy, aging burg cursed with a low-lying overcast that blotted the sun for weeks at a time, the perfect backdrop for the black, ugly B-52 bombers roaring loudly through landings and takeoffs at Fairchild Air Force Base a few miles to the southwest. Everyone Lockman had grown up with hated Spokane, and all the All-American City awards in the world couldn't change the fact that all those people—sane people, Lockman proudly reminded himself—couldn't wait to get the hell out of town.

If old money comforted the brittle genes of Spokane's south side, religion suffocated the north. It reached an asthmatic intensity in Hazel and Al's house, which was just blocks from Holy Name University, "the Powerhouse" to the people of Spokane. Hazel and Al, all their bigotry and dirty-mindedness notwithstanding, were religious fanatics. A crucifix gaudy with red enamel blood hung on the living room wall. An oversized shrine clung to the top of Hazel's dresser, the statue of the Virgin almost as big as a real-life midget. Every Christmas, on the front lawn, lighted every night for a month, stood a life-size crèche that spent the rest of the year hanging by its hooves, horns, and ankles in hilarious sacrilege from a block-and-tackle affixed to the main beam of the garage—in the gloom you had to look twice to be sure you had not entered a real abbatoir.

In grammar school Lockman's classmates used to joke about the noises their parents made during lovemaking, while he could only burn with curiosity about what those sounds might be like. The nights were silent in the home of Al and Hazel Lockman, and if Al hadn't been getting any pussy at the age of forty-seven—this was twenty years ago—it hadn't seemed to matter to him. Al much preferred a night of television and a bowl of ice cream to a tray of martinis and a blow job. That was fine with Hazel, who probably would have chosen to spend eternity fetching Rocky Road and Chocolate Chocolate Chip to giving one more thought to participating in a sex act of any kind. As a child Lockman had endured long periods of loneliness because Hazel thought her own sister was being a whore again and her children therefore unfit to play with her nephew slash foster child. Of course Lockman's natural mother, who had delivered him without benefit of wedlock, was burning in hell for her whoring. Lockman's natural mother had liked It—the big IT—as Hazel had hinted for years before Lockman knew what the fuck she was talking about.

And now, as she headed toward seventy, Hazel rattled through her list of his mother's lovers as mindlessly as a horny teenager reciting prayers in church. What was she really thinking of? Did she imagine that anyone was still listening after all these years? Hazel loved to have the priests stop by, monsignors and a cardinal once as he passed through town, crimson robes gliding smoothly over the broadloom. Never the nuns, who were, after all, women.

For his part, Al loved it, basking in it, as long as it was understood by all that he was not going to have a serious conversation with anybody—ever. Only the practice of dentistry could force Al to behave like an adult. Life was a gag a day, stuff he read in the funny papers, the *TV Guide* crossword puzzle, and a monthly drive to the Liars Club meeting. In exchange for that understanding from the reverend clergy, Al would write a check—tax deductible, as he liked to say, giving his real game away. In his teens Lockman had watched all this with great care. If for Al the expenditure really was the cost of getting to heaven, he wanted to see value for money in this world—in the good opinion of the reverend clergy, or maybe just their well-rehearsed respectful friendliness. Al figured he was paying for a seamless performance, and he turned surly when he didn't get it. No problem. People were spoken to, Al was explained, heads nodded, lips stretched tight in celibate smiles. When it came to Al, Hazel always had an explanation, and her personality was powerful enough to make sure that her vision was imposed on everybody. Hazel and Al were a closed circuit. They wanted their lives exactly as they were without another word about it.

So Lockman didn't hear the sounds of fucking until he was fourteen years old and organized a peep patrol. In those days he kept diaries, and it was all written down somewhere, the names of the members of the patrol, what they saw, the dates and times of the sightings. That definitely included Hazel's sister, who got the teenage Lockman very hot on several nights in the course of two or three years. He kept her off the route of the peep patrol, saving her for himself. One night outside her window he made so much noise attaining ejaculation that she and her boyfriend heard him over their own shouts and cries. Even today, when he was really drunk, on the edge of blacking out, Lockman sometimes allowed his thoughts to drift back over his early fantasies of her. He had a record of them, too, somewhere in all his stuff, how he would force her onto her knees to lick and suck him as eagerly as he had seen her do with the gas-station owner and the bartender from the cocktail lounge downtown. To this day, his aunt and her boyfriends did not know that he had spied on them, compiled dossiers that lived in a box on one of Al's various properties around Spokane.

Lockman had Al by the nuts. Lockman had keys to Al's office, and regularly entered after hours and stole the little schmuck's cocaine. Lockman had been doing it for years, and Al knew what was going on. Lockman assumed that Al covered the cocaine trail by writing prescriptions for what he had "dispensed." Lockman didn't even like cocaine; he just sold it for what it was, medical grade, to his friends when he needed the money.

Al was silent about it because of Hazel, who did not want her foster son slash nephew to have to endure more stress than he had already. She was really talking about herself, of course. Deep inside, Hazel was a psychological wreck, but no one was ever going to see it as long as she had her way. Lockman knew he had them figured when he realized how far Hazel and Al would go to keep from disturbing each other. Hazel made all the major decisions. Al wanted her to treat him like the only real child of the family. The single thing they had to do to make it work was lie to themselves about their nephew/foster child. Now that he was a convicted felon who had served time in Seattle's King County Jail, and no one here in Spokane knew anything about it, Hazel and Al in her wake would do anything he said without asking why. He had a story that they said they believed, but from his point of view it was only a courtesy they extended to him for going along with all their lies. Handling them was so easy that he never really gave it a thought.

They even believed the trip to Atlantic City for the Miss America Pageant had been their idea, when in fact Lockman had suggested it to them after he had conceived his own adventure with camera and fast talk. Al had paid for practically everything, not knowing yet that some of the charges existed, like the two hookers in Atlantic City who had posed for Lockman in his room. Riot! One of the girls had brought her own VISA machine. Lockman liked to spin the exposed thirty-five-millimeter rolls of film on the dinette table under Al's nose, wondering if Al had any idea about the kind of images captured thereon. Like his success in Harrisburg, Martin Jones's opinions to the contrary notwithstanding. Little Chief Sucks Off Dogs was such a neuter that he could not imagine that anyone who would have anything to do with him was capable of functioning sexually. Lockman had gotten the Harrisburg bitch naked to the waist without her figuring out what he was really up to. *Dumb!* No, she had insisted, she wasn't a mother, while he dialed into crystalline focus her distended brown nipples and the white rivulets of her stretch marks. Lockman had put the camera down and stared until it was easier for her to keep her eyes on his hand as he began to caress himself.

Her mouth hung open. He unzipped and exposed himself, knowing that in this circumstance she could not possibly protest.

"What's the matter?" she asked. "Doesn't it get hard?"

He would have killed her at that moment if there had been any chance that he could have gotten away with it.

Lockman stretched his business in Spokane over several days. The nights were cold now, the leaves blowing in the streets. On reflection, Lockman had realized that only one *objet* implicated him in any misdoings, and that was the earring whose mate existed somewhere in the evidence of the murder of Deeah Anne Johanssen, age twenty-two, on August 17, 1976, in the University District of Seattle. And when Lockman had the earring in his pocket, he spent the next several days checking out his other stuff, like his complete collection of *National Geographic*, which he had stolen from one of the south-side mansions a dozen years before, and his Big Little Book collection, from San Francisco, paid for, *Terry and the Pirates, Don Winslow, Smilin' Jack*—very few people could put together a gray autumn afternoon in an attic thumbing through some of the real pop treasures of the early part of the century.

Deeah Anne Johanssen had been Lockman's first murder victim. A spur-of-the-moment deal, almost an accident. Sperm of the moment, he liked to think. He had followed her home, enchanted by the arrogant pitching of her curvy behind. He had been living on the next block over, but in spite of all his prowling, had never seen her before. Lockman Rule One: Nobody could connect the killer to the victim. He had been thinking for a long time about doing whatever he wanted to a woman, seeing early in the game that once you started on such a project, you could not stop, you could not leave behind a survivor to become an implacable enemy and then, finally, your pursuer. You had to kill her. It had been unbearably thrilling and revolting at the same time, especially the moment she realized her life was ending. He had masturbated on the spot, in his pants, achieving one of the most memorable orgasms of his life, one of the highest highs; and afterward, almost instantaneously, dropping to one of his lowest lows. In the crush of his despair he had picked up her body and flung it down a cellar staircase. In the weeks afterward, in the self-loathing that had settled on him with the weight of a building, he promised himself he would stay out of situations that might create that kind of fury in him again, and for a long time he was successful.

Until he met Martin Jones, another guy, like himself, who liked to talk about weird shit. Do weird shit. Brag about the weird shit he'd done. And sure enough, after one especially drunken night of crazy talk six months ago, prison just behind him, a hideous brief memory, Lockman picked up a girl on the Strip and took her down to Portland, where he dared play with her, a cat with a mouse, for more than an hour, before he strangled her with the bar-arm choke hold he had read about in *Soldier of Fortune* magazine. She had gone suddenly limp, dead weight, just as the article had said. Lockman murder victim number two. One of Uhuru's girls, she had said.

He had thought that picking a scrawny black who had not bathed would make the project easier. No. When she saw that he was not joking, she cried like a child, begged, pleaded; and the next day, looking at her dead body, he was drowned by the realization of the senselessness of everything that had ever happened to her, the meaninglessness jigglings of her atoms in the blackness of space. The light inside her might just as well have never been lit. That night, when he drove her naked body back up north again, to a wooded patch in a town on one of the routes he took back and forth between Spokane and Seattle, he was only field-testing

Lockman Rule Two: Feed her to the animals. She would be stripped to the bones in months. Ted Bundy had violated both rules, Lockman had told Martin Jones heatedly on another drunken night. Skeletons told nothing. What was it all about, killing or getting caught?

Lockman knew he was safe after the second one, but that didn't stop the bottom from dropping out of him again as he made his way back to Portland from Enumclaw. And as he slept: some kind of big-time self-betrayal was involved, because thirty hours later, when he awakened, he found himself quaking in terror. And in the next instant he lost the desire to move. He was motionless for what seemed like hours.

In 1976, after the first one, he had been left wondering what he had discovered inside him. Six months ago, after the one he took to Portland, he knew: something coming into creation more savage than any beast. His terror shook his bones and yet he could see at once that this had been inevitable. He began to move again when it became clear he had been given the best reason to date for continuing to live, whether he liked it or not. The thought brought a measure of healing, too: Lockman could feel it.

Monster.

The greatest monster of all time, if he wanted to be.

—

BY THURSDAY LOCKMAN saw he had been hanging around Spokane all this time waiting for Friday evening, when Martin Jones would be home with the next day off. Until now Jones had been a constipated little turdlet of a crook, too afraid even to boost the slugs in the parking-lot machine across the street from the Thirteen Coins, Garrett Richard Lockman's favorite Seattle diner. If Martin Jones had gone thermonuclear and begun a career as a serial killer, Lockman could credit the long nights over coffee in the high-backed brown vinyl booths at the Thirteen Coins, briefing Big Chief Little Penis on what scamming was really all about.

He had Jones's head filled with nutty stuff, like the idea of ordering blank videotapes from the manufacturers on phony credit cards, renting porn tapes to duplicate on the blanks, and then selling the copies for big bucks up in Vancouver. It would make a lot of money, but Lockman had never done it. It sounded too much like work. What he had done after his stint in King County Jail was to take a consignment of porn videos from an Italian he had met inside for resale in Canada. The guy had said he was Mafia, and for all Lockman knew, he was telling the truth. The guy said he couldn't cross the border, not explaining why—he just couldn't. Lockman knew you couldn't get too curious in these deals, and later, driving up the I-5, he drank vodka out of the bottle, worried about getting shit-faced and appearing to look unreliable to the the guy on other end, who turned out to be hardly a tough guy, just a fussy little twerp with a Scottish burr paying cash for the tapes, no questions asked, always ready for more, as he told Lockman.

The Italian waiting in Seattle to return the rental truck thought his thousand bucks was all Lockman was getting out of the deal. *Yeah, right*: Lockman had bought four Rolex watches and an emerald pendant from a burglar on the Strip, and had sold the lot for twenty-five hundred to a Chinese jeweler who planned to take them back to Taiwan. Lockman also had a cache of stolen American Express traveler's checks, and in ten minutes in Vancouver he had passed almost three hundred dollars' worth. Eager to work the exchange rates, Canadians were always glad to get their hands on American traveler's checks.

Al was at his office when Lockman prepared to leave Spokane, and just as well. When Lockman showed up in Spokane early last year before his prison sentence was officially up, he had told Hazel and Al that the original arrest had been a sham to fool certain crooks. For years he had been telling them he had been working under deep cover for law enforcement, all the way back to his days at the Seattle Center during the World's Fair, and then in the navy with the Shore Patrol. Lockman suspected he could tell Hazel he was going to become an astronaut for the next manned shot to Mars and she would believe him—and if she believed him, Al had damned well better act like he believed him, too, if he knew what was good for him.

When Lockman found Hazel in the kitchen and told her he was going back to Seattle, she cried.

"Don't," Lockman said.

"I'm afraid you're going to be in danger again. I worry so. I don't know what you do."

"I talk to people. What they tell me, I pass on to my superiors. Sometimes I'm on surveillance, which means I sit in a car and watch a house a block or two away."

"I pray!" she wailed. "You don't know how I pray! Are you going to Mass?"

"Of course I'm going to Mass. What a question!"

"Are you going to Confession? When was the last time you received Communion?"

"Yes, I am. Two weeks ago."

"You don't want to burn in hell, do you?" She expected an answer.

"No, Hazel, I don't."

"Recite an Our Father. A Hail Mary."

He did, prattling away like a schoolboy. She crossed herself. He never went near a church when he was not in Spokane, but that did not mean that a Sunday went by without him thinking about reinforcing his determination to keep her fooled. They had money, these two little clowns, and no one deserved to inherit it more than he did. Because of her constant weeping and manipulation, being in her presence was like being suffocated under a lilac-scented load of elephant diarrhea. Lockman told her not to make it worse on him than it already was. She sniffed, dried her eyes, and said she would try, because he was right as well as a hero.

He was still enjoying the moment when he passed through Moses Lake, in the middle of the state. Moses Lake was where the chartered plane carrying him from Medford had stopped on its way to Spokane. Throughout his childhood he thought he remembered the place, and years later, when he was able to make the return trip alone, he crisscrossed the little town looking for something familiar. Nothing. Now the town just made him nervous, and he stopped only when he wanted to load up on Big Macs and fries. Not this time. He wanted to hit Seattle's streets lean and mean. Depending on what he found at Martin Jones's house, he could be visiting other friends in the Seattle area for weeks. Two couples knew he was coming; he had told them before he'd left on the long drive east with Hazel and Al. Lockman always brought Chinese food when he dropped in on people. No one could turn you away with the odors of hot Chinese food under his nose.

Lockman arrived in Seattle before dinner, parking in the garage across the street from the library and cruising Fifth Avenue on foot. No passing traveler's checks here. *No nothin'*, in fact. This had been his turf, but not anymore, not since Frogface Boudreau had passed through his life. Friday afternoon? On his normal schedule, right about now Boudreau crossed Fifth Avenue some blocks south of the library, on his way to the bus that took him up to Queen Anne. If Boudreau was still living the dreary life Lockman had observed, when he reached his own neighborhood Boudreau would stop first at a grocery store, and then, because it was Friday, at the Chinese laundry. Lockman knew Boudreau better than Boudreau could ever imagine knowing Lockman, and Boudreau was as much a creature of habit as any other flatfoot. If he didn't go over to the U District to visit his brat in the evening, as often as not he would go back to work, cruising the Pike or Pioneer Square in his beat-up old Mustang. Lockman had to keep his eyes open, because out of habit Boudreau sometimes prowled these streets and the tunnels under them looking for hookers and their customers. Dumb luck had allowed

Boudreau to get Lockman the first time—luck, and Boudreau's innate mean suspiciousness.

Lockman saw himself as doing the same business as Boudreau, only more honestly. When he worked the streets and tunnels, going from hotel to store to hotel, he was looking for a woman who was cruising, too. An adventuress. A sex addict. A woman whose husband didn't know of her secret life: next *Donohue*. Women like that were on the talk shows all the time, sitting in shadow behind frosted glass, their voices disguised. Around here, if a woman caught Lockman following her, she was just as likely to turn and confront him as start to run. If she tried to embarrass him, he turned it around on her, yelling at her, calling her crazy, making sure never to curse. Cursing always got you in trouble with the cops—and they made it worse when women were involved. Where he could be observed, Lockman was careful never to do anything illegal. You had the right to walk on the same side of the street as another person, in the same direction. What was wrong with that? But not tonight. Lockman was much too nervous. He didn't want to go to the Thirteen Coins and risk running into Martin Jones prematurely, accidentally. And with Boudreau so close in space and time that Lockman could almost detect his spoor, Lockman was thinking of the message Martin Jones said he had given to Ron Beale. Lockman would have to check in with Beale soon, but he had to wait until he had a clearer sense of how his situation had changed, thanks to Martin Jones.

If it had changed at all.

Lockman walked down Pike Street to the Market and had a hot dog. The Market smelled of fish, but looking at the water let him drift into reverie. He let himself wonder when he was going to kill another girl. He was trying to stay calm, but he knew he was not being very successful. Off in the distance, a jackhammer rattled.

Maybe he was going to surprise himself!

Another good thought.

Lockman drove through Martin Jones's neighborhood for ten minutes, never taking the same street twice, before stopping the car. No sign of surveillance. From outside Jones's two-story pseudo-Colonial, everything seemed to be the way Jones liked it. Small lamps in curtained windows on either side of the front door softly lit the porch, and on the second floor one even smaller lamp could be seen centered in a window. Normal, normal, normal. Jones always kept the lawn mowed, the hedges clipped. He waved to his neighbors, smiled, said hello, passed the time of day. Good-neighbor, solid-citizen bullshit was easy for him: he *loved* to keep his car waxed, the bank account swelling. If anyone on the block had a question about him, it was only, *Why is he single?*

Jones was a mechanical engineer at Boeing, "a tiny cog in a vast machine working on tiny cogs in vast machines," he liked to say. A part of Jones's mind would be happy trying to build a machine that could put diapers on piss clams. Lockman parked in the driveway. He wanted to walk through Jones's border plantings to the door, but didn't, because that was the kind of thing that got Jones really angry. Lockman stepped up on the porch and rang the doorbell. It was the same as picking up a girl for a date, and the thought made him feel funny. The lights in the windows went out.

"The door is open," Martin Jones called from inside.

Lockman entered.

"I saw you drive around the block," Jones said from the other side of the darkened living room. "You're such a goon. I've been expecting you. When you lock the door from the inside, I'll turn on the light."

" 'I've been expecting you,' " Lockman mocked. "Are you in some kind of a fucking movie?" He locked the door. "Happy now?" He had to get control of the situation. "Where's that audiotape you said you made? You know what I'm talking about. I want to hear it."

"I told you, it's down at your place in Portland. Have you talked to your friend Ron Beale?"

"That's not the way it works and you know it. You said you wrote down what you said to him. Let me see it." In his agitation Lockman had a new realization: had this silly bastard Jones actually saved something in his own handwriting that tied him to a murder?

The living-room light came on. Jones was in the entry to the dining room, champagne glass in hand. He was wearing a white peignoir, stockings, garter belt, panties, and brassiere. A dark lipstick was smeared thickly on his lips. Grinning insanely, he did a little curtsy. "Thank God for mail order. Say I look nice or no champagne."

"You look like a hippo in a tutu—"

Jones stamped his foot. "Say I look nice or I won't give you what I wrote!"

"Schmuck, you look nice." Lockman dipped into his pocket for the earring. "Here, I brought you a souvenir."

Martin Jones reached out for it, leaning forward as if afraid Lockman was looking for a chance to hurt him, like a bully in a schoolyard. "*One* earring?"

"It's from the girl in Harrisburg."

"Thanks, I guess."

"Now do you believe me?" Lockman asked. "It happened."

"If you say so." He put the earring on. A true transvestite, Jones couldn't wait to lock his doors, pull down his shades, and climb into his woman's wardrobe. Mail order? Like Lockman, Martin Jones had a number of postal boxes rented under assumed names. He thought it made him a real criminal.

"The guys down at Boeing should see their savage redskin coworker now. The neighbors. Hey, what would happen if I set the house on fire?"

"More than you know," Martin Jones said. He turned to the dining table and poured a glass of champagne for Lockman. "I have a surprise for you." He swept toward the back of the house, the ribbons of his peignoir flowing behind him like toilet paper stuck to a garbage truck. The desire to laugh was so intense that Lockman dared not focus on it.

"Let me have that paper! *Now*, you little piece of shit!"

"It's on the refrigerator door."

More of Jones's compulsive orderliness. The refrigerator door was covered with schedules, telephone numbers, printouts from his job. In the center of it all was a piece of bond paper, and in the middle of the sheet, single-spaced, was typed:

The girl's killer wants to be like you, only he's too wild. When you find the bullets, look for the strangest cop of all.

Perfect. "Where's your telephone?"

"On the wall, where it always is. So now it's all right to call Beale?"

"More than all right." Suddenly Lockman felt wonderful, absolutely gleeful with opportunity. He grabbed the cordless telephone and shoved it in his back pocket.

Jones opened the cellar door and gestured to Lockman to precede him down the stairs. "Come, let me show you my surprise."

"After you," Lockman said.

"I just love your paranoia. What do you think I want to do, strip you naked and tie you to a chair? How many times do I have to tell you? You're not my type. But if it will make you happy, I'll go first. But don't peek, okay?"

The foot of the stairs faced a wall, so whatever Jones wanted to show him was behind them, in the center of the cellar. Lockman waited until his feet were on the cellar floor before turning around. He was smiling until his brain made sense of what was in front of his eyes.

A woman. Naked, in a chair, tied to it, her arms behind her, something the size of a baseball wedged in her mouth. She was dirty, her dyed yellow hair matted. She stared at Lockman, made a sound, no more than a muffled squeak, and tried to move in the chair. Lockman was electrified, riveted. He smelled feces.

"I saved her for you," Martin Jones said.

Lockman felt a faint contraction of ejaculation. He pushed Martin Jones aside to get closer to her. Her eyes widened as she watched him. Yes, this was the older woman he had heard over the telephone. *He had to get control of the situation!* "Remember me?" He waited, watching her every twitch. "Do you? You told me to call the Seattle police—or do you tell that to all the boys?"

She shook her head and tried to push back from him. He could feel his pants growing wet. He unzipped, careful to keep his eyes away from Martin Jones, who began maneuvering himself around for a better look. So much for the battle for control. Lockman had to keep his distance from the woman; if he dripped semen on her, it could be identified by blood type later. Lockman knew about evidence. He had read all the police textbooks, some of them so many times it seemed as if he had them memorized. "Do you remember me?" he asked. "A nod will do."

She nodded. Her eyes darted to his penis as if to a poisonous snake. He resisted waggling it at her—for now.

"How did you keep her alive all this time? What did you feed her?"

"Diet shake. Through a straw. I had her mouth taped shut, with a little hole in the tape. She couldn't make a sound."

"Very nice." He leaned closer to her. "Do you still want me to call the police?"

She nodded again. He took the telephone from his pocket and displayed it like a magician introducing a new trick. He dialed the King County Sheriff. "Let me speak to Captain Ron Beale, please."

"One moment."

"I'm holding," he announced to his little audience. The telephone clicked.

"Major Crimes."

"Captain Beale, please."

"He's gone for the day. Can I take a message?"

"No, that's all right." Lockman hung up. "Gone for the day," he said to the woman. "But we knew that. *Noooo* problem! When you asked *this* guy to call a cop, you got more than you bargained for!" He dialed Ron Beale's home telephone number from memory. He held the handset to the woman's ear so she could hear the ringing, then drew it back as Beale said hello.

"Hey, it's Garrett Lockman. I've been reading the newspapers. You guys have real problems."

"Lockman! Where have you been? I've been trying to reach you."

Lockman winked to the woman. "I told you I was taking my parents cross-country. I started reading the Seattle papers in Cheyenne." He pulled at his penis. The woman rocked back on the chair, squealing through the sock in her mouth. Lockman said, "I got into town this morning and spent the day making the rounds. The killings are the only thing people are talking about. I think I got something for you."

"What are they saying?"

"As long as you understand that it's just gossip, not the hard stuff you're used to getting from me." He stroked the woman's matted hair. "It's also not the kind of stuff I like to pass on to you for other reasons."

"Why don't you try me?" While Beale was speaking Lockman moved the handset quickly to the woman's ear and drew it back, but not before she was able to make another noise. Lockman heard Beale ask, "What was that?"

"A burp," Lockman said. "I was trying to be polite, and it came up funny. You'd be burping, too, if you were trying to digest all the junk food I've stuffed in myself today. I should bill you."

Silence: Beale was completely humorless. "Tell me what you've heard."

"Hang on a minute." He put his hand over the mouthpiece. "You paying attention to all this, woman?" She stared. He looked to Jones. "Next time get one with nicer tits. This one's aren't even the same size."

Jones's mouth was hanging open. The woman kicked and rocked in the chair. Lockman took his hand away from the mouthpiece again. "Sorry, Ron. I'm calling from a friend's kitchen and her little girl just came in for a soda. What they're saying on the street is that it's a cop, and that he's playing a game with you."

"What kind of game?"

"They don't know. You know what assholes these people are. They hear something, they embellish it, and before you know it—"

"What kind of embellishments?"

"That he's phoning it in to somebody, telling where the bodies will be, that they're disfigured in some special way."

"Like how?"

"I asked, but the people I saw today don't know."

"Let's meet. Tomorrow."

"Okay. In the parking lot?"

"Ten o'clock," Beale said, and hung up. Lockman switched off the telephone and put it in his back pocket. He smiled to the woman.

"Got the picture? That's your cops for you, dumb as they get." She didn't move, her eyes huge. Lockman looked to Martin Jones. "Showtime, Little Beaver." Lockman got behind the woman and looped his forearm around her neck. "This is the way you do the bar-arm choke hold," he said, getting his shoulder up close behind her neck. The smell of feces got stronger suddenly. "Get the gag out of her mouth."

"She'll scream," Jones protested.

Laughing, Lockman reached around and pulled the sock out. Before she was able to get her breath, Lockman applied pressure, all his weight. A moment's kicking, a little jiggling, piddle splattering in the dust on the concrete basement floor, and she entered history. "Here," Lockman said, standing up, filling his chest à la John Wayne, icy ejaculate clinging to his testes, "do what you want with her."

"You didn't see her face!" Jones shrieked. "You didn't see her face!"

Lockman could not help giggling. "Did I miss something?"

"You didn't see her face! You didn't see her face!"

Lockman gave him a smile of perfect triumph. "Then let's get another one!"

November 1982

"He's a puke."

"What?"

"You heard me, a puke," Phil Boudreau said. "Garrett Lockman is a puke."

"Oh, I heard what you said," Special Agent Kevin Donovan of the FBI said. "I just don't know what it means."

Boudreau sighed. He'd known when Dan Cheong called this morning to ask him to "drop by" that he was really being told to report for an interrogation about the killings—the Green River had yielded five bodies now—but he'd thought he'd see a bit more subtlety. After all, these days there was hell to pay, when every voice you could tune in on, every word you could read, was about the possibility of a new Ted and the rapidly expanding failure of the police to do a damned thing about it. Five bodies, the last two on successive weekends. Feminist activists were saying that the cops were dragging their feet because the victims were poor young women. That was correct, as far as Phil Boudreau was concerned. Under the best of conditions he could not get his work taken seriously because he serviced the same constituency. *Street girls* was the usual dismissive phrase, like *stray dogs. Throwaways,* somebody had called them.

Boudreau had thought subtlety was his due. Six weeks had passed since his last contact with Beale, Cheong, Donovan, and the rest of the incompetent gang "investigating" the Green River killings. Boudreau could date it so precisely because the last contact had been the Saturday morning he'd watched Betty Antonelli drive off in that taxi. He hadn't been in her company since. One of the guys in this room, or another member of the team, had told her something about him so ugly, so foul, that it had scared her off.

In addition to Cheong and Donovan were two more King County detectives and another special agent, arrayed around Boudreau like infielders playing a game of pepper, all five avoiding eye contact with one another in the struggle to look casual. After the passage of so many weeks that the clocks were reset to Pacific Standard Time, these guys wanted to chat. Right. Now, after four o'clock, the sky outside darkening, desktops were littered with the fast-food wrappers and paper cups of lunchtime. *Right.* A special agent's idea, Boudreau was sure. Only the FBI would think of trying to fool a street cop with props. *Make it look like we're working hard and this is our first chance to get to him.*

"It's a cop's expression," Boudreau said. "I never heard a civilian use it. My father used it—"

"You just said it's a cop's expression."

"My father was NYPD for twenty-seven years," Boudreau said, barely attempting to conceal his disgust. If they'd done their homework, they would have known about his father. He was beginning to wonder if he had to terminate this "conversation" for a chat with his lawyer instead.

"Why didn't you follow him into that department?" the other special agent asked.

"I met my wife while I was in the service in Panama. Seattle was her home."

"One or the other, eh?"

"No, she thinks New York is terrible."

"You're divorced now, aren't you?" Dan Cheong asked.

"And a father. I love my kid. I don't want to be far from him."

Boudreau saw the FBI exchange glances, as if he had said something strange. He would do no more volunteering, but not so they would notice. One of the King County guys broke the lengthening silence. "Why don't you tell us what a puke is?"

As much as he did not want to seem to hesitate, Boudreau could not help taking another deep breath. "A lowlife, something lower than an ordinary crook, with secret vile habits, things you don't see in an animal. The kind of guy women call a creep. And avoid. In school he was the guy who put turtles in the freezer, or firecrackers up the cat's ass. Crazy Al, Crazy Freddie—behind his back, maybe the whole school had a name for him. He liked to talk about masturbating, or playing the Peeping Tom."

"That doesn't mean anything. A lot of kids are like that."

Perfect. Boudreau turned to stare silently at the special agent who had just spoken. Donovan's partner, a hawk-nosed, prematurely florid coronary candidate. After a moment one of the King County guys laughed quietly and looked away. Donovan wasn't happy. He said quickly, "On the strength of that, you think this Garrett Richard Lockman is the guy killing these girls?"

"It's all in the memo I wrote to Ron Beale after the first body was found. I spent a lot of time with Lockman after I caught him red handed at that gun shop. I knew right away that if I stayed on him, he'd flip. He did, implicating his partner and himself in almost a dozen jobs."

Donovan blinked. "What happened to the partner?"

"Five-to-ten in Walla Walla. Lockman got a year in the county."

"Nice job," Dan Cheong said.

The other special agent asked, "How did you know Lockman would flip?"

"It's all in the file. He was scared to death of jail. He whined, he moaned, all but got down on his knees and pleaded. I thought at the time, this is the most lily-livered guy I've ever met in my life. I hated to be around him. I always thought I had to take a bath after I spent any time with him."

"This is all in the file you sent over."

"Not that so much as the stupid, strange things he said about women, crime, criminals, the way the world worked. His apartment was full of Nazi paraphernalia, porn, scanners, police uniforms, radios, handcuffs, badges. Once he saw he was going to get a break for tossing his pal, he acted like I'd go for being his best buddy. Lockman is a very powerful personality. Extremely. He thought he could get the better of me. He thought he could talk me into something I didn't want to do. Relentless. Persuasive. There were times when I could see he thought he was pouring on the charm." Boudreau had to dig for Lockman's old partner's name. "Brownall. Thomas Brownall. From San Diego. Lockman was there when he was in the navy and I think he met Brownall under conditions that gave the navy second thoughts about allowing Lockman to re-up."

"What gave the navy second thoughts?"

"Suspicion of criminal activity. Stealing navy equipment. They never could prove anything. This guy Brownall was a known fence in the San Diego area. National City. He sold navy electronics to Mexican dope dealers for countersurveillance purposes. The police radio stuff I found in Lockman's apartment here ties in, but we could never prove it was stolen."

One of the King County detectives sitting on the couch said, "All right, all right, the guy's a piece of shit—or a puke, if you want to call him that—but I don't see how any of what you say gets you to conclude that he's a likely murder suspect."

"I said, he wanted me to get the idea that we had entered into a conspiracy together against Brownall. And like it was his own idea. If I gave him that, I also gave him the permission to initiate conversations on other subjects, the Crazy Freddie–Crazy Georgie stuff of junior high. I'm not kidding. For instance, one day he asked me how I thought women could stand themselves—their anatomy and so forth. It was only one negative he expressed about women. Of many. Once it was the odor of vaginal secretions. These comments were parts of a pattern based on the notion that these subjects were part of our private, ongoing agenda. Nothing could be further from the truth, and nothing I said to shut him up had any effect. Relentless, I said. It could have been that he was just testing me, looking for my weaknesses, but his subject matter was always the same. I called him a puke. Women were another species to him. He talked as if it was okay to do what you wanted to them."

"A lot of guys feel that way and they don't consider themselves criminals. Nobody else does, either."

The same guy as before. This time Boudreau looked at the ceiling. And this time Cheong broke the silence. "But you say he could have been probing for weaknesses."

"The guys in my neighborhood who were doing that kind of stuff were always looking for confederates."

"You mean in junior high," Donovan said.

"I should have been clearer. Yes."

"Why were you so close to him?"

"I said, he implicated his partner and himself in almost a dozen jobs, but not all at once. I had to keep him talking."

Cheong smiled knowingly. Crooks loved attention. Once you gave it to them, they worked like hell to keep it. If you worked the right guy the right way, he would rat out his mother. With Garrett Richard Lockman, Boudreau never thought of having been a successful interrogator, mainly because Garrett Richard Lockman had turned himself into an impenetrable morass. Boudreau knew he had heard only a tiny part of what Lockman had done in his life.

Donovan said, "You gave him reason to believe you were entering into a criminal conspiracy together?"

"Did I say that?"

The door opened and Ron Beale poked his head in. "You guys still here?" He stepped in and extended his hand to Boudreau. "Hey, Phil, how're ya doin'?"

A split second passed, no more than a finger snap, before Boudreau took his hand. "All right," he heard himself say. He felt a zap of adrenaline as he found himself dialing into focus the idea that the room was bugged, that Beale had been listening at another location from the beginning. Beale half sat on the end of the arm of a sofa so he remained higher than everyone else. He looked from left to right. "Did you tell Phil about Lockman?" He looked down to Boudreau. "On your tip? Did they tell you?"

"Tell? I didn't know there was anything to tell."

Beale glanced toward the window, taking his time before responding. It was all a show, the only question was where they were taking it. He had to stay blank, impassive. And keep his mouth shut about Betty Antonelli. He had to be careful about what he let on about what he knew of their activities. As long as they thought he was stupid, he had that one slender advantage.

Beale said, "We ran Lockman's name as soon as we got your file. It was one of the first tips to come in. Now we get dozens every day. Anyway, Lockman's credit-card slips for gasoline purchases in the latter part of August and early September put him in Pennsylvania and New Jersey. No question. He drove his aunt and uncle, who also happen to be his foster parents, to the Miss America Pageant in Atlantic City." Beale was looking only at Boudreau as he talked. "We have a tape of the show from the network, and he was in the audience. We made him from the mug shot taken after your bust. Silly-looking character. A woman would have no trouble identifying him." Beale was smiling as he turned away from Boudreau. "The evidence says he's not the character who's killing those girls."

"You can't argue with that," Boudreau said. He knew he sounded lame. Maybe, he thought, he sounded unconvinced—and just that quickly, he realized he was unconvinced, although he wasn't immediately sure why. One of the first tips to come in? *Somebody* had not known he had already sent his file on Lockman to Beale when Cheong and Donovan had visited him after the first find at Green River. Now here was Beale prancing around with an attitude, a little too smug. And somebody had overdressed the set. Sure, the room was wired, remote tape recorders spinning.

Donovan leaned in. "Did you follow the Atlanta child murders?"

Boudreau's first thought almost made him laugh out loud: that they were going to tie those killings to him, too. They were under that kind of pressure. If they failed to catch the killer, they could wind up being saddled with the blame for everything but the killings themselves. "No, not really."

Donovan said, "The FBI broke that case using a brand-new investigative technique. Our behavioral-sciences lab analyzed the evidence on the victims and at the crime scenes to develop a profile of the personality of the killer. As the case progressed they noticed that whenever law enforcement made a statement to the press about him, he adjusted his MO for safety. So the bureau took a proactive role. The press was told that the bodies were yielding a tremendous number of clues. Next thing we knew, the bodies started turning up in the local rivers and streams, where immersion would destroy the evidence. Are you following this? We boxed him in like cowboys! We staked out the bridges over the rivers, and that's where we got him. Wayne Williams is the man. No question. Fits the profile perfectly. It's absolutely astonishing."

Now Boudreau knew from whom Beale had learned the *no question* phrase. Maybe Beale had Donovan going to his church. Another thing to remember. "Sounds to me that you would have gotten him by going, uh, 'proactive' without, what? Developing a psychological profile."

Donovan regarded Boudreau, his lips pursed. "A lot of people who were against this at the start became converts pretty quick, believe me."

"No question," Boudreau said. He was remembering an expression his parents had used for someone who was in the grip of affectation. The literal translation from the French was, "He's farting higher than his ass." Boudreau said, "But what would a so-called psychological profile tell you about our hero here that we didn't learn from Ted?"

Donovan said, "We already know that the Green River killer means to taunt us, that he hates women, that he's impotent, he plans ahead, that in fact he's been planning this for some time."

"How do you know he's impotent?" A safe question for Boudreau to ask, considering what Betty Antonelli could have told them about him. Her exit from his life had hurt like hell. As the old song went, she had found the zipper to his heart.

In the weeks following, to satisfy himself that she was all right, not in more discomfort than just depriving herself of his company could create, he had had to follow up. But because of what the presence of the plain-wrap Chevy sedan that Saturday morning said about these clowns' continuing interest in him, he had had to figure out a way to learn what had happened to her that would not buzz their nerve endings. Of course he had been kidding himself about his motives. Whatever her problems, he'd thought they'd had the spark. *Coulda been a contenda.* Boudreau felt another zap of adrenaline, exactly like Popeye's spinach.

"No evidence of sexual activity. The bullets. It all corresponds with what we learned from interviewing scores of killers who are currently incarcerated."

Boudreau laughed. "Do you actually expect people you put in jail for life to tell you the truth?" He wanted to add, "You fucking assholes."

"That's taken into account. It's part of the study."

Now Boudreau knew how the FBI had gotten in on this case so quickly: they had been waiting for another binge killer, to see if their theories worked.

"Get used to these guys, Boudreau," Beale said. "We're going to do it their way."

Boudreau stared at him. Beale had decided to hitch his wagon to their rising star. He was going to be the behavioral-sciences man in Seattle. They were going to play cat and mouse with a maniac? What made them so careless with the people they were going to use for bait? Was it their commitment to science—or their desire to advance their careers? Boudreau wanted to tell Donovan to look up the definition of the word *deception.* A real crook would tell you anything you wanted to hear, confession, psychological surrender, whatever it took, to get you from where you were to wherever he thought he could take you. Often he didn't even have to gain an advantage, it was enough for him just to be able to practice fucking other people up. That was the damned dumb truth about criminals. If they got bad enough, if they got away with enough, there was no cure, only old age—and even that wasn't enough, in some cases. Garrett Richard Lockman fit the researchers' definition better than they knew—and they said they had evidence that cleared him. Anyone could have used his credit card. And he could have flown to Atlantic City just to be visible in the audience. If he had decided to kill teenagers, five of them now—at *least*—the establishment of that kind of alibi was not so farfetched. The police weren't the only people to have learned from Ted. Boudreau had another thought. "How about the Hillside Strangler? The trial isn't over, but it looks like those two guys. Buono and Bianchi. Cousins. Separately they're garden-variety pukes; together they're a single, two-headed monster."

From the couch, Donovan's partner said, "We have reason to believe this man is close to police work—"

"You mean the bullets?"

"The bullets are part of it."

Ah. There was something else that pointed even more clearly toward a cop. Or these blue-eyed, blond-haired, all-American fatheads thought it did. Yes, that was it. Boudreau got up.

"Boudreau? Where are you going?"

He looked over his shoulder. "Oh. I thought it was over. I'm done. Tired."

"Your first homicide when you were a beat cop up in the University District—what was that about?"

Boudreau stared at the speaker, the other FBI man sitting on the couch. "A young woman, strangled, her body at the bottom of a flight of outside cellar stairs. Johanssen, Deeah Anne. Still open. Never a suspect. Not even a good lead. Okay? Anything else?"

"You're not up-to-date on the use of force," Donovan said.

"What?"

Donovan's partner turned to Boudreau, subduing an ugly little half smile. "One more thing. Why did you visit this guy Uhuru last spring?"

"Missing girl. I don't have the details at hand. What I remember now—" No! What was the use of telling them that? Now he understood the reference to the use of force. The bar-arm choke hold, the rage in law enforcement in the late seventies. He had refused to take the one-day course because he had thought the choke hold was too dangerous. And he'd been proved right: so many people had died in Los Angeles in the past four or five years that the technique had been banned.

"What?"

"I was going to say, What I remember now is that it was the last time I saw Wendy Harrison."

"So why did you stop?"

Boudreau turned for the door again. His hand was shaking. "I got tired of you."

"What?"

"You heard me." The door was open; he was going through it.

The eagle-beaked special agent on the couch, Donovan's partner, called, "Why don't you work with a partner?"

"I work better alone and everybody knows it."

"Why do you tell people your name is Felix?"

Boudreau turned around. "Now I got you, motherfucker! Given what pissant cops you are, who couldn't find water if you fell out of a boat, at this point only Betty Antonelli and her friends could have told you that, which puts you right in the middle of my private life!"

"Now wait a minute —"

"Fuck you, wait a minute! You followed me, you sat in a car outside my apartment like a pervert while we were at our private business, then you followed her home. And took her down here. Why, except to scare the shit out of her, her roommate, and me? Somebody's killing girls out there, that's the bottom line, not your fucking psychological profiles! I drove her roommate nearly crazy that morning trying to make sure Betty was all right. The roommate finally got hold of somebody here who had the common sense, the decency, the human kindness, to put the two of them on the telephone together. Jesus! Never mind what Betty could have told you, what did you tell her? She hasn't talked to me since. She *moved*! I had to be sure she was alive! But I had to go about it so you wouldn't see what I was doing, because, you fucking geek, you'd take it as evidence of guilt of something. I know you're still in my life somewhere, maybe listening to what goes on in my apartment. Do you want her new address?" The special agent looking up at him was blinking rapidly. "Come on, you rat-faced piece of shit! Do you want to know where she's living now?"

"I don't have to take this —"

Somebody grabbed Boudreau's arm from behind. It was Beale, who said, "Easy, Phil, this isn't necessary."

Boudreau wrenched his arm free. "I called her and her roomies told me she'd moved. I wrote her a note and didn't get an answer. Sent a dummy letter requesting address correction. Went around to the new address. First I had to make sure you weren't outside, or following me, and then I had the pleasure of sitting in my car two blocks away for seven hours waiting for her to come out. You put me through that shit only because you're *stupid*! Betty got my name that way because she heard it reported wrong three years ago on a TV news show. I could tell you which one, but I'd rather see you do the work. Better, I'd rather see you go fuck yourself!"

The special agent moved to get up from the couch. "If you're going to rant like a nut —"

Rage jazzed Boudreau like an electric shock. Follow him, mess up his personal life, and then call him a nut? Not up-to-date on the use of force. The bruise on Hot Lily's neck . . . now Boudreau realized that this self-satisfied asshole sitting on the couch had probably listened to him *come*. Boudreau hit him, a hard, clean, heavy right cross that caught Mr. FBI flush on the mouth, sending him back onto the couch, across the two King County detectives who didn't move quickly enough. Blood flew everywhere. Guys bellowed. A good punch, Boudreau's weight behind it, it felt as if it had loosened a cupful of teeth.

He wasn't done. From a desk he grabbed a pile of food wrappers and threw them onto the special agent, whose blood ran freely through his fingers and down the back of his hand. Some of the wrappers spilled on the floor, and Boudreau kicked them up at the guy like a baseball manager trying to throw dust on the umpire's shoes. People reached for him, but he could feel they were halfhearted, afraid of getting hurt. He cocked his fist to throw another punch, then held it back. "If you wanted to know something about my life, all you had to do was ask me and I'd have told you. Not now. Now you get nothing!"

"You could face charges for this!" Donovan yelled.

"Fuck your charges," Boudreau said, heading for the door again. His knuckle was bleeding and it was going to hurt like hell soon—right now, the only thing he regretted. "The public can't wait to see how you guys operate." He stopped and turned around. A couple of them flinched, not knowing what he was going to do next. "You!" Boudreau shouted at Donovan. "Dickhead! I'm making you special agent in charge of me! Make sure everything having to do with me goes right, because if anything goes wrong, you're going to answer for it. I'll see what I can do to your personal life. Maybe I'll just fuck your wife, if you haven't already programmed her to fall asleep in the middle of it."

Donovan had the pained, distant expression of a civil servant roused from a coffee break. "We were told you have a temper," he said. "Now we know."

"No, you don't know shit. You haven't got a clue." He went out, slamming the door so hard behind him he was sure he had broken the glass out of its frame. When the glass didn't break, Boudreau kicked at the watercooler, then had to jump out of the way of the half-filled plastic bottle spinning off the base like an inflated rubber balloon making a brief, exsanguinating flight for freedom.

—

THE FOLLOWING TUESDAY, cold and wet as only a late November day could be, Boudreau walked around to King County Jail. Al Holobaugh of the sheriff's department was in the front office expecting him. Boudreau had heard nothing about his outburst the previous Friday, and if another day passed, he wasn't going to think about it anymore.

Boudreau knew that if there was such a thing as an adrenaline hangover, he was nursing a corker. It didn't matter that he knew that cops threw punches at each other all the time. The incidents were always hushed up, lest the public's confidence in law enforcement be compromised. The FBI certainly didn't want local cops to know that one of their own had popped the arrogance out of a hotshot G-man. It would get around anyhow, but probably as wrong as the FBI and bootlicks like Beale had been about "Felix" Boudreau.

Al Holobaugh was a short, small-shouldered middle-aged man with a large, square head featuring small blue eyes, thin lips, and streaked, straight gray hair. What he had in common with Boudreau was Panama—Holobaugh had guarded the canal in the late fifties. When he saw Boudreau stepping up to the counter of the main office of the county jail, he raised one index finger in salute, then turned to gather up a manila folder. Holobaugh's uniforms were always crisp, the shirts creased as if they had just been taken from the box. Clipped to the file was a sheet from one of those "While You Were Out" pads, and Holobaugh handed it to him. "Message from your office," Holobaugh said. Boudreau read: *Call Wayne Spencer.*

Who?

Holobaugh said, "When I told Sylvia that I was going to see you today, she said I should tell you she'll make up a batch of *lefse* any time you want."

A joke. *Lefse* was the traditional Norwegian potato pancake, a dry, tasteless, lumpy object. Now Boudreau fixed the identity of Wayne Spencer. Holobaugh cocked his head in the direction of the Public Safety Building. "That Fitzgerald fellow is going to remember you."

"Who?"

"Don't give me that. The FBI agent you KO'ed. Too many people saw him leave in an ambulance. They didn't want him bleeding in somebody's private car."

"No comment."

"Good answer. But don't give those pricks an easy way to do you. They will, you know." Holobaugh opened the file. "The first time I looked at this, I thought, Why didn't I hear from Boudreau last winter?"

Holobaugh's words skipped across the surface of Boudreau's consciousness like a little kid's sidearmed stones. Boudreau could see he had been avoiding the idea of retribution by Special Agent Fitzgerald or his friends. This was only the second time Boudreau had heard the man's name. After the first, on Friday, when they had been introduced, Boudreau had promptly forgotten it. What the hell did Wayne Spencer want? "What happened last winter?"

Holobaugh turned the file around so Boudreau could read it. "Your little boy busted out of here."

"You're shitting me."

"No. He escaped." Holobaugh seemed to miss the sudden stress in Boudreau's voice. "The joint's a sieve. Even the plumbing leaks." He tapped a finger on the top sheet. "He was on kitchen duty and somebody left a door unlocked. He walked away."

Boudreau lifted the page while he tried to gather his wits. The second sheet was a negative report from Garrett Richard Lockman's work-release employer, a metal fabricator near Route 99 in the industrial area between the big Boeing facility and Seattle-Tacoma International Airport. Lockman a fugitive? Beale could not have checked Boudreau's tip without learning that Lockman was a walkaway. The employer's report said that Lockman was a poor worker who had a lousy attitude. *The worst of the worst. With him around, it upsets me to think about coming to the shop in the morning. Whenever I give him a job to do, I can see him laughing up his sleeve at me, like I'm not smart enough to see what he's up to. He has me so off my feed my wife thinks I'm cheating on her. Get him out of here.* Boudreau was thinking of the calm, smooth way Beale had told him about Lockman being in the Atlantic City audience. Boudreau's blood pressure seemed to be so high suddenly that he was ready to wonder why Holobaugh wasn't asking, "What the hell is that pounding?" The third page down in the file was the last of the paperwork that had put Lockman into the work-release program just days after his sentencing on four counts of burglary, to be served concurrently—a year, which guaranteed his placement here in the county facility, a roller skate through the buffalo herd compared to Walla Walla. Walla Walla was one of the harshest penitentiaries in the country. Boudreau knew how the work-release recommendation had been made. He dared not lift his eyes from the file. If Holobaugh saw anything not right in Boudreau's expression, he would ask about it, and no matter what kind of answer he got, he'd try to piece it together with Boudreau's connection to Lockman and last Friday's adventure with Beale, his boys, and the FBI.

"Tell me what you remember about the walkaway," Boudreau said.

"Work-release guys are segregated from the general pop. For them, the place is a boardinghouse. But, as you can see, Mr. Lockman fucked up, and getting fired guaranteed he'd be back with the GP. The story was that Lockman was afraid of that because while he was in before trial, he ratted out a lot of people about their outside activities. You gotta remember that this place is an ongoing crime conference—workshops, seminars, guest speakers. If this was the Holiday Inn, we could charge them four hundred a weekend. He must have heard a lot of stuff. When I saw that he was a walkaway, I asked a guy on duty upstairs. Mr. Lockman was scared shitless that he was going to be killed."

"Sounds like the Garrett Richard Lockman I came to know." Boudreau paged through the file more carefully. Lockman had spent less than four months in custody. He had been out eleven months. No, not out: loose.

Holobaugh asked, "Nobody told you anything?"

"When he escaped? No. Why should they? This is the sheriff's jurisdiction."

"Lockman might have called you, you know, to rub it in. You'd think they'd at least check with you, right?"

Boudreau gave his friend his best cop's stare, the one that showed nothing but made the recipient nervous enough to keep talking. Holobaugh got it. "Same to you," he said. "If they're letting guys walk out, they're not telling me."

Boudreau scratched his brow. "The file I put together tells a smart guy how to play Lockman like an accordion."

"Somebody thought he could take 70advantage of his weakness."

"Nobody takes advantage of Lockman's *weakness*. What he's not is weak. Never think he's weak."

"You mean somebody made a deal with him."

"Whether somebody knew it or not. Probably not. He'd try to get you to talk about how much you enjoyed your morning shit if he thought it would give him an edge."

Holobaugh grinned like a kid. "The best day of your life starts with a good shit."

Boudreau pushed the file back at him. "That's exactly what I'm talking about. Only he wanted the details. How hard you had to push."

Suddenly Holobaugh jabbed his index finger at Boudreau. "You be careful. We don't have all the pricks in here yet."

"And you never will," Boudreau said cheerfully as he backed away. He turned and flashed his badge to the guard at the door. Outside, wary, he looked left and right for signs of a tail, but at the same time his lungs suddenly and involuntarily filled with fresh air. A squeaky yellow Ryder rental truck lumbered loudly up the block, as welcome as a robin in the backyard. It was always nice to get out of jail.

Two blocks down the hill, from a pay telephone in a bar, Boudreau called Tom Sheehan, of Holyrood Spring and Axle, identified himself, and asked what Sheehan remembered about Garrett Lockman. The noise in the background caused Sheehan to shout his response.

"That son of a bitch!"

"I have some questions I'd like to ask you!" Boudreau shouted back. "Maybe we'd better meet somewhere!"

Sheehan recited directions to a coffee shop a block from Boeing Field and told Boudreau to meet him there in ten minutes. "You pay!"

Sheehan was a big, meaty, gray-haired man, six feet two inches tall and at least two hundred and ninety pounds. He wanted to sit at a table because he couldn't squeeze into a booth. His hands were thick and calloused, with blackened fingernails. He wanted a piece of apple pie with his coffee. "We do work that's hot and heavy as well as loud," Sheehan said. "It's clear to me now that Lockman took one look at it and decided it wasn't for him. I didn't realize it at the time because he put the con on me. Played humble. Oozed grateful. Wanted to know how I got in the business, as if I'd ooze grateful in return for him taking an interest in me. But whenever I turned my back, whenever he wasn't being watched, he stopped working. If he could have arranged it, I think he would have disappeared. Once he was left unsupervised for an hour, and when we came back, he was in the same spot on the floor where we had left him. Damnedest thing I ever saw."

"What did he do when you spoke to him about his output, or lack of it?"

"He lied. Looked me straight in the eye and told me that black was white, up was down, in was out. I told him he'd have to work harder, and he said yes, he would. But nothing—no change. It was like he was crazy and had figured out a way to drive everybody else crazy, too. I began dreading going in, because I knew I'd have to take him on again. He was laughing at me the whole damned time."

"Do you think he wanted you to fire him?"

"The way he behaved, sure, but according to the guy who told me to put him on, he should have wanted to keep the job no matter how tough he found the work."

"What were you told?"

"That the other prisoners wanted to kill him, if they could get their hands on him."

"Do you remember who told you that?"

"Oh, sure. Ron Beale, from King County Major Crimes."

"What else did Beale tell you?"

"Lockman was a gold mine of information. Important."

"What did Beale mean by that?"

"That's all he said. Beale is a good guy, maybe wrapped a little too tight—"

"When was the last time you talked to him about Lockman?"

"Right after I got Lockman out of here, Beale called to apologize for hanging a loser on me."

"Did Lockman ever talk to you about girls or sex?"

Sheehan's blue eyes clouded briefly with a suspicious curiosity that told Boudreau to ease up, if necessary, and quickly. "Me? Look at me. Do I look like the kind of boy soprano a fruitcake like Lockman would talk dirty with?" Suddenly Sheehan grinned. "I'm kidding you. You heard the noise in the shop over the phone. You can't have those kinds of conversations."

"In your report you said Lockman made you so nervous—off your feed, you said—that your wife thought you were cheating on her."

"I'm a kidder—I talk like that. Lockman wasn't the first favor I've done for Ron Beale and it won't be the last. Usually the guys he ships me are no problem."

"Why did you call Lockman a fruitcake?"

"He'd stare at the women customers. Once, when he was trying to hustle me, he made a comment about not knowing how women could do our kind of work. They don't, really. They're in dealership offices and do pickup and delivery. But I caught him more than once, staring."

"Staring?"

"Well, the women we deal with like a little of that kind of appreciation as long as it isn't pushy—wait a minute, now I remember! A gal named Marilyn, works at a Honda dealership down in Tacoma, she said something about him, now that I think of it. Called him a creep. What else did she say? He gave her the willies. 'Don't leave him alone with me,' she said, 'or I'll gas him. I won't wait for him to do something.' She carries one of them gas canisters."

"I figured it out. They're illegal, so don't tell me anything more about her."

"What's he done?"

"We don't know yet."

"Well, think of something." He picked up the check. "Here, let me get this. You thought I was serious before. You're almost as bad as Ron Beale."

———

THE FOLLOWING FRIDAY night a soft rain swept in across Elliott Bay and up the Pike, bowing pedestrians' heads and quickening their steps past the street kids blowing into their hands in the doorways of the neighborhood's pawnshops, cheap bars, and greasy spoons. Behind the wheel of his well-faded, wheezing '73 Mustang, Boudreau kept his eyes on everything, glancing in the mirrors, his ears twitching like an animal's in anticipation of the urban equivalent of a snapping twig. He had an appointment here while he was looking for Lockman and someone else, a thirteen-year-old runaway who, her mother said, was pregnant. A Mercedes turned the corner for the third time; its driver, an old chicken hawk Boudreau knew well, peered at the doorfront merchandise. Even on a night like this, suburban dads could buy anything that was for sale in the Pacific Northwest, including their neighbors' daughters. Or sons the same age.

By the time the third Green River victim had been discovered, two months ago, Boudreau could have predicted her vital statistics to within a digit or two: a teenage runaway of no fixed address, a big girl's record of prostitution and drug use. A profoundly ignorant junior-high-school dropout equipped with the cunning that came from living on the streets, sleeping in abandoned buildings, eating out of Dumpsters. All of the victims had been seen last on the Sea-Tac Strip, a two-mile stretch of hotels, motels, and bars on South Pacific Highway that ran parallel to Seattle-Tacoma International Airport. Like the Pike, the Strip was a twenty-four-hour outdoor sex festival, where a blow job in the customer's car on a tree-lined side street cost thirty bucks, a half-and-half in a dirty motel room forty and up. If a man wanted something special, or more than one girl, he didn't even have to get out from behind the wheel to negotiate. No matter what the weather, the girls swept down on the cars like Third World beggars. Stupid, rebellious, know-it-all teenage streetwalkers: if someone wanted to kill for fun and get away with it, he couldn't pick better victims. Nobody cared about them. Nobody wanted them except to use. The only way anyone knew they were in trouble was when their bodies washed up in the waste of an open sewer of a river.

And now that the body count was up to five young girls, nothing had changed the way the kids of the Strip and the Pike went about their business, mooching change, scamming suckers, fanning out like a threatened herd of deer whenever they saw a police cruiser. Many of the activists who were blaming the police for not moving swiftly enough to apprehend the Green River killer were the same people who objected to every law-enforcement effort to run the kids off the Pike and the Strip. These self-appointed protectors argued that a curfew could not be imposed because it violated the kids' right to assembly—never mind that the law said the kids were too young to make decisions about what they were assembling for. Every honest cop knew the truth underneath, America's dirtiest secret: too many citizens wanted these combat zones so they could rape and sodomize their neighbors' children without accepting responsibility for the consequences of their acts. And it was true from coast to coast.

Someone rapped on the window of the passenger door. Wayne Spencer, the young City of Kent patrolman, wearing a fur-collared, zippered leather jacket. He was holding the hand of a very pretty, college-age, blue eyed, golden blonde in some kind of shiny blue warm-up jacket. She smiled and waved to Boudreau as if she knew him well. He raised a hand to indicate that he would meet them on the sidewalk.

Spencer extended his big hand to Boudreau and pointed his other index finger toward the blonde. "Say hello to Piper, Boudreau. Thanks for coming out."

Spencer was falling over himself trying to be polite. Boudreau had said he would be here on his own business, and if Spencer wanted to meet him, fine. Piper looked like a milk-fed queen of fraternity row, not so much brassy as overcooked for her age, too sharp and carefully made up. She had been intently examining Boudreau, who was out here tonight also hoping to bump into someone who could give him a line on Uhuru, Hot Lily's pimp, who had abandoned his last address. The landlord there had acted pissed off, as if he did not know the business and character of his tenants. Boudreau had played dumb, as cautious as possible in every direction. That he had told Spencer where he would be tonight could hardly be construed as creating an opportunity to debrief the young cop. Boudreau was curious, but not so much that he was willing to appear to be snooping—not when his brother officers could establish that a man was at the Miss America contest but somehow miss that he was a prison escapee and a fugitive from justice. Boudreau pointed Spencer toward the steamy windows of a doughnut shop.

"Let's do it in there."

Piper's eyes, still riveted on him, showed she liked his style of taking charge. Passing into the shop, he got close enough to her to catch her perfume, so faint he could allow himself to feel, if he wanted to be that kind of stupid, that he had entered into her intimate space. Her eyes caught his again and the corner of her mouth curled in a smile. At the counter he ordered a strawberry-jelly doughnut topped with almonds to accompany his coffee, paid, and moved to the window, leaving the young couple to fend for themselves. He wiped steam from the glass. He had been tough on Spencer that rainy August afternoon at the Green River; something told him now to reinforce the lesson. Piper seemed to be picking up on it quicker, even if Boudreau was avoiding the eye contact that would confirm that suspicion. Piper's interest was the result of Spencer's big mouth, Boudreau didn't have a doubt about it.

When they positioned themselves so they blocked Boudreau's access to the front door, he thumbed them around to his other side. Putting on a bit of the stone face, Piper wanted Boudreau to know she didn't like it. Perfect, he thought, a woman who wanted to make sure the men in her life knew they were supposed to please *her*. Here on the Pike, that kind of behavior had a life expectancy in nanoseconds.

Spencer said, "Story going around about you and a certain FBI agent, that they're keeping quiet about what happened."

Boudreau could see Piper listening carefully, even as she was looking over the multiracial crowd in the shop. A burst of laughter erupted in the back. Piper's jeans were big-label, pressed, and had never been worn for work. Boudreau bit carefully into his jelly doughnut. "They have to gossip," he said with his mouth full. "What else is new?"

"Reason I heard it, they're thinking of forming a task force. This is very early in the game. They're talking about how they need extra bodies for the legwork. But it's going to be multiagency—King County, Seattle, FBI, City of Kent, maybe some other agencies." He stopped. Boudreau gave him the fish eye to keep him talking. Spencer said, sheepishly spilling it out, "They want me to be on it. If it happens. I know the chief let it go to me because he doesn't think the girls were killed in Kent and I'm whatchacallit, expendable, but it looks like a pretty big deal to me. What do you think?"

Boudreau was weighing the fact that Piper might know he had put the slug on a special agent of the Federal Bureau of Investigation. The news would be all over campus by Monday morning. With her wonderful college girl's body, she looked like a natural-born troublemaker. "Sounds like a career move, Wayne. What's the problem?"

"If the story going around is true, I can understand why they didn't ask you, but they should have. You're the one who knows what's going on around here. They know that down below."

"You mean Kent?"

"Yeah. You got a good reputation. People say you're not aggressive. That's what I mean. They should have taken care of you. They shouldn't have pissed you off."

"If that's what they did."

"What happened?"

Boudreau shrugged. Outside, a bus started away from the stop, vibrating the shop floor and window. He didn't like the idea of nonaggression being equated with "good" police work. While the brass might like cops who turned their backs on workaday arrests out of laziness or a desire for time to maintain their private lives, what made Boudreau go was his own, admittedly idiosyncratic view of the job. While the law said that hookers were criminals, Boudreau knew they were really the victims of what the dummies called a victimless crime. Q: How many of these girls had been sexually abused as children? A: All of them. No other factor so powerfully propelled a woman toward this life, where the pimps and johns exploited with equal selfishness her vulnerability, fear, and mistrust. When the law decided to put the johns in jail, Boudreau would be out in the street with a trident and a net. He could get the pimps any time the prosecutors and the courts decided to put them away—*and* protect the girls who testified against them. He asked Spencer, "What have you been told about the murders?"

"Well, the last two didn't have those little trophies with them, if you know what I mean."

His eyes shifted once toward Piper. Boudreau was supposed to assume that Spencer was talking about the bullets. He was supposed to assume Spencer hadn't already told Piper about the bullets. Sure, like Spencer was the first cop since Sir Robert Peel who didn't run his mouth every chance he got. "Were they naked?"

"Yeah."

"Strangled?"

"Yeah. The guy's gettin' better at it, too. The last one was beat pretty bad."

"Can we change the subject?" Piper asked. Now her eyes were locked on Boudreau's head-on. *Your move, sucker.* A player telling the world she had all the aces. She thought. *"Bonne chance, Spencer,"* Boudreau almost said aloud.

"It's played," Spencer assured her. His eyes focused over Boudreau's shoulder just as someone tapped it. Boudreau turned around.

One of his street kids, sixteen years old, small for his size, and thin, malnourished, and underdressed. His name was David, the only name he ever gave. A runaway, he said, but more probably a throwaway, although it would do Boudreau no good to prove it. At this point in his life David didn't want to be somebody's foster child, go to high school, and join the chess club; he wanted to hang out around here and steal and suck dick for money for drugs and alcohol. His unwashed dark hair hung almost shoulder length, and a few wispy hairs on his upper lip suggested he was entering puberty at last. Under the fluorescent lights of the doughnut shop, David's skin had the color of a trout's belly. He shuffled his feet sheepishly. Boudreau noticed that his sneakers had holes in them.

"Hey, Phil. What's happenin'?"

"Just conducting a little police business. Have you seen Uhuru around?"

The kid brightened. "He's up the block, heading this way. He said he was fixin' to get some doughnuts." *Fixin'*. That was the way Uhuru talked, not David, who regarded Spencer and Piper and laughed. "Who are these two, the fucking Mod Squad?"

Boudreau raised his hand to stop Spencer before he responded. "You're sure? I don't want to bag Uhuru. I just want to talk. Should I go looking for him?"

"No. That's what he said. He's comin' here. No shit."

Boudreau reached into his pocket for a couple of dollars, letting David see them. "Did you go to the clinic?"

"Oh, yeah. I'm fine. Sinusitis is all. And underweight. My lungs are clear. They want me to quit smoking, like I'm some old fuck. I ain't lying to you, Phil, I swear. Hold on to your bucks until he shows up, if you like." He wanted the money the way a trained dog wanted his treat, waiting until his master said jump. Boudreau maintained his reputation with the kids by never diddling them. He gave David the money.

"Are you going to get something to eat?"

He shot Boudreau a hustler's grin. "That's why I'm here. You just made it easy."

Spencer said, "What do you hear about these girls that are getting killed?"

David shook his head as if Spencer were stupid. "That's not here, man. That's down on the Strip. Nothin' to do with the Pike."

Uhuru came in the door, all two hundred and eighty pounds of him, wrapped in a long dark fur coat, his head covered with an oversized matching fur cap. Under the coat was a crimson shirt serving as the backdrop for the display of about five ounces of gold. A fan of Mr. T. As Uhuru removed the cap with great care he took notice of Boudreau, frowned, thought of going on by until he saw the head movement hailing him over. He eyed Spencer, and then, more appreciatively, Piper.

"Go eat," Boudreau told David.

"Right . . . right," he answered, trying to be Mr. Hip. He faded away, eyes averted from Uhuru.

"That boy snitchin' on me?" Uhuru demanded with a *faux* scowl. Suddenly he smiled, flashing a diamond in an incisor. "Evenin'," he said to the newly named Mod Squad. "How y'all doin'?"

"What do you say?" Spencer said sternly, for the two of them.

Boudreau said, "Uhuru, I don't want to piss around with you tonight, so I'll get right to it. Have you heard from anybody about Hot Lily?"

Uhuru took the measure of Spencer. "I know the Man when I see him. I was fixin' to get me some doughnuts."

"No problem," Boudreau said. "Talk to me now or after you buy them, your choice. If I have to wait, maybe you have to wait until Monday to eat the fucking things. They'll be as hard as last week's dog turds."

"You got nothin' on me."

"I can bust you for overcrowding the restaurant. Don't fuck with me. I want to know what you know, all of it, and right now. Then we can both have a nice weekend. Otherwise you can talk to the judge about that blade you're holding. No kidding."

"I ain't—" Another smile, a small note of sullen appreciation for the box Boudreau had put him in.

"You got the picture," Spencer said.

"I ain't seen you before."

Spencer rocked on the balls of his feet. "You've been lucky." Boudreau almost winced. Spencer was terrible. The more Boudreau saw of Spencer, the less he respected him. A goofy kid whose timing was a split second off, Spencer belonged in a garage more than in a police uniform. That was it, Boudreau realized: the kid was no cop. He was an embarrassment.

Uhuru said, "I think so. Well, well." He eyed Boudreau. "This gotta be alone. Just you and me, man."

Boudreau looked to the other two. Spencer said, "Okay by me, I gotta take a leak." He gave Piper his Styrofoam coffee cup and paper-wrapped doughnut, then pushed through the crowd to the back of the shop.

"Why don't you move down the counter a little, kid," Boudreau said to her. "I got my eye on you." He nodded toward a farther part of the window counter. She was slow to move.

Uhuru said, "Don't you see she want to ball you, man? You may be the heat, but I be the expert."

Boudreau could almost feel her stiffen. He grinned at her. "You mean, if I slip my card in her purse, she'll call me later?"

"I'm tellin' you."

Sneering at them both, she turned to the steamy window. Boudreau said to him, "What do you have for me?"

"Not as nice as what she got, Boudreau. King County detectives—that Chinese guy?—axed me a lot of questions about you. Same boys that are on Hot Lily's case. They wanted to know about that skinny bitch you axed me about last spring."

"Mona Raymond."

"Her."

"What happened to her?"

"On the wind, man. Could be anywhere."

"Have you heard anything?"

"No. And that's the truth. Those boys were on your case. They wanted to know if you hit on the ladies. You know. I told them you ain't stupid. I never seen it. Or heard. They axed a whole lot of other questions, too, like if the girls been tellin' me about dudes who want to hurt them. The boys don't understand that I run an honest business, that I don't let that shit happen."

Sure. And you give to the church, too, you fat piece of shit. You wash the pope's feet. Boudreau was still watching Piper. She was peeking at them, tapping her foot, doing a little steam. Where she came from, the white, middle-class heart of this part of the world, boys didn't talk about girls as sexual beings in their presence. Everybody had to pretend to be stupid. Two months had passed since Boudreau's night with Betty Antonelli, and before her, too much time for him to dare to think about.

He looked at Piper straightaway, without subterfuge, letting her see him appraising her. No, she wasn't doing a steam, she was regrouping. She moved closer, close enough to hear them. Spencer had no one to blame but himself. The only thing one cop dared say about another to his woman was, *It's his ill-fitting dentures that make his breath so bad.* Boudreau said to Uhuru, "So? Have you been hearing about anything like that? A guy who likes to hurt girls?"

"No," Uhuru said. "No guys like that. Those guys be layin' low now, anyway, you see what I'm sayin'?"

Boudreau thought so. "How about a guy pretending to be a cop?"

Uhuru's eyes widened, as if he had never heard of such a thing. Sure. Even if he was only a pimp, he spent his free time planning robberies, figuring out how to get into banks, breaking into wealthy estates. His fantasies were filled with phony rabbis walking into museums, phony doctors getting into hospitals for drugs—and phony cops conning *what?* "No, I didn't hear about nothin' like that," Uhuru said, all innocence. "And nobody wantin' to hurt the girls. Maybe a few jackoffs like to tie 'em up and take pictures, but that's it, you know, all they want. The girls know who all those guys are."

"I want you to call me if you hear anything."

Uhuru grinned conspiratorially. "You gonna give me one of your cards?"

Piper turned away. Boudreau laughed silently. He could see Spencer making his way back. "No, I've only got one left. You know how to reach me."

"You makin' no mistake. That's sweet pussy. Grind your coffee for you. Check it out."

"Get lost."

Uhuru pushed past the approaching Spencer. Piper handed Spencer his coffee and doughnut. Boudreau said to him, "Look, I want to work with you on this. If I get anything, I'll pass it on to you. It will make you look good with Ron Beale. In return, I want to be kept up-to-date on what they're doing. Two-way deal. We work together. Okay?"

Spencer nodded emphatically. It was going to be a long time before Boudreau mentioned what he knew about Lockman or his prison escape. If Boudreau's tip on Lockman ever made its way to the file of a task force, and Spencer came across it, Boudreau had only to say he had been told it had been checked out and was a dud. That would satisfy Spencer—he wouldn't imagine another layer of meaning. Boudreau said, "Uhuru says there's nothing unusual going on up here. I gotta buy that. But what it also tells me is that the guy or guys doing this might have thought it out very carefully."

"They're saying one guy."

"Yeah, right, and LAPD spent years looking for one Hillside Strangler. Two pukes. And they got Bianchi up in Bellingham because once these bastards start, they can't stop. Okay, I'll give you my card with my home phone number on it. If you have to talk right away, you ask for David. David's the kid who was here just a moment ago. When I call you back, it will be from a pay phone. You may want to get the numbers of pay phones in your neck of the woods. Where do you live?"

"Puyallup."

Boudreau called it Polyp. "Jesus, that's a haul. Here, your hands are full. Piper, just let me put my card in your purse, and you can give it to him later."

She was looking Boudreau in the eye, all but smiling, almost giving the game away. He didn't dare look at Spencer, who was going to have to look out for himself. There were many perfectly good reasons for playing Johnny Ride a Pony with a young lady. Often the young lady's desire to be naughty was more than enough. Boudreau had to recognize a certain naughtiness of his own right now. Being pissed off could trigger that in a man. Being suspected by morons could bring it out. Just knowing you had been spied upon. Wondering what Beale and his guys were going to do next.

Boudreau knew he wasn't doing well with himself. It had occurred to him recently that he was not yet thirty-five and his life was already a mess and he had no idea why. He could not stand to be in the same room with the mother of his only child. Was there anything to be proud of in that? For all he knew, he had frightened Betty Antonelli away with too much authentic behavior. *Something I wanted to eat?* He had been invaded by an ugliness that wanted to curl up permanently inside him. He had been sour on Piper at the start, and only the most perverse of reasons had made him change his mind.

In Boudreau's present mood, being embarrassed by Wayne Spencer, while having to rely on him, maybe even confide in him, made his skin itch. Would Boudreau fucking Piper make a real cop out of Spencer? Being the loser in a round of Afternoon Delight had been the making of cops in the past, had given them an experiential basis for the paranoiac walk and talk. In that sense, maybe Piper was some kind of unconscious offering from Spencer to Boudreau. Anything was possible. Boudreau understood the human animal a thousand times better than that bum Uhuru, and he still didn't have a clue to why anyone did anything. All you did was guess. Did this line of thought mean Boudreau was going to take the trust of young Wayne Spencer and immediately set about to betray it? If Piper picked up the telephone and called him, yes, that's exactly what it meant. Boudreau didn't think he'd have all that much trouble coming to an understanding with the pretty little Princess of the Country Club. He was going to try to fuck her until she was too sore to walk.

After midnight, sure that no one was on his tail, Boudreau took another trip down to Sea-Tac. He had lost track of the number of times he had cruised the airport area now, looking for Lockman driving a covered pickup truck, a van, a panel truck, even a police car. Lockman might think his interest in police paraphernalia and procedures was something completely under his control, a tool he had shaped to further what a prosecutor would call his criminal ambitions, but to Boudreau it was just an infantile attempt to deny his powerlessness. Just as a purse snatcher inevitably graduated from symbolic to actual sex crimes, a Garrett Richard Lockman quickly enough grew numb to the pleasure of strutting in front of the mirror in his police and Nazi uniforms and had to go out in the streets and try to press real power upon real people. Lockman had read police textbooks to learn how to do it. He traded in vehicles that made it possible to transport unwilling passengers.

Boudreau had chased the paper trail as far as it would take him. No driver's license for Garrett Richard Lockman, but he probably had a fistful of licenses under as many different names—law enforcement was only waiting for the computer that could match identification photos. In the same way Lockman had no automobiles or trucks registered under his own name, either. No telephone anywhere in the Puget Sound area. Boudreau had called Lockman's aunt and uncle in Spokane not once but three times, hanging up twice when first the aunt and then the uncle picked up, and then waiting a week to tell the uncle that he was confirming the address for a Garrett Lockman subscription to *Newsweek* magazine. The old guy was a lousy liar, saying as if reading from an index card that he had not seen his nephew in years. Boudreau had also called Spokane directory assistance to see if other numbers were listed at the old people's address. No. Garrett Richard Lockman was a true professional criminal. He knew how to hide.

To protect himself from those who were suspicious that he was one, too, Boudreau was keeping duplicate records of all his moves, making copies of his telephone bills. What Boudreau had told Spencer about keeping good notes was only what his father had taught him. Law enforcement in the United States was government bureaucracy first, and first you made sure you covered your ass. If Ron Beale could have found a way long ago to get rid of Boudreau, he would have done it. Boudreau thought Beale was a clown, not a cop, and Beale knew it, reason enough for Beale to want to be free of him. If Beale had even a clue that Boudreau knew that Lockman was working as one of Beale's informants, he would plant the evidence necessary to put Boudreau in Walla Walla within hours. But in no reasonable way could hanging around the Sea-Tac Strip be construed as evidence that Boudreau was involved in the Green River killings. On the contrary, Hot Lily and Mona Raymond had lived on Boudreau's beat, and one was dead and the other was missing under suspicious circumstances. Until he was told otherwise by his own immediate superiors on the Seattle Police Department, Boudreau was only doing his duty as he saw it.

Tonight he logged an hour and a half, most of it in the elevated parking lot of a new hotel that gave him a view of traffic for five blocks in both directions. Too far away to read license plates, he wrote down a description of every vehicle that could do the job a puke like Kenneth Bianchi or Angelo Buono or a Garrett Lockman would want of it. Boudreau had lists of vehicles from other nights with which to compare tonight's candidates. Sometimes he saw chicken hawks he knew from the Pike, and sometimes he saw girls who worked those street corners. But no nondescript, suspicious vans, no half-equipped ambulances, no ersatz police cars. No surprise. Putting himself in Lockman's shoes, he would not want to work a weekend night. Too crowded, too heavily patrolled. In Lockman's shoes, Boudreau would be pumping Beale for the deployment of deputies—oh, hell, Lockman probably already knew when the deputies were in Denny's, and how they liked their eggs.

Lockman was a gold mine of information? That kind of snitch could make a career, get you promoted, make you chief of detectives. A snitch was a detective's real eyes and ears. The assholes weren't content committing crimes, hurting and killing people for their own pleasure and ease; they had to brag about it, too, show how smart they were, how well they had beaten the system. A cop riding a wave of good collars and the snitch who was doing his dirty work were sometimes closer than husband and wife.

And as with real marriages, sometimes you had to take a second look to see who was really running the show.

That was the easy part.

Where the hell was Lockman?

December 1982

Vancouver, Portland, Seattle, Portland again, in and out of Spokane —
how many miles? Three, four thousand. Cashing traveler's checks, shuffling IDs, license plates, cars. By Christmas, Garrett Richard Lockman
had bought and sold nine police cars and, separately, the radios that
had been left in four of them. There was always a market for police radios. Lockman was keeping his distance from that little prick Martin
Jones, that was the important thing. Again he had Jones where he wanted
him. Under his thumb, like the Stones' song. It hadn't been difficult.
Jones had his regular job, and Lockman just had to take his time returning Jones's calls, let the days pass, keep the conversations as light as possible, never discussing their funny business unless Jones brought it up.
Jones was smart enough to keep his mouth shut most of the time, but occasionally the pressure on him was too great and he needed to whine and
fret. Then Lockman resisted in-depth discussions, and when Jones got
that desperate look on his face, Lockman would just smile, indicating,
"You aren't crazy enough for this." That decided things. Lockman was

saying that not even a perfumed halfbreed transvestite invert could grasp what kind of all-star craziness was required for the run Lockman was making. Lockman knew he was resisting thinking about the things he had done with Jones and then without him since his return to the West Coast. But he believed he was allowing this lapse in concentration only because he needed time to adjust to his new situation. His emerging inner reality. He was becoming a different person, and he was still surveying the internal topography. For the time being, perhaps for a while longer, it was better to stay busy and concentrate on subjects as mundane as automobile transfers and teaching his customers how to use the radios. From his past experience, he knew the concomitant paperwork was the kind of subject in which he could lose himself. Lockman always retained copies of his paperwork. He could show exactly which cars he had owned and when he had owned them, all the way back to his high-school years in unsunny Spokatropolis. He still had his grammar-school report cards, book reports, and research projects from junior high. All of his term papers and tests from college. Garrett Richard Lockman was living one of the best-documented lives in the history of the world.

More important in this period was keeping Jones afraid of him. Back to the old days, business as usual. Lockman knew that the adventure had really started last spring when Jones had said he doubted what Lockman had been telling him of what he had done to Deeah Anne Johanssen, whose earring Martin Jones now wore at home night after night. Remembering her aloud, over and over, even as Lockman measured its effect on Jones, had triggered last spring's adventure with the terrible skinny black kid, of which Jones still knew nothing. Mona Raymond. Uhuru's girl, she had said, as if that could have helped her. Funny, what Lockman could remember most clearly was the feel of her in his arms as the life had left her, the only moment of her life that had had any meaning whatsoever.

Lockman saw now that he had pushed Jones too far. It had taken Lockman a long time to figure out what kind of fruit Martin Jones really was. As smitten as a schoolgirl, but *not* gay. He just wanted to wear women's clothes when the two of them were together.

What a *howl*! And so easy to manipulate if you remembered to pay no obvious attention to the flaming queen struggling to free herself from Jones's suppression. Lockman had realized almost immediately that Jones had not disposed of the clothing of the girls he had killed while Lockman had been away. Getting a confession out of him had not been tough:

Where are the clothes?

Why do you want to know?

Because I know you, you little piece of shit, and the last thing you could ever let go of is a pair of panties with a whiff of pussy on them, so where are they?

In my room. I'm going to put them behind the new shower I'm installing in the downstairs bath.

So these days Lockman was giving Jones underwear, telling him he was paying girls to photograph them, and talking them into giving him their panties. Jones hadn't wanted to believe it, the moron, actually accusing Lockman of buying the underwear in a store. If he was even remotely close to a woman in his behavior and naïveté, Lockman had no problem understanding why so many husbands cheated on their wives.

Lockman had to strip the bodies anyway, leaving no labels, no laundry marks, nothing that could become a clue. He didn't bother with the dental work because it didn't matter. When dental charts became the only way to identify the girls, there could be nothing left of evidence of him.

Allowing Jones to hide the girls' drawers was also the perfect way of preserving the record. Lockman took Jones's participation as true testimony to his enslavement to another man by force of that man's will. Insisting that Lockman had paid for the panties was the perfect way to deny knowledge of how Lockman had really acquired them. All Jones worried about anyway was whether he had ever gotten so drunk that he had sucked Lockman's prick—and that was going to remain Lockman's secret. Watching Jones's anguish was the only way to keep the subject from boring him to tears.

Jones might not be willing to talk about the clothing being evidence of a chain of murders and his own guilt in so many of them, but he couldn't part with the clothing, living literally surrounded by his trophies, sealed as they were behind the Sheetrock of his own assiduous, money-grubbing remodeling. Jones factored every penny he spent into his constant recalculations of the resale value of his house—by his own estimate, tens of thousands of dollars. "My Taj Mahal," he liked to say, leading Garrett Richard Lockman to believe that he did not know that the original Taj Mahal was in fact a mausoleum for a princess. Hysterical. It was great to be loved, Lockman had found himself thinking one day, but by *this*?

SPREE

February 1983

So many miles, in and out of Portland, Spokane, Seattle, Portland twice more, Vancouver, back to Spokane again before the end of winter—thousands and thousands of miles. It was more than just moving around, staying busy. Lockman was expanding his customer list, touching base with men in the Seattle area he had known since high school, letting them understand he was the source for used cars, electronics equipment, and law-enforcement paraphernalia, including tasers and cattle prods. The last time required him to be circumspect around their wives, whom he assumed could not be trusted, each regarding him with suspicion, wondering, he knew, how he was going to crowd her space and disrupt her own secret agenda. No matter. Lockman knew what the men did not want revealed to the wives. Youthful indiscretions. A continuing interest in the forbidden.

And worst of all, an adolescent taste for homosexual activity.

Tom Parkinson in Seattle and Jimmy Dobbs in Redmond always had a couch for him to crash on. Dobbs, a short, pear-shaped young man, was a fuel-oil wholesaler, a father of two who was looking for ways to turn his money over. He wanted to sell police cars as fast as Lockman could buy them. Dobbs knew that Mexicans loved the old Chevies—what could be simpler than shipping them to southern California? Because Lockman had once regaled him with tales of his adventures with Tom Brownall in San Diego, Dobbs thought Lockman knew the southern California underworld inside and out.

It was everything Lockman could do to steer Dobbs away from the subject. Dobbs didn't know that Brownall was in Walla Walla, or that Lockman had been arrested and had pleaded guilty to four lesser counts. But for all he didn't know, Dobbs was clearly afraid to front any money to Lockman, glancing toward the bedroom, where Kathleen, his wife, was watching British mysteries on PBS. Lockman was wary of Kathleen, a tall, always attractively dressed brunette who sashayed around the kitchen like a movie star. He didn't know what she saw in the hapless Dobbs. She wasn't interested in her husband's old friend's adventures, even leaving the table when Lockman was talking about his current undercover work on the Green River murders. Dobbs had been given to understand that Lockman was at the cutting edge in law enforcement's attempt to infiltrate what was really a vicious national racket that had nothing to do with serial killing, the dead girls being those who had refused to become part of what amounted to a traveling show that serviced celebrities, politicians— names so big they never would be prosecuted. As Lockman spun this tale he leaned in, glancing carefully toward the bedroom as if to be sure Dobbs's wife couldn't hear, but sweeping his eyes back as he spoke so he couldn't fail to note Dobbs's reaction. "Homo stuff, too," he whispered.

Dobbs stared, riveted, certainly remembering what had happened between them more than a decade ago in Spokane. A rainy afternoon; Lockman, two years older, had talked Dobbs into a taste of the wonder wiener. Lockman went on with his sex-show story as if he didn't remember a thing.

"You'd recognize every name involved. An absolute nightmare."

Dobbs blinked and swallowed. Wonderful. Nothing more needed be said. But Lockman saw he was getting nowhere: Dobbs was too pussy-whipped to cut a check for as little as a couple of thousand to start up the used-police-car venture. Lockman already had three old police cars stripped down, cleaned up, and ready to sell, but he never mentioned them to Dobbs. If the money had been forthcoming, and Dobbs wanted to see what there was to show for it, Lockman would have driven him down to Portland, where the cars were in storage behind a hurricane fence. That would have satisfied even Kathleen the Style Queen, lying on her bed getting Sherlocked and Marpled until she forgot what country she was in.

Tom Parkinson's wife in Seattle was another matter, the petite, submissive, and codependent Sheila, a bottle blonde with wide hips and an uncertain, honking laugh. Lockman watched her interaction with her husband carefully.

Parkinson was a tall, good-looking, not-terribly-intelligent guy who, in earlier times, would have been under contract to M-G-M. They had two sniveling preschoolers whose names Lockman could never keep straight. No money here: Parkinson clerked in a hardware store, talking about his boss in hushed, reverent tones. Parkinson wasn't smart enough to be crooked. The game here was getting the Parkinsons drunk and seeing them lose control. Lockman wanted to see something intimate. A drunken Parkinson had made an admission in Spokane the summer after they had finished high school. He and Lockman had been terribly drunk on beer, pumping each other about secret desires. Parkinson had said he wanted to do a three-way—two women, two men, it didn't matter to him. Lockman had remembered it for a decade. He couldn't stop thinking about it.

The Parkinsons thought he was an undercover federal cop working on the Green River case. Tom Parkinson was especially interested in what the local cops were not telling the press about what was being done to the girls. With every expression of curiosity Lockman refilled Parkinson's glass with the Johnny Walker Red he had brought for the visit—in addition to the Chinese food, which Parkinson had begun to look for, like one of Pavlov's dogs.

The Parkinsons understood that an undercover federal agent couldn't establish himself in a community and that Lockman had no fixed address in the Seattle-Tacoma area. Since their couch was his, they could all get as drunk as they pleased. At two in the morning, three, three-thirty, it became a waiting game for Lockman, electric and suggestive. When it grew that late he would praise Sheila effusively, encourage her to get up and dance for the two men, but she was usually too drunk to move for long. One night she fell over the stereo. On another, the Parkinsons abruptly went into their bedroom and closed the door. When he thought they weren't coming out again, Lockman tiptoed to their door and listened. Nothing.

He stepped outside into the backyard. That afternoon's rain had frozen on the hard ground and was painfully cold through Lockman's running shoes. The ice was noisy, too, and he had to take care with every step. A full moon made the yard as bright as a movie screen. Small, aluminum-

sided, storm-windowed houses like this stood on every side, and if Lockman's luck went south, some old biddy would feel the cold in her bladder
and look out her window on the way to the bathroom.

A half-inch bar of light showed under the venetian blind that imper-
fectly blanked the Parkinsons' bedroom window, but a dry, leafless privet
hedge five feet high kept Lockman at a distance. Even so, he could see a
bit of yellow wall and a tall, mahogany chest of drawers. An ugly room,
like Hazel and Al's. From the rooftop vent came the whisper of the
swirling water of a flushing toilet, making Lockman's ears prick up and
his palms grow slippery with sweat. Under the blind something swung
into view, white, with little pink figures.

A nightie. A flannel nightie for winter.

And then the light went out.

By the time Parkinson figured out what had happened to his guest,
Lockman was standing on the driveway sighting down the roofs of the
Parkinsons' battered Japanese sedans, a half-smoked cigarette nearly
frozen in his lips. He was feeling very Bogartian.

"Something wrong?"

He detached the cigarette. "Just giving Sheila some privacy, that's all."

"She didn't need it. I sure hope we can keep the kids quiet tomorrow,
'cause she's going to have a sumbitch of a hangover."

"Shouldn't drink so much," Lockman said, phrasing his remark carefully in case Parkinson challenged him: he would say he had been speaking about the three of them—all of them drank too much. But Parkinson
laughed.

"She got pretty nutty in the bedroom," he offered. "Started to talk shit."

Lockman's curiosity leaped like a flushed deer. He showed Parkinson a
friendly grin. "Like what?"

"Nothing. It was just shit."

"Let's get inside. Have another drink."

"No, I'm done," Parkinson said. "I'm going to turn in. You can sit up if
you want to, but just remember that those kids want to see their cartoons
in the morning."

Lockman remembered only late at night, when he was drunk, that
Sheila had talked shit before she had passed out. Try as he might, Lockman could not generate a fantasy about little Sheila, who looked bony
and drained by childbirth. He would try to imagine her naked, but then
he would see the absolutely sexless, romanceless flannel nightie and—
poof! It was all over. Occasionally he would think about the Parkinsons together, but those thoughts occurred during the day, and never had the

same feeling or impact of the thoughts he had late at night, when Lockman had time to draw into one of his most private places.

—

AT THE END of the month Lockman made another run up to Vancouver to deliver videotapes, sell jewelry, and cash traveler's checks. Crossing back into the United States, he used some of his newfound money at a gas station to get change so he could call Portland and access his messages. A call from Hazel, another from Tom Parkinson, and one from Dan Cheong saying he would be in his office late tonight and asking Lockman to call in as soon as possible. Lockman decided Cheong the Moron Chinaman could wait. If Cheong and Beale were tracing their calls, Lockman didn't want them knowing their star informant was anywhere near the Canadian border. As a matter of policy he told them as little as possible about his own activities.

The weather turned bad as Lockman headed south again, snow whirling down out of the darkness and melting instantly on the pavement. Traffic slowed. He turned on the radio. A man was pleading for the donation of food, clothing, and blankets for homeless people. Passing through Redmond, Lockman thought briefly of Dobbs, but he was coming to the conclusion that there never would be any fun or profit in the Dobbs household. He didn't want to deal with Kathleen Dobbs's coldness anyway. Lockman wanted to get Sheila Parkinson drunk again, to see what would happen, but even if he got her dancing naked on the dining-room table, there would still be the Parkinson brats cranking up the television cartoons the next morning when everyone was so hungover their hair hurt.

South of downtown Seattle Lockman turned off the I-5 and headed to the only residence in the world insulated with the bras and panties of murdered teenagers.

Martin Jones kept the chain on the door and spoke through the three-inch opening, as if Lockman couldn't kick the door in.

"What are you doing here?"

"I came to see you. See how you're doing. How are you? Doing?" He giggled.

Jones was playing the Great Stone Face. "You're not funny, Lockman. Did you bring me anything?"

Code for the underwear Lockman had been giving him. "No. I've told you all winter I've been too broke to afford models. Are you going to let me in? It's cold out here."

Jones closed the door, undid the chain, and let the door swing open as he walked inside. Barefoot, in washable tan pants and a white T-shirt, Jones shuffled to the television room in the back of the house, forcing Lockman to follow him like a dog. Jones knew how much Lockman hated following anybody anywhere. Jones flopped in his recliner and tilted back. Lockman glanced at the television set. George Segal and Eva Marie Saint in *Loving*. HBO. Lockman bootlegged cable and always knew what was playing on every channel.

"You're not dressed tonight."

"I'm tired. Never mind this being-broke stuff. Where's the money you owe me? I want to get a new recliner. This one isn't as comfortable as I thought it would be."

Jones wasn't looking at Lockman, but at his big projection television set. He was being cute. Lockman put his foot on the recliner footrest and pushed it down so that Jones popped up like a jack-in-the-box. "Are you going to look at me when you talk, or are you going to sulk like a spoiled papoose?"

Jones pushed himself horizontal again. "Cut it out. You know what I'm talking about. I want to know when you're going to pay me."

Lockman laughed. "What the hell is this? I drive all the way up from Portland to see you, and you treat me like a piece of shit."

Jones glared. "You're up to something. I want to know what, or you're going to have to leave."

"I'm not up to anything. Where do you get this stuff? We're crime partners. We do stuff together."

"I don't know about that anymore. You owe me four thousand, seven hundred, and twenty dollars. I want you to start paying some of it back."

"Not this week. In fact, what I'd like you to do, I'd like you to round it off to five thousand. How much is that? Two-eighty? Let me have another two hundred and eighty dollars. Or I won't give you any more authentic Garrett Richard Lockman modeling-agency underwear."

"I thought you said you were too broke."

"I am."

"How can I believe you?"

"You have to believe me. You have no choice. I provide the only authentic thrill in your whole pathetic life. Do you want it taken away from you?"

"See? You're threatening me! You do it all the time! You think nothing of threatening me! You have no respect for me. If I did it to you, you'd act like it was World War Three!"

"Because I don't like it! And I can threaten you because I have something to threaten with. I know how much you want the underwear. It would break your indigenous little heart if you thought you weren't going to get any more—or that I was giving it to some other cross-dressing primitive."

"You see? You think you can do anything you want to me!"

"I can! Give me the money, the two hundred and eighty, right now! Come on!"

Without sitting up, Jones reached into his pants pocket. Hustling him had been the farthest thing from Lockman's thoughts until Jones mentioned the Lockman National Debt. He forked over a C-note. "Bit hisself in the ass," Al liked to say. Since Lockman was getting only a hundred, not the amount he had asked for, he had a reason for continuing to abuse Jones. Lockman didn't like being treated like some kind of panhandling bum instead of a best friend. Something for Jones to think about, instead of the truth.

Which was that Lockman was still trying to keep Jones calm, distracted from the events of late last summer. It was obvious to Lockman, if not to Jones himself, that Jones was not really cut out for a career in mass murder. For weeks after Lockman's return from Atlantic City, Jones had been hysterical. He was sure to make a mess, letting a girl get away, telling the wrong person the wrong thing. Something was bound to happen, and both of them would be caught.

More important, Lockman did not want Jones stumbling upon the real experience of killing for pleasure. The woman tied to the chair had been Lockman's third, and with her the sensation had been more intense than ever. It was obvious to Lockman that Jones was nowhere near understanding the truth. Lockman had made the decision that night: he wasn't going to share the feeling with Martin Jones or anyone else.

"How about a drink?"

Jones waved his hand toward the bar. "You know where it is."

"You want one, too?"

"No." Now he sat up, but only halfway, as Eva Marie started hitting George furiously. Lockman had seen this movie, but couldn't remember it well, probably because he had watched it on a drinking night. "What do you want?" Jones asked, stealing little glances away from the screen action. "What are you doing here?"

Jones couldn't see Lockman grinning. "I told you. I wanted to see how you're doing."

"Bullshit."

"Wanna cruise?"

"In this weather? You're nuts."

"Tell me something I don't know. Really, you want to go out and see what's going on?"

"No." Silence. Suddenly Jones spun around. "Hey! Have you done anything?"

"Done anything? What do you mean?" Lockman was pouring himself a triple scotch.

"Go easy on my stuff. I mean, have you been cruising?" He hesitated. "Picking up girls and taking them down to Portland?"

Lockman paused for effect. "And killing them, you mean? Say what you mean, Little Beaver."

Jones made a face. "Don't call me those names," he said meekly. "All right, *killing*. Happy now? Are you? Killing? Again?"

Lockman laughed as he raised his glass in a toast. "I don't know why it's so hard to say when you've done it so many times. How many, three?"

"You know how many."

"You did three. That's all, and you quit. And you didn't get off. Not once. You'd rather watch. That's the story of your life." Lockman drank quickly, in the expectation of a sledgehammer rush.

"I guess you didn't get what you wanted."

"Hmm?"

"Now you're in a hurry to get out of here. When are you going to invite me down to your place? The old sanctum sanctorum? Do you know how long it's been since I've been there?"

Lockman knew exactly. Since last August, when Jones had availed himself of Lockman's secret room and made that audiotape, which Lockman had destroyed after one playing. A big nothing. Jones incriminating himself with a lot of hysterical babble, and some grunts that could have even come from him alone. Jones had said there were no other copies of the tape, but Lockman sometimes wasn't so sure. He often wondered if he could kill Jones if he had to. Lockman had never killed a man, but he didn't see how it could be so different from killing a woman. Just not as much fun. Jones wasn't getting in the secret room again anytime in the foreseeable future. Lockman said, "I saw this movie. Before it was over, I wanted to kill them both."

Jones grinned slyly. "You're doing it, aren't you? You never stopped. You've been cruising all winter."

"Yeah, right, in weather like this. What an asshole. I didn't accuse you of having another half-starved woman in the basement."

"I *saved* that woman for you! Are you going to give me my hundred dollars back?"

Try and get it. "No. I need it." Lockman had enough cash in his pockets to pay Jones every cent he owed. He almost smiled.

"I saw that."

"What?"

"That look. You're laughing inside about something. In my house. I demand to know what it is!"

Lockman put his glass on the bar and shook his head. "I'd better go. You know my style. This is the way I am. You knew that when—well, never mind."

"No, what were you going to say? Tell me."

"You don't want to hear it."

Jones almost leaped out of the chair, he bounced so hard. "You wouldn't dare say it!"

Lockman gave him another smile. "You're thinking it. Don't deny it. You're thinking about the leather lollipop. 'Did I do it? Did I?' "

"Get out! Get out! You're an evil human being!"

Lockman laughed. "Look who's calling the kettle black." Before heading for the door, he drained the last of the scotch in the glass. His head would be spinning nicely by the time he got back to the freeway. "Ta-ta."

"You're leaving? Just like that?"

Lockman was out of the room, heading toward the door. He called, "You told me to! Enjoy the woman in the basement, if you have one!"

"Lockman!"

The cold, wet air engulfed him as he closed the front door. He didn't look back as he stepped quickly to his car: of course Jones would be at the window, watching. Behind the wheel, Lockman rubbed his swelling penis through his pants. The scotch was already having an effect. How far to the freeway? Suddenly he was gasping for breath, thinking he could not go fast enough. He was wildly excited. It had happened as quickly as a finger snap, without any more warning than that, while he had been tormenting Jones. The movie on TV? Lockman hated that movie, hated the whining and the fighting. But it hadn't been the movie. No, the animal was loose in him, becoming him, learning how to assert itself that much more quickly with every passing day. Lockman could not help being glad. He had a destiny, a wave to carry him, not just something he had made up, but something that was alive and growing bigger than him, smart and cruel and secret-keeping even from him, as it cleaved to him, as he became it. The lawns and sidewalks were turning white. He was going to have to be careful. Inevitably there would be a long, rambling message from Jones on his answering machine. What Lockman had to remember was to forget about the blinking light until he had the house settled—settled was the word.

Now he remembered Dan Cheong! Cheong had said he and Beale would be in the office late. Waiting for him? Did they know something? The scotch was doing exactly what Lockman had wanted. But he had to call Cheong tonight, act as if he had just gotten the message. The parking lot where they usually met fronted a supermarket facing the interstate where it paralleled the Strip. Cheong and Beale thought Lockman had chosen the location because it gave him a measure of security from the people of the Strip, who did their food shopping at convenience stores within walking distance from the motels they lived in. In fact, the supermarket parking lot gave Lockman the chance to see that he was not walking into a trap, and tonight he followed his routine, cruising past on the interstate, doubling back on the surface streets, and circling the whole complex. He was looking for men sitting in cars, or standing around trying to look busy. The weather was working in his favor. With snow falling, no one could look natural fussing under the hood of a pickup truck. The lot was almost empty, cars rolling in only every ten minutes or so. Lockman used the pay telephone outside the supermarket to call Cheong. The handset was icy against his ear.

"Where've you been?" Cheong demanded. "We called you twice. You're supposed to check your messages."

"Hey, keep your pants on! I was down in Brookings and didn't stop for gas until I got to Eugene—"

"Where are you now?"

"A diner in downtown Portland. You want to see me, right? I'm getting some coffee so I don't fall asleep behind the wheel. I can be there in a couple of hours."

"All right. Come to the Public Safety Building."

"No dice. I keep telling you, somebody will drag in a whore who knows me, and it's all over. Meet me at the parking lot, the usual place. We're getting snow flurries down here, and if it gets too heavy on the road, I'll have to call you."

He heard Dan Cheong sigh. "Call us anyway. We're in a meeting and it will run that long."

Lockman wanted to ask about it, but knew better. Now he had three hours to kill—a few minutes more, counting the time it would take Beale and Cheong to get down here from Seattle. The supermarket had a deli counter and hot coffee. He just had to keep his mind off thoughts of booze until the cops were done with him. Once he started drinking, he always kept going until he passed out. All he could do was keep his cool, move his car to the darkest corner of the lot, and wait to see if the police arrived early—and then, if he had to get away, he could slip out of the car and walk.

The area emptied out, and at ten-thirty he called Cheong again. The conversation lasted less than a minute, but it was almost eleven o'clock when Beale and Cheong finally rolled into the lot in their big Ford. Lockman waited until the headlights went out before he started his own car and pulled up behind them. This was part of the show he always put on for them: they were supposed to think he was using his head, being careful. He got in the backseat of the Ford and closed the door.

"Some night," he said cheerfully. "How are you doing?"

Behind the wheel, Beale didn't look around. "What were you doing in Brookings?"

"Delivering a scanner to a dope dealer. I gotta make a living. Why do you ask? Did something happen?"

"We want you on the street, Garrett," Dan Cheong said. "On the Strip. We told you that."

They were going to harass him? "Oh, come on, except for tonight, I've been out there every night for the past month. Almost every night since last September."

Now Beale turned to Lockman. "And? Have you heard anything new on the killings?"

"Just more of what I've been telling you for months. People are terrified. They're sure it's a cop. These are niggers I'm talking about. Mostly niggers anyway." He was watching Cheong. He loved using the word around him. Lockman had made the trip to Brookings last year; he always kept real information in reserve for emergencies. The dope dealer in Brookings was holed up in a motel, where he was humping the town's prettiest teenagers. Lockman said, "I have something else for you. There's a Mexican gangster in town looking to steal cars, a steal-to-order deal. He's paying people to steal the cars and drive them down to Mexico with his counterfeit VIN numbers and Mexican papers."

"That's good," Cheong said. "Get us some more."

"I got it. His name is Meija." He spelled it. "He's staying at the Kennedy Hotel in Seattle."

"Good. What's the name of the dope dealer in Brookings? We might need a favor from those guys one of these days."

"No can do. He'd know right away who snitched. It's bad enough you're going to tell those guys that he's listening to their radio communications."

Beale shifted his weight. "How about you, Garrett?"

"What?"

"Are you afraid?"

"What?"

"Are you afraid of a cop?"

"Who do you mean?"

"Have you seen any cops lately? Besides us?"

The perfect question. "What other cops do I know?" He paused. Beale glared. "Oh, no," Lockman said. "If I never see Boudreau again, it'll be too soon. That's the truth. I told you that a long time ago."

Beale digested that. "I want you to keep working on this, Garrett. Go back to the people who told you that the Green River killer was a cop in the first place and get them to tell you what made them say that. See if they ever heard if there's a reason why the girls have been taken from the Strip and not anywhere else. Like the Pike. And report anybody, anything, out of the ordinary, understand?"

"Of course. I'm not stupid."

"That's it, Garrett," Cheong said. "Check in with us next week."

Lockman returned to his own car hurriedly, trying to contain himself. Boudreau? Of course they thought it was Boudreau. *The strangest cop of all.* When Beale had first befriended Lockman, he had been sure to let Lockman know that Boudreau was not his buddy. "To tell the truth, Garrett," Beale had said at the time, "I don't like him, don't trust him. There's something dirty about him, and I don't mean crooked. I mean *dirty*." Lockman wanted to tell Martin Jones, but of course he couldn't: Jones would think it put Lockman in his debt. Jones would forget all about what he had originally meant to do, which was to punish his lord and master. Lockman still owed Jones for that, and he was going to make him pay.

But listening to the other two dimwits, Lockman had had another idea. His mind was made up. He'd have to make sure they weren't following him, then he would come back and find a new friend for some fun. A *weekend* of fun. They were so stupid—how many would this make? Not figuring Deeah Anne Johanssen or Mona Raymond. And definitely not counting Jones's three. If he wasn't careful, Lockman was going to lose count. Almost one a week. With the two girls he had dumped in the river with Jones and that older woman Jones had saved for him and Lockman had dumped in the woods, this would be lucky number thirteen.

May 1983

"Let me speak to David," the man whispered over the telephone.

Boudreau sat up in the bed and stroked Piper's exposed flank. The air coming through the wide open windows was cool and moist, but until a few minutes ago Boudreau and Piper had been engaged in a body-temperature-elevation exercise, and had not yet returned to normal. A curtain stirred in the onshore breeze. "Who?"

"David," the man insisted. "David."

Boudreau recognized the voice and remembered why it was asking for David even before Piper bolted up to her hands and knees. "He'll have to call you back," Boudreau said blandly.

"Let me give you the number," Spencer said, and recited a number starting with a downtown exchange.

"Got it," Boudreau answered as he wrote, and hung up. Piper giggled and Boudreau stood up, shaking his head. "He did what I told him." He reached for his clothes.

"Let him wait," Piper whined.

"I told him to ask for David when it was important."

"He can wait ten minutes."

Boudreau laughed. "I need longer than that."

She grabbed his arm and pulled him back to the bed. "I wasn't thinking of you," she murmured, rubbing against him, straightening up to put her nipple in his mouth. She knew she had the kind of firm, athletic body a man loved to play with. Boudreau never asked about Wayne Spencer and she never volunteered anything about what she was up to. Boudreau just assumed she was doing what she pleased with Spencer—and anyone else who interested her. Boudreau didn't care. What she wanted from him was more than enough sex to keep him comfortable, and if the simplicity of the relationship meant also that he had to remember what he was dealing with, all he had to keep in mind for the sake of his equilibrium was that she probably had the same thoughts about him.

But definitely not at this moment, the first time Spencer had ever intruded on them, exercising the only option Boudreau had given him. Piper could figure out that Spencer was probably uncomfortable where he was waiting. It wasn't important to her. The Pipers of the world were willing to accept any rule until it actually crowded them, and then they wanted a new deal. Boudreau sat back. "I don't know how long this will take. I'll be as quick as I can."

She glared, reached for a pillow to tuck between her thighs, and rolled over to face the other way. "Don't be surprised if I'm in the shower when you get back."

Reminding him of her independence: she always showered before she left. But before that she was going to masturbate. It was clear she was going to insist on control under any and all circumstances. Now he said, "Stay as long as you like. Don't lose your concentration."

"You're such a shit sometimes."

He was descending the stairs when he heard her reach orgasm, and that made him tiptoe past the Gunters' first-floor apartment and keep his head turned as he passed under their window. Old Man Gunter had enough to think about without wondering whether Boudreau was using remote control.

The nearest phone booth was around the corner, in a neighborhood tavern. Wayne Spencer picked up on the first ring. "You forgot," he said. "There I am, thinking, What an asshole. What am I supposed to do now?"

"Take it easy," Boudreau said. "I never said I wasn't human. What's up? Did they find another one?"

"No. I almost wish they had. They're not going to do a task force after all. They're going to disband."

Boudreau needed a moment. He chose his words carefully. "The case isn't solved. What are they going to tell the public?"

"I want to talk to you about it," Wayne Spencer said. "Can we meet? Now? I'm in a restaurant near Pioneer Square. I can be up to your place in ten minutes."

"Not a good idea. Do you know Queen Anne?"

"I know where it is."

Boudreau gave Spencer the name and address of a coffee shop too big to miss.

Back in the apartment, under the sheet she had pulled up around her neck, Piper looked groggy as she raised herself on her elbows. He squirmed into his shoulder holster and got a jacket out of the closet. "This is going to take about an hour. We'll be down at that coffee shop where you and I had breakfast two weeks ago."

"You're really something, you know that? Do you ever think of how long it takes me to get up here? It's always me, you know, never you."

Did she really want to argue because her afternoon had been spoiled? If Wayne Spencer put up with her on these terms, he was even dumber than Boudreau had assumed. "I'll see you in an hour."

"Maybe, I told you."

Did she want him to beg? If the telephone had not rung, or if he had not picked it up, Piper would have had a wonderful afternoon, and now she was acting as if he owed her one. "Whatever," he said, and turned for the door.

Walking to his car, he released himself to the pleasure of the spectacular spring day. The sky was dark blue, spotted with a few high, fast-moving clouds. At the corner he could see the snow-covered Olympia Mountains on the other side of the Sound, and as he headed down the hill, snow-covered Mount Rainier rose beyond the downtown high-rises. This was the kind of weather that let Portland to the south see Mount Rainier, too. The two cities were one hundred and seventy-nine miles apart, and on clear days the mountain could be seen from both.

Piper who?

Boudreau had heard her last name only once, and now he could not remember it to save his life.

Ten minutes later Spencer, in his leather jacket and blue jeans, walked past him in the coffee shop to the counter; and when he turned around again with a tray bearing his coffee and a Danish, Boudreau motioned him over to the table. Spencer looked like Boudreau had played some kind of magic trick on him.

"You sit with your back to the entrance?"

"Sit down, sit down. Everybody expects cops to face the door. The first thing a bad guy does when he comes into a place like this is look around. He sees the law, he backs out and goes somewhere else. That is not crime prevention. A guy facing the counter, minding his own business, might even be another graduate of the joint. Even if the bad guy doesn't think anything, he can't head for the cash register without doing another one-eighty there. Gotta be safe, right? But he can't start doing that without me looking somewhere else. He's telling me everything, I'm telling him nothing. Anyway, I'm not going to stop him from cleaning out the register. Unless he starts hurting people."

Spencer waited until he swallowed a wad of Danish. "Come to think about it, you did the same thing in the doughnut shop that night. But where's the crime prevention? I don't get it."

"It's their next crime I'm going to prevent. I follow them out to the parking lot. They're hiding their guns again, maybe even thinking they're getting away."

Spencer smiled as if a lightbulb went on. "And since they're still on the premises, it's still a crime-in-progress. I love it. Did that actually happen to you, or is it something you made up?"

"It happened to my father. In New York. He identified himself and told them to stop where they were, but they were two against one and decided to go for it. So he had to kill them. He shot them both through the heart with his thirty-eight from a distance of thirty feet. The worst thing that ever happened to him, he said. It turned out they were wanted for a murder they did on another job, but that didn't make it easier. One of the other detectives called him Sergeant York, and it stuck. Actually, it was Sergeant Fucking York. It was okay with my old man, being nicknamed after a guy who had killed a lot of Germans. My old man really hated Germans. 'Find one you can trust,' he used to say. All right, tell me what's going on downtown."

"They got themselves all geared up for the killing to start again when the weather got warm. There were those five bodies, then nothing else, from last fall to now. The media and the activists are yelling there's another Bundy out there, but Beale says we'd have more bodies by now. I was in junior high when Bundy was doing his thing, so what do I know? I gotta believe. Cheong says the guy is dead or in jail or out of the jurisdiction. You look like you want to puke."

"It's not that bad. Cheong is saying what cops always say when they have a homicidal maniac who *seems* to stop killing. First, they never stop. Your mother told you not to pick your nose but you did it anyway, and look at you now, you're a nose-picking fool."

Spencer laughed. "It feels good, you mean."

"Right. You couldn't stop pulling your pecker now if someone put a gun to your head. You'd forget the gun was there, sneak your hand to the wrong place, and *boom!* Tell me I'm lying. They never kill themselves, never, ever. 'Stop me before I kill again.' That guy was before our time, but we both know the line. So that means somebody else would have to kill him. A victim? A teenage girl who got lucky? He picks these girls not just because they're throwaways, but also because their need for love and attention can be manipulated to work against their best interests, and they can't stop it. Most of them die young anyway, did you know that? He isn't in jail, either. This guy is weirder than owl shit. Somebody in jail would have noticed, especially another con who would have worked him the way only cons can, to toss him for a break for himself. And he didn't leave the jurisdiction because history shows that this is the best part of the world for him to operate in."

"He was lucky, you know."

"What do you mean?"

"The fifth one? When they did the tests on her, the results showed she went into the water just hours after the cops left the area after the fourth. They just missed him."

"They better keep that quiet," Boudreau said.

"Why?"

"Because it says that even after four bodies were pulled from that scrawny little urinal of a river, it didn't dawn on anybody to leave someone watching the area. It's a pathetic lapse, absolutely incompetent. And those murders are still unsolved, plain and simple. There will be hell to pay if anybody thinks Major Crimes is walking away from the case." The truth was that he had cut his own surveillance sorties down to one or two a week. No new bodies had been found in more than eight months, and Boudreau was involved in a pandering trial that the DA was having difficulty organizing. Boudreau had a copy of Lockman's burglary file at home, although he wasn't exactly sure what he thought he was going to learn from it.

"Nobody has any enthusiasm for this since the bodies stopped turning up. The people who make the decisions say that street girls are a very low priority. But nobody's making any announcements, just in case." Spencer was looking out the window, and Boudreau was about to ask, "Just in case what?" when Spencer rose a foot out of his chair. His eyebrows were so arched they looked like they belonged on a kid seeing his first department-store Santa. "Son of a bitch."

Boudreau decided not to look around. "What?"

"Piper. You remember Piper. She's right out there, stopped for the light. That's her car."

It felt like an electric shock. Boudreau wanted to think through his response, but he had no time, unless he wanted Spencer wondering why his behavior seemed so defensive and studied. Boudreau swung around as the traffic began to move again. No doubt about it, it was Piper and her little red daddy-bought Beemer, rolling down the hill toward the Space Needle. "You're sure?"

Spencer slid disconsolately down into his seat. "Wearing the same baby-blue ribbon in her hair I saw her put on this morning. She said she was coming up here to the University to visit an old high-school girl-friend, but this is a long way from the U."

"Jesus, no, it isn't. Five minutes. Maybe they just had lunch. This neighborhood is full of restaurants. Don't go making trouble for yourself." He dared not say more, and he couldn't avoid Spencer's eyes, either. Even a real-life Baby Huey like Spencer could stumble onto the truth once in a while. Boudreau was wondering if he had to change his telephone number. Piper had taken this route back to the I-5 not so much to check on him—or Spencer—as to present one or both of them with the opportunity to see her. Stir things up a little. Express her unhappiness. And this was just a flash of her fury. He had to ask himself: was there any reason to want to see more? Spencer was in a daze. "Just in case what?" Boudreau asked.

"What?"

"You were saying, they weren't making any announcements about the task force 'just in case.' That's what I'm asking."

"Oh. Yeah." Spencer's shoulders heaved. "Well, if something else happens, they can call everybody in and get back to work."

"You're saying you're going back to Kent."

"I don't know," he said distractedly. "They're going down to three, maybe four guys. Maybe I just had my fifteen minutes of fame. For all I know, I'll be back in uniform next week, writing tickets."

Why did Boudreau feel sorry for him? Spencer understood his situation perfectly. What more could a guy ask of life? Now his eyes narrowed as he focused on Boudreau. "Something I wanted to ask you."

"Sure." He resisted the urge to swallow.

"Why didn't you tell me you tossed in the name of a suspect last fall?"

"There was nothing to tell you. They told me right away that the guy checked out as being back east. I never thought of it again."

"Well, okay. Now they're trying to get everything cross-referenced back and forth. So much stuff, so many tips. Anyway, I tried to find it in the file under your name and came up empty. Whatever you told them isn't there anymore."

Boudreau told him that the guy's name was Garrett Richard Lockman. "Maybe it never got into the file in the first place. Don't get paranoid on me."

"Say that name again."

Boudreau did.

"That's the guy. We saw him. Talked to the guy. You said weird. This is one weird motherfucker."

"Where did you talk to him? Who was with you?"

"Dan Cheong. We were on the Strip. Sea-Tac. Daytime. After the holidays. Remember we got a break in the weather? Dan and I had just finished talking for the third fucking time to the woman who was the last one to see the fifth victim alive. We were headed back up to town. I stopped for a light and this character walked up to Dan's side of the car, called him by name, and started talking. Dan told me to pull over and I did, with this Lockman guy walking alongside the car. I wanted to tell him to get up on the sidewalk, but Dan told me to cool it. He told me to kill the engine and get out, because this guy was so interesting. He was that, I'll tell you."

"What was he doing down on the Strip?"

"Hanging out, he said. Dan asked him what he was up to, and he said, 'Chapter Six.' "

Boudreau wished he could put Spencer on fast-forward. "What the hell does that mean?"

"It's a joke, I guess. Anyway, this Garrett Richard Lockman tells Dan he saw his picture in the paper last fall when they were pulling a body out of the river, so he asks Dan, straight out, if he's still working on the Green River killings."

"Is that what he called them? Did he use those words?"

"Yeah, why?"

"I'm trying to see how dialed into them he is."

"I thought you said he was out of it."

"He was out of town for the first three. All of them, for all I know," he added. He wanted to be careful. He certainly was not going to say he knew anything about Lockman's walkaway from King County Jail. Lockman was Beale and Cheong's snitch, and he and Cheong had fallen into this impromptu performance for Spencer's sake? Why? "What else did he say?" For a moment Spencer seemed distracted again. If he was falling for Piper's mind games, he was on his own. Boudreau could not help thinking that his own relationship with her was over. *Adios!* Spencer said,

"There was the usual long-time, no-see stuff, and then Dan asked him if he had been hearing anything on the Strip about the killings. Lockman said it was just ordinary scuttlebutt."

"Did Cheong tell you how he knows Lockman?"

"You mean later? No, but that's when he said you had tossed Lockman's name in at the very beginning. That Lockman was like a big collar for you."

"It was dumb luck. I rolled past a gun shop while Lockman and his crime partner were doing the deed." Why had Cheong gone out of his way to point out to Spencer that Boudreau was a minor leaguer? *Big collar*. Now Boudreau thought of something else. He studied Spencer, completely certain that Spencer was being as straight with him as he should have been with Spencer. "More coffee? I'm going to get a refill." Boudreau stood up.

Spencer gave over his cup. "Yeah, okay. Thanks."

At the counter Boudreau read the menus over the back bar. If he ordered something from the griddle, he would be given a number and called back later. Something cold, already prepared, would come from the back bar, and while the counter girl put the order together Boudreau could survey the area. Now he was thinking that it was reasonable to conclude that the "chance" meeting of Spencer with Lockman had been prearranged—the dialogue between Cheong and Lockman had been all for show. And Beale knew about Piper. Why not? Boudreau had been under surveillance when he'd picked up Betty Antonelli. After that, in a move that would not have diminished suspicions of him, he'd punched out Special Agent William Fitzgerald of the FBI. So they'd set Spencer up with Lockman perhaps to see how long it took the information to get back to Boudreau. Forever, as it had turned out.

Boudreau ordered a po'boy and a salad and the coffees, caught his breath, and turned around as if he wanted to look at the women. He found one, checked her out, and let his eyes roam over the rest of the crowd. Of all the people in the place, only Spencer could have passed the physical examination for police officer.

Now Boudreau saw them.

This was big time. Across the street, illegally parked, was a dark green van with a fixed, mirror-glass window in the middle of the panel behind the driver's door. Behind the window, Boudreau was sure, was a television camera and a microphone that could pick up every word said inside the restaurant. If the audio recording was too noisy, electronic cleaning would highlight the conversation between Spencer and him. Very big time, the latest from the FBI toy box. His only strategy was to continue to act as if he didn't know they were there. It just happened to be the toughest trick in the world. He paid and headed back to the table.

"You really going to eat all that stuff?" Spencer asked.

"I didn't have any breakfast. If you want my advice about taking them up on their offer to stay on, I'd have to ask you what your career goals are. You don't sound so excited about going back to chasing drunks on the highway or battling them in their homes only to have their old ladies crown you when your back is turned. On the other hand, do you like being a sleuth? Do you like the career opportunities that open to you if you guys do solve this case? You do your twenty, come out, and set yourself up as some kind of rent-a-cop, industrial security, go to work for a major sports franchise, in your off-hours regale the civilians with your true-action cop stories, and have access to some of the world's most entertaining and dangerous women, if you want them, *and* cash a pension check."

"What's the downside?"

"For you? None. You're not calling the shots. If you never even catch a cold, it's not your fault. That's Beale's problem, the FBI. As it should be. They're very big winners for life if they get the guy. They get movies made about them."

"Scary—but tasty, too. I got into police work because I needed a job. I never thought of it as my ticket out."

If his comments were getting on tape, it wasn't Boudreau's fault, and Boudreau felt no obligation to tip the kid to what was going on. A continuing surveillance. They had something they still believed. Did they believe it so much they were missing the real opportunities the investigation was presenting? Was he supposed to give a shit?

Who would plant evidence against him?

Not Beale. He didn't have motivation—or the imagination.

No, there was only Garrett Richard Lockman.

Round and round, Boudreau was thinking as Spencer reached for the po'boy, looking to Boudreau for approval. Boudreau nodded. Spencer tore off a piece for himself. After all, Spencer had to maintain his strength for Piper. He still had the hots for her, in spite of his suspicions, and with Boudreau out of the picture, Piper would focus that much more attention on Spencer. While she looked for other action. And maybe bothered Boudreau on the telephone. A cop did not have to be single for long to get a handle on the possibilities.

———

IN THE NEXT days the situation did not seem so simply sorted out after all. When Piper did not call, Boudreau found how vulnerable he was to her machinations. He had put himself at risk and now he did not like the thought of Spencer's reaction when he learned of his new buddy's betrayal of him. Not *if*, but *when*. It looked inevitable: if Piper herself could not find a reason to bludgeon Spencer with the information, then perhaps Beale would decide it was good police work. Or good religion. Did Beale and Company know about his forays down to the Strip? Holding back while they waited for him to commit a crime? Boudreau could do nothing about their surveillance without bringing about a confrontation that would be worse than the first one in their carefully prepared office. He wasn't ready for that. Not yet.

More likely, their surveillance was intermittent and they hadn't even seen him on the Strip. He understood their budget problems as well as he understood his own, and he couldn't remember ever having gotten there before midnight. Still, they were breathing on him, setting up the meeting with Lockman to see how fast it got back to Boudreau. Had Lockman been in on it—had he identified their suspect? If Lockman really had set Boudreau up in the first place, he was now having the time of his life.

The next month, for the first time since his divorce, Boudreau got out of town. He had vacation time coming, and Paulie's interests gave him an excuse. In south Seattle Boudreau rented a mini–motor home, a converted pickup truck equipped with beds, dining area, kitchen, bath, and built-in television set. To anyone who wanted to observe them, father and son were going camping. In fact, they were stepping outside history. Paulie had his dinosaur books, his father a pile of maps and atlases almost as high.

They headed first to snow-covered Mount Rainier. Paulie's questions poured out: Was this ever a volcano? How long ago? Did Tyrannosaurus rex live here? They took narrow state roads through a tall, silent forest down to Mount St. Helen's, which Paulie knew from television and school. On to snow-covered Mount Hood east of Portland. Then the Columbia Gorge.

They drove south to the Oregon Dunes. Coos Bay. The Rogue River. Down into California to Mount Shasta and then back north to Crater Lake, taking pictures of everything. Paulie started counting the days they had left—he did not want the trip to end. Neither did Boudreau. He could not remember a better time in his whole life. Boudreau's only reminder of Seattle and the problems he had left there was that, like Boudreau's young clients from the Pike and Pioneer Square, Paulie had the attention span of a gnat: if he did not like the sound of a guitar, he pushed a button; and if he did not like what that brought up, he pushed another. For once, Boudreau's experience on the streets served him personally: if he had not seen the phenomenon in others, he might have leaped to the conclusion that Paulie suffered from a mental defect unique to him.

Back home two weeks later, the truck returned to the rental agency and Paulie returned to his mom, the sun setting on a long, tiring day, Boudreau sat down with pencil and paper and played back the messages on his answering machine. The silence gathered close around him again like a ghost, and it almost hurt to be alone. Less than a third of the forty-five-minute message tape had been used. Who was he that he had so little impact on people? Even after his holiday he felt on the edge of spiritual exhaustion. He had not really built a life when he had settled here, but had focused laserlike on making a living. Now he had no choice but to proceed not so much borne up by hope and dreams as buoyed by a confused self-respect. Terrible. And he had no one but himself to blame.

The first message was from a Bellingham vice cop who wanted to discuss a runaway case—he was calling Boudreau at home because he wanted to be sure the message was received. The Bellingham officer, Boudreau thought, had a perfect understanding of the workings of law-enforcement bureaucracy.

Al Holobaugh. Call back.

Perfect. If Beale and his men were still listening, they also knew that Boudreau and Holobaugh had been friends for years.

A reporter from KING-TV. She dated and timed her call at two o'clock on Monday, four days ago. "Please call me back, detective. As you already know, it's important."

Piper. "I'd like to talk to you, Phil. I made a mistake and I know it now. Call me."

"Phil, it's Dan Cheong. Call me when you're back from your trip, will you? I have a new telephone number." He gave the number, and then, after a pause, repeated it. Was he being so courteous because he wanted to lull Boudreau into a false sense of security?

Piper again. "Are you all right? This is the last time I'm going to call, under the circumstances."

A new voice, all business: "Detective Boudreau, my name is Diane Heidt, H-E-I-D-T. Will you please call me at your earliest possible convenience? This concerns the discovery in Enumclaw. I've been told you have original opinions about the Green River murders and the efforts to solve them. Please call." And the number, an exchange in the University District.

Wayne Spencer: "Call David."

And finally, Diane Heidt again, rephrasing her earlier message, finishing, "It's important."

The KING-TV reporter had said the same thing. Enumclaw? Boudreau was too tired to call anybody right now, but he wanted to find out what was going on. He had his laundry bag filled for the trip down the block before he figured out how to do it.

Sleuth!

Downstairs, Mrs. Gunter answered the door. Behind her, a television set played *Family Feud.* Boudreau said, "I've been out of town, Mrs. Gunter. Is there anything I missed?"

Mr. Gunter looked around the side of a wing chair. "They found a skeleton down in Enumclaw!"

Pursing her lips, Mrs. Gunter waved Boudreau back into the vestibule and closed the door behind her. "You heard him. What they found was the remains—that's what they said—of a girl who's been missing for over a year. A prostitute. A teenager. What the genius in there doesn't want you to know is that his daughter—not mine, my kids are just fine, thank you very much—his daughter is a junkie in jail in L. A. for peddling her ass on Hollywood Boulevard. He'd raise hell if he knew I was telling you, but I got a feeling you don't need his bullshit on top of everything else in your life."

"Is there something I don't know?"

"A couple of guys, cops, I guess, were around looking for you on Monday, after the body was found. The remains, I mean. I told them you were away with your son, and they said they'd leave a message on your answering machine."

"Was one of them a tall, sharply dressed Chinese-American?"

She nodded. "Good-looking. Muscles, too."

"They left their message. Thanks." He wanted to get his laundry done while he still had the energy.

—

THE NEXT DAY, Friday, Boudreau rose early. It was the last of his vacation days, so he didn't have to go downtown; but because his bosses had his camping schedule, he was sure Beale and Cheong had it, too. With his list of callers in front of him, Boudreau sat down to the telephone. If Beale and Company had been listening to what went on inside this apartment, they knew who was calling him, too. They already knew everything about his relationship with Wayne Spencer—probably more than he did—and there was no point in going out to search for a pay phone at this hour only to maintain the illusion of a belief in their secrecy. The first number Boudreau dialed was Spencer's. Spencer sounded as if he had been asleep. Boudreau apologized.

"No, no. The alarm is going to go off in ten minutes. Well, you were right."

"Right? About what?"

"A woman walking her dog down in the woods in Enumclaw stepped on the skeleton of a girl they identified as Mona Raymond, that girl you were looking for last year."

"I don't know how you figure that. I was just following up a missing-person report. Have you talked to Uhuru?"

"We talked to him, but he hasn't talked to us. His lawyer told him not to tell us anything."

"What the hell, he's engaged in a continuing criminal enterprise. If he tells you that Mona Raymond was his whore, somebody might decide to seize his assets under the RICO statutes. Tell me how I got to be right, and what about." Boudreau heard water running, as if through a noisy rain gutter. "Are you using one of those portable phones?"

"Yeah, I'm in the bathroom taking a leak. They're giving you credit because the body—well, bones, mostly—tells them that the guy has been at it for a while and can follow different MOs."

Boudreau had to wait until the roar of the flushing toilet abated. "How do they know it's the same guy?"

"The body was laid out exactly like numbers four and five at the Green River—they were found on the bank, facedown, but don't tell anybody. They want to talk to you—about Uhuru, I guess. You've been camping with your kid?"

"We had a great time."

"I wish I could say the same. Piper and I are done."

"Sorry to hear that."

"I just began to get a funny feeling. You remember that day I saw her going by outside the coffee shop. I never mentioned it to her. A couple of weeks later she comes up to town to meet me after work and wants to go to Piecora's because the pizza is so good there. I ask her how she knows about Piecora's and she tells me her friend took her there the afternoon I saw her way the hell over in Queen Anne. Right then and there I said to hell with it, but I couldn't figure a way out until they found those bones." He yawned. "Don't ask me how one fits the other. I told Piper that Beale warned me I was on call around the clock and that I shouldn't make any plans. That did it. Piper isn't into what you call sacrifice."

Now Boudreau knew why she had suddenly decided to call him again.

He had been the one to introduce her to Piecora's. "This is what pizza is supposed to taste like," he had said, playing *l'homme du monde*. If sticking his fingers down his throat could help him puke up his hypocrisy, he would do it. Perhaps indulging the impulse that had gotten him into this trouble in the first place, he did a perfect two-and-a-half gainer into his own perversity. "You know the magic word, don't you?"

Spencer snorted mirthlessly. "What's that?"

Boudreau pronounced the word like a post office worker calling a waiting customer: "*Next!*"

Spencer laughed. "Yeah, right."

Boudreau said, "The shift in MO after the five in the river still points to the idea that there are two guys."

"I'm listening."

"The Hillside Strangler, Buono and Bianchi. From what I understand of that case, Bianchi alone was no killer. He blossomed when he started hanging out with his cousin Angelo Buono. Chances are Buono would have never been caught if Bianchi hadn't fucked up in Bellingham."

"You're still thinking that guy Lockman, aren't you?" When Boudreau didn't answer, Spencer said, "If he was doing those girls, why would he be willing to put himself under our noses the way he did that time?"

Spencer still didn't know about Lockman being his superiors' snitch. "Maybe to gloat. Before I busted him, he never had to submit to anybody's discipline, even in the navy. If he hadn't given the brass a reason to get rid of him, they would have manufactured one. I got that directly from them. Not in writing, of course. They wouldn't dream of putting something in writing for someone as low as a cop."

"Maybe you ought to come in and talk to Ron Beale."

"I gotta call Dan Cheong. If he wants me to come in, I will. Sorry I knocked you out of bed."

He was thinking of Holobaugh. Al Holobaugh wouldn't have called because another body had been found. Only the position of the body tied this one to the Green River killings, and maybe that wasn't enough. And Al Holobaugh would have waited for Boudreau to call him to share what he knew. If cops were the world's best back-fence gossips, they liked to maintain their cool through the process. Holobaugh picked up on the first ring.

"You know, I thought it would be you. You're lucky I'm not out playing eighteen holes. Here's the deal. After they found that kid's bones down in Enumclaw, I decided to have another look at that guy Lockman's file. I was curious. Uh-uh. It's out."

"Missing?"

"No, no, nothing like that. The slip says Major Crimes has it."

"Do you remember the date on the slip?"

"Figuring you'd ask me, I committed it to memory. What is this, the end of June? It's been out ten weeks now."

Boudreau was remembering that Spencer had not been able to find the same file. "Considering he's not a suspect—"

"It's a very long time," Holobaugh finished. "Nice way to keep the file from prying eyes."

"Or the press," Boudreau said.

"Right," Holobaugh said resignedly. "The press has its contacts among my colleagues, and this is definitely going to get nasty. Actually it's going to get so nasty, our asses will be grass if we talk to the wrong people. Like you."

"Al, cops themselves may wind up in jail for this."

"Suits me. I'm just glad I'm not so ambitious."

Boudreau poured himself another cup of coffee and looked at the list of callers. He would wait until he was at his desk before calling the Bellingham cop. The runaway he had called about might have gone home by now. Boudreau was not going to call Piper. Even if he wanted to talk to her, this was the wrong time of day. Piper was a morning girl, but not for talking. Not the KING-TV reporter, either, probably an even more certain route to trouble. For all he knew, he was closer to the top of the suspect list than ever. And not Diane Heidt, whoever she was, or how "important" she thought her business to be.

It was still not eight o'clock. He called Dan Cheong at his new number anyway. Cheong picked up on the first ring.

"Phil Boudreau, Dan. What's up?"

"They told us you were out of town. Are you up to speed on this new body down in Enumclaw?"

"Old body, you mean. The girl I was looking for over a year ago, Mona Raymond."

"Right, right. Anyway, her pimp, Uhuru, has been advised by his lawyer not to talk to us about anything. Since the exact date and time of death can't be established, the question of an alibi is moot. First, given what you know about the guy, do you think he could have done it?"

"What you really mean is, that one and all the others."

"No, no. Just that one."

Boudreau caught himself. "I saw Uhuru late last year and he didn't act like a guy who had something to fear from the cops."

"This from a pimp. For Christ's sake."

"He's always known how to do that without making trouble for himself with us. What I mean is, he wasn't murderer-nervous. To give you the simple answer, no, I don't think he killed Mona Raymond. When I talked to him in the spring of 'eighty-two about her, he seemed honestly indignant about her taking off on him."

"And you saw him late last year, since she disappeared."

"I ran into him in a doughnut shop on Second Avenue."

"What was your conversation about?"

"I don't remember."

"Did you take notes?"

"No. We just passed the time of day."

"You passed the time of day with a pimp."

"I was in the coffee shop and he came in." Boudreau drew a breath. "What's the point of this, Dan?"

A pause. "We want you to talk to Uhuru for us. See what he'll tell you. Do you mind coming down here today?"

"No, I don't, but Uhuru has already made it clear to you that he does. I can catch up with him on the Pike."

"Oh, we want the conversation to take place down here."

"There won't be a conversation down there—"

"Are you saying you refuse to do it?"

"You know perfectly well I'm not saying that. If Uhuru's lawyer gave him the good advice to keep his mouth shut around cops, he's not going to chitchat in a cop shop. But because he's an asshole, and loves to hear the sound of his own voice, he might chitchat on his own turf with me."

"Are you willing to wear a wire?"

"Absolutely not."

"Hold on a minute."

Cheong put him on hold. Someone else had been listening to Cheong's side of the conversation. Boudreau refilled his coffee cup. The telephone clicked again. "Boudreau?"

"I'm here."

"Are you willing to come in?"

"Of course. Didn't I say that?"

"Phil, there's no reason to cop an attitude—"

"Put Beale on the phone."

"He's not here."

"Then put on whoever you were talking to."

"Just a minute." This time Cheong put his hand over the mouthpiece, and Boudreau could not hear his muffled voice as he talked to somebody else. "Phil, Kevin Donovan is picking up the other extension."

Another click. "Good morning, Boudreau."

Boudreau sipped some coffee. "Good morning. The FBI is still working this case?"

"Still as belligerent as ever, Boudreau?"

"No, just contemptuous. You want me to come down there?"

"It would be helpful, yes."

"I don't want to make any assumptions about the agenda. Tell me what will be discussed."

"Can we do that when you get here?"

"No. I don't want to be subjected to the kind of thing I got last time."

"*Subjected* is a funny word for a man who put a special agent in the hospital—"

"You've forgotten what led up to it."

"Boudreau, the fat lady isn't even in the building. You might want to keep that in mind."

"Is that a threat?"

"You know, I'm sick and tired of your attitude. We've got better things to do than screw around with you."

"Then stop screwing around with me! Stop following me, stop bugging my phone, stop listening to what goes on in my bedroom! If I'm a suspect, say so, and I'll hire a lawyer."

"You're not a suspect," Cheong said. "We are not eavesdropping on you."

"At this time," Boudreau said.

They were silent. Admission enough, today.

"Is there anything on the agenda except me talking to Uhuru?"

"No," Donovan said. "But we do want to be sure specific questions are asked."

"Uhuru will know who's asking them. He'll clam up if he thinks I'm running an errand for you guys. That's if he talks to me at all."

"You think maybe he won't?" Cheong asked.

"Uhuru has made a career of accumulating money without working for it, so it's important to him. If he pays a lawyer for his advice and then doesn't take it, he might as well set fire to his wallet. On the other hand, he is an asshole who wants to tell somebody how smart he is. Is that guy Fitzgerald there?"

"He's on disability, thanks to you," Donovan said.

"My tax dollars at work. I'll be right down."

Cheong said, "I'll tell your boss you're working today and should be credited with an additional vacation day."

Putting down the telephone, Boudreau had the thought that he had missed his chance. Talking to Uhuru for them wasn't going to yield anything new. Uhuru would know what Boudreau was up to as soon as he set eyes on him. The only reason to play the fool like this was the opportunity to find out what was being done with Garrett Richard Lockman—but Boudreau could not help believing that he had just fumbled the best break he was ever going to get. He had gotten Cheong and Donovan yelling at him, and if he had sprung Lockman on them, one or the other might have had a momentary loss of control and blurted out something pointing toward the truth.

Downstairs, as he stepped outside, a woman was emerging from a new Honda Accord double-parked next to his Mustang. A good-looking woman, too. Five-six, very slim, her dark hair cut short so it spilled softly across her brow. High cheekbones, little makeup. As she came up the driveway he could see a little spray of freckles across her nose. She smiled.

"Excuse me, do you know if Phil Boudreau lives here?"

"Yes."

"Yes, he does, or yes, you know."

"Both. You can't park where you are, I gotta get out of here."

"Okay, okay. You don't have to be so gruff."

He headed to his car. "Just the way it came out, lady. I meant no harm."

She was following him, almost running to keep up. "You're Phil Boudreau!"

He stopped and looked her in the eye. "Who wants to know?"

She stuck out her hand. "Diane Heidt."

He took her hand and held it with his two hands. Her fingers were long and slim. "Good to see you."

She let him continue to hold her hand another moment. "But not good enough to talk to. I was hoping I'd hear from you."

"I can't talk to you. I can't even tell you I can't talk to you. Don't quote me on that, I'll deny it. I don't know who gave you the idea that I have original opinions—I don't have any opinions. On the Mariners, the 'Sonics, the Seahawks. Nothin'. I'm dumb, got it?" He turned for his car again.

"And very defensive, too."

"What are you, a psychotherapist?"

"Yes. That's exactly what I am."

"That ties it. Move the car, lady, before I write you a ticket."

"It's hard to believe you were just holding my hand with such, ah, enthusiasm. What kind of a handshake do you call that?"

"Don't try to engage me in a conversation, Miss Heidt. Doctor. Whatever. Move it or I'll bust you for interfering with police business. That's much worse than a traffic ticket."

"All right, all right." She walked around to the driver's side of her car, then stopped. "Will you take my card, at least? Let me tell you why I need to talk to you?"

He stared at her. He had her number written down upstairs, but if he told her that, she would draw him into a conversation, maybe into telling her his life story. Now she smiled. "Are you a woman-hater, Mr. Boudreau?"

He smiled back. She had nice, steady eyes. "Nah. I just get surly when I don't have one to fuck."

"You've been alone too long. I'll be back."

"Now that you know what the deal is, I hope so."

She got into her car, but not fast enough to keep him from seeing her blushing. Maybe her panties were just a teensy bit more slippery than they had been. The thought made his mouth water. Her car moved about ten feet before it suddenly stopped. It rolled backward and the passenger window whirred down. He looked in. She leaned across the empty seat.

"Girls are disappearing, you son of a bitch, more every week. Let's see how that sits on your conscience, if you have one."

He decided he was right about her panties, not that it was going to do him any good now. She drove off, smoking rubber.

July 1983

Arresting Officer: P. Boudreau   date: 2/17/81
Name: Lockman, Garrett Richard
Address: 318 N. 143 Street, Seattle
Sex: M   DOB: 6/22/54
Place of Birth: Medford, Oregon   Citizen? Y
Charge: Burglary. Poss./Deadly Weapon (ice pick)
Arresting Officer's Report:
@ approx. 1:40am I was proceeding north on Western Av when I observed subj sitting behind wheel of 1971 Chev. Malibu 2-dr. (Lic. #KHW-
382, reg subj) outside Eagle Guns and Ammo, 1561 Western Av. Subj
covered eyes as I passed, so I circled block and parked corner Clay St
facing Western so I could observe subj from behind. Subj was very nervous, constantly looking around. Suspecting burglary in progress, I approached car on foot with gun drawn and police badge in view. Subj
obeyed order to exit car, immediately claimed to be kidnap victim of second subj still inside gun shop (Thomas Brownall, see attached). A search
revealed an ice pick in subj's jacket pocket. I cuffed subj to steering wheel

of his car, ordered him to remain quiet, and awaited exit of second subj from gun shop. @ 1:53 Officers Sandra Kuck and Robert Bloom approached in radio car on Western Av and responded to my hand signal to pull over. I briefed them on the situation and we took up positions to apprehend second subj.

Second subj emerged from gun shop @ 1:58am bearing an armload of pistols and rifles and was taken into custody. For a kidnap victim, Lockman remained strangely silent in presence of his alleged abductor. Brownall immediately cursed Lockman. The two suspects were kept at a distance from each other until backup arrived.

TRANSCRIPT OF TAPE-RECORDED INTERVIEW WITH
GARRETT RICHARD LOCKMAN
4:10 A.M. 2/17/81

> Conducted by Detective P. Boudreau
> Officer Sandra Kuck, Witness

Boudreau: State your name and address.

Lockman: Garrett Richard Lockman. Three-Eighteen North One Hundred and Forty-third Street, Seattle.

B.: I'm going to read you your rights and ask you to respond to each and every question.

L.: We don't have to go through that.

B.: Oh, yes, we do. You have the right to remain silent and refuse to answer any questions. Do you understand?

L.: Yeah.

B.: Say yes or no.

L.: Yes.

B.: Anything you do say may be used against you. Do you understand?

L.: Yes.

B.: You have the right to consult an attorney before speaking to the police and to have an attorney present during any questioning now or in the future. Do you understand?

L.: Yes.

B.: If you cannot afford an attorney, one will be provided for you without cost. Do you understand?

L.: Yes.

B.: If you do not have an attorney available, you have the right to remain silent until you have had the opportunity to consult with one. Do you understand that?

L.: Yes.

B.: Now that I have advised you of your rights, are you willing to answer questions?

L.: Yes. Do you have to go through this with everyone? Jesus. Don't you get bored?

B.: What were you doing outside Eagle Guns and Ammo at two in the morning?

L.: I told you. That guy kidnapped me. He told me he'd kill me if I didn't watch out for the cops while he went in to rob the place. Boy, was I glad when you came along.

B.: Why didn't you simply drive off? You had the keys to the car.

L.: I told you, he threatened to kill me. He knows where I live. He's a very violent guy, a very bad guy.

B.: All right, how did he come to kidnap you?

L.: I met him in a bar last night. We had a couple of beers, shot the shit — excuse me, officer.

Officer Kuck: I've heard worse.

L.: Anyway, we talked and he said he had a business proposition for me. He wanted to discuss it outside. So we went out to my car, and that's when he pulled a gun on me and told me to drive him to the gun shop, he wanted to rob the place.

B.: If you just met him in the bar, how did he know where you lived?

L.: I told him.

B.: Explain how you did that.

L.: In the bar. I told him in the bar.

B.: Why?

L.: He wanted to know.

B.: A stranger wanted to know where you lived and you flat out told him.

L.: Yeah.

B.: I thought you said he was a tough guy and that you were afraid of him.

L.: I am now. I wasn't then. That was before he pulled the gun on me.

B.: What kind of a gun was that?

L.: I don't know. I don't know anything about guns.

B.: I thought you volunteered in the car that you once were a security guard. You did volunteer that, didn't you?

L.: (Laughs.) I'm supposed to say I volunteered that? Okay, I volunteered that I was a security guard.

B.: You're not supposed to say anything. Do you want me to read you your rights again?

L.: No, no, anything but that. What a lot of shit. Excuse me.

B.: Didn't you have to carry a gun on your job as a security guard?

L.: It wasn't that kind of security guard. It was more like a night watch-man.

B.: Where was this?

L.: Up in Everett.

B.: No, give me the name of your employer.

L.: I forget. It was a long time ago.

B.: Who is your employer now?

L.: I'm unemployed now.

B.: How long have you been unemployed?

L.: Long time. It's hard to find a job. Jimmy Carter's inflation still has the whole economy screwed up.

B.: We searched Mr. Brownall and your car thoroughly and we found no gun —

L.: (Laughs.) He came out of the store with an armload of guns.

B.: All those guns bore price tags with "Eagle Guns and Ammo" clearly printed on them. There were no other guns.

L.: Oh, he must have seen you and taken a price tag off another gun in the store.

B.: The owner of the store has already been here and identified all the guns as his. In the absence of a gun, you'll have trouble convincing a jury that Mr. Brownall forced you at gunpoint to serve as a lookout for him.

L.: What jury?

B.: Your jury. You will be charged with one count of burglary and one count of carrying a concealed weapon. Both are felonies. You could be sentenced to up to ten years in the state penitentiary.

L.: I didn't know that.

B.: What was there about it that you didn't know?

L.: That you thought I was committing a crime. I wasn't. That's what I keep trying to tell you.

B.: We've already taken a statement from Mr. Brownall, and he says that the two of you planned to rob the gun store together. He says we'll find a diagram of the store in your apartment. Do you realize that a conviction of kidnapping could result in your friend going to prison for life?

L.: He's not my friend. I told you, I met him in a bar tonight.

B.: He says you met in southern California when you were in the navy. He says you sold him stolen navy electronics gear.

L.: That's a lie.

B.: He says he has pictures of the two of you together taken at the Hotel Del Coronado in San Diego.

L.: The Hotel Del isn't in San Diego, it's in Coronado.

B.: Then you admit that you knew him before this evening.

L.: No, I don't admit that at all. Look, for all I know, he planted that diagram or whatever it is in my apartment.

B.: But you say you just met him tonight.

L.: Maybe he was stalking me. Maybe he's setting me up.

B.: Why would he want to do that?

L.: I don't know, ask him.

B.: I think we will.

TRANSCRIPT OF TAPE-RECORDED INTERVIEW WITH
GARRETT RICHARD LOCKMAN
1:20 P.M. 2/17/81

Conducted by Detective P. Boudreau
Detective Norbert Walz, Jr., Witness

Boudreau: State your name and address.

Lockman: You're not going to read me my rights again, are you?

B.: This is to identify you.

L.: Garrett Richard Lockman, Three-Eighteen North One Hundred and Forty-third Street, Seattle.

B.: Have you been read your rights and do you understand them as they were explained to you?

L.: Yes.

B.: And you are making this statement of your own volition without any prompting or coercion?

L.: Yes.

B.: Make your statement.

L.: Just like that?

B.: You said you wanted to make a statement about last night's attempted robbery of Eagle Guns and Ammo.

L.: He talked me into it.

B.: Name that person.

L.: Tom Brownall. He talked me into it.

B.: Tell us exactly what he talked you into and what you did as a consequence of his powers of persuasion.

L.: He called me and asked if he could come over, and I said sure. He arrived with that diagram of Eagle. He told me he wanted some ammo to go hunting. He said it was going to be easy. I didn't think it was going to be a big-deal felony, that he was going to grab all those guns. He's a scary guy.

B.: All right, what did you do after you agreed to rob Eagle Guns and Ammo?

L.: I agreed to sit in the car and watch out for the cops, that's what I agreed to. I wasn't very good at it, was I? (Laughs.) I guess it shows my inexperience. We went to that Irish joint in the Market, Kell's, and had a couple of drinks to kill the time until it was late enough to do the job.

B.: And then?

L.: And then we did the job.

B.: What time did you leave Kell's, what time did you get to Eagle, what happened next?

L.: We left Kell's at around one o'clock and got to Eagle at one-ten. We drove around the block a couple of times. He wanted to make sure it was safe. I parked out front at one-thirty and he got out of the car and went into the store.

B.: How did he do that?

L.: He had a key that he stole. I'm not sure how he did that, but he had the key and he knew how to kill the alarm before it went off.

B.: Explain that.

L.: Well, I'm not sure how it works, but there's some kind of time delay that gives the owner the chance to disconnect the alarm after he unlocks the door himself.

B.: All right, now Mr. Brownall is inside the store robbing it. What were you doing?

L.: I was sitting outside in my car watching for you guys.

B.: You were acting as lookout.

L.: (Laughs.) I was the lookout.

B.: Thank you very much, Mr. Lockman.

L.: That's it?

B.: That's it.

TRANSCRIPT OF TAPE-RECORDED INTERVIEW WITH
GARRETT RICHARD LOCKMAN
11:00 A.M. 2/18/81

Conducted by Detective P. Boudreau
Detective Norbert Walz, Jr., Witness

Lockman: You've read me my rights and I understand them as you've explained them to me. There, does that save time?

Boudreau: If you say so.

L.: What's up?

B.: Well, it goes like this, Garrett. The situation has become more complicated than we originally thought.

L.: What do you mean?

B.: Three things. First, your crime partner, Brownall, tells us a slightly different story from the one you told us. Second, we executed a search warrant a judge issued for your apartment, and we found some stuff that we'd like you to clear up for us. And finally, there's a question of some stolen traveler's checks. It all adds up to a lot of trouble if we can't get a clear understanding of what was actually going on.

L.: What do you mean, a lot of trouble?

B.: A very long time in prison.

L.: What do you mean?

B.: You could go to Walla Walla for a very long time. For all intents and purposes, for the rest of your young manhood. Then there's California and the problem with the traveler's checks. You could be in one jail and another for the rest of your life.

L.: The rest of my life? I didn't do anything.

B.: You've already given us your statement that you committed a felony when you were the lookout in the Eagle Guns and Ammo robbery. We have to clear all this up, Garrett. It's the only way.

L.: The Eagle job was only attempted. Nobody actually stole anything.

B.: I'm afraid not. You'll recall that your crime partner actually made it to the sidewalk with the guns the two of you conspired to steal. If he had seen us from inside the store and dropped everything on the floor, you probably wouldn't be here right now. Simple B and E. But we have to follow the law. We have to clear this up.

L.: I didn't conspire to steal any guns.

B.: That's not what your crime partner says. He says that you always knew that the object of the theft was the guns he came out of the store with. Now, what do you think the jury is going to believe?

L.: He's the criminal, the one with the record. I've never been in trouble before.

B.: Where does he have a record?

L.: Arizona. He was in jail a year there before he went to San Diego. He told me that himself.

B.: Now, you see, that's helpful, Garrett. Helping us clear this up will help you. Do you happen to know what he was in jail for?

L.: Same as this. He broke into a bar to rob it. An alarm went off and they got him.

B.: Where was this?

L.: Tucson, before he went to southern California.

B.: Which is where you met him? I'm just trying to understand things.

L.: Yeah, okay, that's where I met him.

B.: Let's talk about the stuff in your apartment. You're not much of a housekeeper, by the way.

L.: (Laughs.) It's hard to get reliable help.

B.: What are you doing with all that police equipment?

L.: Oh, I bought all of that. I have receipts.

B.: What do you do with all that police equipment, Garrett?

L.: Do I have to do something with it?

B.: Garrett, the only way we can clear this up is if you give us straight answers.

L.: I don't do anything with it. I collect it.

B.: You have police badges, police uniforms, caps, radios, paraphernalia, registration slips for police cars.

L.: Not anymore, they're not. The equipment was stripped out of them before I bought them at auction. Did you find my car dealer's license?

B.: Do you ever pose as a police officer, Garrett?

L.: Of course not.

B.: We know now that you did work as a security guard.

L.: That's what I told you.

B.: I wasn't finished. We also know that you attempted to become an officer of the Shore Patrol when you were on duty with the navy.

L.: I submitted an application. I submitted an application for flight school, too. It doesn't mean anything.

B.: What do you do with the police equipment, Garrett?

L.: Nothing, I told you! I enjoy it. I like having it.

B.: Do you ever put on the uniforms and parade around in them? Do you wear the uniforms when you look at your pornography?

L.: (Laughs.) You're one sick puppy, Boudreau. Did anybody ever tell you that?

B.: What about the VCRs? Tell us about the VCRs and the rest of the electronics gear, the stereos and tape decks.

L.: Those are Brownall's. He told me he didn't have anywhere to put them. He said I wouldn't have to keep them long, only until I, I mean he, got a new place.

B.: They're stolen, Garrett.

L.: I wouldn't be the least bit surprised, now. They're his, I'm telling you. He stole them? Lie down with dogs, get up with fleas. My mother tried to teach me that, but I guess I wasn't paying enough attention.

B.: I don't understand, Garrett.

L.: He's a crook. I've been trying to tell you that. I've never been in trouble before. Do you think I want to go to jail? Do you think I'd do anything to put myself there? He told me he was going to steal ammo. I didn't know anything about guns, no matter what he says. Did you search his place? Did you search that self-storage unit he has?

B.: What self-storage unit?

L.: He has one of those little whatchamacallits in a self-storage yard in south Seattle. It looks like a garage? I don't know the name of the street, but it's near the exit off the I-5 where the Denny's and the gas stations are.

B.: Can you show us where it is?

L.: (Laughs.) Not from here.

B.: We'll escort you. Okay, now let's talk about the traveler's checks.

L.: No, let's talk about me not going to jail.

B.: I can't make that kind of commitment. I'll certainly put in a good word for you.

L.: I want to talk to somebody who can make that commitment.

B.: It's too soon for that, Garrett. I'll tell you the truth, you're doing the right things for yourself, working your way up the ladder to an appointment with an ADA.

L.: ADA?

B.: Assistant district attorney. They're the ones who set up this system, Garrett, and that's because they're very busy people. Now, if you continue to help me, then I'll do everything in my power to keep you out of Walla Walla. The traveler's checks were stolen in Coronado, California. I'm a cop in Seattle. What happens in Coronado doesn't concern me. When we ran your prints through Washington, it came back that you were in the navy, and the Pentagon told us you were stationed in San Diego. What we found in your crime partner's place made us have to get in touch with Coronado. They told us that there had been a theft at an American Express office and that the thieves made off with over eighty thousand dollars' worth of traveler's checks.

L.: I'll make a deal with you. You stop calling him my crime partner. I keep telling you, I'm not a criminal.

B.: What's the deal?

L.: What?

B.: You said there was a deal. What's the deal? What are you going to trade?

L.: He told me a lot of things I didn't believe, like the traveler's checks. I'll tell you what, I'll tell you all the things he told me, and I have a good memory, you can count on it, and you get one of the ADA guys in here. I definitely don't want to go to Walla Walla. I don't want to go to jail at all.

B.: Start talking.

L.: Are you going to get the ADA in here?

B.: Let's see how good your memory really is. What about the traveler's checks?

L.: He stole those. I didn't have a thing to do with it.

B.: Where are the checks now?

L.: I don't know. I'm telling you, he stole them. He told me he did.

B.: You've actually seen the traveler's checks?

L.: No, I never saw them. Never. I thought he was bullshitting.

B.: When was this? When did he tell you he stole the traveler's checks?

L.: After we came up here. I didn't know a thing about it until after he told me about them. Up here. In Seattle.

B.: And you came up to Seattle together to commit crimes?

L.: No, I used to live here. I went to the university. After the navy, I was going to settle here.

B.: Let's talk about the stolen stereos. They were in your apartment. You stole those by yourself?

L.: I keep telling you, I'm not a crook. I never did anything wrong before this. He told me to store them for him. I told you, he's a very scary guy.

B.: Garrett, what you have to understand is that receiving stolen property is just as serious a felony as actually stealing it. What you have to do is clear this up for us. Tell us about the stolen stereos.

L.: (Laughs.) In for a penny, in for a pound.

B.: What?

L.: It's another of my mother's expressions. It's like that joke about Pierre the pilot. It doesn't make any difference how many German planes you shoot down, how many buildings you design, you suck one cock, and you know what they're going to call you.

B.: No, what are they going to call you?

L.: You know, it's a joke. Ha-ha?

B.: You said German planes you shoot down. From the look of your place, you like the Germans, the Nazis especially.

L.: What's that supposed to mean?

B.: You have a lot of Nazi paraphernalia. Are you a Nazi?

L.: No, I just collect the stuff. It's not against the law to be a Nazi anyway. But I'm not, I'm a Haywardite.

B.: What is a Haywardite?

L.: We're praying for the return of Susan Hayward.

B.: Susan Hayward the dead movie star.

L.: It's another joke.

B.: Okay, you and Mr. Brownall conspired to steal the stereos.

L.: No, he said he wanted to get a new stereo for himself. I sat in the car.

B.: What kind of car?

L.: A Checker. I have a Checker taxicab.

B.: Why do you have a taxicab?

L.: Why not?

B.: So you were the lookout in this Checker taxicab.

L.: I didn't know. I thought he was just getting a stereo.

B.: *Stealing.*

L.: He said they owed him because they rooked him when he bought another one from them. He said he didn't think it was stealing.

B.: What did you think it was?

L.: I didn't think anything. I wasn't the one doing it. He said his stereo was no good and they wouldn't fix it. I guess that was just more of his bullshit.

B.: This was last summer, 1980, July sixteenth. You sat in the car while he broke into Big Boys Appliances in Bellevue.

L.: I guess that's about right.

B.: And he filled the trunk and the backseat of this big Checker taxicab with stereos and you thought he was only getting one. Why didn't you leave then?

L.: I told you, he's a scary guy. I don't want to cross him. That's why I asked to be put in another part of the jail from him. I really am scared of him.

B.: So what you're saying now is that you served as lookout and drove the car in the burglary of Big Boys Appliances on the night of July sixteenth, 1980.

L.: He did it. He was the one who went into the store.

B.: But you were the lookout and drove the car.

L.: The taxicab. Nobody drives my cars but me.

B.: Thank you very much.

NOTES/MEETING/GARRETT RICHARD LOCKMAN 2/22/81 4:40 P.M.

Subject Lockman telephoned my office at 10am from county jail and asked if he could talk to me face-to-face with no tape recorder or stenographer present. His tone suggested he was in a state of extreme anxiety. When I told him I would not be able to meet with him until the afternoon, he asked why I could not come sooner. I told him I had to testify at a hearing and could not possibly change my schedule, a lie I will explain below. He began to plead and beg that I talk to "the judge" so I could see him earlier. I told him that if he felt he was in any danger, he should tell the guards. I did not ask him what was bothering him and, as noted, I did not have to attend a hearing. My experience with subjects like Lockman suggests that they are most cooperative when they are not getting their own way. When they want you now, you make them wait, etc.

I arranged with the guards to meet with Lockman in one of the attorneys' slots inasmuch as it is jail scuttlebutt that these areas are not "bugged" and a prisoner is free to talk.

When Lockman was led in, I was shocked by his appearance. He was unshaven and unwashed and appeared red-eyed and haggard from lack of sleep. He immediately asked me to get him transferred to another facility. I asked him why. He told me he had been told that his crime partner, Thomas Brownall, had "let the word out" that he wanted Lockman killed and was willing to pay for it. "He's willing to pay a lot of money," Lockman said. As logical as the question might seem, I did not ask Lockman why he thought Brownall wanted him dead. Since I have conducted all the interviews to date with Lockman and Brownall, I knew exactly what Brownall knew about what Lockman has told me about their criminal activities, which is nothing, as transcripts of my interviews with Brownall verify. I told Lockman that if he thought his life was in danger, he would be best served if he reported it to his guards. He said it wouldn't do any good. I asked him why he hasn't arranged to have someone post bail for him. He said he didn't think he was going to be in jail for so long. He then asked me what he could do to hasten the process against Brownall in order to secure his own release. I told him that I would have to consult an assistant district attorney about it. Becoming more agitated, Lockman said he still hadn't seen the ADA I had "promised" him. I told him I had made no such promise and that an ADA was still in the process of evaluating the material I had presented to him. Lockman then offered to tell me where Brownall had hidden the stolen traveler's checks in exchange for his freedom. Since we believe that Lockman and Brownall are responsible for at least a dozen burglaries in the Seattle area in the past year, I told him that I thought he was taking a step in the right direction. I then terminated the interview.

Outside, the guard on duty told me Lockman and Brownall were on different floors and had no contact with each other, nor were there any other prisoners who had contact with prisoners on other floors. Any fears expressed by Lockman were baseless, the guard said.

7:15pm: While writing the above, I was telephoned again by Mr. Lock-

man, who wanted to know what the ADA had said about his case. I told
him the ADA was still evaluating it.

NOTES/INTERVIEW/THOMAS BROWNALL 2/25/81

Mr. Brownall called me and I agreed to meet with him at King Co. Jail.
He was in a highly agitated state, having just been interviewed by Ben
Sumner, with his own public defender present. Apparently Sumner has
told him he is facing thirty years in prison on almost a dozen felony counts.
"How can that be? How can you do that?" I told him I didn't know what evidence Sumner had. "All these things, boom, boom, boom, out of left field,
stuff that happened years ago. What happened to the statute of limitations?" I kept quiet because once I had a suspect who thought birth control
was something that kept the baby from coming out. Brownall thought the
statute of limitations was three years to time of trial. "Who told you that?" I
asked. Brownall stared at me. He said, "The same guy who—" and looked
at me again. "What else did he tell you, Thomas?" "All we had to do was
keep our mouths shut and we'd walk." "Good advice," I said, and told him
I had to run. In the elevator I laughed so loudly the guard came on the
speaker to ask if I was all right.

TRANSCRIPT OF STENOGRAPHER'S RECORD OF INTERVIEW WITH
GARRETT RICHARD LOCKMAN
2:00 P.M. 3/7/1981

Conducted by ADA Benjamin Sumner
Detective P. Boudreau, Witness

Sumner: I'm Assistant District Attorney Benjamin Sumner, Garrett.
Thanks for coming in to help us with our investigation. You remember Detective Boudreau here.

Lockman: Hey, Phil, it looks like you've been demoted.

Boudreau: This is what I promised, Garrett. I told you that an ADA
would get to you just as soon as he could review your file.

S.: Garrett, we want to go over with you some of the details in the statements you've given Detective Boudreau. First, have you retained an attorney?

L.: Not yet.

S.: I suggest you do so. We better read him his rights.

L.: I've been read my rights. I'm here as a good citizen cooperating with
the authorities.

S.: Then you know that anything you say can be used against you.

L.: I told you, I want to cooperate. It's in my interest.

S.: Very well. Now, as you know, you've been charged with burglary, conspiracy, possession of a concealed weapon, and receiving stolen property.

L.: Conspiracy? I wasn't aware of that.

S.: We will introduce evidence at the trial that you and Mr. Brownall planned together to break the laws of the state of Washington. That's conspiracy.

L.: I want to know how an ice pick gets to be a concealed weapon.

S.: You were carrying it during the commission of a felony. It is only logical to assume that you were prepared to do bodily harm with it.

L.: You can't assume that. You should drop that charge. I think you really should drop it. Anybody can see I couldn't hurt a fly.

S.: When it comes to violence and doing bodily harm to others, you're talking to exactly the wrong man. Violence is punished very severely in the state of Washington, up to and including the death penalty. Case law is very specific in support of the state's position. The concealed-weapon charge stays.

L.: (Laughs.) Well, I tried.

S.: California authorities are interested in you and Mr. Brownall in regard to evidence that puts the two of you in possession of American Express traveler's checks stolen from an office in Coronado at the time you were serving in the navy on the island.

L.: Oh, you know Coronado.

S.: As a matter of fact, I do. Let's get back to you and Mr. Brownall.

L.: No, let's talk about my deal. It's totally fucked now. You said I wouldn't have to do any time.

S.: I should caution you about the use of that kind of language.

B.: Nobody said you wouldn't have to do time, Garrett. Nobody ever said that to you.

S.: Garrett, the extent and severity of your crimes requires that you serve some time. As has been made clear to you all the way along, how much time depends entirely on the cooperation you give us now and through the trial phase and what can be recovered of all the stolen property. Note my emphasis on *all*. That includes the traveler's checks. American Express needs to account for every one. They're the same as money.

L.: I don't have any.

S.: Now, that's not what Mr. Brownall says. He says that you have approximately forty thousand dollars' worth of traveler's checks.

L.: He's lying.

S.: If it comes down to his word against yours, it could go badly for both of you.

L.: I don't have any traveler's checks. I didn't do that job. I was just beginning to get to know Brownall when I read about it in the papers. You don't have anything to connect me to the traveler's checks. You know it and he knows it. He's blowing smoke up your ass.

S.: I've cautioned you once about language.

L.: He's the one with the criminal record. I've been trying to tell you how dangerous he is, but you won't pay attention.

S.: We'll get back to the traveler's checks. I have here a list of some of the burglaries that were committed in King County in the past year. Without any further shilly-shallying, I'd like you to identify the burglaries you and Mr. Brownall committed. (See attached Item A.)

L.: Can I just check them off?

S.: If we have any questions, we'd like you to answer them.

L.: Of course. Here, these. I was the lookout on all of these.

S.: The lookout.

L.: I told Detective Boudreau here that Mr. Brownall is a very scary individual. I was afraid of him, but I didn't know how to sever the connection.

S.: You will testify that Mr. Brownall committed all these burglaries, and that you were the lookout?

L.: That's right.

S.: Mr. Brownall says you have over forty thousand dollars' worth of traveler's checks.

L.: And I told you, it's a lie. I had nothing to do with the American Express robbery. I didn't commit any crimes in California. I didn't commit any crimes while I was in the navy. I have an honorable discharge.

S.: I don't have any more questions. Do you have any questions, detective?

B.: Yes, one. Garrett, you told me you have all that police equipment because you're a collector.

L.: That's right.

B.: How did you come into possession of over twenty police badges?

L.: There's a market. People advertise them for sale, and if you want them, you buy them.

B.: You're able to do this during a long period of unemployment and no visible assets?

L.: I have assets. I have all that equipment, all those cars. I buy those police cars, clean them up, and sell them at a profit.

B.: You have the paperwork?

L.: (Laughs.) Boy, have I got the paperwork.

S.: There are no statutes, detective.

L.: Aren't you going to ask me about the Nazi stuff?

B.: There are no statutes covering that, either, Garrett.

S.: What Nazi stuff?

B.: Mr. Lockman collects Nazi paraphernalia, Mr. Sumner.

S.: (Unintelligible.)

B.: I'm done.

S.: See that Detective Boudreau receives a copy of the transcript for his files.

NOTES OF CONV./BEN SUMNER FOLLOWING INTERVIEW W. GARRETT RICHARD LOCKMAN 3/7/81

Sumner asked re. evidence against Lockman in Am. Exp. robbery. There is none, only against Brownall. S. wanted my opinion re. Brownall. I told S. that my own exp. with L. makes it hard for me to believe that Brownall was able to get L. to do anything. If anyone was the boss of the deal, it was Lockman. I said I thought L. was a puke, which I had to define for S., and a manipulative, cunning, self-serving career criminal. Brownall's a puke, too. I said, "If Lockman is willing to toss his crime partner for kidnapping, he'll do anything to get what he wants." S. said he didn't want to pursue the Am. Exp. job as long as L. is so eager to testify against Brownall on the other counts. S. wants to go that route and nail Brownall for mult. burglary. Easier.

NOTES/PHONE CONV./GARRETT RICHARD LOCKMAN
10:45 A.M. 3/12/81

Garrett Richard Lockman called in a state of panic re. the possibility of him going to jail. I told him he had to testify in all matters re. Thos. Brownall and explain the missing traveler's checks. Lockman insisted he didn't have the traveler's checks and that B. was a liar, a manipulator, and a very dangerous person. He knows the talk. I said, "He's your friend. You picked him." Suddenly L. changed his tone, wanted to know what kind of time I thought he would get. "What happens if I don't testify? We both walk, right?" I told him he was forgetting he was caught red-handed, that his apt. contained stolen goods, and that there was evidence they had participated in the Am. Exp. robbery in Coronado. "They just might put you under the jail, Garrett," I said. "I have to get a deal," he said. "Help me get a deal." He asked if he could speak to Sumner again. I asked, "What about?" "My case!" he yelled. I told him that I couldn't disturb Sumner if I didn't have something new to report to him. Then L. begged me to arrange an appointment with S. I repeated that I had to have fresh stuff for him if L. wanted to see him. "Like what?" he asked. I said the traveler's checks. The police equipment is still a problem for me. These are not mere masturbation aids. A career criminal does not "collect" police equipment for no reason. He is up to something, whether he knows it or not.

NOTES/"CHANCE" MEETING/FIFTH AVENUE/GARRETT RICHARD LOCKMAN
(approx.) 6:30 P.M. 4/12/81

After apparently lying in wait, Garrett Richard Lockman stopped me on the street one block from Public Safety Building. I had been told he had been released on reduced bond two weeks before, part of the deal secured by his new attorney. My first contact with him in five weeks, his appearance awful, disturbing. He looks like he's lost 20–25 pounds. Asked if he could buy me a cup of coffee, I said fine as long as he didn't pay for it with a traveler's check. He insisted on taking me to Starbucks, four blocks from where we stood.

In the coffee shop, he began asking personal questions—was I married? what did I do with my free time? did I have any hobbies? I didn't answer any of them directly. Then finally, did I like girls? I asked him why he wanted to know. Lockman: "You just seem to be the kind of guy who does okay with the ladies. Do you ever try to pick up any of the women you see downtown here?" I told him to fuck off. He said he thought we were friends. Weren't we friends? he asked. He said, "I mean, you busted me, for God's sake, and if it isn't obvious that I've forgiven you, I'll say so: I forgive you." No crook has ever talked that way to me before. He asked, "Can't you forgive me for being dumb? That's all it was, you know. We're working together to put Brownall behind bars, aren't we? I'm the only one who can help you do it. I wouldn't mind having you for a friend, and not because you're so useful." I asked him what he meant by *useful*. He said I knew what was going on. I asked him what made him think so. He said a guy in my position had to know the best gossip. I asked him what he thought my position was. He said he knew I was a vice cop—nailing him was an accident, an unlucky one for him. In my previous dealings with Lockman, I never told him I was in vice. I couldn't ask how he found that out, but I am very curious.

He got around to his case. Again he asked how much time I thought he was going to get. I told him I had no way of knowing. He told me he was scared to death, that he had never been in jail before, had never been arrested, never done anything illegal. A crook's classic con. When I finished my coffee I got up to leave. He grabbed my sleeve. When I looked down at his hand he let go. "Let me buy you another one." He sounded desperate, totally convincing. I told him I was on my way out and that this was the time to say good-bye. I was firm and he sensed he was going to be in trouble if he didn't back off.

NOTES/PHONE CONV./GARRETT RICHARD LOCKMAN 10:20 A.M. 4/13/81

L. telephoned to say he wasn't happy with his present lawyer and asked if I knew any good lawyers. I told him it would be a conflict of interest if I recommended a lawyer—he could probably appeal any conviction on the grounds that I sent him to an incompetent or double-dealer who lost his case as a favor to me. I told him I wanted to get off the telephone, and he pleaded with me to hold on. "Look, is there anything I can do, for you, for that guy Sumner, for even the judge, that would keep me out of jail?" I told him that his question was very close to offering a bribe, and that if he bothered me again, I would have to report him to Sumner. L. said, "It's my word against yours." I told him I was making notes as he spoke and that a police officer's notes were always accepted in court as the authoritative version of a disputed event. I expected him to come back with an accusation of trying to frame him. Crooks have tried to manipulate me before, but never with such an intense, in-your-face style. Contrary to what I expected, L. simply laughed and said, "You learn something new every day." If something doesn't work, L. simply abandons it and tries something new. It's so obvious, it's almost an attractive, naive quality. He lets you think you're controlling him, but clearly it's the other way around, if you give him an inch.

August 1983

The riveting terror was worse than imagining falling from a high building. Breathing was hard, almost impossible. Lockman was coming back, or was he back already? Noises in the room. Shambling closer, unshaven, gaunt, wild-eyed. Ready to kill. *This man is going to kill me!* Taking his time about it, savoring it. *My life ends here and he goes on to others.* Not even a heartbeat now, everything locking up in stony anticipation . . .

"*Daddy! Wake up!*"

Boudreau knew where he was, his room, but he didn't know the day, the time—what year?

"*Daddy!*"

Boudreau's confusion blinked away, the dream suddenly swirling below the level of his awareness like a black tide. *Lockman?* Boudreau sat up. Paulie stood in the bedroom doorway. He looked scared as hell.

"I guess I was having a bad dream. I'm sorry."

The kid just stared. Boudreau could see what he was thinking: *The old man isn't so tough after all.* Paulie was thinking that what stood between the world and him was just another frail and frightened human being. Boudreau put his feet on the floor and his arms out, gathering Paulie in and giving him a quick hug. He pointed to the desk. "After you went to bed, I sat up with that stuff I'm going through." *Again:* he had already read the file more times than he could count.

"Mom watches the demonstrators on the news. She's on the phone all the time talking about it with that Annalisa."

Groups of women with placards protesting police inaction on the murders were showing up more and more frequently at the Public Safety Building. Boudreau knew Annalisa, one of Adrienne's oldest friends, but why did the whole business make him want to think of something else? Paulie was visiting for the weekend, the highlight of which would be a trip down to the Kingdome to watch Kansas City kick the Mariners' butts, as usual. Boudreau kissed his cheek. "Go to bed. We'll talk in the morning."

"It is morning."

"Later, smart-ass."

After he heard Paulie close his bedroom door, Boudreau shuffled out to the living room and anchored himself on the arm of the sofa that let him see the lights of downtown. The clock on the VCR said 4:12. If one was looking for trouble even at this hour, it could still be found, but with some difficulty, on the Pike and around Pioneer Square. Or the Sea-Tac Strip. Girls were still disappearing? None from Boudreau's beat, and no new bodies had been found since the discovery of Mona Raymond's remains, but that did not mean that girls were not still disappearing. But girls disappeared from this part of the world all the time. The cities of the Northwest were so far apart, in so many different jurisdictions, that cooperation was spotty and communication often seethed with bureaucratic and personal antagonisms. Boudreau was as much a part of that corruption as anybody else who had ever lost his temper over being sent the wrong file, or being bullshitted by someone who wanted to seem more important than he was, or worst of all, living in the expectation of being backed up, discovering he had been forgotten about. Over the years Boudreau had made enemies. In the years since the start of the Green River killings he had made more. And he thought he was a *good* cop.

Better than Beale, anyway. A study of the conduct of the Green River case so far that had been commissioned by the sheriff himself said that many, many mistakes had been made, that leads now cold had never been followed up, that the processing of tips was chaotic, and that evidence had been allowed to become disorganized. The trouble with the sheriff's study was that it was highly confidential, and no changes in staffing were contemplated. If the fears of the activists were correct and girls were really disappearing, instead of simply having removed themselves as far south as Vegas or Laughlin, Nevada's new, growing, low-rent hot spot, then law enforcement was absolutely helpless anyway. It didn't have a shred of evidence to work on, not one real clue in the whole case. Mona Raymond's body had been found facedown—and the first three girls had been found *in* the Green River. Mona Raymond had been identified by matching photographs of her teeth with the dental charts of recently disappeared young girls. Uhuru had sent her out for beer. After that, you were looking into eternal darkness.

This was the first time Boudreau had seen Lockman in a dream. He could remember the dream better now, his arms tied behind him on a bed or a sofa, too heavy to move, unable to speak, Lockman moving around the bare, harshly lit decrepit room at his leisure. In dreamland Boudreau had made himself the victim, and he knew why: going through the notes he'd made while Lockman had tried to insinuate himself into his life, Boudreau had been reminded too clearly of the driving, crushing, oppressive relentlessness of the guy's obsessions. Lockman had not gotten to trial until summer, and his telephone calls downtown, "accidental" meetings, a vaudeville of pretexts, stepped up over the months from less than one a week to more than three, finishing with calls to Boudreau's apartment here, heavy breathing, hang-ups—a dream? Victim? Boudreau had made himself a *woman*?

A perfect victim. What Lockman would have made of Boudreau in the months building up to the conviction and sentencing of the hapless Tom Brownall. Brownall had taken most of that time figuring out what Lockman was doing to him. Brownall had acted like a forlorn girlfriend, going through all the phases of the end of a romance, pain, denial, bargaining, never facing the fact that Lockman was operating on another wavelength. The afternoon of the sentencing, Boudreau stood at the back of the courtroom, watching. Lockman was not doing anything to Brownall that Boudreau had not seen before. Civilians rarely believed that criminals behaved this badly. If the law-enforcement community had a secret, it was because people wouldn't face the truth about real career criminals: they were utterly irredeemable. A disgrace to the species. Lockman was squealing like a pig, doing anything just to stay out of jail. He would argue with that, of course. He would argue anything and everything if it meant there was a chance he could get what he wanted at the moment.

The sexual element between Lockman and Brownall was not new to Boudreau, either. Uhuru had spent his youth boning his kid brother—Boudreau had that information on no less an authority than Uhuru himself, who saw nothing wrong with his behavior because he had played the male role. Criminals often had gender-identity problems, using sex to control their crime partners. With Brownall, Lockman perhaps had taken it one turn tighter on the wheel. If Brownall in fact once had been a practicing heterosexual, as he still claimed to be, Lockman by sheer force of his own remorseless will had reduced him to a profound depth of creepy dysfunction. In custody Brownall had compounded the problems caused by his blindness to Lockman's true motives, responding to police questioning according to some nutty code of criminal honor, strutting a silent, stupid lack of cooperation. He seemed unable to absorb the consequences of what was happening to him, like the killer who trudges sheepishly to the electric chair, muttering, "I guess I was born to die young."

All that ended when the sentences were pronounced. Brownall blasted through the bargaining and denial and pain to flat-out rage: in leg irons, he had to be carried out of the courtroom, cursing, yelling, screaming himself hoarse. He would have bitten Lockman if he could have gotten close enough. Five-to-ten in Walla Walla while his crime partner was thanking the judge for being so fair. *Smiling!*

Now Boudreau knew exactly why he had pushed Lockman out of his mind so quickly thereafter: if you spent enough time even with just your own notes about him, you wound up dreaming that he was going to fuck you up the ass and then kill you with his bare hands. Lockman would laugh out loud at the idea. How did that make him crazy? And if somehow that did make *him* crazy, and not everybody else, how could you lock him up for it? With the inessential stripped away, the basis for the argument was only the common knowledge that he scared people.

Boudreau was awake for the day now. Tiptoeing around the apartment, he fetched the Lockman file and made coffee and two slices of rye toast and then juggled his breakfast and the file back to the sofa, where, braced on its arm, relishing the butter melting in his mouth, he watched the morning's metallic light limn the northern flank of Mount Rainier. He wondered what Dr. Diane Heidt would think of his analysis of the processes at work between Lockman and himself. In the two months since she had tried to ambush him, Boudreau had heard from Heidt only once. She had given him every reason to believe she was going to be in his face, but no: only a note apologizing for her behavior that day in front of his apartment.

Right. He thought he remembered perfectly what had happened between them. And that she did, too. Did she need so desperately the information he had that she was willing to do a little rewrite of their personal history? Something else had made her put him on her back burner. Just as well: he couldn't talk to her about official business and knew he had embarrassed the hell out of himself in their first meeting. He expected zilch from her on a personal level, where his mind kept wandering nevertheless. He remembered her coming up his walk, moving with self-confidence and languid grace. He remembered liking her skin and the charm of her freckles.

Boudreau knew that what was missing from his notes on Lockman was innuendo. From the moment he first saw the heavily laden Brownall trying to tiptoe out of Eagle Guns and Ammo, Boudreau wondered about the nature of his relationship with Lockman; and after Lockman began to spin his tale about Brownall terrorizing him, Boudreau assumed that Lockman was only reversing their roles. By June of that year Boudreau had no doubt that that was how Lockman functioned with Brownall. By June Lockman was occasionally calling Boudreau "Frenchy." Boudreau could have gotten rid of Lockman at the beginning, but he had not called Sumner, had not prepared a memorandum for him, out of curiosity about Lockman, about the police equipment, about Lockman's peculiar and opaque lifestyle. Maybe Lockman had even suckered him in with his occasional, sly hinting at a deeper weirdness inside. Boudreau was willing to think so.

> 7/13/81/1:20am: Lockman again, this evening, in a tunnel under Fourth Avenue. He was nonchalant, even cheerful, insisting, as he has in the past, that our meeting was an "accident"—and he was sufficiently self-contained to acknowledge that he was out of line speaking to me.

Boudreau remembered. A rainy summer evening, humid and sparkling, with hours and hours of daylight remaining. Boudreau had been heading home, cutting across town through the tunnel system toward First Avenue and the bus that took him within walking distance of home. Lockman stepped out of the doorway of one of the underground storefronts. Boudreau saw him right away, looking as well dressed as seemed possible for him, in a sport jacket, white shirt, and well-pressed wash pants. Immediately Lockman waved him off.

"I didn't mean this! Strictly an accident! I'm just trying to do a last little bit of Christmas shopping, seeing where I'm going to be when Santa comes to town. Come on, let me buy you a latte."

"Not tonight, Garrett," Boudreau said. "I have a date and no time to spare."

"A date, eh? Who with? I still don't know what kind of women date cops. Let me treat you."

Boudreau had no date, and now he regretted having lied, because it was going to be difficult to sustain it under a Lockman-style bombardment. It was as if Lockman could zero in on a lie faster than on any other weakness. "No time, Garrett. I mean it, I have to be going."

"Come on, come on, don't send me away like this. I've got nothing to do, nowhere to go. I just want to be sure that if I deliver for you guys—"

"You know I can't discuss any deals, Garrett."

"That's not what I'm asking. Let me finish. I want to be sure Brownall really is going away for a long time. I'll tell you, without us working together, anything could have happened."

"What are you talking about?"

"I'm talking how dangerous Tom Brownall is. No telling how he was going to go if we hadn't caught him."

We? "I want to hear this. I'll have coffee with you, dickhead, but I gotta pay my own way."

Lockman laughed. "You act like I'm wearing a wire. You wanna frisk me?"

"I don't want to touch you. It has to do with the ethics of the situation."

"What the hell can happen over the price of a cup of coffee? You guys are too much!"

"Just setting a proper example, Garrett."

Lockman hardly paused for breath. "I really am concerned about Brownall. I know, I know, he's in jail where he belongs, but I have this fluttery *thing* in my chest about what could happen."

"Like what?"

"Like suppose he escapes, gets loose, whatever you want to call it, and comes after me. He could have a knife. The jail is full of knives—or is that something you know?"

"Let's not talk about what I know." Boudreau ushered him up a short flight of steps that led into a hotel, Lockman talking about the possibility of the impoverished Brownall hiring someone to kill him. Nonsense— and if it wasn't nonsense, Boudreau couldn't bring himself to care. If Lockman was going to be murdered, it was only because of what he was doing, and no cop in the world could prevent it. Most wouldn't want to try.

Boudreau led Lockman to a little lobby café where they could have coffee and Boudreau could watch the traffic. More and more of the world's peoples were passing through Seattle, doing business with the port, making arrangements with shippers to move cargo inland, preparing to take delivery from Boeing—the money for one of the big jets changed hands at sea, where sales taxes could be avoided. Whatever their business, many people away from home tended to leave their personal obligations and responsibilities at their front doors, but in the last analysis, no matter how much fun it was, vice was bad for the community, the personality, and the soul. When one of Boudreau's kids was promoted to call girl, and he saw where she was making her calls, it didn't take much detective work to get a line on the desk clerk or bellboy providing that little extra service for his guests. Boudreau had followed one of his girls into an elevator where he knew the operator was serving as her pimp. Boudreau said hello, she said hello, and her eyes darted furtively toward the ugly little gnome in the theme-park uniform. Boudreau flashed his badge. "Close the door, but keep the car right here."

The guy did it.

"Give me your dough," Boudreau said to him. "Now. Don't fuck around."

"What?"

"Come on, come on, give me your dough or I'll shoot your dick off. She won't say anything. I've got enough on her to put her in the can until she is a very old lady. Don't I, honey?"

"Give him the money," she said to the elevator operator.

The guy pulled out a roll of bills. He thought Boudreau was shaking him down. Boudreau produced a Bic lighter and set the wad on fire. The gnome let out a yell that could have been heard throughout the hotel, then fell back against the wall in furious resignation as the car filled with expensive blue smoke.

"Thus endeth the lesson," Boudreau said. "Would you like to tell me what you have learned?"

"You fuck."

"Don't make me charge you with pandering and resisting arrest. The kid here has a sheet longer than your middle leg and *noooo* credibility in the courts. You'll lose your job and spend your old age mooching on the Pike, trying to steal business from her. Now, what is today's lesson?"

"Don't break the law?"

"That's exactly right, because if I catch you peddling her ass again I'm going to put you where you can get a taste of that kind of life for yourself. Be grateful she's over eighteen, or you wouldn't be getting this break."

Boudreau waited until the coffee was in front of them before he said he wanted to know what Lockman had meant by *we*. Lockman stared at him, his eyebrows arched goofily.

"We worked together. You wouldn't have had any kind of a case if I hadn't helped you."

"You keep forgetting you were caught red-handed. Your apartment was full of stolen goods."

Lockman laughed. "You're a hard man, Frenchy."

"That police equipment of yours doesn't help."

"I'm a police buff."

"What do you mean?"

"I like cops. I wish I could have been one. I've had security jobs, I've read all the textbooks, probably more than you. I applied for a cop's job up in Bellingham, but they were very discouraging up there."

This was what Boudreau had wanted, to get him talking. A pretty girl passed ten feet in front of them, young, dark-haired, with a curvy figure proudly displayed in a sheer, close-fitting dress. Out of the corner of his eye Boudreau picked up Lockman's intense staring as she headed to the elevator bank. Boudreau stayed silent. Finally Lockman asked, "Do you want me to guess if she's a hooker?"

Boudreau shrugged. "What do you think? You're the one who wanted to be a cop. Let's see if you had the makings."

Lockman smiled. "If she is, she's out of my league."

"I don't understand."

"I couldn't afford her."

"More than you know," Boudreau said. "She's a civilian."

"How do you know?"

"Trade secrets."

Lockman let his eyes drop as if in disappointment, then he looked at Boudreau and grinned. "Isn't that more than you need to know?"

"I don't understand."

"I mean, you don't arrest anybody until a crime has been committed. This isn't just girl watching."

"What is it?"

"You study women. It's much more than a professional interest." There was a split second's pause. Boudreau braced himself. Lockman asked, "Haven't you found that brunettes have the strongest vaginal odor?"

Boudreau looked away. Lockman gave that little laugh of his. "Never mind. Answer this—you've been asking all the questions, so let me ask one—have you ever? You know."

"Nope, not if you mean what I think you mean."

"Do they ever offer?"

"Of course. They're criminals, same as you. They wriggle and squirm to get away. Same as you."

"Why do I feel you didn't answer my question?"

"I did. You just didn't like what you heard."

"I don't care what you do," Lockman said. "To tell you the truth, I don't believe you."

"That makes us even."

He looked alarmed. "What do you mean?"

"I don't believe the shit that comes out of you."

Lockman laughed in Boudreau's face. "You're a pisser, do you know that? You're a real pisser. Have you ever heard of Freud's theory of opposites?"

"What about it?"

"You're just the type. All cops love crime, that's why they get in the business of sticking their noses in it, and vice cops love sex crime. You know what you like to stick your nose in. Ipso facto. I can't say I share your appetites. Women do themselves up as luridly as they do to conceal their underlying disgustingness. Humanity's greatest secret. A dope dealer I knew once told me that because he's destroyed his nose, the only three things he could smell were burning tires, rotting corpses, and cheap pussy."

"Where is he now?"

"Who?"

"Your dope-dealer friend."

"Terminal Island, San Pedro, California. It's a federal pen."

"I know what it is. Your friend is the reason we build places like Terminal Island." Boudreau was sure Lockman had invented the "friend." "What I don't understand is how a guy who wanted to be a cop at one time—"

"Oh, I still want to be a cop. I will be, too, one day."

Lockman had to know that was impossible. In any event, it was pointless to discuss it with him. Boudreau said, "What do you do with all that police equipment? Tell me the truth. Do you dress up and pretend to be a cop? As long as you stay in your apartment, you're not doing anything wrong. Do you put on the clothes and put a porn tape in the VCR and pull your joint all night?"

"What are *you* pulling?"

"I asked you a question about the police equipment."

"No, you're up to something. Are you trying to get me to implicate myself in some criminal activity? If I've told you once, I've told you a thousand times: Brownall intimidated me, he forced me to do the things that I have to go to jail for, thanks to him, and now you're playing Inspector Javert and trying to get me to incriminate myself. You seem to have it in for me. Everybody else understands that I'm the victim in this and that I'm doing the best I can with a miserable, difficult situation that has probably ruined my life. I'd watch myself if I were you, Frenchy. One day Freud's theory of opposites is going to catch up with you, and the powers that be will find your nose in a warm, wet one—and then, *bang!* You'll be on your way into the pen, just like Mr. Thomas Fucking Brownoff, who is getting what he deserves. You see, what I think is that you secretly hate these girls, and that, for all your protests about caring about them, you want to punish and humiliate and degrade them. You're in the position to do exactly that, and I don't think it's an accident. You're a woman-hater, Frenchy. You're in it for the revenge."

"You told me you went to the U. What did you major in?"

"Oh, psychology. What did you think, schmuck, electrical engineering?"

"Well, genius, what you know about police work you learned only to facilitate the commission of crimes, no matter what your fantasy life lets you believe. Everything you told us about Brownall being the mastermind is bullshit. You reversed the roles so you could weasel out of the heavy time you deserve, and now, of course, this crap about me is just another projection of your fevered imagination. You're the woman-hater. In all the digging we did into your life, we didn't find one. No women at all. No girlfriend visiting you at the county jail, no little black book of telephone numbers, no pictures of you with girls, no souvenirs of weekends out of town. Just some tapes and a couple of split-beaver magazines for you to whack off to. A few minutes ago you were carrying on about why women do themselves up. I know a lot more about you than when we met outside Eagle Guns and Ammo. In fact, I think I may even be wise to you. I'll be watching for you, because I know this experience isn't going to stop you."

Lockman laughed in his face again. "You're a fucking asshole."

Boudreau stood up. "If I catch you in the commission of a crime again, you piece of shit, just as sure as you're sitting there, I'll get you. I will follow you into hell if I have to, but I will get you."

A momentary loss of control, Boudreau thought in his living room as the sun rose into view. How much of Lockman's success with the criminal justice system could Boudreau blame on himself for having been so clear about the advantages of ratting out one's friend? He had seen Lockman's little wheels spinning. That afternoon in the hotel lobby, Lockman had made the mistake of overstating his case, like all sociopaths. Boudreau knew he wasn't alone in his complete contempt for Lockman. Sumner loathed the guy. A dirty, vicious criminal who would be a problem to the community one way or the other until the community was able to put him away for life, was the best thing Sumner could say about him.

Boudreau closed the file and lay down on the sofa to catch another hour's sleep before Paulie wanted to turn on the television set again.

The telephone awakened him.

"It's Dan Cheong, Phil. I'm sorry to be calling you at this hour, but we have another problem. I'm calling from South Two Hundredth Street, south of the airport. Do you know where it is?"

Boudreau tried to shake his head clear. Paulie came out of the bedroom. "Is that Mom?"

"No, no, it isn't. I wasn't talking to you, Dan. My son is with me this weekend."

"We want you to come down here, Phil. Is it going to be a problem?"

Boudreau sighed. "Paul is too young for me to leave alone for long. Let me see what I can work out."

Cheong hung up. Boudreau was thinking of Mrs. Gunter down on the first floor. No. Boudreau didn't want to expose Paul to Mr. Gunter. Boudreau called Adrienne. And hung up after the seventh ring. A girl could get lucky, too. Good for her, he thought. Good for him, too, for as long as she was involved with someone else, she was not focusing on him. Paulie was staring at him. "Was there another murder?"

"Maybe. They want me down there. I can't get your mother—"

"I know. She's up in Victoria with Mr. Travers."

"Oh." Travers? This was a new player on the field. "So I figure you come down with me, but you have to stay in the car, know what I mean? Bring something to do so you don't get too bored."

"I have a book. It's pretty good, too. All about Stone Age kids."

"We'll stop for breakfast on the way down."

"I get to pick."

"Right, let me guess: jet-engine eggs and cow-pie sausage patties on a squeaky foam plate."

Paulie laughed. "Don't forget the potato brick."

He knew all his father's jokes. Hot dogs and peanuts this afternoon while watching Kansas City cleaning the Mariners' clock. A day of *cuisine minable*. Boudreau was trying to give his son some sense of their family's love of food. He thought of his own mother steaming the fat out of a duckling before sliding it into the oven. He had not tasted anything as good since he had left home. Actually, his early-morning toast could hold him for at least another three hours. "Well, get yourself ready, kid. And remember that you won't be able to go to the bathroom."

Paulie crossed his eyes and did his robot walk back into the bedroom.

It was not a bad day for trooping through the brush to examine human remains. The story wasn't on the news yet, but that didn't mean it hadn't been picked up from the police bands by some enterprising snoop. Paul Boudreau was having no trouble scarfing down his take-out *petit déjeuner* as they rolled past Boeing Field and its many samples, in a variety of colors, of the house jumbo, the 747, a.k.a. the Honolulu Bomber, a.k.a. the

Flying Slum. Why did Beale and Company want Boudreau on the scene again? Why hadn't Boudreau heard from Wayne Spencer—or was the fact that he *hadn't* heard an indicator of how important this was? He glanced at his son, to see if his concern was showing. No: Paul was smearing his slab of hash browns in his blob of ketchup, trying to keep his book out of harm's way.

An MD-80 cruised in toward Sea-Tac, landing gear down, as Boudreau rolled the Mustang up to the line of sheriff's vehicles up on the side of South 200th Street. Boudreau bundled the breakfast debris into a ball and stuffed it behind the passenger seat. Paul was deep in his book. Boudreau could see a crowd milling about down the hill, about thirty yards into the trees. Who would wander in there, kids looking for adventure? A geezer walking the dog he loved better than any human? Months, even years, could pass between such visits. Boudreau kissed Paul on the top of the head. "Remember, stay in the car. Don't even roll the window down if somebody wants to talk to you. If somebody bothers you, lean on the horn. I'll be right over there. See?" Paul didn't look up from his book. "I'm going to lock the doors and take the keys, okay?"

"Okay."

You couldn't ask for more. Boudreau was halfway to the crowd in the woods when he saw Dan Cheong, in jeans and a U sweatshirt, detach himself from the group and head in his direction. Since it was obvious Cheong wanted to talk to him privately, Boudreau slowed down, and then, after a few seconds, stopped.

"Were you able to take care of your son all right?"

Boudreau raised his thumb to point behind him. "He asked if it was another murder. I said maybe."

"How old is he?"

"Seven. What have you got? All of a sudden you think I can help you?"

"What we have are the remains of two people, probably young girls, one possibly as young as twelve or thirteen, and the different conditions of the two bodies say they were killed and dumped here at different times in the past year. There may be more. We gotta dig up the whole area. We need the Explorer Scouts."

Boudreau let his eyes roam over the scene. No sign of the media. "You still haven't told me why you hauled me down here."

"You're not making this easier. You'll know in another split second why I'm the one talking to you. We—I mean the guys on the Green River case—have reason to believe that you're one of the many, many people the protesters are trying to get to for information about what we're doing. We'd be much obliged to you if you continued to shine these people on."

He had his eyes locked on Boudreau's now. "In other words, don't talk about the case."

Boudreau grinned. "You know what you just did?"

"What?"

"Admitted you've had me under surveillance more or less continuously since this crap began. Tapped my phone. Bugged my apartment—"

"Phil—"

"And I'm supposed to roll over?"

"Phil! It goes with the territory."

"Where does it say that I signed away my civil rights?"

"Phil, listen to me! We had a tip!"

Lockman! Boudreau had already told them all about Lockman, and he could not be held accountable for their stupidity. Two cars pulled up behind the Mustang. "Tell me about it."

"I can't." Cheong's eyes darted toward the road. "Shit! Shit! They listen to our radio transmissions, did you know that? The media people won't be far behind. Don't get pissed off again, will you? You tell the television clowns we're finding evidence of spaceships, they'll have the guy who plays Captain Kirk and film at eleven."

The car behind the Mustang was a Volvo sedan, and a fat woman with stringy blond hair got out from behind the wheel. Boudreau turned back to Cheong. "You dragged me all the way down here at this hour on a holiday weekend to tell me not to talk to people I never talk to anyway, but you won't tell me what kind of a tip you got on me. Motherfucker, you intercepted me right here so I can't get near the crime scene! Who identified the first body?"

"Lower your voice, they can hear you." Cheong nodded toward the road.

Boudreau stepped closer. "This quiet enough for you? You've got eight bodies now and these women are right, you're pussyfooting around with somebody who may not just be the equal of Ted, but much, much worse—"

"We can't say that. The community might panic."

"Then what? They're going to overthrow the government? The worst thing that can happen is that somebody might lose his goddamned job! And who would that be? You're just a grunt, like me. Stop covering for these sons of bitches who think they can play the politics of this thing."

"I'm not you, Phil. I have a family."

"You're just an errand boy. So I got an errand for you. Go back and tell Beale and that FBI piece of shit that if I catch you guys snooping in my life again, I'm going straight to the press to tell them exactly how you boys are blowing the case!" He turned around to keep Cheong from answering him. A woman in black slacks and a white blouse stood close to the passenger-side window of the Mustang, leaning over, talking to Paul. Now Boudreau saw that the window was halfway down. "*Hey, you! Get the fuck away from that car!*"

She straightened up and turned around. Diane Heidt. She showed him a playful little smile. She waved.

"You know her?" Dan Cheong asked.

The lady who made my mouth water? Sure. He almost said it aloud. Instead, he said, "Check the file on me and you'll see that somebody already knows I know her. I'll see you around."

"Don't talk—"

"Fuck you," Boudreau cut him off, and headed toward his car. As he got closer he saw that Heidt looked even thinner than he had remembered. Her smile became a little ironic twist of the lips. "Sorry I yelled like that," he said.

"Perfectly understandable. Paul told me you didn't want him talking to anybody, but I told him I was sure you'd make an exception in my case."

"You know my son?"

"Oh, sure, we're old, old friends."

"Oh, you know Adrienne. Figures. No exceptions. Get out of here. No, wait. Why did you write me that note? It made me think I was going to hear from you again."

"You were, but I got caught in a revolving door." She stood on her toes to look over his shoulder at the doings in the woods. "You will, now," she said. Boudreau noticed that Paul had his face back in the book. What did he care?

"I just got told—again—not to talk to you."

"What do you call this, taking a chance?" She glanced over her shoulder. "This is a hell of a place to bring a child his age."

"Well, to tell you the truth, doctor, I'm not that deep in baby-sitters. Paul was just fine in the car reading his book, and by the look of him, he's still fine. So excuse me. This is a hell of a place for a guy my age."

She stepped aside. "If they told you not to talk to me, you can be sure I want to talk to you."

"You've never worked for the government, have you?"

"I teach at the U."

"Not the same thing. They think you're people up there."

"Are you really that upset that I know Adrienne?"

She knew she had him, but he was going to tough it out anyway and ignore her remark. "Take it up with the big Chinaman in there. He'll straighten you out."

"Chinese."

"What?"

"Don't call him that word."

"Is that worse than motherfucker? 'Cause that's what I just called him to his face." He walked around to the driver's side of the car.

"You're still very surly, detective. I'm sorry you're having such bad luck."

It wasn't until he had driven back to South Pacific Highway that her reference came clear to him. Good thing he was so slow-witted, or he might have responded with another obscenity, and he might have been called onto the carpet to explain why he was being so difficult with the taxpayers. One very easy way to lose a job—especially within a year of telling the press that the victims had rocks in their *vagyynuhs*. But if Heidt reached out for him again, knowing he had been told not to talk to her, and made another sexual reference . . .

"Why do you have that funny look on your face, Dad?"

He had lost track of himself. "I think I'm going to get something to eat, kid."

"Then we go to the ball game."

"Right," Boudreau said, as he hauled himself back into the real world, "we have some time to kill, but that's the schedule."

September 1983

"You lied!" Martin Jones cried. "You plain lied to me! Again!"

Lockman laughed. He pushed away from his backyard picnic table and stood up. "I did not. You're such a flaming asshole, Martin. You ought to take a look at yourself in a mirror someday." He had to be careful with Jones, who had driven all the way down here from Seattle listening to a KIRO All-News Radio roundtable on the Green River killings. Lockman drained his beer and tossed the empty into the trash barrel. He said, "What happens, Martin, is that you redden up. Your whole face and your neck get red. Maybe that's where the redskin stuff comes from, because you people really are kinda brown, know what I mean? Maybe the cowboys never realized how pissed off all of you were."

Martin Jones squinted at him in the afternoon sun. Lockman had lived in the house for only a year and a half, but he knew the angles of the sun well enough to be able to place the table and chairs to put his guests at a disadvantage, unless they were willing to assert themselves. Jones said, "I hate you. I never hated anybody before. You are the worst human being I have ever met. You lie, cheat, steal—"

"Kill. Don't forget kill."

"I was getting to that."

"And then you're going to tell me how all that makes me different from you? Or is it something else that does that? Do you think it's something else? Because God knows I'm different from you. The last thing I would want anybody thinking is that somehow we're alike, or a team, for Christ's sakes. Brothers under the skin!" Martin Jones blinked, apparently shocked by the intensity of the assault. Lockman sometimes wondered if he even knew how deeply he was being insulted, he was willing to absorb so much. Lockman popped another can. "The answer is no, I didn't kill the girls they found last week. For all I know, they're trying to tie a whole bunch of different murders together so that when they do get their hands on some dumb bastard they can manipulate him into confessing, or making a run for it so they can shoot him. They can clean a whole bunch of their files at once and then tell the world what heroes they are. Maybe there's a real serial killer out there and not a couple of pissant dilettantes like us. For all I know, it's another one of my madcap fucking friends! Like you! You *started* this, and now you're acting like your feelings are hurt. Get real, Martin, we're talking about murder here!"

Martin Jones frowned. Lockman loved it when Jones got suspicious of some new surprise. "Another friend? What are you talking about?"

"This isn't the only freak relationship I have. I've told you about Tom Parkinson and Jimmy Dobbs, earlier friends, if you will, of Mister Jim."

"Have you been trying to make killers of them, too?"

"As well as cocksuckers, you mean? What do you think? Look, as long as you're here, I'll build a fire and we'll have a barbecue. I've got some nice steaks in the freezer."

"Where did you get the money for nice steaks?"

"I cashed a check."

"You always say that. What does it mean?"

"What do you think it means?"

"You're full of shit, that's what it means."

The first late-afternoon breeze came up, a brisk herald of fall making the treetops bow and thrash. If he and Jones stayed outside, they would be glad to have the heat of the barbecue. At least the house was clean, a bit of luck. Nothing to see, nothing to know. Jones had not had the effrontery to demand to go downstairs to the basement to see the secret room. There was nothing to see down there between adventures anyway, and this weekend was definitely between adventures. The cops had told him long

ago that the holiday weekends were trouble's prime times. If they thought
so, it was reasonable to assume they responded by stepping up their own
activities. Another of Lockman's rules: Know The Enemy. For that reason
Tuesday morning was much better than Friday night, but Sunday night
had a certain dangerous charm. "So? Are you going to stay?"

"Sure, I'll eat your food. I may even spend the night. Drink your booze.
Listen to your lies. When are you going to start to repay me?"

Garrett Richard Lockman stretched. No truth to be told on this subject,
either. The fun would end. Across the shallow valley another house was
under construction, the third since his arrival, and he had heard talk at
the supermarket that Sunset Highway was going to be widened. Overhead, the tallest branches whipped about in another chilly gust. "You
know I'm working on a deal to get even, Martin. One big deal, I'll have
the money to pay you, and then it's off to the next adventure."

"Just make sure you pay me first. Before you start building your own
town. It's really not sane, Garrett. You can't just build your own town."

"Of course you can. It's done all the time. Levittown back east. Disneyland. Look at all those mining towns in Montana and Idaho. You want to
go to Idaho and take a look? Right now. I'll drive."

Lockman filled the barbecue with coals and splashed starter fluid on
top, watching Jones watching him work. What do you do for amusement
with a guy like this? You couldn't get drunk with him. Jones opened another beer. He would nurse it for an hour. Across the valley, one of Lockman's new neighbors was barbecuing, too. His yard sloped down toward
the back of Lockman's house and was completely enclosed by a shiny
new aluminum fence. From his bedroom window Lockman had an un-
obstructed view of all three yards and into the windows of the houses beyond. Nothing to see. This side of the valley was dotted with houses, and
although most were hidden in the trees, their lights at night created an urban effect—and left the people on the other side feeling as if they were on
the stage of a giant amphitheater.

Lockman knew two people who lived on his block, and he knew that at
least another three were aware of him, or could identify him in a lineup.
"That's Cliff Lloyd," they'd say, because that was the name they knew.
Clifford Lloyd owned this house. Ten thousand dollars down, five hundred a month to the former owner, as in OWC, *Owner Will Carry*. An extra taste for the real-estate agent, to encourage Mr. Owner Will Carry to
go for the deal. A balloon payment was due after six years, and if Lockman
didn't want to make it, he would walk away with as much equanimity as
when he'd walked in.

The two neighbors who knew him were women. One, a single woman in her fifties, gave him a wide berth. Lockman was used to that and had learned not to think about it too much. The other woman, who was also single, was in her thirties and a bit of a hippie and was curious about him. He did not detect any sexuality in that interest, but he had learned not to think too much about that, either. Dorothy Gold. Dottie, she had told him to call her. She was short with a narrow face and big Jewish nose and she was beginning to pack weight on her hips and thighs. He had already told her that he worked for the government and would be out of town often. She had seemed impressed. Another one who didn't drink. He'd asked her if she would like to have a drink, and she'd said no, she didn't drink. What do you do with a woman like her? How did you warm her up?

"Let's wait until dark and take a ride around Portland," Lockman said to Martin Jones. "Maybe we'll find true love."

"You're such a goon, Lockman."

"The steaks are in the refrigerator, all defrosted."

"Oh, you've had them awhile."

"You're still wondering where I got the money?"

"No, I'm wondering when I'm going to get some."

"Don't be a bore. Put a potato in the microwave, if you want one. And put some more beer in the refrigerator."

"When Oscar cooks, Felix jumps."

"Oh, now you do want to play *Odd Couple*. Go get the stuff, my faithful Indian companion."

Lockman had found himself wanting to think more about Dottie Gold. He always studied her house as he rolled by on the way out to the street to the highway. Where did she work? Downtown, at Merrill Lynch, in one of the big high-rises where she could see Mount Hood, she said. No one was fucking her, Garrett Lockman was reasonably sure. Hello, Mister Jim. *Why, helloooo, Garrett!* He had thought of walking over to her place when it was very late, but because his house was below the street, and hers was well set back on the other side, he had no way of getting information about her schedule. When she went to bed, for instance. Or did she suffer from insomnia like so many other single women?

Martin Jones appeared in the kitchen doorway. He almost dropped the tray in his hands. "Are you pissing in the fire?"

"No, I just wanted to feel the heat on it."

"My God, you're masturbating! Those people across the valley can see you!"

"They're too far away." With a smile, Garrett Richard Lockman tucked his tumescent penis back in his pants.

———

THEY WAITED UNTIL nine-thirty before they left the house, and then they headed for the other side of the Willamette. Lockman did not know what Jones expected tonight, but he really could not take the chances that went with getting busy here in Portland. Not the least of which was the emotional problem he would create for himself if he violated one of his own rules. If you did it once, you'd do it again; eventually all discipline would collapse, and the result would be capture.

Finally Lockman steered Jones to Digger O'Dell's, where he talked Jones into ordering some boiled shrimp to go with their ice-cold beer. Lockman was intrigued by Digger O'Dell's, a dark-wood-and-red-leather re-creation of a turn-of-the-century seafood bar in an historic Victorian building. He liked to imagine that the place was filled with the ghosts of the pretty Chinese hookers and other characters of the building's one-hundred-year history. Lockman was sure people had been murdered in the building, and when he'd had enough to drink, as he had been able to do on two or three other occasions here, he had seemed able to look backward in time, had seen the ghosts, had heard their laughter.

Not tonight. The little Indian expected Lockman to talk to him. He had forgotten he was an uninvited guest, no matter who was picking up these tabs. Which was only fair. Lockman was down one excellent steak and three beers and it was possible that the feast was far from over. He couldn't piece his thoughts together. He switched from beer to Rusty Nails, then to Long Island Iced Teas. Digger O'Dell's was a great bar, a wonderful bar. Martin Jones's face came closer and asked Lockman if he was fit to drive. Of course he was fit to drive. Jones was saying he wanted to go home—and not just halfway out to Beaverton, either, but all the way back to Seattle. Wasn't he enjoying the evening? At this point in the proceedings, Lockman wasn't all that sure he wanted to be left alone again.

The car was parked around the corner, only Lockman wasn't exactly sure which one. Jones said he knew where the car was. Lockman stopped in his tracks. "Is that the reason you think you're more qualified to pilot said machine?" Always better to ignore him, Lockman thought as he lurched behind the wheel. He never got tickets, or almost never, not for years, and certainly not for DUI. You did not want cops searching your car. You never knew who was all tied up in the trunk. He had actually forgotten about one sweet young thing. Too drunk to drive that night, coming down from the Strip, with the girl kicking from the inside of the trunk against the fenders. No one could hear her. Lockman checked on that, riding next to another car while she screamed at the top of her lungs.

When she became really annoying, Lockman raised the volume of the radio until he was afraid he was going to split the speaker cones.

"I did that, you know," he yelled at Martin Jones as they climbed the hill toward the zoo.

"Did what?"

"Never mind."

"You're really drunk, man! Are you sure you don't want me to drive?"

"Yes. What did you do with the body in the trunk?"

"What body? Hey, you killed them! You killed them and a whole lot more! You never stopped!"

"Once you start, you can't stop. True stuff. So what? What are you going to do about it? Suppose I'm bullshitting you again? What does it matter anyway, since you're cursed to believe whatever makes you craziest? You are, you know. I believe you're a hermaphrodite. Cut you open, you'll find a secret, stinky little pussy inside." He giggled. "That should hold you for a while."

"You son of a bitch, you've been killing girls right along! Why did you cut me out like that?"

Lockman dismissed him with a wave of the hand as he turned into his street. A strange car was parked in front of Dottie Gold's house, its lights on. Lockman braked his car until it rolled very slowly past the front doors of the other car. Dottie turned in the passenger seat, saw Lockman, gave a little smile, and waggled her fingers at him. Could she see that he was drunk? He tapped his horn as he continued to roll. In the driver's seat, next to Dottie, was a skinny bald guy. *Figured.*

"You look like you have a crush on her," Martin Jones said bitterly.

"Shut up."

"What are you up to?"

"Who said you were in charge of my life? I don't have to answer to you." He turned into his own driveway. Now he wanted Martin Jones on his way. "How do I know you're not still doing stuff, Little Beaver?"

"Oh, no. You're not doing that to me again."

Lockman set the hand brake and shut off the engine. "What are you talking about?"

"I'm talking about you putting everything in reverse, blaming me for the things you're doing. I stopped. It got too scary for me. You know that."

"Don't you forget it, either. There's nothing to link me to anything *you've* done. They nail you, I'll leave you twisting in the wind. It's the way it has to be."

"You want me to get caught, don't you?"

"It's one way to be rid of your whining. All right, you wanted to go home. There's your car. Go home."

"Jesus, Garrett, I have to go to the bathroom."

"Too bad. I have to go to bed." He got out of the car and fell face-first onto the gravel. His first thought was that he was on the wrong side of the car to have been seen by Dottie. He got to his hands and knees, gravel dropping like bird shit from indentations in his face. His hands, knees, and forehead began to sting. Martin Jones had him under one arm, trying to lug him to his feet. Not the time to start yelling. He didn't want to attract the attention of the neighbors, especially Dottie, although Lockman was beginning to have bad thoughts about her now. She was too old to kill, too close to home, and too ugly: could she imagine that all three elements were blessings? Lockman wondered about her appetites. In what ways was the skinny bald guy going to be pleasured? Martin Jones guided Lockman into his house, then closed the door behind them. Did Dottie now think Lockman was a fairy?

"Tell me how many girls you killed this year, Garrett."

"Where are you? I can't see you. What have you done?"

"Your eyes are closed, you stupid son of a bitch. If you want to see what's going on, you have to open your eyes."

You're taking advantage of me, Garrett Lockman thought, and passed out again.

He awakened on the living-room couch in daylight, and when he moved, his head burst into pain. His palms and knees hurt, too, and in an other moment he vaguely remembered taking a header on the gravel outside. Dottie—had she seen him? What had he done to her? What had he done in her presence? He couldn't be sure of anything. He sat up. He had slept without a blanket, and now he felt chilled—sick. Martin Jones seemed to be gone. No car in the driveway. What had he done while Lockman had been out cold on the couch? Lockman couldn't even remember what he had planned to do yesterday before Jones's arrival had thrown everything up in the air. Lockman was going to spend the rest of today sick. In the kitchen he poured himself a tall vodka on the rocks. What day was it? The only way to find out was to turn on the television set. He didn't have the newspaper delivered. He didn't like *The Oregonian* anyway. *The Oregonian* covered the whole state, and he was one person who didn't care what happened in Corvallis or Bend.

He slept through the day and in the evening walked the length of his street to check out who was parked at Dottie's house. The sky was faint purple and he was still terribly sick and definitely coming down with something, which he blamed on Martin Jones. Jones was out of the picture, Lockman was deciding, and not because he had barged in yesterday and then had left his host uncovered on the couch. As long as Jones was incapable of understanding what the big adventure was really about, Lockman did not want to bring him back into the process, even just to keep him calm. No one was parked outside La Gold's palazzo tonight. Lockman had to keep walking to the corner, lest someone figure out what he was really doing. He was past her house when he heard a screen door slam.

"Cliff! Cliff Lloyd!"

Standing on her concrete stoop, Dottie waved him over. He raised his hand and started in her direction at his own slow pace.

Her hair was in braids and he thought he could see a softness in her face that wasn't usually there. He could not help believing that she had spent the night fucking and sucking Mr. Skinny Bald Guy. Perhaps God had done Lockman a favor, leaving him passed out on the couch. What was interesting was that he had no desire for her, just some lesser, and vague, *feeling.*

"Look, I want to thank you for slowing down to see if I was all right last night. It's nice to know that there's a guy like you living on the block. I feel a lot safer."

"Okay. You might as well know, some of the work I do has to do with those murders up in Seattle. He uses a car to get his victims. That's why I was checking."

"I didn't think you were a cop."

"I just don't look like a cop. Actually, the agency I work for is positioned—well, never mind. Very advanced work, going to change everything. Now, please don't spread it around. There are always people who think they have a right to know everything. I could be put in an awkward position."

She nodded. He wanted to be invited into her house, but there was nothing he wanted to do if he got in there. She had nothing he wanted to drink and he was much too sick to eat. He didn't like to romance any woman so soon after her last sex bout, as aroused as it might have left her. "I'll see you around," he said, starting away. "Don't forget to keep your doors and windows locked."

"Thanks, Cliff."

"Good night, Dottie."

———

A WEEK LATER he drove to Spokane, up through the rolling farmland of The Dalles and then past bleak Walla Walla, where he held a good thought for Tom Brownall, and eventually past Fairchild Air Force Base and under the slow-moving B-52s to the home of the Spokane *Spokesman-Review*, a.k.a. the Spook. Lockman wanted to hit Hazel up for more dough. She was always good for a couple of hundred, and Lockman was in the process of executing a new scheme.

He had called the Scottish-accented pornographer in Vancouver with the news that he was coming into a stash of X-rated tapes of his own — any interest? By all means, came the reply; twenty dollars Canadian for every one. Lockman dickered for more, but the buyer was firm. It didn't matter, because it was all pure profit for Lockman.

He had been applying for credit cards under dozens of names, and now the cards were coming through to postal boxes all over the Pacific Northwest. With three cards — just three, because he would never be able to use them again — he had begun ordering porn tapes from the biggest advertisers in the back pages of *Hustler*, *Chic*, *High Society*, and *Velvet*. The cards worked; the tapes were pouring into the postal boxes. When he had a trunkload, he would make the run to Vancouver. And Hazel's two hundred? Not for paying off the credit cards — he was never going to do that. The big deuce was for gas, food, and lodging. The last thing he wanted to do, on this run, anyway, was leave a paper trail from Portland to British Columbia.

In return for the two hundred dollars, Hazel made him sit down with her on the plastic-covered chairs in the living room with iced tea on coasters on the glass-topped coffee table and tell her everything he was doing. Sometimes he wondered if the creepiness of the situation and the persistence of her questions had not turned him into the wonderfully skilled and polished liar he was simply to keep himself entertained instead of being driven insane. So he told her about the role he was playing in the undercover work being done to trap the Green River killer, and how law enforcement suspected the killer was somebody important in Seattle political circles, maybe somebody who had worked with Ted back in the seventies. Old Hazel lapped it up. Lockman never spun these tales in front of Al, who made his opinion felt by pursing his lips and taking his copy of the Spook into the next room. Lockman stayed a couple of nights anyway, long enough to break into Al's office to steal a quarter ounce of pharmaceutical-grade cocaine and sell it within the hour to one of his old Spokane pals.

The night blossomed into another drunken brawl. His friend was one of the biggest coke dealers in the city, surrounded by coke-hogging young females willing to do anything for toot. He offered to show Lockman, but Lockman resisted, saying he was just as allergic to that kind of sex as he was to the little item he had just exchanged for his host's cash. Besides, there was a new disease going around, and until doctors knew more about it, Lockman said he was going to be careful. His dope-dealer friend didn't know what he was talking about. One of the girls finally spoke up. "He's talking about the fag's disease," she said, "and straight people don't get it." That made the dope dealer laugh loudly, too pointedly for Lockman, who was out of the apartment soon thereafter, getting drunker, making his way back to Hazel and Al's, where in his room he continued to drink, propelling himself into his most vivid fantasies, until he passed out.

He waited another week in Portland for the last of the tapes to arrive, and then, with a driver's license and registration made out to Steve Maddox, he started up the I-5 to Vancouver, a six-hour drive if he didn't stop to eat.

Lockman's misgivings began in Redmond, and by the time he got to Bellingham, he was sick to his stomach. He had gone over the plan a hundred times and could find no fault with it, but now he could not help thinking there was something he had overlooked, had not thought of, or plain did not know. Like changes in Canada's customs regulations and procedures. Had they changed? How would he know until he got to the customs inspectors' station? Then it would be too late. He had no friends like Ron Beale in Canada. Two hundred pornographic videotapes! All he would be able to say was that someone had put them in his trunk when he had left the car unattended. In the absence of other evidence, he would have trouble getting anybody to believe him. He could go back to jail, real jail, and not for just a couple of weeks, either.

At the border he handed over the license and registration to an apple-cheeked, uniformed Canadian. These were real documents, not forgeries, based on a birth certificate he had stolen years ago from a sailor's duffel bag in San Diego.

"Would you mind pulling over, Mr. Maddox?"

"What's wrong?"

"Just routine. Would you pull over to that area on your left, please?"

The area was the parking lot in front of the RCMP station. They wanted to search the car, no doubt about it. Lockman was having trouble keeping his bladder closed. The building was practically windowless, long and low, extending almost all the way back to the American border. Lockman saw that if he backed into the parking space, the driver's side of the car would be out of the inspector's view. The inspector had the driver's license and registration in Maddox's name, but also bearing Lockman's own photograph and thumbprint. So what? This was Canada. At least

Lockman knew his mind was working. After what he had told Hazel, he wouldn't be able to let anyone in Spokane find out that he had been arrested at the border for smuggling porn. He couldn't let Beale know this about him, either. He couldn't have anyone thinking about him and illicit sex.

He backed into the most distant parking space and walked steadily around the side of the building, ready to tell anyone who stopped him that he only thought he was doing what he had been told. He kept going around to the back, ducking below the windows, stopping only when he reached an overgrown bushy weed to relieve himself. Burglars had told him they often had the overwhelming urge to defecate after they had broken into a house or apartment. When he was clear of the building he just kept on to the American side, blending himself into the crowd.

What had he lost? A car. A perfectly good set of documents. And the cargo. The cargo had no value except at that one location in Vancouver. He couldn't think about the profit he would never see. He had sensed that something was going to go wrong—how? What had tipped him off? Was he developing psychic powers? Once he was clear of the U.S. Customs and Immigration facility, Lockman put his thumb in the air to get a ride south again. An eighteen-wheeler stopped and the driver leaned over to open the passenger's door as Lockman climbed up.

The driver was a beefy, bearded country boy who wore a cheap straw cowboy hat. The cab smelled of his sweat.

"How far yer goin'?"

"Portland, but if I can't get there tonight, I'll stay with friends in Seattle."

"Good thing you're not a girl, if you do much hitchhiking. The radio just said they found two more girls."

"Girls? Bodies?"

"Well, not exactly bodies. They've been dead awhile. I guess there ain't much left of 'em."

"Where was this, at the airport?"

"Oh, no. These were down by Star Lake, if you know where that is."

"No. Sorry. I never heard of it."

The driver glanced over as he shifted gears. "That sumbitch has his body count up to ten. He's doin' better'n me in Viet fucking Nam, and I killed a bunch."

"He's crazy," Lockman said, but it came out not as he had wanted. It sounded halfhearted, a mumble.

"What do you do, cowboy?"

"I work for Boeing. I'm just a small cog in a very big machine. I was up in Vancouver visiting my kid and somebody stole my car, probably my ex-wife's boyfriend. That's why she's up there—she's Canadian—to discourage me from seeing my own kid."

"Now there's a bitch. The law can't do anything about a thing like that, everybody bein' in two countries and all."

"I just want the kid to know I tried. When she's grown up, she'll know her father didn't run out on her."

"That's the way. How old is your little girl?"

"Four. We're very close."

"Hey, if you work for Boeing, how come you're going to Portland?"

"That's very observant of you. Portland is where my mother lives. She has a car I can have until I get straightened out. It had to happen while I'm moving, too."

"Always, the way. Hell, I can take you to Portland. Hell, I can take you clean through to fucking Modesto. I can take you right to your mother's door, if you like."

"No, no. I told her I was flying down to PDX and was going to take a taxi home. I don't really have the spare dough for airfare, but I didn't want her to worry. If you let me off at the Morrison Bridge, I shouldn't have any trouble getting home from there. Listen, thanks, I really appreciate this."

"And you never heard of Star Lake?"

"Oh, I heard of it. Knowing that we have another maniac on the loose is just very upsetting to me."

The driver nodded, but Lockman did not think he was completely convinced. Lockman realized that he had to stay quiet: trying to sell himself was absolutely the worst thing he could do.

"You got a picture of your little girl?"

"That was in the car. I wouldn't be surprised if her mama's boyfriend knew that. Mama would have told him. I used to use my glove compartment as a catchall for personal stuff when we were still a family. There's nothing I can do. I guess I wasn't exciting enough for her."

The driver laughed. "Hell, even I can understand that. Exciting is what you ain't, cowboy."

"Thanks a lot." Lockman looked out the window. At the slower speeds the truck made, it was going to take at least ten hours to get to Portland. That included a meal break. Did the driver expect him to pick up the check? Maybe not, considering Lockman's car had been stolen today. Lockman thought again about what had happened at the border. How had he known there would be trouble? If he was developing a true gift of precognition, he was afraid to put himself at risk to prove the point to himself. The fact was that he had committed every crime in the book except incest and had gotten away with all of them. How? By being cautious.

And now that he was making history, he was going to stay that way.

The truck didn't cross the Columbia River until nearly midnight, and by then the driver was only too happy to let Lockman off at the Morrison Bridge, where it was a short walk to a telephone to call a taxi. Lockman and the driver had had enough of each other. At dinner in Tacoma the driver had questioned Lockman again about the fictitious daughter and ex-wife, a tedious exercise that had left Lockman feeling uneasy again about today's losses. Morrison Bridge was within walking distance of Digger O'Dell's, but Lockman felt too grubby and used up to want to celebrate anything. Standing on a dark corner in a bad neighborhood at midnight to wait for a taxi was all the adventure Lockman could handle. He could feel himself sinking into an ever-deeper depression. He was thinking of that little prick Martin Jones. Jones wasn't responsible for the remains found at Star Lake, but that didn't mean he wasn't out there running around like a maniac without the slightest idea of what the adventure was really all about.

The taxi was late. Lockman was on the telephone with the dispatcher again as the taxi rolled around the corner, and as Lockman got in the backseat the dispatcher was whining over the radio about a nervous customer worrying about getting raped. The driver turned the radio volume down and gave Lockman the eye through the rearview mirror, daring him to make a comment. Lockman looked out the window as they crossed the Willamette and plunged into Portland's tidy, tree-lined downtown. If he kept his mouth shut, the driver would do the same.

Lockman made the driver stop around the corner from his street. He had left by car—why should anyone see him return by taxi? With more bodies found today, people were justifiably tense and excitable. Tip? He had to do nothing unusual there, too, so he calculated fifteen percent almost to the penny. He waited until the taxi was over the hill before setting out for his house, where at least he would find something to drink.

He heard voices even before he turned the corner. He stood still and listened: women's voices, two of them, and their tone did not indicate unhappiness. A party at this hour? Now he recognized Dottie Gold's voice—and she sounded drunk! Lockman pushed his hands into his pants pockets and started walking again.

"Cliff? Is that you?"

He stopped, making his moves step-by-step: carefully turning, looking, taking a step in the direction of her house. The light beside the front door was on, showing her sitting on her front steps with another woman, a bottle blonde.

"Dottie?" He thought he hit the right note of surprise. "Hi!"

She waved him over. He hesitated, the paradigm of shyness, then started walking again, flashing a seemingly self-conscious grin. The other woman was in her late forties, maybe older. She had a row of beer cans on the walk in front of her and she was smoking a cigarette. Dottie was holding a glass of white wine, with the bottle next to her. "Myra, this is the guy I was telling you about, Cliff Lloyd. I saw you leave this morning, Cliff. Say hello to Myra Goss."

"Hello to Myra Goss."

"Hi."

Dottie asked, "So what are you doing, wandering around so late at night?"

"I was not wandering around."

"Oooh," said Myra Goss. He saw that he had answered without thinking, too quickly.

"I've been walking back from downtown," he said. "My car crapped out on me."

Dottie Gold laughed. "Why didn't you take a taxi?"

"I felt like walking."

"You walked all the way from downtown?" Myra Goss asked.

"I've done it before. It's not a bad walk."

She snorted. "I wouldn't climb that hill for free money."

"Well, I don't smoke. What's the occasion?"

Myra Goss dragged on her butt. "Does it have to be an occasion?" He almost expected her to blow the smoke in his face.

"I've never seen Dottie do this before. That makes it an occasion."

"You are one very defensive young man," Myra Goss said.

"You are one very angry woman."

"Hold it, you two," Dottie said. "Don't get off to a bad start with each other, *please*."

"I am not an angry woman. *And* I've been insulted."

He stayed silent. Myra Goss stared up at him. She was drunk. She wanted an apology? The only thing he was sorry about was that she was too old to kill. Who would want to look at her? He had her figured out. No man wanted even a blow job out of her. She knew it. That's why she was drunk, so she could let out her bitter disappointment. "Well, nice to meet you. See ya, Dottie."

He was turning away when Myra Goss said, "What gas station is your car in?"

He stopped and looked back at her. "What?"

"I *said*, 'What gas station is your car in?' "

"What's the matter, don't you believe me?"

"Frankly, no."

"That's your problem."

"*Please*, guys!" Dottie cried.

"No, no," Myra Goss said. "I'd like to see the receipt from the gas station."

"I don't have to show you anything."

"I'm calling you on this. If you can't show me a receipt, I say you're a liar and you're up to some kind of shit. Are you a peeper? Is that your game, Mr. Lloyd? Are you a Peeping Tom?"

"You'd better watch your mouth. You can get sued for saying things like that."

"Sue and go fuck yourself. I say you're a phony from baloney."

"Maybe you ought to leave, Cliff," Dottie said.

"I only came over because you called me. A guy can't even be out after dark without somebody accusing him—"

"After dark, my ass," Myra Goss said. "It's after *midnight*."

"And you're drunk," Lockman said.

"And tomorrow I'll be sober—"

"Thank you, Winston Churchill—"

"But you'll still be a creep." Myra Goss was looking him straight in the eye. "Stay away from him, Dottie. For all you know, this is your Green River killer standing right here in front of us."

"You can make real trouble for yourself with that kind of talk," he said.

"Exactly what kind of threat is that, mister?"

"Go home, Cliff. I'm sorry. Please go."

He turned again. Myra Goss muttered something he couldn't make out. He kept walking, suddenly realizing that his hands were balled into fists so tight they actually hurt. What had happened today? He would have to talk to Dottie. He would have to caution her not to spread the kind of poison that old bitch had on her mind. What was he going to do about the car he had left in Canada? If Dottie had been paying any kind of attention to him, she knew he always had two or three cars in the driveway and changed them frequently. But now she might wonder why this particular car was out of the picture. She had seen it this morning. He had just let her understand that he had left it in a gas station. At least his mind was working again: all he had to do was keep quiet about it, wait for her to ask. When she did, he'd tell her he sold it. He couldn't have an unreliable car, could he? Then he would mention Myra Goss and how dangerous her confrontational style could be for someone in a position as sensitive as his. Dottie wouldn't ask more—and she wouldn't say anything to Myra Goss, who would only want to know why Dottie was still talking to him. He had it figured right. He was covered.

But something continued to gnaw at him. This had been an awful day. Awful thoughts pressed against a dam hidden within him. Once inside his own house, Lockman quickly bolted the door. He could see part of the street from the front bedroom, and he wanted to be sure La Goss had not followed him. Why would she? Because she was drunk and belligerent. That was reason enough. He turned on the lights in the living room even though it was his style to sit in the semidarkness, relishing the atmosphere created by the glow of the television screen. Tonight everything had to be what was normal for the ordinary people, just in case. Upstairs, he peered around the curtain at the little bit of the street in view. Nothing—no one. He had not collected his mail from the box up at the curb, but now he was afraid that doing so would just attract more attention from Gorilla Goss. She had actually said it! Green River killer! Did he have to get rid of her? He didn't know if he was capable of killing a woman as old as she was. Dottie would figure it out anyway, and he'd be in jail before the day was out. How well did she know Goss? Well enough to get drunk with her after she had told him she didn't drink. Lesbos. End of story. He grinned. He didn't have to think about killing some ugly old broad. He was a specialist, and he didn't have to see himself any other way.

He had not checked his telephone messages, either—not that there were that many people who had his telephone number. He filled a tumbler full of scotch and went back to the living room. The answering machine indicator light blinked two times fast. Two messages.

The first was from Hazel, who wanted him to tell her everything the police knew about the discovery at Star Lake. "It's hard to feel sorry for those girls," she said. "They chose their lives, and they certainly knew he was out there. Take care of yourself, Garrett. You're very brave, but remember you're still my little boy."

The second call was from Martin Jones, and it, too, was about the discovery at Star Lake, although the language Jones used was far more circumspect. "How many, Lockman? How many is it really? Should I tear my walls apart and count the panties? If I don't hear from you soon, and if you don't start leveling with me about what you're up to, I'm going to get very, very nasty. Call me."

But the last two words sounded more like a plea than an ultimatum. What did Jones want to do, watch? *Level* with him? It was plain that he wanted to be in on it, whatever it was, but how could he be in on something he was constitutionally incapable of understanding? It took a special kind of intelligence, insight, imagination. Even if Lockman explained it to Jones, he still wouldn't get it. Jones was not transcending death. Jones was not interested in achieving immortality on his own terms. Power was for those who wanted it badly enough. How could Jones become a god when he could not even imagine it? How could he risk pressing life to the limit when he wasn't ready to acknowledge that there was absolutely nothing on the other side? The world was full of Martin Joneses and Myra Gosses and truck drivers who smelled of stale sweat denying the nothingness, wondering why they were unhappy. Frenchy Boudreau! Did Boudreau ever suspect how much Garrett Lockman knew about his tiny, wretched existence?

Lockman wasn't going to let Boudreau enter his thoughts tonight. He filled the tumbler again and turned on the television set.

In another hour Lockman was dreaming of the town he intended to build where he would be mayor and chief of police. One day. Blue-and-white police cars, blue-and-white fire trucks. Blue-and-white parking meters, too, the proceeds of which would go directly into the mayor's pocket—no bagmen as in the rest of America. When Lockman first started to plan his own town he thought he was going to call it Lockmanville, then for a while he was fixed on Lockman City, and most recently he leaned toward White City, but now he was undecided. The first two sounded too small, and he remembered there was a White City in England. He wanted something with heft and mystery, a name that would make people want to visit and stay. He was thinking he was going to have to make up a name. All he knew so far was that it would start with the letter Y.

An hour later he was really drunk, thinking about going downstairs to the secret room. The room was spotless, clean to the point of antisepsis. There was no other way to do this business, no other way to go on and on, as Lockman hoped to do. He could remember the heaviness of Deeah Anne Johanssen's breasts when he'd wrestled her into the alley, the amazing huge round firmness of her buttocks. For all his many experiences since, he always returned to her and that first thrill when he wanted to excite himself.

The lights in the living room were off now, the television screen flickering with *Carefree*, starring Fred Astaire and Ginger Rogers. It was curiously unsatisfying, but he couldn't tell if that was because the film was not their best or his own inner processes were too disturbed by the events of the day. He filled the glass again and downed it and used the remote to turn off the set and then he sat in the silent dark to wait for the alcohol to smash him unconscious like the fist of a giant.

He heard the telephone ringing several times in the next days, but he stayed away from it, stayed distant from the yapping of the answering machine as it recorded the callers' messages. He was too sick to want to deal with anybody. He stopped drinking only because he ran out of booze and was too shaky to go out and too frightened of the gossip that would start if a delivery boy saw him dirty and hungover. There would be gossip, too, because most people had no other reason to live. Star Lake. Two bodies. Everybody was thinking about it, even this far south. What would it take to get people thinking about him, like that Myra Goss, in her cups and raving, but dead serious?

When he was not quite so fragile and able to clean himself up, he drove out toward Beaverton to a Jack in the Box and got some bacon cheeseburgers, fries, and a large shake. The place seemed crowded for the middle of the afternoon, so he asked the sweet young thing behind the counter for some change for an *Oregonian* from the machine outside. From there, with the breeze giving him chills, he watched her through the window. She was a wonderful-looking kid, a petite, curvy brunette with just a soupçon of baby fat, very clear creamy skin, and pale blue eyes, about seventeen years old. He wanted her, but this was too close to home. He folded the paper under his arm and walked quickly, a little unsteadily, back to his car.

The dateline was Saturday. He had lost four days. On the inside of the main news section was a wire service story datelined Seattle saying that the remains found Wednesday off Highway 18 had been identified through dental charts as those of fourteen-year-old Etta Mae Newman, who had been last seen ten months ago on the Sea-Tac Strip. Her mother said that she had sent Etta Mae out to the 7-Eleven for bread and milk.

No, Lockman thought. Etta Mae had told him that Mom had sent her out for an hour because Mom needed privacy in their motel room so she could turn a trick. Lockman had gotten Etta Mae's attention by asking her how much money Mom got from her customers. "What do you wanna know that for?" the kid had asked. "Because I want to pay you twice as much," Lockman had purred. "I know it will make you give me the nicest ride." "I like that," Etta Mae Newman had said with the kind of sexy smile only a fourteen-year-old could muster, and had gotten in the car.

Another bony, undernourished body!

Disgusted by his easy capitulation to temptation, Lockman had made quick work of her. And, finished, he had been overwhelmed by a rush of self-loathing worse than anything he had ever experienced.

From the Jack in the Box he hurried home. Time to listen to those telephone messages. Hazel again, wondering why he hadn't returned her call. Hazel a third time, after Wednesday, apologizing for bothering him when he must be so busy with the murder investigation, but then, almost in the same sentence, demanding a call back to put her mind at ease. Typical. The woman was a bundle of chaos and cross-purposes, yet she insisted on maintaining control of everything at the expense of everybody else—except Al, of course. Lockman didn't want to think about calling her, but he knew that if he didn't do it, he would hear her squawking in the back of his mind until he wouldn't be able to sleep.

The third message was from Martin Jones: "I thought I would have heard from you by now, but you probably don't even know what I'm talking about. You're drunk, aren't you? Passed out on the floor? Your head in the toilet, hailing Ralph? Selling the Buick? Or are you out somewhere, doing your *thing*? Whatever you're doing, you'd better believe that if I'm dragged into it, I will do everything I can to extricate myself, and to hell with you, do you hear me? To hell with you!"

Garrett Lockman laughed out loud. He knew exactly what he had to do to get Martin Jones back in line. "As a matter of fact, Martin," he said aloud as the message tape continued to run, "you're the very next thing on my agenda."

Next was another baritone, and it took Lockman a moment to recognize the voice of Dan Cheong. "Garrett, are you there? Pick up. It's Dan Cheong." Suddenly, surprisingly, he laughed. "Garrett, what do you think you were doing, trying to get a load of porn into Canada? After you skipped, and the Mounties saw what was in the trunk, they sent the license and registration to the FBI. You handed this office the biggest laugh it's had in months. You've supplied the RCMP with enough dirty tapes to keep them entertained for years. And a free car. If you're worried, relax. Canada doesn't want you and you didn't commit any crime here that we know of, as long as you didn't steal the tapes. The border guard saw you hotfooting it back to our side and told his sergeant that you were going so fast you looked like you were about to crap your pants. Look, Ron wants you out on the street. Call us before the end of the week."

Lockman removed the little reel of tape and put it in his pocket. He wasn't going to wait another minute. In downtown Portland he had a safe-deposit box under the name of C. F. Gardner, with a postal drop for an address, and in the box was a copy of the key to a locker in a self-storage facility on the other side of the Willamette—a copy, because a copy bore no identifying marks that would allow police to trace it. As long as the bill was paid, the contents of the locker were safe, even if he went to jail. The bill went to Spokane and Hazel paid it out of her household account, with Al knowing nothing about it. Hazel thought the locker had to do with Lockman's undercover work. The tape was going straight into that locker, to join the many other artifacts of his connection to Dan Cheong and Ron Beale. If the cops thought he was stupid, Lockman had only to remind himself that they thought he was relatively innocent, too. The last thing Ron Beale could tolerate was a scandal. What had Myra Goss called him? A creep? Creepiness was his ace in the hole.

November 1983

Boudreau set aside what he knew about Garrett Richard Lockman to see the perspective that developed out of an examination of the rest of the case. After the discovery of the seventh and eighth bodies, Boudreau began to add to his home file, cross-indexing what was known about the victims, collating his notes from interviews with street people like Uhuru and David. Victims nine and ten, like seven and eight, were not immediately identified, but the release of the name of victim number eleven, Etta Mae Newman, allowed Boudreau to make some headway. He knew Etta Mae's mother and knew that the story about the errand to the convenience store was a lie. The kid had been sent out on the street while her prostitute mom turned a quick trick. That meant that before her death the kid had been wandering around the Strip, bored and ready for a little fun of her own. Fourteen years old? With her background, she could have lost her virginity before kindergarten. People thought they had to read Dickens to find humanity at its most suffering and pitiful, but the truth was exactly as Willard Motley had written in this country, in our time: *Knock on Any Door.*

The personality and behavior of the victim always told volumes about her killer. The FBI and its sycophants would have the public believe that this was new "science" in police work, but it was as old as London's Metropolitan Police. Show a crook's wife pictures of his girlfriend and she'll rat him out on the spot. Thieves brag; work your snitches. If a husband is found in the kitchen with a butcher knife in him, detain his wife. Etta Mae had been fourteen years old, black, streetwise, looking and acting more or less like the other Green River victims. The killer was trawling the Sea-Tac Strip. The victims kept getting into his car. He knew how to talk to them. No magic words or phrases. Whatever else he was, the killer was a crackerjack psychologist, fast on his feet. Definitely a *he*: women probably couldn't kill with the bar-arm choke hold, a relatively recent innovation in police work. On the street Boudreau was asking: "Anything unusual? Two guys looking for three-ways? Couples? Women?" The answer was always no.

Boudreau felt safe eliminating cops, or ex-cops, because it would be too difficult for a serial killer to sustain such murderous intent around other police officers for long. He would bubble over, badmouth women, talk shit. Other cops would have already noticed, and would be gossiping about him now. Again, nothing. There was no such talk.

But a police *buff*: someone who knew the work and how to talk the talk. Someone fascinated by the streets. Someone who was yellow, too. The victims weren't only throwaways, people the rest of society couldn't be made to care about: they were young, most of them, physically vulnerable, easily controlled if psychological manipulation failed.

The killer was a planner. It was not an accident that no one had seen him driving off with any of the victims or that the recent discoveries offered so little evidence of what had been done with them. Now that they had the benefit of hindsight, maybe the detectives assigned to the case agreed with Boudreau's opinion that the bullets found in the girls dumped in the Green River had been meant to mislead. Beyond those untraceable bullets, there was not enough evidence in the case to fill a business-size envelope. Whether he was a police buff or not, the killer had made himself knowledgeable about the limitations of law enforcement. Why? He wanted to be in the girl-killing business for a long time to come. The Green River killer was giving King County Major Crimes the old humpity-bumpity, with sand in the Vaseline. And he knew it.

Always Sea-Tac, never the Pike. What was the difference between Sea-Tac and the Pike besides Boudreau himself?

Boudreau got up from his desk and sat on the arm of the sofa and poured a scotch and sipped at it for most of an hour as he absorbed the thought and all its ramifications, and then he cried.

It always came back to Lockman. Lockman may have tried to frame Boudreau or maybe he had taken advantage of one peculiar circumstance to cast the shadow of blame on Boudreau, but Lockman was finally so afraid of Boudreau that he dared not come near the Pike.

The bullets and that peculiar circumstance, what Dan Cheong had called a *tip*, pointed to two killers. Lockman and a junior partner, Lockman and somebody who had set everything in motion, who had pushed Lockman into a rampage, pukes, two pukes . . .

What puzzled Boudreau was that his Lockman file showed no other names besides Thomas Brownall, who was still in Walla Walla but up for parole at an early date. If the emerging record on serial-killer pairs was valid, then there had to be a *relationship* between the two men, and not homosexual — homosexuals, when they took up this particular passion, killed *men*.

But the relationship between two killers of women was just as certainly *homoerotic*. A courting. Two pukes in a grotesquely evil pas de deux.

Like the relationship between Lockman and Brownall. *Again* Lockman. Boudreau pulled Lockman's mug shot out of the file and stuck it in his wallet.

The fourteenth body was discovered the week after Halloween and brought the protesters out in force again. Boudreau watched them on television, but did not see Diane Heidt or the other women he had seen at Star Lake. These were new women, and more of them.

Understandable: the victim this time was no throwaway kid, but a thirty-two-year-old white, single, working mother of two who had disappeared from a bus stop on Fourth Avenue in Seattle at the time the first bodies had turned up, fifteen months ago. Pansy Borland had been on her way home from an evening work session at the law firm where she had been a paralegal. At the time the community hadn't been in an uproar over a maniac, and her disappearance had been treated only as another missing person.

At ten o'clock the night after the discovery of her body, Boudreau walked around the corner and pumped eight quarters into the pay phone to call Wayne Spencer at home in Polyp. *Puyallup*.

"Facedown. Nothing but bones, Phil. And teeth. We'd be dead without the teeth. You know, we can't even take credit for that. One of the guys down at the ME's office rounded up the dental charts of all the missing girls and women in the area and memorized them. We're not even sure that this one is part of the series, but we've got ourselves in such a bind, PR-wise, that we can't say anything." *PR-wise?* Boudreau could not help thinking that Spencer was still being victimized by the company he kept. Spencer said, "He could have just done a better job with this one. When she didn't come home that night, her daughter called her aunt, the dead woman's sister, and the aunt called the police. And you know what they told her? Call back in twenty-four hours. There's something wrong with the system there, Phil. It doesn't do the job."

"It does for us. We don't have to go look for everybody who finds a card game or has a flat tire. Even if we had deputized ten thousand citizens, it wouldn't have done her any good. What else do you know?"

"Besides her not fitting the profile? Nothing. Not a damned thing. No clothing, no bullets in her . . ."

The way his voice tailed off was suspicious. Boudreau asked, "Have you got company?"

"Yeah," Spencer answered, his tone suddenly sheepish. "Piper is here. We're giving it another try. Look, since this Pansy Borland disappeared from your turf, maybe you could ask around among those street people you know."

"Every time I see them, Wayne." Boudreau hung up, contemplating, among other things, the return of Piper. On impulse he picked up the Seattle telephone book. D. Heidt was listed, no address. She picked up on the first ring.

"Jesus," he said, "I thought I was calling your office. I was going to leave a message."

"I don't have an office." She sounded sleepy. He heard movement, as if she were sitting up in bed. "So how are you, detective? Have you gotten lucky yet?"

"How the hell do you know it's me?"

"I'd recognize that New York accent anywhere."

"What are you doing in bed so early?"

"I'm alone, if that's what you mean—"

"I should have said asleep. Sorry."

"No harm done. Why did you call?"

"The Borland woman. Something you need to know. You're going to hear that she's not part of the series. Don't believe it. And you didn't hear that from me."

"Fair enough. Anything else you want to tell me?"

Yeah, but not over the phone. The words simply jumped into his consciousness. "What the hell," he almost said aloud. "Yeah, but not over the phone."

"Are you making a pass?"

He was silent for only a moment, but it was a moment too long. "You have to say it, detective."

"Yeah." He said, "You were Adrienne's therapist."

"I can't discuss that with you, you know that. Never."

He heard a pot *clunk* on a stove burner. Everybody had a portable telephone these days. "Are you making coffee?"

"You're not coming over. Don't even think about it."

"You know, going to bed early is often a sign of depression. Let's have dinner. I'm right about the depression, aren't I?"

"Go fuck yourself, detective."

"We've already established that having to do that makes me surly."

She giggled. "All right, dinner. 'The faint aroma of performing seals.' "

"What?"

"The song. I'm not going to say the title."

He knew it. "I Wish I Were in Love Again." He said, "Can you stop calling me 'detective'?"

"I like saying the word. It's romantic."

"Dinner. How about tomorrow?"

"Next week. Thursday. I'd like to say I'm making you suffer, but it's because I have patients. Really."

"Do you have my telephone number?"

"Not anymore. I got mad at you. All right, I have a pencil. Go ahead."

He recited the number. "Call me."

"I will. I have to figure out how to handle Adrienne. It's a professional problem, but I'm not going to let it bother me when I should be enjoying my life."

"That sounds right to me."

"I wonder if you really understand what I'm saying."

"I'm not an asshole, for Christ's sake—"

"Sure you are. And you know it. That's what's so cute about you." The teakettle started to whistle. "Time's up. Next week, detective, and we'll talk beforehand."

He said good night, hung up, and checked his watch. He was wide awake. If he picked up a container of coffee at a 7-Eleven, he might be able to log three or four hours on the Strip. And now that he had a list of the locations from which the victims already found had disappeared, he knew that the Green River killer wasn't working the same street corners over and over. He loved what he was doing. He planned to be at it for a long, long time.

———

DAVID DIED. BOUDREAU heard about it from a girl named Terri, an unbathed sixteen-year-old with yellow hair and heavy mascara who shuttled between her divorced parents' homes and the Pike. With the words "David's dead," Boudreau thought at once that it had something to do with Green River and he, Boudreau, was at fault. No. David had been stabbed by a drifter, a white man in his thirties, in an argument in an abandoned building when David thought his familiarity with the turf gave him territorial privileges. According to the hearsay, David stared as the knife slipped between his ribs and nicked his aorta. Then, crying, he watched himself bleed to death. The drifter was on the run, out of the state by now, and probably would never be caught. Terri had considered David to be her best friend, she said, but as she talked to Boudreau she showed no emotion.

She told Boudreau that David's family could not be located, that the little about them he had told his friends here in Seattle had turned out not to be true. The result was that he was going to get a pauper's burial, no gravestone, no marker, not even a prayer said over him. Boudreau did not see the point to telling her that he had already heard that more times than he could count. The deadness in her eyes said she was an even bet to meet the same fate.

He gave her his card and told her to call him anytime. And then, to make her think it was an afterthought, he took out the picture of Garrett Lockman.

"Do you know this guy?"

She took the photograph and held it a foot from her face and squinted. She needed glasses. "No, I never seen him. I'm not around that much, to tell you the truth. And I'm not gonna be, neither. Better to go home and let my folks kick the shit out of me."

Just talk. She didn't know where she'd be tomorrow. Boudreau retrieved Lockman's picture and then his card and wrote the address of a clinic on the back. "Go there. Tell them I said to test your eyes."

She squinted up at him. "David said you were a good guy."

"Don't make me have to put you in jail."

"Yeah, right."

"And if you see that guy, let me know."

"What's his name?"

"You know his face. Remember it."

"Let me see the picture again."

While she squinted again Boudreau looked over her head across the street to a new purple Coupe de Ville with a white vinyl top and landau bars pulling up to the doughnut shop. Uhuru came out of the shop with a large white bag and got in on the passenger's side and the car pulled away.

It took Boudreau another four days to run Uhuru down again. The pimp was ensconced in a large apartment in a high floor of a luxury building looking down on the Market and the bay. Boudreau was admitted by Uhuru's new factotum, a well-muscled ebony gentleman with a shaved head and wearing a tank top, shorts, and Ray • Ban Wayfarers. Apparently Uhuru was making his contribution to society by hiring ex-cons. The living room was furnished with only a lurid butterscotch-colored, oversized leather couch, a folding canvas director's chair, a big, rear-projection television set, one floor lamp that was not lit, and a small plastic TV table with nothing on it. The bare hardwood floor was littered with doughnut-shop bags and coffee containers. No pictures on the walls, no drapes on the windows through which the lowering sky cast a gloomy, gray-blue light. The condition of the living room suggested to Boudreau that Uhuru was a heavy user of heroin. The doughnuts satisfied his sugar craving, the TV table all he needed to do his cooking. A heroin addict could go on forever as long as he had a steady supply of quality stuff, but as Uhuru was demonstrating, the addict's horizons tended to constrict severely.

"I got furniture on order," he lied. "Want something to drink? We got beer, scotch—what else we got, Marlon?"

"Got Kool-Aid."

"Nothing for me, thanks."

"Sit down, sit down," Uhuru said, waving at the director's chair. Now Boudreau got the way things worked around here: the couch was Uhuru's throne, and Marlon got the director's chair when Uhuru wasn't conducting audiences. "My attorney told me not to talk to you guys, you know."

The caveat meant Boudreau was to accept anything that followed as a beneficence for which gratitude was the only appropriate response. "You know Yolanda Newman."

"Oh, yes. Too bad about her kid."

"What do you hear about that?"

"The River dude got her. She be turnin' tricks, too, you know. Old Yolanda turned her out about two years ago."

"Didn't Yolanda work for you at one time?"

"Nobody work for me but Marlon here."

"Stop the crap. Did you have a business relationship with Yolanda Newman?"

Uhuru shifted his weight. "Not really, and I'll tell you why: the kid. I am the expert. I told you. Yolanda was one of those mean mamas who wanted their kid in trouble. I figured it was gonna spill on me if I let her hang out. Now here it is, not the way I thought, but it's the worst trouble there is."

"You heard about David, the white kid."

"I know he's dead, if that's what you mean. One of those psycho homeless offed him. A hobo. Did you get him?"

"The eyewitnesses gave us pretty good descriptions, but they fit a lot of people."

"All you white people look alike." Uhuru grunted as he reached for the picture of Garrett Lockman Boudreau extended to him. Uhuru frowned. "I know this cat." He passed the picture to Marlon. "Help me with his name, bro'."

"That be Murdoch."

Uhuru beamed as he took the picture back. "Yeah, Murdoch. Walter Murdoch. I see him sometimes with a Mexican, some kind of Mexican. That guy is scary. Ain't he scary, Marlon?"

"I never seen no Mexican."

"Come on! You never seen that funny-colored dude?"

"No, I never."

Boudreau said, "Are you saying he's funny and he's colored, or he's a funny color?"

"The second," Uhuru answered, studying Lockman's picture again. "Funny color, like this couch here. Nice on a couch, but not on a tubby little fella."

"How tubby?"

"Tubby—and pear-shaped. What do you want with these faggots?"

Boudreau reached for the picture. "Just tell me how you know them."

"They hang out on the Pike, you know, like weekend hippies? They don't live around here, but once in a while you see them, oh, around."

"What have you talked to them about?"

"Oh, I never *talked* to them."

"Then how do you know this one's name, or that they're faggots?"

"That's the name he told me, the big one."

"I thought you just said you didn't talk to them."

"I *didn't*!" Uhuru protested. "He talked to me."

"What about?"

"I dunno. He started this *weird* stuff, and I just turned away from him."

"Where was this?"

"In a bar down on the Pike."

"Was the other one with him that night?"

"No, not that night."

"But you know his name."

"No, never heard it. I just see him around."

"When? When was the last time?"

Uhuru shook his head. "It's a long time now."

"What makes you call them faggots?"

"No girls! They just look and point and laugh, you know, like faggots."

"So you don't know that they're faggots."

"They are in Folsom," Marlon said suddenly, with authority. Uhuru's belly shook with laughter.

"That's it?" Uhuru asked.

"Just confirm that name again. What did he say it was?"

"Murdoch. Walter Murdoch. You mean that ain't his real name? What a bitch! I don't dig that shit at all."

"His name is *punk*," Marlon said. "You get a candy-ass white boy like him inside, he be a pump to the whole yard."

Remembering Lockman's desire to stay out of the can, Boudreau smiled. Uhuru and Marlon smiled back. Boudreau wondered if they would be smiling if they knew how desperately he wanted to put them both in jail. *Walter Murdoch.* And a Mexican. Lockman liked to have a boyfriend, no matter what he thought his sexual preference was.

"One more thing," Boudreau said. "I've been telling the girls to be careful. I don't want to hear that you're telling them to take more chances. If I do hear that, you're both going to Walla Walla—I will work it out."

"You got no cause to talk like that. One of the first girls what got killed was a friend o' mine."

Boudreau turned to Marlon. "See that he listens to reason, kid. You know exactly how long a fat tub of shit like him would last."

The soft, sleepy quality of Marlon's smile allowed Boudreau to understand the situation at last: for all of Marlon's macho bluster, Uhuru was boning him just as he had boned his kid brother.

———

WIRED ON STARBUCKS' best again, Boudreau perched on the arm of the sofa and stared through his little window at the downtown high-rises. Last night, after still another tour of the Strip, he had slept out here, as if afraid to go to bed. In the times in the past when he had been restless and fearful like this, he had known the cause: his marriage was about to break up, or, years ago, he had had to make other life-changing decisions. Now was the cause the death of David? He had seen street kids die before. The mounting Green River body count? He had lived through the years of the Bundy rampage. His own life? He was steadily employed, living within his income, and his son did not seem to be suffering from the deprivations Boudreau thought his own mistakes had inflicted on him. The entry of Diane Heidt into Boudreau's life had fanned a spark of hope, even if it had led to the realization, appropriate to his age and experience, that he dared not make too much of it.

What Boudreau knew he did not want to accept was that when he cleared his mind, Garrett Richard Lockman entered it. A jailhouse walkaway who used aliases and manipulated supposedly clever people, a felon convicted four times over who may have never had a successful or enduring sexual relationship with a woman, a troubled, disorganized individual who proclaimed bizarre fantasies and ambitions, somehow had imprinted himself on Boudreau's mind in a way that left him feeling helpless and victimized. Without so much as a hair of solid evidence, Boudreau believed that Lockman was behind the systematic slaughter of so many females, with more to come—Boudreau believed that, too. And in spite of the evidence to the contrary, that Lockman had been on the other side of the country when the first girls were killed.

And worst of all: no matter how Boudreau tried to shake the question, no matter how he tried to create doubt and uncertainty, even to the point of telling himself that the Green River killings and Garrett Richard Lockman were *none of his business*, he came back to being sure he was right.

———

"I CHICKENED OUT," Diane said over the din in the bar. "I told your wife—excuse me, ex—that I was seeing you on Green River business."

Green River made Boudreau look around to see if anyone was eavesdropping. No. "Is that what you call a Freudian slip?"

"The tip-off of a reversion, actually." The corner of her mouth came up in a quick, wry smile. "Years ago, before I went back to school, I used to choose ineligible men. Sometimes, other women's husbands. Disappointed?"

"With what?"

She frowned. "Oh, I see. I didn't tell her because I thought it was premature. If we decide some night that you should wear a gorilla suit—in private, of course—then I'll tell her Mom's on the roof."

"I know that joke."

Diane sipped her kir royale. She was still a little tense, he thought. They were in Shuckers. He had planned to take her someplace less expensive, and when she had insisted on going Dutch, he had suggested the upgrade. "So you're not going to judge me for once having dated married men, eh?"

"What you wanted me to understand was that you learn from experience. I know I do."

She got her elbow up on the bar. She had said she liked bars, and now she was proving it, animated and relaxed at the same time. She was wearing a muted glen-plaid suit and a pink blouse with a thin edge of pink lace on the collar. "Give me an example."

"One of the first things I learned was to keep my mouth shut. If I ever talked two sisters into a three-way, I'd never tell you."

Her eyebrows shot up. "Did you?"

"You asked for an example. That's it."

"You're not going to tell me? Dirty pool! I—"

"Know a lot about somebody's perception of me. We ought to talk about that."

"You mean the sexy stuff? I'm here. I'll leave it to you to figure out whether I liked what I heard, and how you should conduct yourself." She toasted him. "See? You've taught me something already."

"Serves me right. I tell myself I like to be the teacher. A carryover from my job."

"What are you doing these days?"

"It's what I'm *not* doing. We were going to conduct a sweep, but we'd just drive the kids down to the Strip, where they're more at risk. A couple of times a week we've been parking a beat up old cruiser on the Pike to scare off the customers. The kids think they're hustlers, but even they believe cops are hiding somewhere, taking pictures of them. But that's it for the duration."

"Your idea?"

"Yeah. It worked, too."

"I asked around about you. Counselors at Juvie Hall think the world of you. The kids don't hate you, which is a real step up out of the swamp."

"It's not just my idea. Stan Pfeiffer—"

"Ah, the master politician."

"What do you mean?"

"He knows the patter, tells you what you want to hear, and leaves you in the hall wearing only your smile. 'Thanks for a productive exchange of views.' Always."

Boudreau thought her assessment of Pfeiffer one-dimensional. "He and I had a conversation two or three years ago about breaking the whole wasteful cycle of playing bad guy. Unclog the courts. Cut down on the paperwork. All while serving the community better. But this is the police you're talking to, not the welfare. I like busting the bad guys. Watch me sometime."

"I'm sorry, but it seems more and more like an unlikely career choice. You're a round peg in a square hole, Boudreau, don't kid yourself about that."

"I fell back into the family business. My father and his brother didn't want to be waiters in French restaurants, which is what happened to most French émigrés in New York between the wars. My grandfather saw World War Two coming, and shipped his sons to the United States. My grandfather lost all his brothers and cousins in World War One, fifty-three members of the family. When I got to Seattle I needed a job."

"Do you speak French?"

"I *thought* in French until I got to high school. My parents insisted on speaking both languages. English on Thanksgiving, French at Christmas. How old are you?"

"I'm thirty-nine. You're thirty-three, aren't you?"

"Thirty-four."

"I'm not exactly robbing the cradle. Still, there is an element of thrill-seeking in this for me. Before last week, I always caught you at your worst, meanest, nastiest. Very entertaining. You have charm, Mr. Boudreau. Detective."

"And your walk fires my imagination and burns in my memory."

She gave a little growl of pleasure and signaled the bartender and pointed to her glass. "These have promise," she said. "Two more." She reached for Boudreau's hand and squeezed it. "I'm glad you called."

Their table was ready. When the waiter opened the menus, Diane put on glasses, large rimless bifocals with a little floral pattern etched in the upper outside corner of the left lens, like the kind of tattoo women were beginning to wear. She modeled the glasses for him, turning her head left and right. "What do you think? I got these last week. The optometrist's assistant said they had *glam*—that's the word she used. Do they? Have glam?"

"Absolutely. You're going to wear them when it's your turn in the gorilla suit."

"You have a deal. You know what the assistant told me? She said if they slip down, I should dab a little antiperspirant on the bridge of my nose. I tried it, it works!"

"And your nose doesn't offend. What a deal."

She shook her head in mock dismay and looked down at the menu, then closed it. "You know food, I heard. Order for me. How is a man like you able to work with a flaming hemorrhoid like Ron Beale?"

He winced. "You don't want to hear about police politics. Under the circumstances, I can't—"

Diane reached across the table and squeezed his hand again. "Stop. The question was unfair. You told me you couldn't talk."

"I brought it on myself when I told you about Pansy Borland."

"Only because you wanted my attention."

"I had that, if you threw away my phone number because you were angry with me. Let's back up. Originally you sought me out because Adrienne heard from Paulie that I had my own ideas about the case. I do. Why does a guy who dumps bodies in a river suddenly start burying them in remote locations? All the victims but Borland were living on the streets. I think more than one man is involved and Borland was a mistake probably made by the lesser of the two."

Her eyes widened. The waiter arrived and Boudreau asked about the origin of the Dover sole and the waiter said he would have to ask the manager and excused himself. The manager stepped up and said that the fish had come from the Billingsgate fish market in London directly by cargo jet, just as the John Dory had come from New Zealand. Boudreau told the manager to select a California sauvignon blanc and to serve it with their salads.

"I've never been able to get the food thing," Diane said when they were alone again. "I do a lot of my eating on the run."

"If you're going to eat like an animal, eat like a cat, not a dog."

She sat back.

"My mother used to say that. She said Americans ate like dogs."

"She taught you to cook."

"More like I learned by watching her. She taught French at Long Island City High School, then came home and cooked from scratch every night. I've tried it, and it takes a great deal of skill and planning."

A movement to his side caught his attention, and as he turned he saw Diane look up. A young woman, a little plump, with her dark hair swept up in a retro forties style. For a moment his mind was blank, then he realized that the last time he had seen this woman she had been wearing blue jeans instead of an elegant black dress and pearls. He rose.

"Hello, Betty. How are you?"

"I see you finally got here. I work in the hotel now." She nodded toward the rear door and glanced indifferently at Diane. "How have you been?" she asked him.

"Good. Let me introduce you to Dr. Diane Heidt. Diane, this is Betty Antonelli."

"I know your name," Betty said. "From the U."

"That's me."

"I'm sorry about the trouble you had last year," Boudreau said. "I wanted to get that message to you, but it proved difficult."

"Well put," Betty said stiffly. "I had the crap scared out of me. I did not like it."

"That had nothing to do with me."

"That's not the conclusion I came to." She turned to Diane. "A pleasure to meet you. I hope you really like cops, because you're going to see a lot of them. But who knows? In your line of work, you may be the right woman for him." She gave Boudreau a tight little smile. " 'Bye." She headed to the entrance that led into the hotel. When he looked to Diane, she was watching him merrily.

"I'm sorry, but it's very funny. Here I was worried about your ex-wife."

"I haven't seen this kid in more than a year. And then only once."

"Some once. You left an indelible impression on the little bitch. Oh, well. We already know you're capable of tempestuous relationships."

He rose. "Excuse me. I'll be just a moment."

She laughed at his distress. "Better watch the clock. You don't want to come back to a cold fish."

She was looking up at him, her eyes on his. He stroked her earlobe lightly with his fingertip and started toward the hotel entrance. In the lobby he found Betty talking to the concierge. He moved into her field of vision and waited the few seconds it took her to finish her business and step up to him. "What?"

"What did they say to you? Last year. I thought—"

"You thought wrong. I've done a lot of living since last year and I imagine that a man who sees more pussy than a dentist sees cavities can probably say the same thing. They think you're a bad guy, and now that I see you in here with her, I at least have to wonder. What's the next step in your program? What's the last? Good-bye. Hit the road. If I ever see you again, I'll call a real cop."

She turned and walked away, and after a flash of rage, he did the same thing, heading back into the restaurant. She'd had a year to think about what had been said to her and to rehearse her speech, and in his anger he had to ask himself if he would have heard something like it even if she had never met Beale and Company. Thinking that he really knew how to pick them, Boudreau sat down as the waiter arrived with the wine and their salads. Diane was staring at him again with an eyebrow raised. He went through the wine-tasting ritual and indicated his approval to the waiter, who nodded and backed away.

Diane raised her glass. "Well, if I go any further with you, I can't say I wasn't warned."

"Yeah," he wanted to say, "I'm the fucking Green River killer." "I'll tell you all about it—except the part involving her sister."

It took her a moment. "Performing seals. God help me, I do love it."

———

AS HE DROVE home later a light snow began to fall, and he was in his apartment only a few minutes when the telephone rang. He knew who it was before he picked up.

"I wanted to make sure you were safe. Thank you again for a good time."

"I enjoyed it, too. Thanks for taking the thorn out of my paw." He was referring to what he had told her about Betty a year ago. She had confirmed his first thought after the exchange in the hotel lobby: that Betty might have said the same thing to him anyway, for whatever reason. "And thanks for being so understanding about the blank spots in what I could tell you."

"Perfectly understandable. Don't bother to say more." He had told her that his telephone had been tapped and his apartment probably bugged. "I called for another reason. I got so comfortable with you that I lost track of the fact that you never tried to tell me your side of what happened between Adrienne and you."

"Side?"

"Shhh. You have no idea how rare that behavior is."

"I know I shouldn't have married Adrienne in the first place. What I still don't understand is why I did it."

"If you're really curious, I could direct you to a competent therapist. But my professional opinion is that you would be wasting your time."

"From you, that's a fine compliment."

"Want another? You kiss nice."

"You make it easy. And hard."

"I noticed. Sweet dreams, detective."

"Same to you."

"I'm looking forward to mine."

He made coffee and drank the first cup at his station on the arm of the sofa, where he could see the indistinct shapes of the skyline beyond the whirling haze of the snowfall. He was going to be awake anyway. The good feeling he had taken away from her front door, where they had kissed good night like teenagers of another era, only covered a quickening sense of dread over the rest of what was happening in his little corner of the planet. There was nothing he could do about what he felt as a result of the collision with Betty Antonelli. Beale and Company had smeared him probably only to see what he would do next—was that their idea of proactive police work? From Diane's point of view it might seem that he had already had enough turmoil for a lifetime—except that her own story was only more vivid. In the sixties she had been in San Francisco for the summer of love. "I smoked weed and dropped acid," she had said. "I laid everybody, a regular Who's Who of famous penises."

If this was a test, all he had to do to pass was keep his mouth shut. A few minutes later she wanted to know how Boudreau had gotten so secure that he was not upset by the notion that a woman had an identity that had nothing to do with him. It wasn't his business, he said. In his world, not even Paul was really dependent on him. As the rest of the world was evolving, not all that differently, very few people seemed to find needs and satisfactions in their interactions with others. It was the perfect milieu for the Garrett Richard Lockmans of the world, senseless self-seekers for whom the rights and needs of others had no more moral consequence than fast food. By today's standards he was maybe even a cool guy, but the fact of the matter was that he did not like it very much. What he really wanted was a family. Family life. Nothing else was real.

December 1983

In the middle of winter there was only a slight chance that hikers and campers would stumble across more remains, and Lockman thought he could visit his little Injun friend Martin Jones without having to ride out another of his media-induced storms of suspicion and paranoia. No. Without any prompting from Lockman, Jones did a two-and-a-half gainer into a swamp of depression, bemoaning what had become of his orderly life.

"Nobody cares about your feelings but you, Martin. Listen to your pooh-bah talking."

"I don't get it," Martin Jones said. "How does a remark like that make any sense? You've taken my money, drawn me into your schemes—"

Lockman made Jones wait while he sipped some of his Black Label. "What don't you get? Nobody told you to kill those girls, Martin. You chose to do that."

"You were the one who kept talking about it. You were the one who said he'd already done it. You're the one who kept hinting there was some special thrill—"

"And?"

"And what? Did I feel a special thrill?" Jones leaned forward. "I hate thinking about it. I dream about it."

"All this is happening to you because you didn't do it right, Martin. I tried to tell you, didn't I? Didn't I? That you weren't taking the right attitude. That maybe you weren't temperamentally suited for it. So what happened? While I'm out of town you lose control of yourself and throw a murderous tantrum. No wonder you didn't get it. You didn't deserve to. This is an exploration. A religious quest. You have to think of it that way." He chuckled. "You have to trust to a higher power. Like your pooh-bah."

"What didn't I get? Your remark just now? Or your mysterious thrill? And you can lay off that pooh-bah stuff."

Lockman drained his glass and rattled the ice cubes. "You didn't get me the first drink. Now get me this one, thank you."

Jones snatched the glass out of his hand and went to the bar. Lockman could see that the little geek was burning to be inducted into the next level. A hopeless case. Jones was a degenerate, but the wrong kind for big-time adventure. Lockman smiled when Jones returned with his drink.

"You've been killing girls all along," Jones said. "All those bodies."

"Bones. Dem bones, dem dry bones."

"All right, bones. Who knows how long you've been at it? You told me you weren't—"

Lockman laughed again. "I'm not! Somebody else figured out the way to get away with it."

Jones's eyes narrowed. "Exactly the way you described to me? Don't be silly. How many people could have the same dementia?"

"No, you have it wrong. As usual. You saw me do that woman downstairs, the one you saved for me, you said, because there was no way we could let her go without you going to the gallows."

"You forgot the one we got later that night! And the one we did the following weekend!"

"So I did. So what? Did it ever occur to you, by the way, that I could have untied that first one? I would have been her hero for life! Jesus Christ, Martin, put yourself in my shoes. I don't know that you even did the first three they found in the Green River, that you haven't just been taking credit for them. And you have the nerve to question my friendship."

Jones almost leaped out of his chair. "Oh, no! Oh, no! You saw their clothes! I showed you the clothes."

Lockman pursed his lips and looked away, then back again. "Didn't you accuse me of buying the clothes I've given you? That very thing? I brought you the panties of girls I talked into giving them to me, and you said I'd bought them—"

"You *killed* those girls!"

"There you go again. Who started it all? No matter what you think you may or may not have done in the past while drunk, you really ought to suck my dick now."

"My God, you're a terrible human being."

"I'm going to offer you a deal, Martin," Lockman said. "One of these days—very soon, I promise—I'll kill another one. And you can be a witness."

"Where? Here, or there?"

"Both. I'm going to let you listen over the telephone. Maybe you'll be able to figure out what's going on—what the big thrill is."

Jones shook his head. "First you tell me you're going to kill another one, then you tell me the others were done by some mystery man. Which is it, Lockman? Or are you just a complete phony?"

"I am a criminal mastermind, you impotent little dwarf! The last thing I'm going to do is admit to crime of any kind! That's part of my quest."

"Like trying to convince me that I've—"

Lockman laughed again, drawn away from what he had just said about himself. But it was true, he had been killing girls every ten days or so since he had killed the woman downstairs. "You can't even say it!"

"Why should I let you define the terms?"

"Because you have to follow without knowing. That's your quest. Yes. That's who you are."

"And when is this great event going to take place?"

"Soon. You know I haven't finished my Christmas shopping. I have to go up to Redmond one of these next two weekends with presents for all. You know I have to maintain those relationships. Someday they may have to be character witnesses for me."

Now Jones obviously thought it was his turn to laugh. "If it ever happens that you need character witnesses, the last people who will come to your aid will be Dobbs and Parkinson. They'll do whatever their wives tell them to do. It will look like the women are pussy-whipping them, but they won't care. Who'll take care of them? That's what guys like them worry about."

"What about you?"

"I've already proved myself," Jones said.

"To be what? I mean, besides a cocksucker."

"Read your newspaper clippings."

"You're the one who keeps the scrapbooks!"

"Don't fuck around, Lockman! You're saving everything!"

"My lifetime project, you mean? I explained that to you a long time ago. No one else has ever done what I'm doing. A complete record. I can tell you exactly what I did in the second grade. Do you wanna hear?"

Lockman dug into his hip pocket. Jones leaped back. "*What are you doing?*"

Lockman giggled. "I was getting a quarter out of my pocket to give to you. So you could buy a clue. You haven't got one, you know."

———

BEALE AND CHEONG wanted him on the Strip. He had to hang out, circulate, look busy. The guys who worked the Strip, hillbillies and niggers mostly, complained that the Green River killings were screwing up their business. He continued his own scams, trading in choice jewelry and fur coats, chasing a traveler's check here and there, trading police equipment and other collectibles, and refitting and selling cars he bought at municipal auctions around the Northwest. Beale and Cheong were pressing him for information on the Green River case, but there wasn't any. Just before the holidays he told them there was a rumor that a girl had gotten away from the killer after he had tried to push her into a station wagon. What had alerted her was the absence of handles and lock buttons on the interiors of the rear doors. Beale wanted to see him immediately. Lockman said he needed twenty-four hours.

His problem was that the whore who had given him the story had heard it from another, who had assured her that the girl to whom it had happened had left town. At this stage of the game, Beale and Cheong wanted names. Lockman was going to have to give up his source, and she would figure out who had talked to the cops. He was going to have to think of something, and this was not the kind of pressure that spurred his imagination to its best efforts.

He made sure he was late getting to the parking lot, pumped up when he got into the backseat of the big Ford.

"Sorry. I know you want the name of the girl who told me about the station wagon caper, and I have that, but let me ask you something—"

"No jokes, Lockman," Cheong said. "We have no time for fooling around."

"No, no. You have plainclothes guys out on the Strip, right? Well, one of them has been spotted. Drives an old sporty coupe, a blue Cougar or Firebird, something like that. Tattered black vinyl top. I heard this from a couple of the girls, and I checked it out with one of the pimps, a guy who calls himself Grover."

"We know Grover," Cheong said.

But not to talk to, Lockman knew. When he was drunk Grover liked to brag that he had done three years for possession with intent to sell when he could have given up his homeboys for no time at all. A real moron. "Anyway, according to Grover, every player on the Strip knows that this sporty-coupe guy is the heat, and when they see him coming, they run for it. Either get him another car or another assignment." He did not pause. "The whore who gave me the information about the station wagon is named Tiny Parker. She told me that she knows the name of the girl who had the problem, who left town. You won't have any trouble finding Tiny. She has a record under that name, and a new tattoo, a kind of a vine, around her left wrist. She's about five-two, stringy blond hair—"

"We'll pick her up," Beale said. "Considering all your experience with cars, I'm surprised you don't know what kind of a car our guy is driving."

"I didn't see him! I'm just relaying what I heard from several people. I know every car that's been built since World War Two. Try me."

"See what else you can get us on both items," Cheong said. That was dismissal. Lockman got out of the car.

He had given up Tiny because he had seen her regularly over the last three months with his real source. If Lockman knew the station-wagon story, so did Tiny—and Tiny had certainly told enough people on her own to keep her guessing about who had snitched on her.

What was interesting to Lockman was that he had thought of her after he had driven up to Queen Anne to Boudreau's street to make sure the Frog was still driving the '73 Mustang clunker he had owned in the summer of '81. Identifying Boudreau's car precisely would not have worked. If anything, in fact, it would have directed suspicion back to him. Beale and Cheong still had Boudreau on their list of suspects, he was sure of it.

Lockman avoided Spokane at Christmas, telling Hazel that the case required that he work long hours of overtime, often undercover. Snow in the mountains in January postponed a belated visit to the eastern part of the state, and when he finally got home, at the end of the month, Al was in the hospital with a pneumonia he had caught from a patient, and Hazel was agonizing.

Al was not all that sick when Lockman made the obligatory trek up to his hospital room, which was filled with a half-dozen priests and members of the faculty of Holy Name University—limits on the number of a patient's visitors did not count when applied to the overripe and malodorous knights and footmen of the church. Old Al was sitting up in the bed, quietly suffering their presence. It was hard for Lockman to tell if they were there because Hazel had told them to come, or because they knew they had to show up to demonstrate to Saint Al of the Purse Strings their concern and friendship. Lockman could tell by looking at Al, propped up against his pillow like a wizened chimp playing Queen Victoria's death scene, that he was not much fooled by these nattering, desiccated turds. Lockman decided to play the role of faithful stepson, and asked Al first, then the others, if there was anything he could get for them from the shop in the lobby. Coffee? Coke? No. No, no, and no, around the little room, a clean sweep. Lockman allowed himself a small, private smile, and when he looked around, he was on the receiving end of the glowing "Hello, sailor!" grin of a two-hundred-and-ten-pound fruit, one of the law-school faculty. He nodded to Lockman as if he had him bedded already. Lockman looked away, determined not to encourage the balding old auntie. Lockman wanted to step out into the hall, but he knew that would only draw the guy into following him. They had been introduced—what was his name? Charles. Anton Charles. Charles was about forty-five, dark-haired and tall. More nervous than ever, Lockman turned his attention to Hazel, who fluttered back and forth among the reverend clergy like a spastic hummingbird. Al was staring at him.

"What are you looking at?"

Al beckoned to Lockman with a crooked index finger. Lockman drew close. Al looked at him gravely. "I've been thinking about you," he gasped.

"You have? What about?"

"You know." His lip curled sourly, Al suddenly put his hand on Lockman's brow and pushed him back with surprising strength and violence. The room fell silent. Lockman looked around. He laughed aloud.

"Last tag! Al! You've been reading *Mad* magazine!"

Al turned toward the window. Hazel moved in. "What's going on? Al! Are you tired?"

"Yeah, he's tired," Lockman said.

"We should leave," Anton Charles said. Lockman didn't have to look around. The others said good-bye and Lockman nodded without looking at anybody. He waited until he was sure the elevator had begun its descent before going out into the hall. He did not say good-bye to Al—later, when Hazel asked why not, as she inevitably would, Lockman would tell her that he wanted Al to rest. When it suited her Hazel never looked below the surface, and trying to interact with her was like being trapped in two dimensions. Lockman was sorry he had come home, but he thought he could make it worth his while if he could put the arm on Hazel for money or steal some of Al's cocaine to sell. The pneumonia might be the start of Al's decline. Lockman certainly hoped so. He did not want to see Al outlive Hazel. If Hazel inherited Al's estate, she would certainly pass it on to Lockman, no questions asked. There was no telling what Al would do—Lockman was not even sure Al would not give it to the buffoons of the cloth and their attendant twits.

That evening Hazel took a telephone call, chatted for a few minutes, then turned to Lockman. "It's for you."

"Who is it?"

"Anton Charles," she said as proudly as if she had been announcing the Vicar of Rome.

"I'll take it in my room," Lockman said.

"Hang on," she said into the telephone, "he's going to take it in his room."

I'm going to take it up my ass, if he has anything to say about it, Lockman thought. He closed the bedroom door behind him. "You can hang up now, Hazel," he said when he was ready. The telephone clicked at once.

"Hi!" Anton Charles sang. "I thought you might like to come out for a bite of supper, if you haven't already made plans with your mother."

"My foster mother."

"Ah. I'm sorry, I didn't know. But it does explain your use of their first names."

"Where do you propose to have a 'bite of supper' in a lunch-pail dump like Spokane?"

"You've been out of town. There's a new place down by the river. It closes early, so we'd have to meet at seven."

"I have to tell you, I don't have any money."

"Didn't you hear me? I *invited* you! You're my guest!"

Chump. "Give me the address, and I'll see you there at seven."

"Why don't I just pick you up? I know where your parents live."

"Uh, no. I have to run some errands, and I may want to drop in on some old friends afterward."

Anton Charles hesitated. "Ah, yes. I see. Well, let me give you the address."

In the living room Lockman told Hazel that he would be meeting Anton Charles at seven o'clock.

"You're not going to visit Al again?"

"I just visited Al. Who is this Charles guy?"

"He's one of the most distinguished members of the faculty of the Holy Name Law School. He must be impressed with you. I can drive myself to the hospital, but what if it starts snowing again?"

"I'll tell Charles I have to pick you up. He'll understand. We'll go back for your car tomorrow. No problem."

Lockman wanted to tell her to spend the night under Al's hospital bed, snow or no snow.

He timed his travel so he would arrive at the restaurant ten minutes late, but then, confused by the old streets near the river, he went around the same block three times before realizing he had to turn left where he had been turning right. He made his entrance at seven-twenty, and thought at once that he had made a mistake. Anton Charles stuck out like a lavender gorilla, and his face lit up like a jack-o'-lantern when he saw Lockman. Lockman took a surreptitious look around to see if anyone knew him. No—he hoped.

"Are you one of those people who's always late?"

A struggle for control? Charles didn't have a prayer. Was he a little oiled? His small eyes looked red-rimmed. "I had to run an errand for my aunt. You know her. She's very upset about Al."

"I thought you said she was your foster mother."

"She is. My parents were killed in a plane crash when I was five years old, and Hazel and Al took me in."

"I'm sorry," he said with genuine contrition. "I imagine you don't re-member your parents very well—"

"But I do. I remember Christmases—everything."

"I'm sorry." The bartender arrived. "What would you like to drink?"

"Johnny Walker Black," Lockman told the bartender. "On the rocks. A double."

Charles leered. "That sounds more like the person I thought you'd be."

"You'll tell me all about it, I'm sure."

"Don't take offense. What I mean is, now that I know that Hazel and Al are your foster parents, I can see how it's possible that you're a cop. They're almost comic relief, aren't they? These tiny people scuttling around so busily trying to buy their way into heaven—"

"I think you ought to stop right there," Lockman said. "Don't say any-thing you don't want me to repeat to your dean or the president of the university or the monsignor."

Charles looked like he was about to wet his pants. "I am sorry. Please. Cheers. I thought—"

"What? What did you think?"

He was quiet, his mouth hanging open. Lockman could see the fillings in his lower molars. Lockman took a good swallow of scotch—he wanted to drain the glass. He looked at Charles again. "You old tart." And he grinned.

Charles stared, pop-eyed. "You're very good! You actually had me fooled! You must be very good at the work you do."

"The best." Now he finished his drink and waggled the glass at the bartender. "You owe me this one," he said to Charles.

"Yes, I do. How did you wind up doing undercover work? You obviously could do so much more with your abilities."

"There's more to me than meets the eye."

"Are you saying you're gay?"

"Like you, you mean?"

"Careful, Spokane is against straight sex, for God's sake. You should know. Hazel and Al aren't all that far from the norm."

Lockman had another drink. "You're hilarious. You invite me out for a bite of supper, in your precious phrase, in the hope of throwing a lip lock on my joint—isn't that right?—and you start off by defaming the people you thought were my parents."

"Well, you're gay."

"Uh, no."

"Guess again, my young friend."

"I'm not that young—and I'm definitely not your friend."

"Ah, but you aren't taking the opportunity to deny that you're gay."

"Whatever I am, if you want to do the deed, you have to say so."

"That's what I like, a control freak."

"Now! I want you to say it now!"

"If you wish."

Lockman waited.

"I want to suck your cock," Anton Charles said calmly, and smiled.

"It's probably not going to happen, actually," Lockman said. "I've never performed a homosexual act, and I've never allowed any to be done to me, either, while I'm sober."

Charles smiled again. "Why, have another drink, you sweet young thing."

"I'm more interested in that bite of supper."

"My God, a hustler, too!"

"How much do you know about undercover work?"

"I know I don't like it. I know that there have been times in my life when I have put myself at risk, wondering whether the person I was with was in fact a police officer working undercover."

"There you are. Undercover takes a special kind of person."

"And you're the best, as you say. But you're still gay."

"If it entertains you to say so, okay. If I were, I'm not sure you would be my type. Let's get a table, I'm hungry."

"Why am I not surprised?"

"Would I make a good lawyer?"

Charles laughed. "You certainly are duplicitous enough. You'd lie to God Almighty—and act surprised when He didn't believe you."

"Makes you hot, eh?"

"Freud said we should understand our complexes because they direct our lives. Maybe it's a lesson I can teach you. Are you thinking of coming back to Spokane, coming to Holy Name? Plunging yourself into the pietistic milieu?"

"I can handle Catholicism."

"Catholicism, Lutheranism, High Church Episcopalianism—it's a nasty mix."

"Don't forget the Baptists."

"Someone in my position never forgets the Baptists. Well, are you thinking of coming to Holy Name?"

They followed the hostess to a table with a view of the Spokane River and the city's eastern-bloc skyline. If Charles wanted the view, Lockman didn't let him have it. The hostess put the menus in front of them, told them to enjoy their dinner, and withdrew. Lockman had not forgotten that he had been asked a question, but he opened the menu anyway. "What's good here?"

"Wonderful!"

"Hmm?"

"You. You're such a manipulative bitch! Everything's good here. Are you thinking of entering law school or aren't you?"

"Given what you just said about me, it doesn't matter what I say, you're going to believe what you want anyway. I am thinking of making a change. It's clear to me that I'm in the wrong end of law enforcement. No satisfaction. You arrest people, you see them on the street a week later." He looked up from the menu. "The good news is it's nice to make somebody hot."

"What's the bad news?"

He had no idea; he was making it up as he went along. "You don't want to hear it."

"Don't get too drunk," Charles said.

"If anything ever happens between us, it won't be tonight. It won't be anytime soon. Can you accept that? I'm just not somebody who moves very quickly. I live with the worst of the human experience, and some of it—no, a lot—has rubbed off on me." He looked out of the window at the lights in the distance, like an actor playing a scene. "I don't know where my life is going. I have a lot of decisions to make." He turned his gaze to Charles, who was lapping up Lockman's performance. "Look, if I do want to make a change, would you be able to help me? Could you put in a good word for me?"

"With your pa—excuse me, foster parents, you don't need my help."

"Your help will get me taken seriously. I know what the priests really think of Hazel and Al. Better still, I know what Al really thinks of the priests."

"I love it! Is he that worried about going to heaven?"

"He doesn't give a shit about heaven. It's keeping Hazel in line that's important to him. He gives a little in the spiritual realm, he takes a lot in the material."

"You definitely don't mean sex."

"I definitely don't. I'm talking about being waited on hand and foot. I've never been more than the foster son because Al is really her baby. Watch them sometime."

"Are you so resentful?"

"It's nothing compared to my parents dying because some mechanic forgot to turn a wrench. He admitted to that. I think he was drunk. The case was mishandled—I'm penniless. *Maybe* Hazel and Al will leave me something. If I have a reason for wanting to become a lawyer, that's it. Did Freud really say that about complexes? I don't know anything about Freud, but from my own life I know that what you said is the true stuff."

"Give me the inside poop on the Green River killings."

"You have to understand that I'm a very small cog in a very big machine. If they tell me to stake out the brass pig outside the Pike Market, that's what I do. The truth is that he's got us running around in circles. The thinking now is that he's a cop. Smart enough to change his MO. The way we're going, the only way we'll ever get him is if we get lucky."

"What is he doing to the girls?"

"The girls who were found in the river had objects in their vaginas—"

"I heard rocks."

Lockman shrugged. "We can't tell much with all the discoveries since because there isn't that much to work with. He's that clever."

"If they catch him, they'll hang him, no matter how crazy he is."

"That sounds very tough, coming from someone who teaches law."

"I'm thinking of Ted. Bundy. He humiliated the police, and they definitely do not like that. As a lawyer, I have had some experience with the police myself."

"They must have loved you."

Anton Charles wanted to clink glasses. "You're a very interesting man."

Lockman wanted to say "Maybe I'll let you get me drunk," but inside he was afraid. He didn't want to think about it. He would need to control the situation far more than Loverlips Charles might be willing to accept. The person Lockman wanted to think about was Deeah Anne Johanssen. Deeper inside, where he was not afraid, she was still alive, smart and sassy, swinging those big, perfect hips. He had acquired her soul. He was full of souls, and he knew exactly how many.

"A penny for your thoughts," Anton Charles said sweetly, a would-be seducer with his hopes still soaring.

All the more reason to let him down with a thud. Garrett Richard Lockman decided to order the New York steak.

JANUARY 1984

On their third date Diane asked Boudreau to pick her up at her apartment in Bellevue, on the other side of Lake Washington, and then she directed him to a sushi bar three blocks from her house. He held sushi in low esteem, but on the telephone she had seemed subdued. He already knew that she was capable of a range of moods, but always for cause, so if she had something important to tell him, like *good-bye*, he wanted to give her the opportunity to express herself on her own terms. They weren't lovers yet, had not discussed it. Like a lot of other people their age, he imagined, they had decided they had nothing to prove to themselves. In the sushi bar, Kiku, Diane asked for a table and ordered sake for two.

"You look so unhappy," he said. The place was brighter than a subway station. "If our genders were reversed, I'd think this was the kiss-off. A woman wouldn't dare break down in a place like this."

"Sometimes you're too smart. No, no. I definitely do not want to call it off. I called Adrienne. The way we're going with each other, it's just a matter of time before I see you in the gorilla suit. I want to function honestly with you. Honorably." Diane stopped while the waitress poured the sake. "I asked her to meet me for lunch. Since we don't see all that much of each other, she arrived at the restaurant understandably apprehensive. I told her that I had seen you on Green River business and that something *had* sparked between us. I said I wanted to continue to see you without feeling I was going behind her back." She looked up and blinked, suddenly trying to compose herself. "She became very upset. In her view I have betrayed her completely. She attacked my professionalism. She said she couldn't trust the counsel I had given her two years ago, when her second marriage collapsed—" Her eyes welled up.

"You don't have to do this to yourself."

"Hush." She found a tissue in her purse and used it. "Finally she said that if I weren't a mental-health professional, she would do whatever was necessary to revoke your visitation rights. Because I am who I am, she knows she wouldn't have a chance against us, she said. I misjudged the situation, Phil. I've made trouble for you and I'm sorry. If I could go back and undo it, I would."

"I'm the one who started this. Please don't forget that. She hasn't called me. And she's not a person who holds back."

"I can't discuss her beyond what I've already said."

"What good would it do? Since she said she knows she couldn't get my visitation rights revoked, I'm not going to worry about it. And I'm not going to get into a confrontation with her if I can avoid it. She knows Paulie loves me. He already knows a lot of fathers disappear on their kids before the divorce is final."

She smiled. "That's one of the things I liked about you a long time ago."

"Let's get out of here."

"Want to go back to my place?"

"Not to fumble around trying to screw. This isn't my idea of foreplay. I really do want to get out of here. This isn't food as I know it."

"I hope you're not too picky to come home and sleep with me. I want to be held. Foreplay for next weekend."

He shook his head. "Next weekend is Paulie. But come for dinner. And a movie. That's what we do."

"Let me think about it."

"Fair enough."

———

DIANE AGREED TO come after all, and when he told Paulie in the car on the way back to Queen Anne that Diane Heidt was waiting at the apartment, the boy never asked how Dad knew her. The sky was overcast and threatening. Maybe he thought the confrontation on South 200th Street was all it took for adults to become friends. His only comment was that he didn't want to see a movie with a lot of kissing in it. Boudreau had made a pot roast, which had filled the apartment with warm, mouthwatering fragrance. A few moments before, Diane had said she loved the apartment, the bright color, the clever assemblage of midcentury junk. When she had opened Boudreau's relatively new photograph album he had suggested that she wait for Paul to guide her through it. "He's the star," Boudreau had said.

"No pictures of you?"

"Oh, sure, when I can find an old lady willing the push the shutter release."

"An old lady?"

"If I have to run after someone for my camera, I want to make sure she's slow and harmless."

"How can I ever forget you're a cop?"

When father and son entered the apartment, Diane was talking on the telephone. Today she was in black slacks and a white blouse—she seemed to have assortments of both. "He just came through the door. Hang on." She put her hand over the mouthpiece. "Wayne Spencer. He wanted me to identify myself. I told him I was bleep of the month. Hi, Paul!"

"Hi. I don't want to see kissy stuff."

Eyes wide, she looked to Boudreau, who said, "He means the movie. Spencer is a cop."

"I know. Paul, will you show me the photograph album?"

"Let's pick the movie first."

Boudreau turned away. "Wayne? What's happening?"

"Another one. Hasn't hit the news yet. South of the airport, where they found the two last September."

"I was there." He looked around. From the sofa Diane watched him as Paulie attacked the newspaper. Paulie knew where the movie ads were.

Spencer said, "You might have stepped on this one. She was like a hundred yards from the others. A dog sniffed her out and dug her up. Now Beale and the FBI guys are wondering how many more are buried there."

"It's about time."

"You can't talk, I guess. She sounds like a nice lady. Bleep of the month? Pretty hot. Here's the deal. They're going to have a meeting Monday morning and decide once and for all whether they're going to put together an interagency group for this case. Big deal, a big-bucks budget. If you want in, I'll say so."

Diane was standing next to him now. Boudreau said, "I don't think Fitzgerald would want to work with me—"

"He's in Dallas, permanently. You want in?"

"Go ahead, recommend me. But I don't think Ron Beale and Kevin Donovan want me, either."

"Fuck them, all they can say is no," Spencer said. "I'll do my best."

"You're learning a lot, Wayne."

"Christ, I hope so. We ought to double-date sometime."

"That might be complicated. Tell me how it goes Monday." Boudreau hung up.

Diane rubbed his arm. "I could hear some of what he said. How could double-dating be complicated?"

"They're kids."

"No problem. I like what's left of your youth—"

"Thanks, I think."

"I wasn't finished. What's left of it in there under your brokenhearted-ness—"

"Brokenheartedness?"

"That's all that's wrong with you, detective. Report me to the Freud-ians. They found another body, didn't they?"

"South of the airport, where I yelled at you for talking to Paulie. Now they wonder how many more are there. How many more are at Star Lake?"

"I want to see *The Right Stuff*!" Paulie shouted.

"It's three hours long," Diane said to Boudreau quietly. "The radio said it might snow later. But if you're up for it, so am I."

"*The Right Stuff* is cool," he called. To Diane, he said, "No kissy stuff."

Diane nodded. "He got me. I admit it. Cool is in your vocabulary? Why won't this Fitzgerald work with you?"

"Let me tell you later. I want to pick your brains anyway. Now it's time to eat."

"Thank God. I've been drooling, it smells so good. I began to wonder if you were conducting some kind of fiendish sensory-stimulation ex-periment."

Three hours. Three hours of thinking the directions an interagency group could take, which would be determined by the size of its big-bucks budget. With several agencies contributing, there would be an endless battle for control. The direction of the investigation wouldn't matter. Here was a chance for the bureaucrats to build an empire. After a year and a half all that had changed was the body count. And it was going to rise. Ted Bundy had been caught because he had gone over the top, at-tacking a sorority house full of girls and then, still not satisfied, going after a little girl. If his choice of victims was a clue, the Green River killer had gone to school on Ted. Bundy had taken his victims from a variety of locations. With the single exception of Pansy Borland, who had been taken from a Seattle bus stop, the Green River killer had fixed on the Sea-Tac Strip, not traveling far with some of the victims. So it *seemed*. Was he clever enough to want the police to think he had murdered impulsively and disposed of the bodies immediately, when in fact he had planned everything with care? Everything else pointed to planning, didn't it?

Outside, a light snow swirled down, melting on the ground. Paulie was tired enough to go to bed without argument. Diane paged through the album while Boudreau fixed her tea. He poured the last of the dinner wine, Fetzer nonvintage cabernet, for himself.

"This is the Rogue River, isn't it?"

He looked over her shoulder as she shifted to the side to give him room to sit down. "Yes. I forget the name of the town."

"Grant's Pass. The locals call it Grant's Pants, among other things. One of my classmates practices in Medford. She has patients who live in Grant's Pass."

"What's the book on serial killers?"

"They do it for sexual pleasure," she said calmly, turning the page.

"Keep talking."

"Symptoms of personality disorder surface in childhood: fire starting, bomb building. Ted Bundy secretly hated his mother. Some men need power over women simply to function sexually. There's a lot of social complicity. Every society thinks its mating custom is the only possible way to do it. My friend in Medford says she sees relationships that are nineteenth century—the men consider the women property, the women submit. It's the same dynamic that makes young women so attractive to so many older men. Begging your pardon, but didn't you say you like to play the teacher?"

"Begging yours, you said you found what's left of my youth attractive."

"Touché." She leaned toward him and lightly kissed his lips.

"What broke my heart?"

"Life. And you'll get over it. I'm old enough to see what will happen to people. You'll be fine."

He put his glass on the table and gathered her in and kissed her. She felt light in his arms. They kissed again, tasting each other. She held him, her cheek against his. "I love to kiss and touch," she whispered. "And I can't keep my hands off you." She kissed him again and moved back. "Who is this Fitzgerald and why won't he work with you? You said you'd tell me later and this is later."

"Are you going home?"

"Eventually. The snow isn't sticking. You need more necking practice anyway. You're ducking the question."

"If you say so. Fitzgerald is a special agent of the FBI. I sucker-punched him and put him in the hospital. He's been transferred to Dallas, Spencer says."

She was sitting up straight. "You got away with hitting an FBI agent?"

"Cops hit each other all the time. Who's going to arrest us?"

"You put him in the hospital with one punch?"

"I'm a New Yorker. I know how to do it."

"What else am I going to learn about you?"

"When I was Paulie's age—my dinosaur period—I thought I found the reason why I was smaller than everyone else. Why I looked the way I do."

"What are you talking about? You're gorgeous."

"My parents took me to French movies. I didn't look like Fernandel or Jacques Tati, God knows, but there were a lot of others I did look like."

"All right, I'll give you that. You look like a certain kind of good-looking Frenchman."

"Well, all by myself, at the age of seven or eight or maybe nine, I decided that we were descendants of Cro-Magnon man—"

Diane laughed out loud.

"You asked what else you were going to learn—"

She was still laughing. "Caveman. Of course. I've been going out with cavemen all my life. Here I am with someone who believes he really is one. I'm sorry, you don't know how funny this is to me."

He tickled her. He had learned at her place last week how sensitive she was. The lightest of touches could set her off. She pulled away. "Don't! No!" He reached for her again. "Oh, God! Stop!"

He did. He was hearing something else. So was she. From Paulie's room. Was he moaning?

Boudreau was up, Diane right behind him. He threw open his son's door. Paulie was sitting on his bed, his face contorted in anguish.

"Don't hurt her, Daddy!"

Boudreau lifted him into his arms. "No, Paulie. We were playing."

Diane brushed the hair out of Paulie's eyes. "He was making me laugh, baby, that's all."

"Diane and I are friends. I wouldn't hurt her—ever. I'd never hit her."

Paulie looked to her for confirmation.

"No, Paulie. Your father is not that kind of man."

"Mr. Travers hit Mommy. Two times."

Boudreau held him tightly, looking over his shoulder at Diane. She shook her head, which he took to mean she didn't know anything about this. She stroked Paulie's head. "Would you like to come sit with us in the living room awhile?"

Paulie nodded against his father's shoulder. Boudreau felt himself sinking. "Is Mommy still seeing Mr. Travers?"

Diane shook her head vigorously—a warning.

"Not lately," Paulie said.

"We don't have to talk about it now. Come on outside. I'll make you some hot chocolate."

"Can I stay awhile, detective?"

"Please," Boudreau said.

She saw something in his eyes: she reached up and stroked his head, too. She understood him correctly. He was going under. The dread he had somehow lost sight of rolled over him in a terrible black tide.

———

ON THE STRIP at a quarter past three, Boudreau saw the first car roll into position at the end of the block in front of him, then the second across the street; he had to look around behind him to see the third, a rusted old Malibu, two guys in the front seat. He got out of the Mustang and leaned against the front fender and waved them in, six deputies from all three cars, and then stood still waiting. They were just getting out of their cars when Boudreau heard the helicopter approach. If he didn't feel so sour, he would have laughed out loud.

"Turn around and assume the position!"

Boudreau obeyed. The helicopter's light came on, the beam darting toward him. With Boudreau finally in the center of the blue-white oval, the helicopter started circling overhead. From the corner of his eye Boudreau could see one of the detectives who had been in the office the afternoon Boudreau had punched the FBI agent. The detective flinched as he recognized Boudreau. He reached for his radio.

"Call Ron Beale!" Boudreau shouted.

"Shaddup!" the deputy nearest him growled as he moved in for the frisk.

Boudreau identified himself. "I'm carrying a nine, under my left shoulder, and a twenty-five on my ankle. My badge is in my hip pocket."

The deputy went for the badge first, something Boudreau would not have done in his situation. "What the hell are you doing here?"

"Following a lead in a kidnap-murder."

The detective who knew him was close enough to hear. "You've put your ass in it this time. I'm calling Dan Cheong. You might get a break from him."

"He won't get a break from me," Boudreau wanted to say.

In another moment the detective was patched into Cheong's home phone. As he spoke he turned away from Boudreau, then turned back again to look Boudreau in the eye as he listened. "Are you kidding?" He listened again, then switched off. "We're going up to town, Boudreau." He turned to the deputy. "Did you get his gun?"

"I was waiting for you to tell me. He says he has two."

"Go ahead. I'm not going to put you in cuffs, Boudreau, but it's that kind of a deal. I'm officially informing you in front of witnesses. Do you want me to read you your rights?"

Boudreau raised his hands to give the deputy access to the guns. He thought of Lockman saying no to having *his* rights read. "What about my car?"

"Give me the keys."

He did, then got in the backseat of a cruiser. As he expected, he was taken straight to Ron Beale's office. They had officially informed him of nothing—this had stopped being a good bust as soon as it had started. Cheong arrived at four o'clock, Beale at four-thirty. "This finishes you, Boudreau," Beale said. "You were told repeatedly to stay out of the Green River case."

"I'm not talking to you until Seattle Chief of Detectives Stan Pfeiffer gets here."

Beale glanced at Cheong. "Have you called him?"

"This is the first he's said."

Boudreau checked his watch. "Let's wait until Pfeiffer comes in. He's usually at his desk before seven."

Beale was looking at Boudreau. "Go ahead and call him now. I want to see what happens."

"You don't understand. He told me to tell you to let him get his sleep."

"What? You're the one who has to explain what you were doing down there. Bringing in Stan Pfeiffer is a courtesy to you. If you don't call him, I will."

Boudreau gestured to the telephone. Beale got one sentence out of his mouth when he suddenly stopped and handed the telephone to Boudreau.

"I gave him the message," Boudreau said to Pfeiffer. "Sorry to wake you."

"We know what we're dealing with," Pfeiffer said groggily. "He's had my memo sitting on his desk for ten days. I'll be down as soon as I can get there."

When Boudreau put the phone down, Beale said, "What do you think you're doing, sandbagging me?"

"I told you, I'm not talking until Pfeiffer gets here."

"Then wait outside so I don't have to look at you."

Pfeiffer was at his desk early to beat the rush hour, which lengthened his trip from home to an hour and a quarter. Under the best of circumstances the trip was still forty-five minutes. If Boudreau had known he had been setting himself up for an all-nighter in an outer office, he would have thought it through again. At least there was coffee.

At the time of the announcement of the formation of the investigative team, Boudreau had told Pfeiffer what he knew about the case, the steps that had been taken against him, and what he knew about Garrett Richard Lockman. "All right," Pfeiffer had said, "throw his name in again. I'll write a memo recommending you for inclusion on the team."

"Wait, there's more." Boudreau told him about Lockman being spotted on the Strip, his own trips there, and why he thought he was on safe ground with his tactics. Pfeiffer eyed him.

"I'm going to continue to do it."

Pfeiffer was a baldish, argumentative fireplug of a man who spent more time taking classes at Quantico than any two other men in the department. He read seven books a week, recommending them as if everyone followed his reading schedule. Recently he had been among the top five finishers for the job of chief of the Long Beach, California, Police Department. He entered the office with his necktie slung over his shoulder and a bag from Winchell's under his arm.

"What did they do, run you in?"

"They took my guns."

"Cheap intimidation. You didn't fall for it, did you? Did they read you your rights?"

"I talked them out of it."

"Good boy. Is the coffee fresh?" He tossed the Winchell's bag to Boudreau and poured himself a big cup of sheriff's coffee. He opened the door to Ron Beale's office. "Ready?" he asked the two inside as he motioned to Boudreau to stay close behind him. "What's going on?" he asked as Beale and Cheong looked up to him. "Share the doughnuts, Boudreau. Let 'em get their own coffee."

"There's nothing funny about this, Stan," Ron Beale said.

"Oh? Not funny ha-ha or not funny weird, as in an illegal arrest, confiscation of property, and what Groucho Marx called *mopery*? Phil had every reason to be down on the Strip. What was your victim's name, Phil? Rita something?"

"Mona Raymond."

"That's our case," Cheong said, taking the Winchell's bag from Beale.

"Prove it," Pfeiffer responded. "Where's the paperwork? Show us your copy of the receipt for Boudreau's file."

"Aw, come on," Ron Beale whined with his mouth full. "You know what kind of pressure we've been under. You can pull this on anybody."

"None of this would be happening if you had read my memo," Pfeiffer said.

Beale glanced at Boudreau. "I read it. I'm not going to discuss it in front of him."

"You don't want to discuss your connection to Garrett Richard Lockman," Boudreau said.

"Connection?" Beale moved toward him menacingly. "What do you mean by that? Are you inferring something?"

"Implying," Pfeiffer said.

"What?"

"The word is *implying*. When I say it, I'm implying. When you say it, I'm inferring. I want to hear what you have to say. Phil, do you mind waiting outside?" He looked back at Beale. "And give him back the tools of his trade."

Beale turned to Cheong, who nodded. With the doughnut bag Cheong gestured Boudreau toward the door and pulled it closed behind them. Across the larger room, a couple of deputies eyed the bag of doughnuts hungrily. Cheong got out a ring of keys to unlock a desk drawer. "You've been a pain in the ass from the very beginning, Boudreau," Cheong said. "You don't know how lucky you are, having Stan Pfeiffer going to bat for you."

"You violated my civil rights—"

"Don't start that again. I told you, we had a tip—"

Boudreau checked his guns. "Garrett Lockman?"

"As a matter of fact, no. But Lockman has given us almost thirty good arrests, robbery, burglary, even a murder in Walla Walla—"

"He'd rat out his mother."

Cheong smiled. "Easy. You're talking about *our* Garrett Lockman. Seattle is going to bust a major car-theft ring, thanks to him."

"He's your Green River killer—"

"Phil! He couldn't hurt a flea! He's scared of his own shadow!"

"That's an *act*, you stupid son of a bitch!"

Cheong's head snapped around. The deputies on the other side of the room looked up. Cheong saw them. "I'm sick of you calling me names, goddammit!" He threw the doughnut bag. It bounced off Boudreau's arm, splitting open and flinging jelly and sugar doughnuts in an arc over his head. The other deputies moved closer. Boudreau stood up. If he threw a punch, not even Stan Pfeiffer could get them off him before he was stomped senseless.

"Have you checked out where he lives? He used to have an apartment, but probably a house now. Check out his cars while you're at it."

Beale's office door opened and Pfeiffer stepped out, waved Cheong in past him, and led Boudreau toward the outer door. In the elevator, he said, "Wait until we're outside." He brushed powdered sugar off Boudreau's shoulder. "I know you're dedicated, Boudreau, but rolling in your doughnuts really isn't necessary."

"Maybe we ought to go down to the Market for breakfast to discuss this."

"That won't be necessary," Pfeiffer said as the doors opened on the lobby. "I've got to go back upstairs. They're still putting together the Green River Investigative Team and it's obvious someone from Seattle has to be in on this phase of the planning. Here's the deal as far as you're concerned: stay away from the Green River case, the Strip, and any contact with Garrett Lockman. Especially stay away from Lockman. He's the snitch who got both Beale and Cheong promoted. If they turn on him, they're going to call into question everything he has led them to so far, and the questioning could get to cases they've made, cases-in-progress, the reputations of prosecutors. Until and unless something positive turns up about Lockman, he's an untouchable—and as of now, you're a pariah—"

"There'll be hell to pay if the papers get wind of the fact that Lockman walked away from King County—"

"They won't get wind," Pfeiffer snapped, "and if they do, we can handle them. You don't understand the precariousness of your situation. Beale wanted a pound of your flesh. You were lucky I could talk him out of it—"

"Don't side with them, Stan, they're building a disaster—"

Pfeiffer raised his hand like a traffic cop. "You're not getting it. I was lucky to get out of there without an interdepartmental firefight. You've never been an administrator, Phil. This kind of decision can be easy or it can be difficult. It's up to you. Easy, you promise me you go back to your turf, stay there, and continue to do the excellent work you've been doing. Difficult, well—" He paused, studying Boudreau.

"All right, I won't make trouble for you."

Pfeiffer broke into a sudden broad smile and clapped Boudreau on the arm. "I knew I could count on you."

Boudreau grinned. He'd been had, and it had happened so fast he hadn't been able to see it coming.

Mᴀʀᴄʜ 1984

Lockman turned off the I-5 where it paralleled Sea-Tac and then he turned west. The snowfall that had started at dusk was heavier now and he was beginning to worry he would find the Strip completely deserted. The side streets were white, tracked black where cars had traveled, building up on the sidewalks, parking lots, and unpaved yards. He was desperately excited, unable to focus. He couldn't get the heater setting right. The temperature that was comfortable for him allowed the snow to build up on the windshield. The snow silenced everything, too, and made him more nervous and sweaty. Were the cops out tonight? Would plainclothesmen stand around in the wet, falling snow to protect a collection of teenage cocksuckers? Not if the grumbling that Lockman had heard meant anything. That so many of the girls were black only made things simpler. "These people are animals," one guy had told Lockman. "All I'm going to get for stepping between two of them is a knife in my gut."

A block from the Strip, Lockman stopped for a light, the windshield wipers thumping. A woman ran up to the passenger side of the car and rapped her knuckles on the window. Without looking her way, but smiling to himself, Lockman let the car roll toward the curb. He reached across the seat and opened the door.

She didn't get in, just held the door open and tilted her head toward him. A white girl, oval-faced, her snow-speckled straight hair parted in the center. Now Lockman allowed himself a big grin. A Ted Bundy All-Star, the kind Bundy loved, and Lockman hadn't even had to go as far as the Strip to get her. He would send old Ted a note, except that right now Ted Bundy would trade anything to save his own life. Lockman knew Ted Bundy's *soul*. Bundy was, after all, the guy who had starved himself in jail so he could squeeze between the bars to escape. The cops had watched him lose every pound and had been too dumb to believe their eyes.

"Get in," Lockman said.

"Don'tcha even wanna say hello?"

Now he knew why she was down here—in the snow, yet. *If I only had a brain.* "I'm trying to get you in out of the weather. Come on. You want to party, right? I got a place just south of here."

She got in, her eyes on his eyes. Her mouth widened in a tentative half smile. "How much do you want to spend?"

She was trying to act sexy, but it was clear she didn't know anything about sexy. The real reason why she was a whore. She might have had sex with two hundred men, but she didn't have a clue to how to really get a man *interested* in her. Worthless. It made him want to kill her right now, but he wasn't going to be tricked that way. He had already decided that the one he harvested tonight was going to last. His penis swelled. "I have a hundred," he murmured, knowing what her reaction would be. *Phony bitch!*

"Oooh," she moaned, "you want to have a *gooood* time!"

Exactly what he had expected, a cheap imitation of the late, unlamented Jayne Mansfield. He could have written the line himself. Did they go to a bad school somewhere? "You got it, babe." He had already prepped himself and the car and now he pulled a hundred-dollar bill from his coat pocket. "And you're going to get this." He balled it up in his palm and shuddered. "But not now," he gasped.

"You sound like you just came."

He had, a little, but she couldn't possibly imagine why. The hundred went back into his pocket. "So what if I did? I'll come again. What's your name?"

"Debbie."

Debbie? He wanted to vomit. Jayne Mansfield had given him an idea.

He took his carefully folded handkerchief from the other coat pocket, put the car in gear, and pulled away from the curb and made a U-turn. "Unzip me, I want to wipe up. No, wait a minute," he added, doing the kind of acting he wished she was capable of. "There's a bottle of vodka in the glove box. Get it for me, will you?"

She fell for it. "Got any coke?"

"Not here. Give me the bottle." They were doing twenty-five as they neared the I-5. He slumped in the seat so she could work his zipper. As her head disappeared below the window line he took both hands off the wheel to unscrew the cap on the vodka bottle. She had his pants open and was looking around for the handkerchief, which he had palmed, and was now dousing with chloroform from the vodka bottle, his hands well away from his face. Debbie looked up.

"Hey, what are ya doin'? What's that smell?"

Too late. He had the handkerchief over her nose and mouth as he pulled the car over to the curb, braking down to a crawl. She struggled, but he was much too strong for her. She dug her nails into his flesh as she held her breath. *Go for it, bitch, you'll only need to take a deeper breath.*

Lockman knew from trial and error that the falling snow made it impossible for passing drivers to see what was going on in here. Debbie kicked the passenger door, still trying to hold her breath, which was good; when she finally inhaled, she'd get enough chloroform to put her out until he got her into the garage in Portland. He held her more tightly. It would never occur to a girl in her situation that he had practice. She was like an animal that had sprung a trap: all she knew was panic.

At last her lungs heaved. In another moment she went limp, floppy as the corpse she was soon to be. He pushed her into the footwell on the passenger side where no one would ever see her, her head down against the transmission tunnel, her butt against the passenger door. He didn't have to worry about cops pulling him over for a traffic violation on a night like this—they had told him as much themselves, Beale and Cheong and the others, in one of the many casual conversations into which he had drawn them when they thought he was fawning over them. Cops were like any other civil servants, unwilling to put themselves out under even the best of circumstances. In this weather, cops who were supposed to patrol the interstate were parked under one or another of its underpasses, reading girlie magazines. Lockman hadn't needed Cheong and the others laughing their asses off at stories of cops' antics to know that much. He had seen it himself when he hadn't even been looking for it.

Lockman got the cap back on the bottle, his arms out straight, the car filling with the smell of the chloroform. He held his breath, working as quickly as possible. Always a splitting headache, no matter how little of the stuff he breathed. If he lost his concentration, he could slip into a depression that would make him think he was losing his mind.

He got rolling again and cranked the window down. Melting snow pelted his cheeks, and he realized he was smiling. Dumb as she was, he was thinking he was going to make her last, at least until Jayne Mansfield time.

On at least three occasions he had been so excited he hadn't bothered to take the girls anywhere, but had crushed their larynxes here in the front seat of the car. Once he had killed one with the body of another in the trunk. His first doubleheader, he had gone back to Portland barely able to keep his eyes open, and then had slept around the clock, his car in the garage, one corpse in the trunk, the other staring dead-eyed through the windshield. Garrett Richard Lockman knew how to do it. He was the maestro. Fuck Ted Bundy, who equaled him only in passion. Caught because his teeth matched a bite taken out of a victim's backside? More than passion, reckless abandon, which was stupidity. *Maybe* Jayne Mansfield. Lockman had a Filipino machete in the closet of his bedroom in Portland, carbon steel so sharp his breath could set it singing. Jayne Mansfield had been beheaded in an automobile accident. Like La Mansfield, Debbie would see it coming. Guillotined heads sometimes lived for minutes after they rolled into the basket.

He hoped. He wanted to see the expression on her face.

In the end, he decided to let her live for a while. He worked his way through his chloroform headache by carrying her from the garage down to the secret room, the sanctum sanctorum, as Martin Jones had called it, and after she was secure on his obstetrician's examining table, stripped, bound and gagged, her feet firmly in the stirrups, Lockman went back upstairs and drank a beer with a defrosted pizza. He was promising himself that he would not get drunk this time. When he grew tired of watching *Star Trek II: The Wrath of Khan* on Showtime, he went back to check on her.

Still out, her head flopped over to one side. The table was in the center of the little room, which was fitted into the downhill corner of the house, as far as he could get it from neighbors' places. When he had built the room, Lockman had soundproofed it top and bottom and all four sides. When she awakened, Debbie would be able to see the soundproofing on the ceiling and walls, deeply scalloped Styrofoam pads nine inches deep. She would not be able to see the floor—she would never see a floor again—but under the plastic sheeting the floor was the same as the walls and ceiling, making it necessary for Lockman to remove his shoes before he entered. He had thought the floor, as uneven as a cow pasture, would make moving around too uncomfortable, but in fact only the sheeting, a cleanup necessity, interfered with his mobility. The seven-by-nine-foot area was really cozy, the up-against-the-ears silence more erotic, in Lockman's estimation, than oppressive.

Attempting to play with her while she was unconscious got him nowhere, so he checked the knots on the kerchiefs with which she was bound and then went upstairs to bed.

———

DEBBIE STRAINED TO raise her head to see him. He was sitting on a kitchen chair in the corner. He had cleaned and fed her and covered her with a sheet. "If no one can hear me, why did you put the gag on?"

"Control. You don't do a thing without my permission."

"Let me up. Come on. I can't feel anything in my arms. I'll do what you want, I swear."

"This isn't what the adventure is all about."

He doubted her authenticity. It was much too soon for real bargaining. She was still in the disbelief phase. He took a belt of vodka, then set the bottle on the floor.

"What is it about?"

He didn't answer. He was thinking that he was beginning to get in the mood again. He had awakened with a headache, but it was gone now and she was beginning to interest him. Sitting at her feet allowed him to look up under the sheet, and there was nothing she could do about it. "Do you know who I am?"

"No. I never seen you before."

"No. Think." This was the test. As long as she played dumb, she was not really bargaining. "Tell me who I am." He moved his hips up between her thighs. "Tell me, it's good for the soul. You'll be amazed how purified you'll feel. It's the only way to the other dimension."

She tried to squirm away. "Come on, don't. Let me up. I'll scream. I really will."

"Look around. Do you think anyone will hear you?" She was dry. The K-Y was on the shelf under the examination table. She kept her eyes toward the ceiling. She wasn't going to give him the satisfaction of looking him in the eye. She felt rough inside. Did she have a disease? Now her eyes were squeezed shut. She was getting the idea. She knew who he was. How long this lasted depended on how entertaining she was. He knew what waited on the other side: the monster he was becoming, the discovery he had begun with Deeah Anne Johanssen of blessed memory, with having done something he could never tell anyone, the thing that had isolated him forever. This time he was going to relax about getting to the other side. He hoped. Having the monster fill up in him was terrifying, but it was the only way to understand why the monster was feared by a community of millions.

Now he ejaculated easily and quietly. When he grew soft again, he withdrew and positioned the pail for her urine under the foot of the table. "I'm going back to bed for a while," he said. He had more vodka upstairs. A few more swigs would help him pass out. He wanted to wake up with no memory of having her down here even if for only a moment. He loved the bowel-grabbing realization that he was a being in the process of becoming another being. He now understood the ancient terror of evil creatures. He had attempted to explore the terror from the inside and thus had given himself over to myth. His appetite for the process presently and powerfully overwhelmed his slow-simmering disgust and fear. What he loved, in the final analysis, was the unsolved mystery of why the monster was growing. The part he couldn't see and was only hinted at in the greatest of legends was happening to him. He had entered the world of ancient times, the world that was bound to return in the last days, soon.

The Aztec calendar had run out.

The world had entered the age predicted in Revelations.

He, Garrett Richard Lockman, had made of himself a man so evil he could not look in mirrors.

Demigod.

———

"I GOTTA HAVE my arms free. Please. I can't feel anything above my elbows."

"I'll rub them." He put down the brush with which he had been doing her hair. Her forearms were cold. He was very drunk. And getting to the threshold. The desk telephone with the speaker was on a chair behind her head where she couldn't see it. Martin Jones was listening on his telephone one hundred and seventy-nine miles away in Seattle. "Are you ready to tell me who I am?"

"Please don't. Look, I'll do anything to get out of here. Anything you want."

"Eat my shit?"

"Yes, I'll eat your shit."

"Say it again!"

She did.

"Are you going to tell me who I am?"

"No!"
Getting closer!

———

"MY ARMS HURT!" she gasped. "Cut me free!"
He entered her. "Say it again."
"Please!"
"Again."
"You're that guy."
"Say it."
She closed her eyes. "Green River. Now let me go."
His penis very hard now, he set an easy rhythm. He was remembering Deeah Anne, dreaming of her, his eyes closed. Martin Jones was listening—Lockman could feel the eyes of the misbegotten papoose coming right through the speaker phone. The girl was already dying because of the lack of circulation in her arms for so many days. Garrett Richard Lockman was at the center of the world—or would be, if the world could see what he was doing. "You're still not saying who I am. You have to say that last word."
She let out a wail of pure terror. He had to be careful or he would have his orgasm too soon. "Say it."
"Killer."
"The secret word!" Martin Jones boomed. "Say the secret word and the duck will come down and give you a hundred dollars!"
"Who's that?" Debbie shrieked.
"That's Igor, the monster's only friend. Say hello to Igor." He leaned over her, stroking slowly, and braced his forearm under her chin. "Say hello!"
"Hello."
"Hello, Debbie," Martin Jones said. "We're making you famous. This is your fifteen minutes of fame, only it's not going to last that long. Are you listening?"
"Yes."
"Good-bye, dear."
Garrett Richard Lockman drove himself up into her as he threw all of his weight forward onto his forearm. No scream. Just the eyes, the sudden horror of realizing she was about to die, until, in fact, she did exactly that. Lockman saw again that he had the touch. He was getting to be an absolute expert. He was looking directly into her eyes at the very moment she could no longer look into his. The fear rushed out of her expression and in another moment the look on her face could almost be taken for

love. Surrender. Patiently he waited as her nerves began to twitch as her body died. He moved his hips rapidly as her spine lashed and her vaginal walls contracted.

He ejaculated copiously. The monster roared. Lockman already wanted her back. The love for the adventure ebbed suddenly and familiar oppressive self-loathing flooded into him. Lockman groped for the phone and pushed the button that disconnected Martin Jones. He floated out of his body up to the ceiling and looked at himself sprawled in obscene sexual repose over a corpse. He became all the people in the world looking down on his hideous spectacle and experienced their revulsion.

A scream tore out of his chest.

Debbie was the forty-seventh girl Garrett Richard Lockman had murdered in the past seventeen months. He had done the last twenty in roughly this fashion, which was becoming increasingly difficult to bring to a sexually satisfying conclusion. He had known for some time that he was going to need even more intense adventure to satisfy his jaded taste. Now he promised himself—again—to begin to explore a different fantasy. Not immediately: he had to wait for the whole beautiful and terrible cycle to begin again before he could build the foundation of new desire.

April 1984

Lockman was napping on the Parkinson couch when Tom Parkinson prodded his shoulder to awaken him. "Okay, kids, Garrett and I are going to take over the television now."

Lockman sat up. "What's going on?"

"While you were asleep Sheila called me at the job to say you'd pulled a surveillance all-nighter. What I heard on the car radio on the way home may tell you what you were really doing."

"Nothing would surprise me." Lockman wiped his face with his hands and took the can of beer Tom Parkinson had popped for him. Parkinson clicked the remote until one of the anchor desks blinked into view. A Chinese bitch was earnestly reporting the budget crunch at a suburb's school system. Lockman kept his voice casual and sleepy. "Did they find more bodies?"

"Yeah. And it looks like what you said about the sheriff playing politics is the real scoop. This morning they announce the formation of the

Green River Investigative Team, and this afternoon they find a new dump site with two more bodies. What a surprise!"

Lockman's heart raced. When he had heard the news this morning, he had reeled with the shock of the triumph and challenge. An investigative team! He feigned a yawn. "How do they know it's a new dump site? Where?"

"Highway 18, between Issaquah and North Bend, just south of the I-90, your road to Spokane."

"Don't even say that as a gag. I told you, we haven't eliminated the possibility of the killer being a cop. Two bodies? How does that make it a dump?"

"It doesn't, just that they think it is. They say. Thanks for the invitation to Disneyland, by the way. It's really nice of you. I thought you would find it very suspicious, the discovery coming so soon after this morning's announcement."

Lockman hit on the beer. "What did they say this morning?"

"Just what you've been saying about them having to form an interdepartmental team. King County, the FBI, Seattle, Washington State."

"How do you figure last night's stakeout was politically motivated?"

"Why would they have you sitting in a van all night outside a house where nothing happened?"

Lockman glanced toward the kitchen. This was what he had told Sheila. She must have gotten on the telephone with her bubbleheaded hubby just as soon as Lockman had dozed off. He swigged the beer again. "They told me it was a real lead. According to the behavioral-sciences people, he was supposed to roll last night. Maybe the guy I was watching wasn't the right guy. But nobody told me about any bodies. I hate to disappoint you, Tom, but I think what happened today was reported in the order of occurrence."

Parkinson grinned. " 'Order of occurrence.' I like that. It sounds legal. We're going to see what we can do to take you up on Disneyland. You know we have a baby-sitting problem."

They had to go to the kids' grandparents. Lockman said, "It might be a good idea if you told the baby-sitters that you weren't taking off for a weekend to go to Disneyland. People could wonder about it, see what I mean? Tell them you're just going to L.A., that I have tickets for the *Tonight Show.*"

"That sounds good."

"Okay, but you have to let me know when."

"Just as soon as we can." He toasted Lockman with his beer. "Thanks.

You want to check your messages? Under the circumstances, they might want you coming in."

Lockman waved vaguely toward the television set. "Let me see what the circumstances are, first."

"Oh. Right."

Lockman had to know how serious this was. He had dumped three bodies off Highway 18, one at a distance from the other two—he might be able to judge how effective the new investigative team intended to be by the speed with which it recovered Highway 18 body number three. If it recovered that one at all. Lockman couldn't remember a thing about her, except that she had been black. One of the quickies. There were three more stiffs at North Bend, but it was impossible to predict that the discovery of a new dump site would encourage civic-minded saps to beat the bushes surrounding Puget Sound for more. The spot that concerned him was the emergency dump in Portland. Beale and Cheong knew Lockman was living in Portland—if they found bones there, would they regard Lockman's proximity as too much of a coincidence? Maybe the time had come to move. Or to tell them he was moving, which would work just as well. Where would he tell them he was moving to? Did he have to tell them anything? Snitches disappeared all the time.

Sheila came out of the kitchen to announce that the kids were having their dinner early. "Make a lap," she said to Lockman. "I gotta be nice to you. Tom says." She was wearing a sweatshirt and jeans. She sat with her arm around Lockman's neck and kissed his forehead. "He better watch himself, I might get carried away."

"Well, I won't," Lockman said.

"You're blushing!" she cried. She hugged him tightly, allowing him to feel her soft, small breast against his cheek. "You're so *cuddly* sometimes!" She looked to her husband. "Didn't know that, did you?"

She stayed on his lap as they watched the news program grind through the day's stories. Sports. Weather. Consumer fraud. The New York stock markets, then the Vancouver market, followed by the prices of local issues, starting with Boeing. One of the kids called her mother, and for a long time after Sheila was gone Lockman kept his eyes on the television screen. If Tom wanted to see a reaction to Sheila's friendliness, Lockman was not going to show it. After she had gone to bed during Lockman's last visit, Tom had gotten very drunk and told him how frequently she gave him oral sex. A revelation—the girls of the Strip had nothing on her. Lockman was sure now that her husband was still stuck on the idea of a threesome, even if he couldn't remember it sober. The television screen suddenly lit up with familiar faces, the leaders of the demonstrations against police inaction. The dirty-haired overweight blonde and the skinny shrink from the U. To the overweight blonde, the announcement of the formation of the investigative team just hours before the revelation of the discovery of two more bodies was a little too serendipitous.

"What the hell does that word mean?" Tom Parkinson barked. He knew that Lockman would know.

"Lucky. In the right place at the right time."

"Why the hell don't they say so?"

"Well, look at her. If she didn't use big, fancy words, it would be too easy to see what a big, fat, unwashed tub of shit she really is."

"Look at the other one."

"A lez," Lockman said. A cut to a tape of Highway 18, according to the graphic. Lockman recognized nothing, having seen the area only in summertime. The victims were not named, pending notification of next of kin. Lockman's concentration on the television screen suddenly faded.

They had the names so quickly? He couldn't help noting that only a couple of hours had passed since the police had arrived on the scene. The teeth? Lockman knew he had left no other evidence—these girls had been dead for months, their bones picked clean. Dental charts of missing females were at the fingertips of the police. If they could not figure out what he was going to do next, at least they could put together a list of possible victims—missing girls. Somebody had spent hours going over their dental charts, learning the difference between one whore's mouth and the next.

Beale and Cheong had not mentioned dental charts to him. What else were they up to that he did not know? And the investigative team had just been announced. The station's commentator expressed the hope that the formation of the investigative team would lead to a swift conclusion to this sorry affair. *Pious asshole.* Lockman stood up.

"I better check my messages after all. I'll use the phone in the kitchen."

"Bedroom's all right, if you want privacy."

"I don't need privacy from you guys." He stifled a deep, emotion-purging sigh. He had to get out of here. How close were the police? For all he knew, they were on their way.

At the kitchen table the kids slurped at plates of SpaghettiOs. Sheila gave Lockman a game little smile. Was she getting hot for him? Had she and Tom entered into some kind of a deal? There were guys who liked to watch their wives with other men—if they didn't have Tom Parkinson's background, then whose?

Only Hazel and Martin Jones had called. Hazel wanted him to know yet again that she was very proud of him, and Martin Jones wanted to taunt him about this afternoon's discoveries. "It's just a matter of time before you slip up, Captain Kirk, and then the Klingons will be upon you."

Lockman hung up and punched the exact-time number. It rang twice before the line opened.

". . . you hear the tone, the time will be five forty-two and twenty seconds." *Beep.*

"It's Garrett, checking in." He listened until the woman got to forty seconds. "All right." He checked his watch. "Ten minutes. I'll be there before six o'clock." More listening. "Really? That's great. I want to hear all about it." He cradled the handset and said to Sheila, "You heard. Back to the salt mine. Something may be breaking."

"If I hadn't heard it for myself, I'd have thought things were getting too s-e-x-y around here for you."

"Never." He let her kiss him lightly on the lips.

"I can't wait for that weekend. I've never been on a plane, can you believe it?"

"Well, look, we're going to have to hold off until this case is cleared up. You heard me on the phone. Something's up. We could have somebody very soon."

"Okay, we'll wait for you to say when." She looked to the floor. "We're just kidding, right? All the hugging and kissing. I'm just playing."

"I never thought it was anything else. Geez, if I did anything to make you think otherwise, I'm sorry."

"No, I just embarrassed myself, that's all."

You should know what your husband says about your sword swallowing. He blew her another kiss, waved good-bye to Tom, and slipped out the side door to his car parked in the driveway. He was around the corner before he banged his fist on the wheel. That snotty, skinny, broad-beamed bitch! Was she afraid Lockman knew her husband too well, and was trying to stave off the inevitable? Or had Parkinson kept his real nature hidden from her, and she still thought she was the mom in her own little sitcom heaven? For all Lockman knew, the cops were after him. And he had almost talked himself into taking those two clucks away for a weekend? Hundreds of dollars! Forget the money, what was he going to do when he wanted to talk to a human being?

His hands were shaking! Why were his hands shaking?

May 1984

Three bodies were found in the beginning of the month, two more before the holiday weekend. Two of the girls had been dead only since December of '83, so there was no doubt that the killer had been able to do his work all through the year, if he had wanted. Two disappearances in December that had turned into Green River killings raised another question, asked in editorials in newspapers and on the air: how many Green River killings were there going to be? How many missing women fit the Green River victim profile? One story had it that the investigative team was calling for millions of dollars for, among other things, a computer. Pfeiffer had placed three of his detectives on the team, all staunch allies; Boudreau was surprised it wasn't more. Spencer wasn't calling him now: perhaps he had been cautioned against it. If not, going to ground was the appropriate stratagem for a member of an outfit that did not want to confirm the obvious. After all, how much police training did it take for one to see that calling for a computer meant that the Green River Investigative Team did not have a clue? If the public didn't seem to be getting that message, surely it was being transmitted to a killer who had already demonstrated an effective grasp of police work.

Boudreau knew he could drive himself crazy over the investigative team's waste of what he had to offer. No one in that whole gang knew the streets and its players as he did. Did the investigative team know that even scumbags like Uhuru were scared to death? The Green River killer was destroying Uhuru's livelihood. With girls disappearing and johns afraid to cruise, all that was left to a smackhead pimp was to trust the police who knew him. What the Uhurus of the Pacific Northwest were telling Boudreau jibed with the investigative team's signals: nobody knew anything.

On one issue Boudreau had been completely straight with Spencer: what the Green River case meant in terms of career advancement. The cops who caught the Green River killer would be national heroes. Books, movies, television talk shows—if Ed Sullivan were alive, he would be introducing the intrepid detectives in his studio audience. One had only to reflect on the fates of Eddie Egan and Sonny Grosso of the French Connection case. Egan had become a movie actor, Grosso a television producer. Compared with what they had made as cops, they were rolling in dough.

Boudreau did not tell Diane about Stan Pfeiffer's double shuffle—she knew nothing of Boudreau's suspicion of Lockman, had not even heard Boudreau utter his name. Maybe the internal politics of a college faculty were just as treacherous as those of a quasi-military organization such as the police, but college faculties rarely dealt with issues of importance, much less life and death. Why risk an argument, maybe even a falling-out? He and Diane were in agreement on another issue much closer to home. When Paulie calmed down after his misperception of their horseplay after *The Right Stuff,* he told them that he knew of only the two instances of Mr. Travers hitting Adrienne. Boudreau saw that, in the ugliest possible scenario, Paulie's testimony alone was probably insufficient for Boudreau to take Paulie away from her. And if it were sufficient, then what? Boudreau knew that Paulie loved his mother and his mother loved him. By separating them, or even threatening them with separation, Boudreau would make an implacable enemy of her and a possible emotional cripple of Paulie. If Adrienne's self-esteem was so low that she would let one man get away with hitting her, chances were good that she'd let another—or worse, if she lost custody of her child. Boudreau of all people knew exactly how those processes worked. But he couldn't leave his kid in a situation that his own life experience told him would almost certainly grow worse, and Diane understood that, too. Paulie was much too young to express himself clearly in business like this—but he could be told that if his mother was ever hit again, he should tell his father. For now, that was all a little boy needed to hear. After all, his father, Diane said, was this big, tough, FBI-agent-slugging cop who could protect everybody. And if Paulie ever came to the conclusion that he couldn't talk to his father, his father would be the first one to notice a change in his behavior.

By the end of June Boudreau couldn't resist his curiosity any longer. He called Wayne Spencer early one morning at home.

"I'm glad you called, Phil," Spencer said. "I never heard a word after I gave your name to Dan Cheong. I figured I'd wait until I heard something before I talked to you, but then so much time dragged by, I felt embarrassed."

"No problem. Can we get together and talk?"

"Sure. You ready for lunch at that joint we met in last time? Maybe you'll sit facing the door, so at least I can see you when I come in. You still with that nice lady?"

"Yeah. How're you doing with Piper?"

"Off and on, and you can take that any way you want."

Boudreau had not seen Spencer in over a year and might not have recognized him if they had passed on the street. As it was, what drew Boudreau's attention to the window table Spencer occupied was Spencer's waving arm. New clothes and a haircut made him look like a yuppie asshole television reporter instead of the hillbilly flatfoot Boudreau had met almost two years ago. Spencer rose a little from his chair to shake hands. "I got you a po'boy, salad, and coffee. If you don't want it, I'll take it back to the office. We have a new administrative executive, a guy named Norm Chapman. Maybe he'll want to send the sandwich out for analysis."

"I know Chapman. This is official? Chapman's a budget guy, a bureaucrat. He was head of the sheriff's tech services. The SWAT team, the marine patrol—"

"And helicopters. Chapman is very big on helicopters. Things were bad enough before we got a guy who wants us in our own building, with new furniture. And results. He wants us 'to put something on the board,' like a baseball team. What the fuck is that?"

Boudreau said, "I'll tell you, but first I have to clear the air. That nice lady, as you call her, the one who answers my phone, is Dr. Diane Heidt."

Spencer's eyebrows went up. He smiled. "We never know what you're going to do next, do we, Phil? 'Nice lady' is not what she's called at my place of business. Swell walk for a skinny woman, though, I'll give her that."

"Slim."

"What?"

"Lithe, lissome—she knows all the good words for thin, and *skinny* isn't one of them. If you don't want to talk, that's okay. I had to tell you. Full disclosure."

"I don't disclose shit to Piper. I learned that the hard way, but I live it now. Always will. It's the way life is. You don't disclose police stuff to Heidt, do you?"

"She doesn't ask," Boudreau said gently. "I had to tell you or Beale, or one of those other dickheads accuses you of consorting with the enemy—"

"Tell me about Chapman. What do you think?"

"His presence says that somebody on high thinks Beale has screwed up."

Spencer shrugged, looking out the window. "Life would be a lot easier if you could just shoot guys in the parking lot. What the fuck, I've always gotten an honest count from you. More than I can say for some of the guys on the team. I'm with the sheriff now—transferred when they set up the team. The longer I stayed on the Green River case, the bigger liability I became for the city of Kent. When the transfer paperwork came down, I got the word that some of the guys tried to get the deal undone. They knew how good I was doing, how much I liked it. They wanted to make room for more Seattle guys. Three Seattle guys, then four. They were talking about five, now they're down to three again, and they're talking about two. In, out—fuck those people. Donovan, the FBI guy, stuck up for me. But you have it figured right. Let me tell you what's been happening. I don't know how long Beale is going to stay in charge. We've checked thousands of letters and telephone calls, most of them from nuts, people carrying grudges against their neighbors, people who have no idea how America is supposed to work. If this investigation is screwed up, just about half the blame goes to the good citizens of the Pacific Northwest who are trying to screw each other over maybe just because somebody has an RV in the driveway and it louses up the look of the neighborhood. Hey, man, if the neighborhood can get loused up over what's in one stinking driveway, maybe it was on the edge to start with, and the assholes shouldn't have moved there in the first place."

Boudreau decided to think about the meaning of Stan Pfeiffer's machinations another time. "Spoken like a true cop."

"So let me tell you the other half. Remember that I'm new to this. This case started when that first girl's body was found, where I was first on scene. Everything that has happened since has been put in that case—all the other murders, all the damned letters and phone calls. We had victims on one side of the room, possible suspects on the other side. When they announced the Green River Investigative Team, what we had was just a big fucking mess. The office looked like some weirdo's mobile home. So much shit we couldn't find anything. So they called in this guy from San Francisco. A retired hotshot, an old friend of Ron Beale's. Beale fought for him instead of some others who were being recommended. I thought, This guy is going to save our asses. So he tells us to get our files in order, and when we do that, he'll come back and tell us how to run our case. So we do it and he comes back six weeks later and hates what we've done. Instead of working with us, he files a report with the county executive telling him that we're doing everything wrong. With the report was a bill for fifty thousand dollars. They paid! I couldn't believe it! Beale's pal comes in, reams Beale, and makes off with fifty grand! For wasting our time! I thought sure that that was the end of Beale, but no, the county exec hires another expert who charges the county twice as much and takes almost twice as long. His answer? Put the victim files on one side of the room and the suspect files on the other, and divide us into two teams. In theory we're supposed to meet in the center. In his dreams! He didn't give us a process for exchanging information. Maybe we're supposed to do that on our own time, like in the bar across the street. But thanks to your girlfriend's girlfriends, we can't even do that. We can't go out for a fucking beer without having some dried-up lesbo militant bitch setting up a fucking picket line. Now we got Norm Chapman."

Boudreau grinned. Spencer had changed inside as well as out, that was clear. No one could doubt he was becoming a cop. "Diane told me she wouldn't mind double-dating."

"If you want to go out with Hitler, that's your problem. Include me out."

Boudreau wanted to say, "Look who's talking," but Spencer might have it figured out before he reached the door. Boudreau said, "I'll tell her what you said."

"What the fuck. The thing that gets me is that Norm Chapman went from a patrol car to inside sergeant to inside lieutenant to inside captain without ever working a case."

"Have you seen that guy Lockman since that time on the Strip?" Almost a year and a half ago, Boudreau thought.

"His file from County Jail, now that you mention him."

"Where?"

"On top of a file cabinet. The name jumped out at me. I don't know what it was doing there and I don't know what happened to it after that. This was last fall sometime, and I wanted to call you, but I put it off. Then it slipped my mind until just this moment. Now I'm not even sure when it happened. September? November? One of the things I'm learning on this job is that human memory isn't worth shit. I didn't think to look inside the file, so don't waste your time asking."

"I have to make a call." Boudreau got up, fishing in his pocket for change. The telephones were in view outside, near the street. He had the telephone number of the County Jail memorized. Al Holobaugh picked up his extension on the first ring and Boudreau identified himself.

"Stranger! What's this about a woman in your life?"

"Who told you that?"

"Sylvia Holobaugh, and she never lies. She got it from Adrienne—who is *not* pleased, by the way. All the gorgeous women in Seattle and you have to pick your ex-wife's former shrink? On the other hand, your lady is one of Sylvia's heroes. Sylvia sees your friend giving TV interviews outside the Public Safety Building and she's just thrilled to pieces. Used to be my wife hated that kind of thing. Made her uncomfortable. Pushy women were to be shunned. Well, time marches on, and so does Sylvia. I'm not surprised. By you, I mean. You never go the easy way. If you liked a female Black Panther, you'd be doing the fish in a biker bar and thinking you'd found heaven."

"Maybe you'd like to double-date."

"Screw that. I don't even single-date anymore. When Sylvia wants to see a play, she calls a girlfriend. She says, by the way, that since you're not Adrienne's only ex anymore, Adrienne's complaints are like the kid who murders his parents—what's the word you tried to teach me?"

"Chutzpah."

"Right, he killed his parents and then wanted mercy because he was an orphan. You used to hear a lot of Jewish words on television, but all those guys died, I guess. What can I do you for?"

Boudreau asked him to see if the Garrett Richard Lockman file had been returned. It was going to take a few minutes, and the booth was located where Spencer could see him. Boudreau turned his back to Spencer in time to see a bright flash of inner thigh as a college-age redhead leaped over a puddle against the farther curb. The redhead turned around again to her friend and showed the world a gloriously freckled face. She headed up the street as Holobaugh picked up on the other end. "Phil?"

"Right here."

"It's back. I'll mail you a photocopy, if you want."

He wanted to look at it again. The redhead turned the corner and vanished forever. "Okay. Good."

"Does this girlfriend of yours like *lutefisk*?"

"Nobody likes *lutefisk*, Al. Thanks."

In the restaurant, Spencer was grinning. "Redheads are so much nicer than blondes."

"RPH is the standard for close tolerances the world over. Even the Russians use it."

"RPH," Spencer repeated.

"Red pussy hair. When an engineer says it fits to an RPH, he means it can't get closer."

Spencer shook his head in silent mirth. "Meanwhile we got a guy cruising the city in the death van wanting to try out his new screwdriver."

"That's an awful thing to say."

"Somebody came up with it when we were out drinking one night, and it stuck as a kind of rallying cry, like the Pittsburgh Pirates and Sister Sledge singing 'We Are Family.'"

Boudreau wished he had kept his mouth shut instead of playing good ol' boy. It had made him sound like Garrett Lockman. "The Pirates had something on the board."

By the look on his face, Spencer didn't like that. Boudreau didn't give a damn.

THE TALK BETWEEN Paulie and Diane about camping intensified, and Boudreau wondered about Paulie's response to the idea of inviting her to join them, and whether she would accept an invitation if it was offered, until they sat him down and told him that they were going as a trio—that is, if *he* felt like joining *them*. Boudreau kissed them both, thinking that he had not felt so loved since his own childhood. Paulie was proud of this little foray into self-assertion, even if, at the age of eight, he wanted to maintain a certain reserve about it. He was getting to be a big kid. He had big hair, down to the base of his neck. The kids in his class had big hair, and he was not going to be different. Boudreau *père* had to be careful around Boudreau *fils*'s tender and growing ego. Boudreau looked to Diane as if to ask, "Are all males like this?" She looked back as if to answer, "No. You're worse."

She gave Boudreau a check for her share of the rental of a four-wheel-drive vehicle and camping equipment. "I'll make a list of what we need," she said. "From what your son tells me, you really don't know much about camping."

"What about food?"

"I'll leave the food to you. But no snails or other snotty French things for me."

Boudreau spent his free time the rest of July buying and renting equipment, and when school ended the three of them drove east through the Cascades into apple country and then parallel to the Columbia River north to Grand Coulee Dam, stopping to see Indian artifacts and fish ladders for salmon headed to their spawning grounds in the river's headwaters. Paulie was past dinosaurs and not ready for Indians, but the mystery of salmon going by instinct thousands of miles to their birthplaces wowed him. He wanted to spit over the edge of the dam. Boudreau told Diane he had had to do it himself, off of most of New York's bridges.

"Marking your territory," she said.

"That's not how you do that."

"The immature have no way of knowing." She did the navigating without a map. Working from her list, Boudreau had acquired a portable CB radio, jerry cans of water and gasoline, emergency rations, fishing rods, and flares. In a padlocked tackle box was his police .38—not Diane's advice, but Al Holobaugh's. They were headed into bear habitat, but bear were less of a problem than crazy humans. "If you're going off on your own," he had said, "keep the gun at hand. Better you make a mistake you can bury rather than one that will bury you."

The next day they followed the river north across the border and turned east in Canada into rugged, heavily forested country through Creston and Cranbrook before turning south again into Montana. As they made their way through the mountain passes, radio stations drowned in great hissing tides of static. Paulie had his chin on the dashboard as he watched the sun travel over the trees.

The pavement disappeared and they slowed to fifteen miles an hour. Where the dirt road forked Diane turned onto the narrower of the two tracks. It wound uphill through pine and fir as thick as Boudreau had ever seen. Diane engaged the four-wheel drive and they ground forward so slowly the speedometer needle only twitched on the peg. Diane looked in the mirror at Boudreau sitting behind her.

"How are you doing now, city boy?"

"Fine. Are you going to tell me where we're going?"

"We're here. It's called Little Bitterroot Lake."

They had run through setting up the tent in his living room, and so they were able to erect it again easily in a clearing on a little bluff overlooking the lake. For dinner, when the purple sky revealed Venus under a crescent moon, they had small steaks with the maître d'hôtel butter Boudreau had prepared two nights before, fire-roasted potatoes, romaine with oil and vinegar, and red wine. Paulie fell asleep with his head in Diane's lap and his father carried him into the tent. When Boudreau stepped outside again, Diane was packing the litter into a plastic bag. The night was fierce with insects' singing and, down at the lake, the croaking of frogs.

"Let's not forget to put the bag in the Jeep before we turn in." She poured what was left of Paulie's wine into their glasses. "I'm going to have the camera ready when father and son are sipping their wine again. He copies your every move."

"Thank you for bringing us here."

"You're welcome. Tomorrow we fish, explore, look for animals." She touched his glass with hers. "Thank God we brought the cook."

"Maybe we'll catch some fish and see some animals, but we will definitely eat and drink well, until our bellies are well distended."

"Yuch."

Boudreau broke a dry branch over his knee and threw the pieces into the fire. A thousand orange sparks churned up toward the canopy of cold white stars. "A literal translation of a treasured compliment. I want Paulie to know how to live well, and this is something I couldn't have arranged myself. I'm grateful to you for making it happen."

"I don't want to get married, Phil. I don't want to live with you, either. I love you and can't imagine ever being so intimate with anyone else, but I don't want to do your laundry. Can you live with the way things are?"

Boudreau studied her in the firelight. He had thought of marriage, but he had also asked himself if their relationship was a problem that needed solving. "I have to tell you that I've learned a lot about patience since I've met you. I don't know why. With you I'm happy keeping my mouth shut. You're the shrink. Why?"

"Who we are depends on who we're with." She put her hand between his legs. "You've heard the expression 'She brings out the best in me.' It's a true thing."

"I didn't have that with Adrienne."

"I know. Put the trash in the Jeep and clear off the backseat while I go get my cough drops."

"You're not coughing."

"For the menthol. You haven't lived until you've had a mentholated blow job."

"Is this another Heidt household hint?"

"What are you talking about?"

"If you have that antiperspirant on the bridge of your nose, you'll be able to see how you're doing."

She stared at him, speechless. He doubted she would get the chance to finish what she wanted to start. The Jeep's windows were going to be closed, so they could make some real noise together without scaring Paulie.

They awakened in the Jeep and stumbled giddily into the tent and crawled into their double sleeping bag. Boudreau was almost asleep again, his nose against the back of Diane's neck, when he felt her stirring. She was reaching for Paulie, to hold him close through the sleeping bags the way his father was holding her. "Puppy," she murmured.

On the night before they were to head home Boudreau cut up the last trout and sautéed it in a pan with some butter, oil, onions, chopped celery leaves, and bits of bacon, poured the mixture into a pan layered with torn-up stale bread, then added eggs mixed with Gruyère and cream. He covered the dish with foil and put it in the Jeep, which had been vented earlier of the hot air of the day. At this hour the Jeep was a nearly perfect refrigerator.

"Another friggin' omelette?" Diane asked. She was organizing the backseat to accommodate Paulie's Little Bitterroot Lake trophies. Paulie was reading *The Cay,* by Theodore Taylor, and wanted to finish it so badly he was using a flashlight as a reading lamp.

"Tomorrow's breakfast. My mother used to prepare something like it on Saturday night for Sunday brunch, with leftover vegetables, ham, bacon, a mixture of cheeses, whatever we had."

"Right," she said, "another friggin' omelette."

"Another friggin' omelette," Paulie called gleefully.

"You're going to get me in trouble with your mother if you repeat that word in front of her."

"I know what it means," he said.

"All the more reason," Boudreau said.

"I know," Paulie answered, going back to his book.

"Last year you couldn't listen to the same radio station for two minutes."

"This is a good part," he said without looking up.

Diane leaned over his shoulder. "No wonder. Listen to this." She pretended to be reading. " 'Lord Charles swept young Becky up in his arms and passionately kissed her hungry, wet lips.' Pretty good. Me next."

"It doesn't say that! It's about this little kid on an island with an old guy trying to survive and stuff."

"Does the old man make friggin' omelettes?" She was looking at Boudreau. Paulie didn't answer. Two days ago Boudreau had made the mistake of counting the hours until the time they could be alone, and that had made the day seem long indeed. Now they were going to have to wait until tomorrow night in his apartment before they could do some serious fooling around. "I want to hear more about young Becky," he said to her.

"You will."

Paulie didn't look up. "You two are nuts," he said. "You think I don't know what you're really talking about."

The next morning they headed south to I-90 and then west through Coeur d'Alene, where they stopped for gas. While Boudreau waited for his credit-card receipt he picked up a copy of the Seattle *Times*. According to the story bannered across the top of the front page, the remains found near South 146th Street earlier in the week had been positively identified as the work of the Green River killer. South 146th Street was at the north end of Sea-Tac Airport. The gas-station clerk told him that the public telephones were on the wall outside the office. At the door Boudreau mimed to Diane where she waited with the Jeep next to the pumps that he was going to make a call.

"There's more to it than what the paper says, Phil," Spencer shouted across a bad connection. "It's all still very hush-hush. What I can tell you is that we have a suspect. We're bringing him in for a lie detector test tomorrow. He agreed to do it. He wants the attention. It fits the profile."

"Is it Garrett Lockman?"

"I can't tell you anything. Get back here to Seattle and we'll meet for lunch. By that time we'll have the whole thing wrapped up."

"Have you seen Lockman recently?"

"I'll tell you everything when I see you."

Boudreau hung up and turned around. Diane was standing three feet away. Her eyes were locked on his. "They have the killer?"

"Spencer wouldn't tell me anything."

"You mentioned a name—Lockman? In everything you've said to me about the case in all these months, you've never so much as hinted you had a name."

"I couldn't. Under the circumstances. Are you going to drive?" He headed for the Jeep, forcing her to chase after him.

"You don't want to talk?"

"I can't! Not when all I have is a suspicion that no one will take seriously."

"That the investigative team won't follow up on, you mean?" She glanced at the Jeep, where Paulie was in the backseat with his new collections of rocks, ferns, and mosses. "What do you think all our protesting has been about?"

"That isn't the way the police operate."

Her eyes rolled heavenward. "Oh, Jesus."

He stopped. "Look at me. If any of these guys got the idea that I was using you to promote my ideas about the case, my career would be over—"

"Don't you see that this is exactly what's wrong with the whole damned country?"

"I wasn't finished. I was going to say, and no one would follow up on my candidate. Ever."

"And he'd keep on killing until he died of old age. I rest my case. Jesus Christ. I don't know when the hell I've been so upset. I've always assumed—"

"I don't ask you about your patients."

"My patients aren't *dying!*"

She glanced again at the Jeep and back at Boudreau, who was thinking that they should have stayed in the woods. He stayed silent. Anything he said now would only upset her more. And make him forget—however briefly—about what he could not tell her about Ron Beale and Dan Cheong and what they knew about Garrett Lockman's walkaway from King County Jail. Boudreau had been living with all of it for so long that he had almost forgotten that if it ever became public information, it could burn the city of Seattle down to the bedrock.

Maybe.

Who was this bird they were going to question?

October 1984

"I'm sooo glad you could come," Anton Charles purred, swinging the door open. He accepted the bottle of wine Lockman thrust at him. Lockman was just a little drunk. And cold. On most nights so late in the year Spokane was cold enough for snow. Ever since their meal together last winter, Charles had been gently badgering him over the telephone for what he called a "rematch," calling Lockman the most seductive piece of rough trade he had come across in his life. "Let me get you a drink," Charles said. "Vodka? I remembered, you see." He swept inside — toward the kitchen? Suddenly Lockman realized he was experiencing memories of this place, its old mahogany furniture and kitschy oil landscapes on the walls.

"I was really drunk last time."

"They all say that," Charles sang. He reappeared with two glasses packed with ice and handed one to Lockman. "But in your case, it's true." From under his arm he produced a bottle of vodka and covered the ice in Lockman's glass. "When we got back here last time I offered you my humble brand of scotch and you told me you really preferred vodka. Which of course led me to the conclusion that you were running up my tab at the restaurant. You are what you are, and I've put myself in a position where I can't complain. So. Cheers. Tell me everything about this man your colleagues have been questioning, this suspect."

"Oh, you know I can't contribute to the rumor mill."

"I forgot, you respond only to bribery." Charles smelled of bay rum. "Tonight I'm feeding you a mountainous shrimp cocktail and all the T-bone steak you can eat. So tell me—how do they say?—everything at once."

Lockman had been following the story day and night since it had begun to surface in the Seattle *Times* in September. The first item had reported that sources were saying that the Green River Investigative Team was "talking to" a Seattle man. The team would neither confirm nor deny the report, but would say there had been no arrests. The next week one of the television stations had a name, Robert Marks, and that night all the stations were saying that Marks was a cable installer with his own van.

Now Robert Marks was a full-blown national story, identified as a suspect in the Green River killings by none other than Ronald Beale, head of the Green River Investigative Team. Marks was thirty-one, a little guy who wore glasses, a bachelor who lived with his parents a few miles from the airport. All of the newspapers and radio and television stations were interviewing people who knew him, and their reaction to Marks's new fame ran from deep disbelief to the feeling that their long-standing suspicions were confirmed. Several described him as a loner, which was American code for being a failure with women. Lockman couldn't help laughing. While Marks was in custody Lockman would lay off, and when the dust settled, Lockman would start up again with a different MO. Lockman had killed sixty-two girls and women so far. He wasn't going to worry about Mr. Marks: when the smoke cleared, Marks would be a rich man, courtesy of all concerned, after he sued the pants off them.

"It's tied to the discovery at the airport in August," Lockman said.

Anton Charles's eyes glowed. "I saw that. I thought of you at once. I followed the story with keen interest."

"You should have. I was the one who developed the lead. If you really followed the story, you noticed that there was no mention of how the remains were found. Usually we say a hiker stumbled across them, or a dog dug them up, but this time we said nothing. That's because we didn't want to compromise a potential witness we can't name now, someone whose life would be put in jeopardy."

Charles laughed. "You're wonderful. Just marvelous."

"What do you mean?"

"Even when you're telling the truth, as I'm sure you are, you have the enthusiasm of the born bullshitter. One of the world's greats. No one else even comes close."

"I didn't come here to be insulted."

Charles patted him on the shoulder. "No, of course not. You came here for the sexual teasing. Perhaps, if you get drunk enough, you'll allow a repeat performance of the last time, which I'm sure you don't remember. You don't remember, do you? I can tell by your expression."

Garrett Lockman took a big drink. Charles couldn't know how well Lockman played this game with Martin Jones. "Shrimp cocktail? Do you know how to make a decent sauce?"

"I bought sauce. And horseradish. I was sure you were in a state of blackout last time, although it didn't affect your sexual performance. You told me about an Indian companion, as if you were the Lone Ranger. You really are quite bizarre when you want to be."

"What about law school?"

"Too late for this year, my boy. You won't be able to start until the fall of 'eighty-five."

"But you'll help me get in."

"Everybody will help you get in. I told you that."

"What about the paperwork?"

"I brought an admissions application home with me this afternoon. You'll make an interesting lawyer. You certainly won't be worse than most."

"Let me have another drink."

"Of course. I want to hear more of your adventures."

Lockman felt a bolt of panic, but it subsided as quickly as it had come. *Adventure* was the code word he used with Martin Jones to refer to his Sea-Tac forays, and he had spoken of Jones when he'd been here—but Anton Charles would not have chased after Lockman as he had done if Lockman had told him any part of the truth about Green River. One thing Lockman remembered of the night they had met for "a bite of supper" was that he had arranged to take Hazel home from the hospital, but he couldn't remember actually doing it. He slurped the top half inch of his vodka refill. "All right, I confess. I drank more than I usually do last time. Tell me what happened."

Charles sipped his own vodka. "I performed oral sex on you, as you commanded. You're quite the little dominator."

"You weren't very memorable, I guess. I'm trying to fix the onset of my blackout."

"That's rather hard for *me* to say. We parted company at the restaurant because, you said, you had to pick up Hazel. The idea was for you to come here after that. Don't you remember endlessly going over the directions from your house to here? How special! I was out of my mind with lust and you were so drunk you couldn't retain two lefts and a right. You really don't remember, do you?"

He didn't remember leaving the restaurant. All through the spring, whenever Charles had called, Lockman hadn't been able to remember anything after the waiter had set the steak before him. He couldn't remember chewing the thing. Since he often blacked out when he drank alone, he hadn't given it any real thought. And since June his mind had been on other things, like the expansion of the Green River Investigative Team. Lockman had not seen Beale and Cheong in months. They had not called him, had not told him to call them. They had dropped him—lost interest. Lockman had not been very productive for them lately anyway. And then Marks, the suspect. For all Lockman had learned since the story had broken, Marks was just a piece of police disinformation—a trap.

Lockman had allowed his paranoia to feed on him for weeks, worrying that everything was only a smoke screen to give the investigative team a chance to get closer to him. But nothing. No sign of anything before or after Lockman had gotten Tom Parkinson to record the announcement on his answering machine: "Cliff Lloyd here. Leave a message." Letting Parkinson make the recording had helped ease his frustration over having the Disneyland trip postponed again and again.

The number had always been listed in the name of Clifford Lloyd—and now he had a voice to go with all his credit cards and IDs. The only connection between Garrett Richard Lockman and Beale and Cheong had been Clifford Lloyd's telephone, with its number in the 503 area code. Anyone checking out the number would find that it did, indeed, belong to Clifford Lloyd. Lockman had a roommate? How do you kill all those girls with another guy watching Johnny Carson in the next room? That would stop most cops, or at least slow them down. The investigative team could not reach into Portland without the permission of the Portland PD, and you did not have to be an expert on police business, as Lockman considered himself to be, to know that the Portland department wanted to keep its distance from the people who had fucked up the Bundy investigation and were only doing worse this time around. No hard evidence of Green River killings had been found within a hundred and twenty-five miles of Lockman's Portland address, all the justification the Portland PD needed to keep the investigative team north of the Columbia River.

But if the team went farther, if by some miracle it got the cooperation and assistance of the Portland PD, if he was put under surveillance, if a friendly judge gave the team permission to tap his telephone, Lockman would be the first to know it. A tap always caused a drop in line voltage, and in all that police electronics equipment Lockman had the device to measure his telephone's line voltage. He used it every other day or so. The voltage was as steady as a rock.

That left only Hazel needing to know why there was a strange voice on his answering machine. Lockman told her that he had gone under deep cover and that his partner, Cliff Lloyd, would forward all his messages. An unexpected bonus: deep cover gave Hazel more to worry about, less he could tell her. Al was still recovering from his pneumonia, or pretending to: when he wasn't in his office, he was horizontal, napping on their plastic-covered couch, or on a chaise in the backyard taking the sun, or going to bed early, or sleeping late. Lockman could not help enjoying this turn of events. Al was in denial. He wasn't as strong as he had been before the pneumonia, but whatever had been in his fevered little brain that after-noon in his hospital room was now being systematically avoided. He didn't want to go up against Hazel, especially on so serious a question. Lockman wanted to rub Al's nose in it, but restrained himself not because he was afraid of Al, but because there was no point: Lockman had every-thing he wanted.

But he could lose the battle being fought here, if the noises this old fruit was making had any truth to them. Lockman's notions about law school had gotten more serious as the investigative team had taken root. A convicted felon couldn't possibly become an attorney, of course, but that wasn't the question. Lockman was eligible for veterans' benefits. He had a place to live, his old room in Al and Hazel's house. He would be over thirty-five before he would have to figure out what to do next—and per-haps by that time Al would be dead, and Hazel ready to leave their estate entirely to her nephew/foster son.

Lockman asked himself if he could actually kill her, if he felt he had to hustle the process along.

"What are you smiling about so slyly?"

"I was thinking of my aunt."

"Your *aunt*? Oh, yes, I see. The sight of your Mister Jim ready to frolic would probably kill the old girl dead as a doornail."

Mister Jim? No chance now of Charles lying about what happened last time. Lockman finished his drink. He didn't want to black out again tonight—it would be much more fun if he didn't. "I don't know if she'd die, but she certainly would scream, jump up and down, and pee her drawers."

Anton Charles smiled. "You're so sick." His eyes dropped. "I thought of you so much after the last time."

Lockman grinned. He was beginning to see the potential of this situation for the very first time.

———

No physical evidence of the Green River killings had been found near or in Portland, but that didn't mean that physical evidence did not exist, at the golf course three miles to the south of Lockman's Portland house. Whatever his reasons, the self-disgust brought on by seeking his pleasure too intensely and often, maybe even just the damned weather, Lockman had disposed of three of the less interesting subjects in a ravine a hundred and fifty yards west of the back nine of a municipal golf course, rugged land backing onto an industrial park, the kind of cutoff, littered swath nature lovers went out of their way to avoid, rather than explore. He hoped. The fact was that he had made a mistake, and if anything was found so close to home, and Beale or Cheong thought too much about his 503 area code, at the least it meant that the time he had after such a discovery for the purpose of making absolutely sure there was nothing in his house to feed their curiosity would be cut down to an unacceptable minimum.

Lockman took Anton Charles's law-school application back to Portland. He had shown it to Hazel, who had wept. "How soon will you be coming home?" she had asked, and he had answered that it could be as soon as Christmas. What mattered was his energy, or how he used it.

The following Saturday he rented a truck to back up to the garage doors for the big items from the basement. The meat locker door was well hidden in the truck by heaps of soundproofing when Lockman saw Dottie Gold approaching from her house. In sweatshirt and jeans, perfect gear for the all-American Jewish spinster to wear when slogging through the wet, yellow leaves of her neighborhood. She thought they were on good terms again.

Last spring he had stopped at her driveway while she was washing her car. She had waved, and he had gotten out from behind the wheel and waited for her to come to him.

"Uno momento," he'd said. "I just want to apologize for giving your friend so much trouble last summer."

"This is a long time to have a thing like that on your mind. Anyway, it was more like the other way around. Myra sometimes gets belligerent when she has a snootful."

"You told me you didn't drink."

"She has to have company. Wine just puts me to sleep."

"Nobody's perfect," he'd said, getting back in his car.

Now she smiled as she peered around his rental truck. "Cliff? Are you moving?"

"Yes, depending on when my new orders come through."

"New orders? Are you leaving Portland?"

"I never know what I'll be doing. The preliminary order to decommission this facility came down Thursday. Could be anything between thirty and a hundred and twenty days before I hear anything."

"Decommission this facility?" She tried to look in the truck. "Who talks like that?"

"*They* do. They also specify crap like that." He gestured to the piles of foam. "Talk about government waste! Anyway, what can I do for you?"

"Actually, if you are moving, a lot. My landlord is going to raise my rent after the first of the year to five hundred, and even though it's a nice house and all, I can't afford that much. So I was wondering, if you're leaving, maybe you could arrange with the owner of this house for me to take it over for you. I'd be the new tenant, is what I'm saying. It would be perfect for me. I wouldn't even need a truck. I could walk my stuff over on a weekend. I like this house. I used to be in it all the time—"

"When? When were you in this house?"

"Take it easy. Before you—"

"Take it easy? You scared the crap out of me."

"I'm sorry! This was before you moved in! I'm sorry I scared you, but—"

"It's okay, it's okay. What? Were you going with some guy who lived here?"

She frowned. "No. A college professor and his wife lived here. She and I became friends—"

"Where are they now?"

"Back in Eugene. He was up here on a grant. They had a short-term lease on this place. God, you're nervous."

"I just have to be careful, that's all. For me, until Thursday, having other people in here was prohibited. You know, as guests. The people you did see around here were part of the organization."

"You'll tell me when you're leaving so I can talk to your landlord?"

"I'll work it out for you, don't worry."

"What happened to that fellow Marks? If you're leaving, the case is over. Why haven't they arrested him?"

Lockman had forgotten exactly what he had told her about Cliff Lloyd's business. "I can't discuss it with you. It's much too sensitive."

"I mean, they had him in for questioning, they gave him lie detector tests, he complained that he was being kept under surveillance, that his business was ruined."

"That's a lie."

"That's what I thought. These guys are all the biggest liars. Why don't you arrest him?"

"I just told you—"

"All right. Be sure to call me." She turned to leave, looking back over her shoulder. "And next time don't be so nervous. You acted like I was going to rape you or something."

He couldn't move. He couldn't take his eyes off her fat rear end as she headed across the lawn toward her house. She couldn't possibly imagine all the things that had gone through his mind while talking to her these past few minutes. He'd tried to think of Anton Charles, trying to find something that would give him a laugh, but his mind wouldn't hold, he couldn't focus on the possibility of Sheila Parkinson, either, playing hot and cold over a plane ride and *Pirates of the Caribbean.* Not even Deeah Anne Johanssen. What crowded out everything else was a sudden, deep hatred of Dottie Gold herself. He was grateful now that she had been in the house in the past; if she had wanted to take a tour, anything could have happened. He would have tried to talk her into staying awhile, and if she had agreed, he would have exposed himself—a wild, first-time idea. If he had done it, she would have headed for the door, running, for all he knew, and he would have tried to kill her. It was absolutely clear in his mind. He would have had to wave Mister Jim at her, and then he would have tried to kill her. Tried. She would have gotten away. If she had gotten as far as the lawn and he had been able to grab her, he would have pulled her back into the house no matter who would have seen them, heard her screaming. *Why so nervous?* Had she actually said that?

She wanted to rent this house?

———

LOCKMAN DROVE UP to Redmond with every intention of picking up Chinese food and dropping in on Jimmy Dobbs. He had not seen Dobbs in a while, which was reason enough to pay him a visit, but in the end it was the reason Lockman stayed in the car and studied Dobbs's house, facing the fact that he was saying good-bye from where he sat. These two years had been the most vivid time of his life, and he didn't know if anything in the future could ever match it.

He drove down to Parkinson's. Again he stayed in the car—here, because he did not want to have another conversation about the trip to Disneyland he had promised and never delivered. *This is kidding, right?* Had Sheila been able to see through him? How much had Dottie Gold seen? Could a woman see something like an encounter with Anton Charles? Provided Parkinson hadn't been trying to make his life sound better than it was, his Sheila and old Anton had a lot in common. *Kidding, right? Hello, Mister Jim. Why, hellooo, Sheila!* A three-way might be all right with Parkinson, but Lockman did not know how far Sheila could be pushed. He decided that the situation was still too volatile to be walked away from. He would call the Parkinsons later and tell them he had to leave town quickly, and would be in touch.

No stopping at Martin Jones's. Lockman had not talked to Jones in two months. No interest. Lockman did not want to hear the guy's possessive whining, his accusatory and guilty moaning, his craven terror. The last round had been over the discoveries at the north end of the airport, a week before the team's announcement that it was questioning Robert Marks. Jones said he had never thought that Lockman had killed so many girls. The community reaction was going to be horrible—terrible. Lockman laughed in his face. What bothered Jones was the possibility of arrest, of being the focus of the most intense unhappy attention. What he couldn't see was that if the intensity wasn't surfacing with the discovery of more and more bodies—eighteen, so far—it wasn't going to surface later, either. It didn't exist, and perhaps that was a tribute to Lockman's planning: you could have your fun killing girls like these at the rate of one a week for a thousand years, and in time people would rather change channels than hear another word about it.

He was headed back for Portland at one in the morning, sober and alert. Driving had done that for him, as he had hoped. He was now operating inside such close personal limitations that he had had to structure a routine that would enable him to stay sober for a job that could be done only at three-thirty or four in the morning, when he was usually drunk or sleeping it off.

Not tonight, thanks. Tonight he was in the mood for a little head— three of them, actually. No moon. Lockman had driven past the place a dozen times, driven the golf course in electric carts carrying rented clubs. He hated the game, but the starter kept putting him into foursomes with old geeks or eighty-pound Japanese women who could not hit the ball forty yards. He would drive ahead to the woods where he had buried the three girls, study it, leave a golf club behind, then return for the club for another good look, to make notes and take compass headings.

He remembered where he had put the three bodies, and it was no surprise they had not been found yet. But he thought he would be able to get in and out without using a flashlight. At the graves he would be able to keep the light low enough so it would not be seen unless someone was well into the woods, looking in the right direction.

Shovel, pick, hunting knife, flashlight, compass, plastic bag, work gloves, rubber gloves, a surgical mask: in all, not a good package to get caught with. What would he tell a cop, that he was looking for mushrooms? He was driving the ambulance tonight, lights off, interior dark. He could park with the back of the ambulance facing the woods, move through the vehicle, and slip out through the rear doors without anyone seeing him go. He figured an hour and a half at the most. He was absolutely certain he knew exactly where he had buried all of them. With nothing to compare with dental charts, the bodies would never be identified. He did not get far before he realized he needed the flashlight. Suppose he stepped on an animal, and it bit him?

The surgical mask allowed him to hear his breathing, like the crewman who took the space walk in 2001. Getting to number one turned out to be as easy as crossing a room. Under the carpet of leaves the ground was hard but not frozen. She was just under the surface, facedown. The awful smell came through the surgical mask instantly, as sharp as a razor. After only fifteen minutes he was covering her up again, spreading the leaves evenly. It was approximately three hundred and fifty yards on a heading of one hundred and thirty-five degrees to body number two, close to the edge of the golf course for about a third of the way. He wound up walking into a wire fence he had not seen during his daytime reconnaissances. He was off line, and didn't know how far. The only way to correct was to go back up to the edge of the golf course where he had taken compass readings by day and do it all over again. By the time he harvested his second trophy, he suddenly had no time to spare, and no confidence in his direction finding.

The sky was purple when he found the third body, and he had to hurry to get back to the ambulance before daylight. Two hours to the Puget Sound area again, the interior of the ambulance dark, one red light on the rack rotating. He was in and out of the woods near Star Lake by seven-thirty, rolling south, all lights out, doing a steady sixty.

He could still smell what he had unearthed. He had never seen anything so terrible in all his life. But it had had to be done. If the bodies were ever found, the first agency on scene would be the Portland PD. Now, with no ID possible, trying to tie the remains to the Green River case only amounted to looking for trouble. Lockman had to forget about it. In the next two weeks he had to rent another truck and load his stuff for the trip to Spokane. He was going to need another self-storage bin there, too.

Dottie Gold was at the end of the driveway picking up her newspaper when he turned the corner. She was wearing a maroon corduroy bathrobe and her hair, unkempt now, looked more gray than ever. She flagged him down, eyeing the ambulance. "I've meant to ask you about this."

"Ever ride in one?"

"No, thank God."

"Smoothest ride there is. Has to be."

"You seem calmer. Did you talk to your landlord?"

"Yeah. You got a deal. Make out the check for first, last, and the security deposit to Walter Murdoch, and I'll leave you the keys when I go before the end of the month."

"Three-fifty, right?"

"Exactly. With the security deposit, it comes to a thousand even. It's some kind of magic number with him. I'll leave you all the phone numbers with the operating instructions for the dishwasher, the washer and dryer, and the microwave. You have to call the cable yourself."

Her nose wrinkled. "What's that smell?"

"What?"

"There's a smell coming out of the ambulance." She leaned forward, her nose twitching delicately. "It's on your clothes! My God, what is it?"

"I spent yesterday at the junkyard."

"Oh, no. Really? Still, that's not right." She ventured close again, only to back up, fanning the air in front of her face with her hand. "Some kind of toxic. Burn those clothes. I'll bring over the money later."

"Just stick it in the mailbox. Walter Murdoch."

"I remember."

He smiled and nodded as he put the ambulance in gear, and she waved good-bye without the slightest idea why he was smiling. *Because you just gave me a thousand bucks, you dumb bitch!* All but begged him to take it, he thought.

———

ONE OF THE bodies at the golf course was found on Tuesday afternoon. The television newscasts gave conflicting accounts of who had first come across it, which made Lockman sit up. Police often failed at getting the story straight for the press. He wanted to call Martin Jones to have him monitor the Seattle television news, but Jones would only freak and bawl. Lockman didn't ever want Jones to see Lockman's own weakness or vulnerability, especially now, when Lockman was leaving the area and Jones wasn't going to be told until the last possible moment.

Dottie Gold was another problem. She had smelled death on his clothes, but apparently had no experience to which to connect it. He had her check—did he want to cash it after all? Maybe it was enough simply to have hustled her out of it. He wanted the money—he could always use a thousand dollars. Lockman positively itched with curiosity about the conclusions of the Portland PD. He considered the wisdom of another round of golf, just to scoot past the site on the electric cart. No—absolutely not. If the Portland police had a brain cell working, they would be photographing everyone who came by.

The doorbell rang at nine o'clock. There was no way he could not answer; the television set could be seen from the front yard. He peered through the blind. Dottie Gold, the collar of a plaid jacket turned up against the cold.

As she rang the bell again Lockman ran to the kitchen and looked into the backyard. Empty. Still not completely convinced she was alone, but seeing he had no real options, he went to the door and opened it.

"Hi," she said, swinging her arms to stay warm. "Did you send my check to the landlord?"

"Oh, yes. I drove it down to the PO."

"You didn't have to do that. May I come in? Actually, that's why I'm here. I should have had a look around before I gave you the money."

He was still holding the doorknob, blocking her way. "Do you think I can't keep house?"

"No, it's not that. It's just good business."

Her hair was sticking out at all angles. Why did gray hair announce itself so boldly? He stepped out of her way and then closed the door behind her. "Come in! Have a look around! Check out anything you want! I'll be in the living room, watching television. The Portland police found a body not too far from here, and I'm watching to see how they handle the press."

She looked alarmed. "Is it a Green River killing?"

"We don't think so. Of course, we don't have to deal with the press, but I personally don't think Portland wants to mix it up in the Green River mess."

"What about Marks? He's still running around loose."

"I just follow orders. Go ahead, take your look around." He headed into the living room. He had wanted to say "case the joint," but that might arouse her suspicions.

"Can I look in your bedroom?"

"Sure, whatever you want." He lowered the television sound so he could listen, remembering a vodka bottle under the bed. He hated the idea of her knowing that he drank alone, but there was nothing he could do about it now. He called, "If you want to go down to the basement, the door is in the kitchen."

"I didn't know there was a basement!"

In another moment he heard her on the wooden stairs. He hit the mute button and listened, rubbing the head of his penis. The basement was empty now, all but spotless. He didn't hear her again until she closed the door in the kitchen. "Okay! You're quite the housekeeper!" She stepped into the living room before he could hit the mute button again. Was she going to say anything about him listening? "Why do you have a telephone extension down there?"

"I don't understand."

"I mean, that's the only thing down there."

"Well, now. That's where I had my office."

"Why not use the den up here?"

"Right where somebody could do some electronic eavesdropping? Train a microphone on the window and hear everything that goes on in the room? That makes a lot of sense." He reached for the remote control, but it seemed to fly out of his hand. It landed in the middle of the room. He stood up, his hand shaking so badly he had to hide it behind him. His lower lip was trembling. "Everything all right? You happy?"

"Uh-huh." She backed toward the door. "I was just thinking again that you haven't been so nervous lately. I guess I was wrong."

"I'm just not comfortable with somebody in the house, that's all. I told you I would have been in serious trouble a week ago if I had let any unauthorized personnel in—"

Dottie pointed to the television set and Lockman turned to it. The station had cut to a news brief with a videotape of cops carrying a stretcher on which bounced a fairly empty body bag. Dottie picked up the remote as the tape cut to a head shot of a Portland PD detective.

"No, no," he was saying. "These remains are in such bad shape that we can't make a determination of the sex of the individual, much less connect it to other crimes."

The offscreen female reporter asked, "How was the body found, detective?"

"Anonymous tip. We're speculating it was a person who walks her dog on the golf course before dawn."

A lie! In all the times Lockman had been on the golf course, he had never seen so much as a single turd!

"You—you can't take a dog on a golf course without leaving a mess."

Dottie Gold didn't turn around. "The dog's owner could clean up as they went along. A lot of people do that."

She was right. He wasn't thinking. Why? Lockman started to feel the stirrings of true sexual excitement. Dottie had the kind of ass he liked, but she was too old. He hated imperfections and the aging process, but he rubbed himself anyway, shuddered, quickly wet his pants, and sighed. Dottie looked around. "You don't agree?"

"What?"

"You don't agree a case like this is hard to solve?"

The cop had said that? "It's a bad idea to give out that kind of information. The less the crooks know about how we do our business, the less business we have to do."

"I have to remember that." Before she turned for the door, she looked him in the eye, faintly smiling. Did she know what had happened to him? Was she making fun of him? Or did she want some for herself? All he knew was that he hated her. Barging into the house when she had already done the deal? Her money was gone! If she had changed her mind about taking the place, he would have given her a phony address for Walter Murdoch and gotten out of here in thirty-six hours. Either way, it was going to take weeks before the real owner showed up for his interest payment and told her his name was not Walter Murdoch. Dottie could consider herself lucky—less than fifty dollars a day for what could prove to be the most notorious house of the twentieth century? A bargain! It even came with a bargain *basement*!

Suddenly Lockman needed air, a lot of it, as a darkness rose up from the floor. He could feel himself becoming dizzy. He wanted to reach for the chair for support, but he was afraid to move. Had she come that close to dying? Yes. He did not know why, or how, but he had almost surrendered without a struggle to the monster. Why? He *knew* Dottie Gold. He did not want to kill someone he *knew*.

The dizziness passed, leaving him gasping. His heart thudded against his chest, actually skipping a beat. He whimpered. He felt he was as close to the edge of eternity as it was possible for a man to bring himself, and he could not see it—he felt denied, turned away, made unworthy by hateful human limitations. If he had killed Dottie Gold, he would have had to eat her heart to let her live on inside him, to console her spirit, to commingle hers with his, to let her find immortality in the monster.

DECEMBER 1984

Now that Robert Marks was consulting a lawyer to file a multimillion-dollar suit against King County, the Green River Investigative Team, and Captain Ronald Beale for ruining his life, the team was telling the press it was pursuing "strong new leads." Before it had announced that Marks was no longer a suspect and "deserved a clean bill of health," he had been fired from his job, someone had burned a cross on his parents' lawn, his father had been hospitalized for a recurrence of heart problems, and the windows in Marks's van had been broken, his tools stolen, and the tires slashed. You did not have to be a Supreme Court justice to know that Mr. Marks would have no trouble tapping into the main arteries of the agencies and individuals at the root of his torment, and if he chose to spend the rest of his life on a tropical isle sipping a Mai Tai the size of Tacoma, Phil Boudreau for one thought he had earned it.

What Boudreau had gotten out of the Marks fiasco—in exchange for coming more or less clean with Diane about Garrett Richard Lockman—

was another window, however distorted, on the workings of the Green River Investigative Team. From what Boudreau was able to infer from Diane's conversation, the protesters had their own sources of information about the team's maneuverings, and the sources had persuaded a majority of the protesters for a time that Robert Marks was indeed the murderer. Throughout, Boudreau saw his own situation as remaining extremely delicate, and he consciously decided not to tell Diane that it was possible that the information being fed to her colleagues had been designed to mislead. On the surface it might seem that the authorities would not want women picketing the Public Safety Building, demanding to know why Marks wasn't being charged, but if the politicians really wanted a swift closure to the case, even if it meant railroading the wrong man to the gallows, they could claim later, if the real killer turned up, or more bodies were discovered, that the protests had pressured those in charge into the hasty, bad decisions that had caused poor, innocent Robert Marks to have his neck snapped. By then so many years would have passed, and the causes for the outrageous miscarriage would have become so muddied, that there would be nothing to do but cut a check for Marks's heirs. Diane was not naive; but if it ever occurred to her that her government might be willing to throw one of its honest citizens into the volcano, she wasn't saying so to Boudreau. If it really was beyond her imagination, it was a measure of the difference in their life experiences: Boudreau could see that framing someone was not only a way for the pols to keep themselves in office, but also had the charm of cost-effectiveness. Compared with the price tag of the ongoing Green River investigation, a couple of mil for the Marks family was a hell of a deal.

In the meantime, while he tried to figure out what Stan Pfeiffer might or might not be willing to do for him now, and while he calculated what he could not tell Diane about Garrett Lockman, including his walkaway from King County Jail, subsequent conversations with Green River detectives, and his curiosity about the Green River case, Boudreau wanted her professional opinion about all the rest, the Nazi paraphernalia, Lockman's interest in police work, the nature of his relationship with Thomas Brownall, his comments about women. In private Diane expressed her professional opinion succinctly: "The guy's a nut."

"The kind who could be the Green River killer?"

"Does he hate women enough to kill them? I don't know. Maybe he hates women more than he did when you knew him, but maybe since then he found a woman who's relieved him of his, ah, surliness. Mental illness, for want of a better term, doesn't stand still, meaning you either get better or you get worse, and it's easier to get worse than better. Somebody else with his symptoms and experience might live his whole life without ever hurting a fly, but that doesn't define a successful life. Chances are your harmless guy would be numb inside, gray, unreachable. In the case of Lockman, his experience with you probably made him worse. What happened to him after jail?"

Boudreau shrugged. He told her that Lockman had had an intense curiosity about his personal life. She laughed.

"If I had come into your life sooner, he might have said you chose a flat-chested woman because you really wanted a boy."

"You did the choosing as much as I did."

"Well, I have always loved rough, hairy guys, and you are a rough, hairy guy. Bitchin', as the kids say. You scared the hell out of him, I'm sure. You're everything he doesn't understand and wants to be, reason enough for him to hate you, and you got the better of him."

"I love your body."

"That's nice." She glanced at her watch. "But the next time the word *flat-chested* gets said in your presence, be a little quicker with the worship, hmm?"

He kissed her on the lips. It was an icy, wet Saturday afternoon. Paulie was with his mother. Boudreau's living room smelled of the potato-leek soup he had reheated for their lunch. He was wearing a sweater she had given him. She was curled up in one corner of the sofa under the quilt she had told him to buy for himself, her tea close at hand on the end table.

"What did you ever find out about Lockman's family?"

He had been looking over the file again only two nights before. Lockman's background was in the probation report filed with the court prior to sentencing on the Eagle Guns and Ammo burglary. Lockman had been born out of wedlock and his mother had surrendered custody to her brother and his wife in Spokane before Lockman had started school. Boudreau remembered something else. "He liked to quote his aunt—his foster mother. 'Lie down with dogs, get up with fleas,' was one of the lines he attributed to her."

"You quote your mother. Wasn't 'Americans eat like dogs,' something she said?"

Boudreau blushed. "I hope you heard affection and respect in my tone."

"I did, as a matter of fact."

"I didn't hear it in his. If anything, he was annoyed by the memory. He was trying to convince me, by the way, that his partner was the real bad guy, not him."

The telephone rang. Boudreau and Diane had taken to screening their calls through the answering machine when they had an afternoon or evening of doing nothing. They stared at each other as they waited to hear who was calling.

"It's Wayne Spencer, Phil. Are you there? Pick up. We've got some new developments. If you're there, pick up."

Diane rose from the sofa, wrapping the quilt around her. "Maybe he doesn't want Hitler listening in."

Boudreau picked up. "Hold on, Wayne. Hitler is going into the bedroom to give us some privacy."

"Jesus Christ, you told her?"

"She's laughing right now." Diane waved prettily as she closed the door behind her. Boudreau said, "Go ahead, what new developments?"

"Beale is out. Clearing his desk. He's taking early retirement. Dan Cheong is being reassigned. Norm Chapman is taking over."

Pfeiffer wouldn't object to putting Boudreau up for consideration by Norm Chapman—unless Pfeiffer thought the incompetence of the investigative team so far was going to rub off on his own reputation. "I think Mr. Marks can expect an early settlement to his suit."

"If he wants to take short money. See? I'm learning more every day. I wanted to ask you some questions about your boy Lockman. I was hoping we could get together."

"Not tonight. We were just gearing up for a nap, and then we're going to see *A Chorus Line*. It's only going to be in town a couple of weeks, and we were lucky to get tickets."

"Can we get together afterward? I need to know more about Lockman now, and I can't go through normal channels because the investigative team is playing mind games with the Portland PD."

"Hang on." Boudreau put his hand over the mouthpiece and opened the bedroom door. Diane was on the bed, the quilt up to her neck. "Can we meet with this guy later?"

"Let him hear my answer," she said. He held the phone up. She cried, "I'm still going to get laid, aren't I?" Boudreau rolled his eyes. She flipped him a bird and pulled the quilt over her head.

—

FROM THE SIDEWALK Boudreau pointed out Spencer at the end of the crowded bar.

"I'll look at him when I'm inside," Diane said. "I'm freezing."

At the door the maître d' raised his hand to keep them from entering. Over the roar rising behind him, he said, "We're booked for the evening, sir. Sorry."

Boudreau flashed his badge. "Police business." He nodded toward Spencer. "That guy's waiting to see me." The maître d's eyes widened. "Relax," Boudreau said to him. "It doesn't concern you."

Closer to the bar, Diane squeezed his arm. "You did that to show him yours is bigger."

"I only showed enough to beat him."

Spencer was displaying his goofy grin of recognition. "Hey, Phil, look at this crowd. Reagan's really fixed the economy, huh?" He blinked at Diane as Boudreau introduced them. "You're something else," Spencer said to her.

"Just call me Adolf."

Spencer shook his head. "Okay, I'm a dumb shit. Piper just went to the john. What are you drinking?"

"Irish coffee."

"Make that two," Boudreau said. He felt a stab of apprehension. He hadn't thought of Piper being here. She liked attention, and it was hard to see how she was going to get it from this group. Unless she demanded it. Yes. How would she be able to resist? "What have you got, Wayne?"

Spencer glanced at Diane. "This makes me nervous."

"Relax, you work for her."

"Lockman. I wanted to reach out for him because Cheong said that he was good for stuff on the Strip. I was with Dan one day when he called Lockman, so I figured when that was, and looked up the number in the telephone logs."

"You're turning into a regular sleuth."

"A junior G-man, I'm telling you. Listen, the number's disconnected. I called the phone company down there—"

"Down where?"

"Oh, yeah. Portland."

"Cheong was calling Lockman at a Portland number?"

"I didn't know it was Portland at first. They got only the one area code for the whole state. I called the phone company, and they had it under the name Clifford Lloyd. What I want to know from you is, does Lockman use aliases?"

"Yeah, sure," Boudreau said distractedly, "he's a real asshole." Given what he knew already, the location could even have been Beale and Cheong's idea.

"As opposed to a fake asshole," Diane said.

"Plenty of them around, too," Spencer said. "Full of phony shit."

"Of course, I wasn't thinking."

The Irish coffee arrived and Spencer reached over the bar to take them from the bartender. "Put these on my tab."

Boudreau nodded his thanks. "Your next step is to see if Clifford Lloyd is Garrett Lockman. Pull his driver's license. You know what Lockman looks like."

"I told you, we're not getting any cooperation from Portland PD. I can ask them, but then they'll want to know why. Green River is out down there in every way."

"All you said to me was that you were playing mind games with them. What happened?"

"That headless body they found down there?"

"What headless body?"

"They found remains, no skull, in a little woods near a golf course. We think it's a Green River, but Portland PD is telling us to go fuck ourselves. They say it doesn't have a head and all the other Green River bodies have had heads. We pointed out to them that he changed his MO after the first five, but that's no never mind to them. Here comes Piper."

And wearing a black cocktail dress that perfectly displayed her tempting cleavage. For a panicky moment Boudreau thought it was his place to make the introductions. He couldn't remember Piper's last name and, rocking with déjà vu, decided he wasn't sure he had ever known it. Spencer introduced Diane by saying maybe Piper had seen her on television. Piper's last name was Thompson, and Boudreau concluded he had never known it. As Spencer handed Piper her drink from the bar, she gave Diane the once-over. "What do you do on television?"

"Oh, he's talking about the news—the Green River protests. I'm a shrink."

"Seriously?"

"Well, sometimes it's fun."

Piper turned to Boudreau. "Phil's just trying to save money. How are you, Phil? We haven't seen you in a while."

"I've been busy."

Eyes back to Diane. "I guess so."

Boudreau said to Spencer, "I'll give you the number of a detective on the Spokane PD. Jack Murphy, older guy, about to retire. Tell him I told you to call. He'll get you what you want—you won't even have to tell him why."

"Nice. Thanks."

"While you're at it you can ask Murphy if he knows anything about Lockman, who comes from Spokane. His foster parents still live there."

"You know a lot about this guy."

Boudreau suddenly remembered that Spencer had said he had only seen Lockman's file. He knew nothing about its contents, nothing about Lockman's walkaway from King County Jail. "Getting the name of the person who owns the property at the Portland address might take a trip down there. In the meantime the telephone company can give you the name attached to that address now. That person might be able to give you some information about Clifford Lloyd. Check with the credit-card companies on both names. I've got a third name in my notes. Murdoch." *Help me with this name, bro.* "Walter Murdoch. Meanwhile you might get a line on where this Clifford Lloyd is by sending a letter to him at the address you have and putting on the envelope, 'Address Correction Requested.' The PO will inform you of the new address, if any." Now he saw that Piper was staring at Diane, who was paying attention to him. He said to Diane, "If you're under a rock in Burma, I *will* find you."

"I admit I am kind of wowed, Sherlock."

Spencer said, "Let's call the foster parents now."

Boudreau didn't want to leave Diane alone with Piper even for a moment. "It's late."

"So what? We call them, ask for Lockman."

"You do it. He doesn't want to talk to me anyway."

"Why is that, Phil?" Piper asked.

"I put him in jail. I'm wise to him and he knows it." He said to Spencer, "Just make sure you know what you're going to say to him, in case he's there."

"What do you do, Piper?" Diane asked as Spencer moved to the rear of the restaurant.

"I'm student-teaching, but I'm not sure I'm going to bother to get my license. I'm thinking of going to New York." She turned to Boudreau. "You're a New Yorker, aren't you, Phil?"

"Yes, but I haven't been back there, except for funerals, in a dozen years. And what I saw I didn't like."

"Why not?"

"It's dirty, crowded, noisier than I remembered." She wanted attention, all right. He turned to Diane. "You've been there. Tell her what you think."

"It's exciting. It might be just her speed. Does that expression date me?" She was looking Boudreau in the eye. "I don't know. She should go and find out. At her age, it might be great fun. Unless she's going to marry her friend here. But I don't think so. Isn't that right, Piper?"

She shrugged. "It's a long time until June."

They were silent. Diane looked at her watch. Boudreau said, "I want to hear what they say to him."

"Thank you." Stiffly. She was not happy.

In another moment Spencer pushed through the crowd. "They were awake. I said, 'May I speak to Garrett Lockman, please,' and the old guy said, 'Just a minute.' Then she got on the phone and asked who was calling, so I gave my name. She asked if I was a friend, and I said I was an acquaintance, which is true, and she said, let's see, I want to get it word for word, 'I'm sorry, but we haven't heard from Garrett for many, many years.' "

Boudreau nodded. He drank a little more of the Irish coffee, wondering how much sleep it was going to cost him. "We have to get going. Thanks for the drinks. I owe you."

Spencer looked disappointed. Diane nodded good-bye, and Boudreau let her lead the way to the door.

The car was a block away, and the misery of the walk through the piercing cold was followed by the misery of waiting for the car to warm up.

"I think I'm going to go home tonight," Diane said.

"All right."

"Well, at least I know why you thought double-dating would be complicated. How is she?"

"What?"

"Can she fuck? If she's as good as she looks, she must be terrific. 'Oh, Phil's just trying to save money,' " she mimicked, " 'How are you, Phil? We haven't seen you in a while.' She could have sent me a telegram. And staring! I thought she was going to ask if I still liked doing it at my age."

"I stopped seeing her six months before I called you."

"I don't give a shit! You betrayed your friend!"

He put the car in gear. It stalled. He started it again, took a breath, and stepped on the gas.

She rubbed her forehead. "It doesn't make any difference if he was your friend or not," she said almost to herself. "You betrayed him. And instead of telling me something, anything, you froze, like a damned kid. Stonewalled? Is that what you were doing? Jesus, is the opinion I formed of the police back in the sixties, when I was smoking dope and protesting the war, all I really had to know about you guys? What did that Lockman say? 'Lie down with dogs, get up with fleas'? I certainly felt that way after dealing with condescending shits like Ron Beale and the sheriff. I thought you were a cut above, but all you cops are alike, aren't you? That big tub of guts called me *Hitler*? What do you call her, Stalin? Vlad the Impaler?"

"I was in a lot of pain at the time."

"So you consoled yourself with that jerk's bimbo?"

He sighed. "That he was a jerk made it easier."

"He's not a jerk now?"

"He's a different kind of jerk. He's hanging around the wrong people."

"Cops, you mean."

"Cops. Stop, please."

She shook her head. "That cunt. You knew she'd try to pull something. That's why you didn't want to go to the telephone with what's-his-face."

"If I'd thought she was going to be there, I would have arranged to meet him next week."

"So your secret would be safe. You were acting like a kid. You conceal things, Phil. This has been nagging at me since last summer, when I finally found out you had your own suspect. Lockman uses aliases? Spencer is acquainted with him? That other cop knew him? What the hell is going on?"

"Ordinary police work, Diane. I told you last summer I threw in Lockman's name at the beginning. He was traveling in the east when the first five girls were killed. Look, the guy is an asshole, one of hundreds I've come into contact with. Thousands. They're our clientele. They lie, cheat, steal, swindle. Most civilians never do get it about them, but you of all people ought to."

She shook her head. "Tonight of all nights—"

"Don't say it."

"I'm forty years old. I don't need this shit. Stop the car. I'll take a taxi to my car."

"Diane, *please!*"

"Stop the car!"

He did.

———

THE FOLLOWING WEDNESDAY, Spencer left a message on Boudreau's machine: "Phil, it's Wayne. I followed those leads you gave me. The person living in that house down in Portland is a woman named Dorothy Gold. I spoke to her on the telephone, told her I was with the government, gave her my employee ID number and a lot of mumbo jumbo about why I was calling. Maybe I really am getting good at this shit, because I'm beginning to scare myself. She's been in the house not quite a month. She knows

Clifford Lloyd, who lived in the house for roughly two years. Kind of a funny guy, she said. He told her he worked for the government in some kind of hush-hush capacity. She actually said to me, 'I didn't know whether to believe him, but I guess I do, now.' You'll love this. She gave Lloyd her check for first, last, and security deposit to forward to the landlord. He told her the landlord's name was Walter Murdoch. Jack Murphy called Portland PD for me. Good guy. They ran Clifford Lloyd in the DMV down there and faxed Murphy the result, and he faxed it to me. It's Lockman. Murphy remembers Lockman as Spokane's leading young nut. When Lockman was a kid he built a bomb that made so much noise a woman who had been diagnosed as stone-deaf actually heard it. Lockman made news of a kind when he got home from the navy. When an officer is discharged from the service, the government will ship a sea-land container home full of his personal stuff for next to nothing. Lockman shipped home a container full of Mexican sombreros and serapes, which he spread around Spokane on consignment. Started a local craze that made the Spokane newspaper. I queried the credit-card companies on the names Lockman, Murdoch, and Lloyd. In the Northwest alone they have thirty guys with those names, and I won't have time to check them, but for all I know, he's all of them. A couple show very many gas and meals charges, like the guys are on the road. If they aren't real people—besides Lockman, I mean—I'd like to match them up to see if they could be the same guy. It's a lot of work, and then what? No crime there, if he's paying his credit-card bills. And it wouldn't be my jurisdiction if he wasn't. As for scamming Dorothy Gold out of first, last, and security deposit, I can't notify the Portland PD without telling them how I learned of it, and why, and I don't think they want us digging up work for them, not with our track record. So La Gold has a problem, and there isn't a hell of a lot we can do at this stage of the game to help her. This Lockman is some character.

"It was nice seeing you and your lady. I hope we can do it again real soon. If I don't see you before Christmas, have a merry. Oh, yeah. Piper sends her regards."

Boudreau already had a call in to Stan Pfeiffer, and the next evening he found an answer, of sorts, on his home machine. One of Pfeiffer's lieutenants. "Stan has your message, Boudreau, and he wants you to know that he appreciates your continuing interest. But for now, and the immediate future, he wants you to sit tight. If you have any additional comment or insight, put it in writing and funnel it through this office."

Put it in writing? At this point, only a fool would put anything in writing, and Stan Pfeiffer knew that better than anybody. *Keep quiet, Bou-*

dreau. Don't call us, we'll call you—and why don't you hold your breath while you're waiting?

—

ON SATURDAY NIGHT, after Paulie was in bed, Boudreau broke out the scotch and drank himself stupid, as much as he hated hangovers. Paulie had asked about Diane, and Boudreau had told him she was busy this weekend. The truth was that Boudreau had not heard from her, and what he had been trying to hold together inside him was beginning to fall apart and blow away.

February 1985

Martin Jones stamped his foot. "Do you know what I've been through? I've been sick with worry. How did I know you weren't dead? How did I know that one of your clients didn't get the better of you and stick a knife in you?"

"Don't say things like that. Don't even think them. I see you bought yourself a new recliner. Looks expensive. Are you comfortable now?"

"It's a BarcaLounger. And I'm very." Jones lowered himself into the thing and pushed back on the arms to put himself in a near-horizontal position. "In my house, I'll say anything I please. I called your house, the number was disconnected. I drove down there, the house was empty. Some crazy woman came running out from across the street, raving about somebody I never heard of. Was I looking for him? Who was I? When I started to leave, she grabbed my arm, tried to restrain me, yelling about her money and calling the cops. I was lucky to get away from there. I'm not sure she didn't get my license number. I'm still not sure that I'm not in real trouble!"

Garrett Lockman grinned and sipped his champagne. "Makes you mad enough to kill, doesn't it?"

"Don't even make jokes like that around me anymore. I'm trying to survive you. So what is this? What are you doing here? What are you up to?"

Lockman sipped again. Jones was wearing a black peignoir, mesh stockings, and high heels. Draped across his precious BarcaLounger, did he know he looked like the luau in a Hawaiian vampire movie? Lockman had called from Spokane and said he was bringing champagne and this was how the little twerp responded. *Dressed to nag.* "I'm going back to school," Lockman said now with carefully affected calm. "I'm going to study law."

"You can't become a lawyer, you stupid shit! You're a convicted felon!"

Lockman giggled. "So far, so good. I've been admitted to law school."

"Probably only because you lied on the application."

"Maybe I let a member of the faculty suck my dick."

"Oh, well, now you're talking," Martin Jones said. "That sounds like your style. Where? Where are you going to go to law school?"

"Holy Name."

"So you're going back to Spokatropolis."

"I *am* back in Spokatropolis."

Jones's eyes widened. "With Hazel and Al?"

"With Hazel and Al."

"They should know what you think of them."

"They do. They know I love them very much."

Jones was quiet a moment, his lips pursed. "So what are you doing in Seattle?"

"I'm here to see you."

"Sure. You drive five hours in uncertain weather to split one bottle of cheap domestic champagne with me."

"The best domestic there is, according to *Consumer Reports.* Thank you for dressing for me, I suppose."

"I didn't dress for you. This is how I relax."

Lockman couldn't help laughing. "Right, and you accessorize for a trip to the 7-Eleven. How butch! Do you want to go out?"

"And do what?"

"Kill some time, if nothing else."

"You just love doing this to me, don't you?"

"Doing what?"

"That's what I mean! Playing your little games, denying that you're doing it, laughing at me when you can see me suffering."

"Do you know what you sound like? You sound like a woman scorned."

"Don't start that stuff again!"

"I wasn't starting anything. In fact, you're the one who thought of it first. I drove here all the way from Spokane to see if you wanted to have some fun, when I've got only until tomorrow afternoon—"

"Why? What are you doing tomorrow afternoon?"

Lockman examined his fingernails. "Another adventure. It doesn't concern you."

"Why did you mention it?"

"Why not? What I'm trying to tell you, in the context of all this censorship you're imposing, is that I care about you and want to know how you're doing."

"Then you taunt me with the idea that your time is limited. What are you doing tomorrow?"

"The weekend, in fact. Can't I have any privacy? I'm going to be out of town."

"You started out of town, if you're living in Spokane!"

"How do you get fixed on these things, Martin? Come on, put some real clothes on, and we'll cruise for a while."

"I don't want to pick up any girls."

"Under the circumstances, that would be silly."

"What circumstances?"

"Relax. You're jumpy as a cat. The circumstances I'm talking about are the circumstances you initiated two and a half years ago. Those circumstances."

Martin Jones's eyes drifted toward the far corner of the room. "I don't think so."

"You don't think so about what?"

"About cruising. That's what you mean, isn't it? I don't think it's a good idea to go out and allow ourselves to be seen soliciting prostitutes. Maybe the police have women working undercover. Maybe they're taking pictures of cars and checking licenses. I don't need the trouble. I think I'll stay home."

Lockman got to his feet. "Then I'll see you around."

"Where are you going?"

"Now? Or tomorrow afternoon?"

Martin Jones didn't answer. He was looking toward the bar, near the floor. He looked like he was about to cry. Lockman said, "I'm going to southern California tomorrow."

Jones's head snapped around. "With the Parkinsons?"

"Did I mention them to you?"

"You know perfectly well you did." He pushed himself to an upright position. "My brain is by no means as addled as yours, as booze-soaked, as sex-crazed—"

"I almost forgot, you've never had sex."

"Better never than to have had it with a corpse!"

"That's what you think."

"I was saying, you hinted about them a long time ago, how 'Old Tom' used to tell you how much he wanted to do a three-way. Maybe he doesn't want the kind you want. Maybe he wants you to be a girl, too. I'd love to see that! One way to stop your raving! You'd do it, too, if you could get Sheila to watch, just to drive her nuts!"

"Give me some money."

"Get it from Parkinson. Wait a minute, where is an impoverished schmuck like him getting the money to pay for a trip to southern California? You bastard! Pay your debts!"

Lockman laughed out loud.

Martin Jones was up. "Give me my money! You're paying! You're paying for that trip! Give me my money!"

Giggling, Lockman dodged out of his way, skipping around the recliner, out into the living room to the front door. "You want your money? Come and get it!"

"What are you doing?"

"The air is stuffy in here." Lockman stepped out onto the dark porch, leaving the door open behind him. Martin Jones quickly closed the door again and parted the curtain to peer at Lockman with one large, round, brown eye. On the front walk Lockman reached into his pocket and pulled out his Detroit. He fanned the roll and put it on the damp pavement. The street was empty. Silently he gestured to Jones to come out. The eye seemed to grow bigger—huge. Was Jones tempted? Lockman danced in circles, fluttering his hands, rolling his eyes, waggling his tongue. He bent over and wriggled his butt at Jones. He couldn't help laughing. He crooned like a coyote. He bent over and picked up the money. His blood rushed to his head as he tried to get another look at Jones's eye. Disneyland again! Lockman could hardly wait!

—

DRUNKEN MONSTER SLEEPING on the Parkinsons' couch—in his dream Lockman knew who he was, where he was. He was visiting a children's home where work was being done on the playground near the wall that kept the adult world out. But the world was in, like it or not. Standing high on a ladder inside was Michael Caine, the English actor, hanging something over the door, not a picture but a placard Lockman couldn't read—a warning? Caine looked down at him contemptuously with his girlish, blond-lashed, pink-lidded eyes. Lockman had taken all the psych courses—Caine was supposed to represent somebody else. The thought skittered away. Caine glared at him as Lockman passed out into the yard again, where the dirt was raked smooth, where no one watched now—or ever would see. It was a dead place.

The dream of the monster, Lockman knew. Lying on his side, he could feel his limp willie lax in his bed of crispy curlies. Sheila hadn't sat in his lap tonight. Since last summer she had been a little huffy around him, thinking, apparently, that the promise of a trip to the House of the Mouse had been a scam. She didn't know the half of it—maybe she would be sorry that the trip was real. Above suspicion, Walt's Acres were criss-crossed underground with concrete catacombs, where, according to a Disneyland employee he met at a bar not far from the park, the so-called clean-cut all-American "youngsters" who worked there did their dope and fucked, like real young people the world over. Lockman looked forward to gamboling in the sunshine over an underworld of sweaty, copulating teens. Lockman had already decided he was going to get very drunk Saturday night in southern California. If he worked it right, he and the Parkinsons would party all night. He hadn't told them that he had reserved adjoining rooms in the motel in Anaheim or about the cocaine in his suitcase that he had stolen from Al. He would get these folks jumping like marionettes, maneuver them into a private performance. . . .

Nothing so fancy in Lockman's silent gravel dreamyard. Nothing grew, not even his dick. Maybe one glaring foreign eyeball.

April 1985

Je t'aime, Boudreau wrote on the card accompanying the roses he sent to Diane, realizing only later that he'd written in the language of his childhood, using words he'd said only to his mother. So be it, he thought.

No response—for a week, anyway. Then, unusually, Mrs. Gunter's voice down below, followed by footsteps ascending the stairs. Boudreau was on his feet before the knuckles rapped on his door. On the landing stood a man of seventy, toothless, wearing a lightweight plaid jacket and knitted watch cap. He worked his lips. "Boudreau?"

"That's me."

The old man thrust a bottle in a paper bag at him. "Olympic Liquors."

"Hang on." Boudreau pulled some singles from his pocket. "Thanks."

"Have a nice night," the old man said, and turned to go down again. Boudreau locked his door and pulled the bottle out of the bag.

Wine, a Robert Mondavi vintage cabernet. The card with it showed a bluebird with a little branch in its beak. Inside, in Diane's handwriting:

Next time make it a six-pack of Henry Weinhard. Let me think.

D.

I *will* be in touch.

Boudreau saw the last not so much as an afterthought as a clarification. When four weeks passed, he thought of sending the six-pack, but then decided to wait. After another week, he sent six Bohemia.

More silence. Paulie knew they had had an argument. He was more than capable of expressing himself.

"I like Diane. So? We're not going camping this year?"

"Look, if you like her and miss her and want to see her, call her or write her a letter. I'll give you her address. Whatever happens between you is your business. I'm not going to hang our problem on you." Boudreau stopped. He had been going to say, "But don't be surprised if she doesn't answer," but he didn't believe it himself. Paulie might have hard lessons to learn about his fellow humans, but Boudreau really didn't think Diane was going to teach him one.

"I know where her office is," Paulie said. "If I write to her, I can deliver it myself and save a quarter."

Paulie's last words on the subject, and Boudreau forgot about them. Then, in May, more than six weeks after he'd sent the beer, she called.

"I'm sorry I've taken so long. Come out for dinner. My treat."

"After all this time, is there anything to talk about?"

"I know you're hurt, but yes, I think there is. Paulie wrote to me and I've talked to him on the telephone at his mother's when she wasn't there. He said you encouraged him to get in touch with me if he wanted to."

"That's right."

She could not fail to hear the guardedness in his tone. "Thank you for that. Please, Phil, let me see you."

Was he going to hurt her when his stupidity had precipitated this in the first place? He owed it to himself to see what she thought was so important. "Sure."

She suggested they meet at the brass pig at the Pike Place Market the following Tuesday night. On Monday morning the Seattle *Times* bannered the story of another headless body discovered in Portland, less than a hundred yards from the location of the remains discovered last fall. Quoted in the second paragraph were "members of the Green River Investigative Team," who were absolutely certain that both bodies were the work of the Green River killer. Boudreau didn't have to talk to Wayne Spencer to get confirmation that the team was fighting its battle with the

Portland Police Department in the press. Diane knew Garrett Lockman had lived in Portland until recently. Boudreau did not want to spend his evening with her talking about Green River or Garrett Lockman, but some conversation was necessary. Whatever she thought of Lockman, Boudreau did not want to have to deal with accusations that he had deliberately divulged police business to her. There were other ways to ensure that Lockman would be investigated again, and Boudreau was going to let her know what they were.

On Tuesday afternoon he walked down to the Market with time to spare. It had been a blustery spring day, the damp air redolent with fresh growth. Since they'd talked, Boudreau had gone over what had happened to them another dozen times, and while he could see that nothing had been said that could allow him to get his hopes up, at the same time he did not want to sink into stony bitterness. He wanted to have a good time. He wanted to see her smiling.

She was waiting, early, too, wearing the plaid suit she'd worn on their first date eighteen months ago. She grinned and then, something she did when emotion filled her—the tiniest gesture—she bowed her head and turned away. He took her hand. He wanted to kiss her, but he reminded himself again that this was her party. She looked tired. "You look good," he said, happy to play the sucker again. She squeezed his hand.

"You're a dangerous man. Still."

"What the hell." He kissed her cheek. She turned her head and found his mouth with her mouth. He had forgotten how thin her lips were. Her eyes were on his, and bright.

"Go for it," she said.

He kissed her again. "I'm sorry I hurt you."

"I know. Thanks for that beer. Mexican beer. I thought maybe I picked a lousy wine and he's trying to tell me something—"

"No—"

She touched his lips with her finger. "Let me finish. You know I'm not the food maven. Drugs and booze, yes, from my misspent youth. As soon as I tasted the beer I knew it had come from the real you. Did anybody ever tell you you're intense, Boudreau?"

"Detective."

"Yes, that, too." She gave a little shrug, looped her arm in his, and steered him into the building. "I made a reservation. We can sit by a window and watch the sun go down. I've got an appointment with the governor. With seven other women. Do you want to be on the Green River Investigative Team?"

"Are you trying to seduce me?"

She pulled him along. "Maybe. Who knows?" They climbed the stairs and he followed her into the restaurant. She ordered martinis. Because it was only late afternoon, the room was mostly empty. Amber shades had been pulled down to diffuse the glare of the sun. The wind had cleared the air and they could see across the Sound to the snowcapped Olympias. Boudreau waited for the drinks to come before speaking again.

"Don't mention my name. Argue that the victim profiles demand that the team have people who have worked with those girls when they were alive. If only because we know how to talk to them. You met Spencer. The other team people I know are no better, and one or two of them may be a lot worse. You see, I've been asking girls who knew some of the victims what kinds of guys those girls attracted. Lockman is definitely among those who would be interested in them."

"Tell me some of the questions you asked."

"Only the one—what kind of guys were attracted to so-and-so. I didn't lead them, I let them tell me."

"Atta boy. What do you know about the Portland bodies?"

"What do *you* know about the Portland bodies?"

"Headlessness? Removal of identity? Theft of identity. The victim may be already dead, but the act is still an attempt to do violence against her. Lockman has identity problems, although I doubt he thinks so."

"Didn't you tell me that we change in the presence of others? We become different with different people? Your profession is giving the customers a big hand job on the issue of identity."

"All right," Diane said, "he's not happy with the people he becomes."

"Look, you don't get it. All I want to do is take a good look at what he's been up to. The team is the best way to do that. I'm not saying he's guilty of anything. I never did. To me, Lockman is a *suspect*. If I've given you the wrong impression, let me nip it in the bud. If a story starts going around, it can be a career killer. As it should be. Okay? You get it now?"

She sat back. She looked out toward the water, quiet a long time. "I forgot how much I loved you loving me. But I was beginning to live your life."

"No, you were sharing my life. I was sharing yours. You said you didn't want to get married. I wanted to think I had accepted that, but maybe I really wanted to win you."

"What does that mean?"

"I wanted you to think the best of me. That was the identity I wanted to have in your mind. I made a mistake. But apparently you had put yourself in a position where it wouldn't take much from me to push you over. I remember how you reacted when you found out about Lockman. My interest in him. I didn't tell you? What made you think I had any obligation to you like that?"

"Why did you want to win me?"

"I loved having you love me back. It was the happiest time of my adult life. What did I do that was wrong?"

"Nothing. I didn't know where we were going. Where you wanted to go. You were always so comfortable—"

"Do you mean it was easy for me? I was grateful, but it wasn't easy. Do you think I cook like that for myself?"

"I did think that you should have told me about Lockman."

"Why?"

"Because of the way we were together. How we got. The closeness. You acted like it was perfect. I thought so. I was delirious for months. You have no idea how vulnerable." She stopped, looking into his eyes. "Ya wanna do it?"

"Oh, you saw that movie." *Prizzi's Honor.*

"I thought of you the whole way through. Noo Yawk. Come on. Let's go to my place."

"What happens after?"

"We order a pizza. Sit around naked. Try to do it again. On the Oriental."

"I don't want to go through a lot of crap with you. I don't want to bounce off walls."

"You want to win me."

"I won't play the sap for you."

"I have *that* movie memorized."

"I'm not kidding. I'm as afraid as you are. More."

"I know. Phil, please. Can we just sit quietly?"

"I'm embarrassed."

"It's all right."

He couldn't raise his eyes. "No, it isn't."

She reached for him. His instinct was to withdraw. He hated it. If he thought about it, he knew, sitting there would suddenly become the hardest thing in the world to do. She'd already offered a way out. What was he going to lose, his self-esteem? He already saw himself as a slimeball. "Pepperoni."

"No pepperoni. Sausage. You give me the pepperoni."

No, as it turned out. In his tension he couldn't talk, and when he tried to turn his silence into a game, she acted uncomfortable, and he withdrew. He sat up in the bed and put his feet on the floor and so did she and that was the end of it. The sky wasn't even completely dark. As he dressed they made eye contact once or twice, sadly. They had nothing to say. And then he was ready to go.

"I really wanted to try with you," he said.

She shook her head and sighed, her head down, then gave him a small smile. "Okay. Kiss me good-bye and go home."

He kissed her and she pulled herself closer to him when he rubbed her bottom. But they weren't looking at each other as he went out the door.

Three months later he saw a T-shirt with a legend that reminded him of *Kiss me good-bye and go home*, something that ended, *Tell me you love me and get the hell out*, but the time that had passed and where they had left it made him think she might misunderstand. If there had been a meeting with the governor, Boudreau had not felt the impact of it. He was in San Francisco when he saw the T-shirt, passing through with Paulie on their way home from Mexico. Boudreau had traded up from the Mustang to an '82 Plymouth Colt, a Japanese car that made thirty miles to the gallon, which had made a Mexican trip possible. Without a real clue or inspiration, he had decided that Paulie was old enough to see how the rest of the world lived. Mexico was not as poor as Panama, but it was poor enough to make Boudreau's point—and make Paulie unhappy enough for his father to see that his own attitude was too grim for Paulie's good.

Not so much depressed as joyless. If he saw a woman who interested him, he contrived to dull the pleasure of the experience. He reminded himself that he had no money—true enough: he had run up two credit cards with Diane and the Mexican trip. He had learned enough about AIDS to be quite frightened by the possibility of infection. And the Green River body count was up to twenty-nine.

One result was that the Sea-Tac Strip was a ghost town. The Green River killer had easily accomplished what the county had found impossible. Bars were shuttering. Motel owners were seen on television news complaining about their loss of income. "What can you do?" said one civic-minded entrepreneur with a shrug. His story was one of dozens of angles covered as editors kept the story alive between discoveries of new bodies. *Time* reported the departure of Norm Chapman. The BBC and Australian television did feature pieces about "the greatest manhunt in American history." Writers flew in and out of town. The continuing discovery of bodies made the hysteria routine. Stan Pfeiffer accepted an appointment as chief of police of Santa Rosa, California. Word came down that his position on the Seattle PD was not going to be filled anytime soon. In August, almost three years to the day of the discovery of Hot Lily, Spencer telephoned to tell Boudreau confidentially that he was being considered for the Green River Investigative Team.

"About fuckin' time," Spencer added. "They had to get rid of Norm Chapman, but this new guy ain't cuttin' it either, let me be the first to tell you. So don't be surprised if it gets bogged down while everything else goes up in the air again. Do you know how many times down here we have reinvented the fuckin' wheel?"

Doesn't matter. Boudreau almost said it aloud. He had learned something on his own about the Green River killings, and if nothing else, he wanted to see how long it took the investigative team to learn it—and get the information to the public.

He thanked Spencer and said good-bye without telling him anything, not even thinking—for a half hour, anyway—that he was violating the basic agreement between Spencer and him, that they were to share information. What made Boudreau think of it at all was the realization that Spencer had told him, in one of those moments when Boudreau's attention had wandered, that Piper was out of the picture for good. Boudreau caught himself reflecting on the idiocy of wishing he'd never meet another Piper in his life.

Two weeks later Chapman's replacement was reassigned and the new man's publicity photograph showed him in the usual dress uniform and cap too small for his head. Boudreau had never heard of the man, and had to force himself to read the PR-generated copy synopsizing his career. What the general public would not see in the catalog of promotions and commendations was the possibility that the man had never made an arrest.

Boudreau was in bed that night when he called Diane.

"It's me, Phil Boudreau."

"I know." She sounded sleepy. "What's up?"

He was silent a moment. "They're considering me for the investigative team. If you had anything to do with it, thank you."

"Did you want to hear my voice?"

"What?"

"Did you want to hear my voice? You have to say it, detective. Don't you remember? We started this way, with you calling me on a pretext."

"Yes, I wanted to hear your voice."

"Paulie says you're not doing so good."

"That—may be an exaggeration. I'm—"

"Do you want me to come over?"

"You'd do that for me?"

"I want your friendship. I missed you."

"Why didn't you call?"

"It was just a matter of time. Screwing up the courage to tell you what I put into what happened, being forty and scared —"

"Stop."

"I'll be there in ten minutes."

He sat up. "Hafta unlock the door."

"Stay where you are. I still have a key."

Diane was undressing in the darkened bedroom when he told her that his informants were saying that the disappearance of street girls and prostitutes had all but stopped in the Seattle-Tacoma corridor. She stayed silent until she was under the covers next to him. "We'll work this out." She nuzzled him, letting him feel her lips and tongue wet on his nipple. "*Je t'aime* yourself, asshole."

OCTOBER 1985

Garrett Lockman was getting a buzz on. He was in a bar three blocks from the Holy Name campus, a hangout for law-school students and faculty, with Anton Charles's contracts class. In the classroom and out in public, Lockman kept his distance from Charles, who showed gratitude for the protection of his privacy in private, where he could express himself most appropriately. Now, six weeks after the start of the fall semester, Lockman knew he could make the problems at the law school at Holy Name University work for his benefit. The law-school faculty was riddled with old aunties like Charles, and out of necessity a polite fiction was maintained. One was supposed to believe that it was only a coincidence that so many professors were lifelong bachelors, never able to rustle up a female dinner companion. The whispered joke among students was that one professor in particular wanted an appointment to the U.S. Supreme Court so he could redecorate it.

All the hush-hush and tiptoeing around reality made it less likely that it would ever get out that Lockman occasionally let Charles belly up to the love spigot, and for that Lockman was grateful. He was having enough difficulty adjusting to the chicken-coop qualities of campus life. Lockman had been out of school for almost ten years, and in spite of his best efforts, he was developing a certain reputation. People thought he was a little— well, insane. He was still driving the ambulance. People thought his giggle a shade too maniacal. And he had a past that included police work and the navy as well as his government assignments. The people who wanted to laugh at the last, that he had ever worked in a confidential capacity for the federal government, were on his "dirty tricks" list, and in his own way, he was letting them know it. In just these few weeks he had figured out how to get into the university's central computer. It was possible, he was telling people, for the wrong sort of person to log on and delete whole academic careers. The same trouble could be made for faculty, too, as Anton Charles was beginning to realize. Charles was already on notice that Lockman did not want the sexual attentions of the other faculty queens. "I don't ever want to find out you've been bragging about this," he had said to Charles at a wonderfully apt moment. If Charles had given him a killing look, Lockman had missed it. How would one know with Charles's face distorted by a pair of wide-open jaws? What could Charles do now? Why would he want to do anything, when he could go on giving private performances of his impression of Toulouse-Lautrec entering a voting booth? As far as Lockman was concerned, the situation was perfect.

When Waldo Starr came in and took a stool at the bar, Lockman was quick to get up from his place at the Charles's class table and join him. Starr was a heavyset Corn Belt Billy with straight yellow hair, and he was another outsider. His problem was a certain intensity of mien: the young women of the law school were calling Waldo Starr the "Janitor Rapist." Lockman had seen Starr around the campus since the start of the semester, registering what were probably the usual thoughts about him. Starr was an odd duck, with a driving, bent-over walk, as if he wanted to get where he was going as quickly as possible. He had small, darting eyes set deeply under an abnormally thick brow that would have made him look like an asylum inmate even if he had somehow turned out to be easygoing and happy-go-lucky. But he was not those things. Starr was the sort of man who picked his nose and then cleaned his nails on his teeth. He was always unkempt, often unclean, frequently unpleasant, regularly argumentative, sometimes abusive, and occasionally, to the women, frightening. For all of that, Lockman saw in Starr the charm of being one of the front-runners, with certain members of the faculty, in the student-faculty race for strangest guy on campus. It took much of the heat off Lockman. He stuck out his hand and introduced himself. Starr glared.

"You're a freshman. Why should I talk to you?"

"And you're a big-deal sophomore—but I'm the only guy in here who knows how to have a good time in Spokane."

"Impossible. Spokane is an Indian word meaning 'White Boys' Slum.' "

"Ever try the hookers on the east side?"

Waldo Starr winced. "Don't even whisper that word around this crowd. The women here don't want you even looking at them. How are you supposed to fulfill your biological duty of spreading your DNA?"

Lockman giggled. "When I'm done with my DNA, I don't give a shit what happens to it."

Starr eyed him, then broke out in a grin. He raised his hand in a high five. "My man!"

"Buy me a round."

"Put your own money on the bar. I want to be sure I'm going to get one back."

Lockman reached into his pocket. No Detroit here, but a roll big enough to make it look as if the years he had been away from school had been well spent.

An hour later, when the conversation turned to guns, even though it was obvious that Starr knew a lot about guns, Lockman was drunk enough to argue with him about the stopping power of the .45 versus the .357 Magnum. Starr offered to take Lockman out to a range.

"Let's do it now," Lockman said.

"Are you kidding?"

"I know where you can fire a gun around here at night without bringing the cops down on you."

Starr laughed. "How do you know what you hit?"

"Well, we can always hire a hooker and tie her to a tree. When she yells, you know you've hit her."

"That's cold. You like hookers?"

"Hate 'em. Now they have a disease that makes your dick fall off before it kills you. Not a lot of fun in that. No, they're always hustling you. The idea is to separate you from your money while delivering as little sex as possible."

"All women do that," Waldo Starr said.

"You sound like the Green River killer," Lockman said. He watched Starr jump, alarmed. Lockman laughed in his face. "Are you somebody I should worry about?"

"About that? I was in North Dakota. I can prove it. But you shouldn't even joke like that, right? I mean, they're saying that there haven't been any new killings in a while, but that doesn't mean that there won't be more."

"Damned straight. He's out there."

"You've been following the case?"

"Shit, yes. I was living in Portland. Spent a lot of time in Seattle. The cops are never going to solve the case."

"Why do you say that?"

"No forensics. They're finding skeletons. They've got a new DNA matching test, but it's worthless if you don't find a guy's load. Somebody knows evidence. But that's enough of that. I think I'll go find some chick with vacuum chops who wants to make a fast thirty bucks. Then I'll sleep like a baby."

"It's just that easy for you? I've been in town over a year and I haven't been able to find a woman I'd want to touch. You just get here and know where everything is."

"You're not supposed to touch them. I know where everything is because I grew up here."

Starr grinned maliciously. "Just terrible."

"But it didn't make a killer out of me. Now, do you want to go for a ride? I'm not kidding." He had to overpower this guy. "I want to see how you talk to the girls."

"I want to be a prosecutor, you know."

"Like a politician never had a private party with the best ginch in town? You have to learn your way around the scene in more ways than one. I want to see your gun collection. Maybe you'll even sell me one sometime."

Starr got up. "Let's do it."

Lockman kept his eyes away from Anton Charles as he followed Waldo Starr to the door. Starr was going to be fun, if not as easy as Martin Jones. Lockman was twentieth-century America's reigning champion serial killer, and had gotten away clean. Nobody would ever catch him. He had to keep reminding himself that he was living a new life. Even if by some freak accident he was ever accused, it was going to be impossible to make a case stick.

———

STARR WANTED TO save money by getting only one girl and taking turns, and when they found a not ugly light-skinned black girl named Sonya, he told Lockman to go first. Lockman got the picture—did the big goofy farmer think he was an original? Because of AIDS, Lockman told the girl, he wanted only oral sex. When Starr did not volunteer to leave the motel room, Lockman moved the girl around to give him a better view. Some prosecutor. Was he trying to jump in Lockman's pocket? Whether Starr knew it or not, he was a case of misery loving company, wanting to put people in jail because his psyche already had him in the worst of all possible prisons. Not as easy as Martin Jones? Lockman was making his plans for Waldo Starr, and they were *wonderful*!

NOVEMBER 1985

Phil Boudreau and Diane Heidt knew now how their defenses had risen up out of the general fear everyone was heir to. Diane had decided long before meeting him that she was going to remain autonomous. She was the daughter of an alcoholic father and a mother who had spent most of her adult life in denial about what she had allowed to be done to her. The payoff had come on her mother's deathbed, all reason for denial finally stripped away, with her father leaning close for her mother's last words:

I hate you.

The ultimate last tag.

At the beginning, when Diane had told Boudreau she could see what he could become, she had hinted that the difference in their ages allowed her to see what was left of his youth. She loved looking at him, thought he was beautiful, occasionally hilarious or, when his attention was turned to police work, terrifying. If he had seduced her, and not the other way around, it had been after their second meeting, south of the airport, when she had seen a loving, protective father. She had known then it was just a matter of time.

Their celebration of themselves left Boudreau thinking that he was temporarily as crazy as a shithouse rat. He called her one morning at her office on the university campus, asking her to allow him to take her to lunch. He brought the lunch with him, locked the office door, and pulled down the shades. She wanted to act peeved but couldn't help laughing, even when he muscled her over her desk and pulled up her skirt. "Don't I get lunch first?" He didn't answer, too busy getting her panty hose down and slipping his hand between her legs, insinuating it ever . . . so . . . slowly, taking notice again, not incidentally, of her small, soft buttocks. She moved the telephone and a penholder to the far corner of her desk. "You just like to see terror in my eyes."

"I can't see your eyes."

"I'll get the mirror out of my purse—"

He entered her and she yelped, steadying herself with her forearms on the desk blotter.

"Anybody in the hall heard that," she murmured.

"Everybody in the hall."

"I'll get even. Tonight. Your house. Your downstairs neighbor. That dirty-minded old goof. He'll hear *you*."

He had her by the hips, lifting her up to him. The blotter slipped, the telephone crashed to the floor. Someone knocked on the door. "Diane?" A woman's voice.

"Come back later!" Diane cried.

"You all right?"

"Not yet!" The off-the-hook tone sounded from the telephone. "You'd better hurry," she whispered. "The campus cops are going to come."

"Them, too? It must be in the air."

Paulie knew what was happening between them. One night in Boudreau's living room, he asked, "Are you two going to get married, or what?"

She crossed the room to kiss Paulie on top of the head.

A replacement for Stan Pfeiffer was named, and before Boudreau could call him about Green River he learned that his new chief of detectives was a member of Ron Beale's church. Had Pfeiffer been working more angles than Boudreau had imagined? In the middle of December Boudreau got another call from Wayne Spencer. "You're in. Kevin Donovan is going to call you next week."

"The case is ice-cold, Wayne."

"I can't say anything, Phil. Listen to him."

The next week, in the darkness of late afternoon, a telephone call Boudreau thought would be from Donovan turned out to be from Diane. She never called him during the day, so he asked her what was wrong.

"Paulie came by my office."

Boudreau had long recognized that Diane was Paulie's first adult friend and he was going to talk to her before either of his parents. "He's got a problem," Boudreau said.

"He wants to move in with you," she said.

"I'm listening."

She drew a breath. "Travers is back. Moved in. From what Paulie says, Travers is an alcoholic, and Adrienne would rather join him."

"Has Paulie said that Travers has hit her?"

"Not in so many words, no."

"What has he heard?"

"Fighting, he says. Loud, drunken arguing with name-calling. He can't bring himself to say he heard this asshole hit his mother and it's not wise to push him on it. What would be the point?" She paused to give Boudreau the chance to respond. He didn't. She said, "It isn't going to do Paulie any good to see his mother hit, and nobody can stop Travers from doing it except Adrienne. You have to do something first."

DECEMBER 1985

"No, listen to me," Lockman said to Waldo Starr over beer in the law-school hangout. "Sonya stole my wallet. I went around to the motel and asked for her, but the guy behind the counter said she moved. The mistake I made was in not making up a story about why I needed to see her."

"This doesn't have anything to do with me," Starr said.

"But that's exactly the point! Go to the motel, tell the person behind the counter you're a lawyer and you represent a member of the Spokane Police Department who doesn't want to go through the embarrassment of making an official complaint against Sonya. Look, it's a chance for you to try on your game face. You act tough and determined, he'll tell you everything you want to know. The very last thing a motel owner wants is trouble with the police."

"I still don't get why you can't do it yourself."

"Because I blew it! They know my face! If I tell them now that I'm a member of the Spokane PD, the first thing they're going to ask is why I didn't say so the first time."

"But they already know about the wallet," Starr said.

"No! They don't! That's the point! When the guy said he didn't know where she was, I just left. I never mentioned my wallet. They know nothing about it."

"They're going to be suspicious, two guys asking about her in the same time frame."

"No, they won't. Guys are always asking about hookers. I was there ten days ago. In the morning. If you go in the evening, you won't even get the same clerk."

Waldo Starr sighed. "I don't know."

"My law career is going to be just fucked if anybody ties me to a prostitute. Suppose she dies? Prostitutes get killed all the time."

"I know, you told me."

Lockman had told Starr his theory of the Green River killings, that they had been done by two guys and the killings had stopped when the two guys had had a falling-out. Lockman said, "If my wallet is found with her possessions, bingo. I can't go to anybody else about this. You're the only friend I have. I need your help."

"Well, I'm going to my sister's for the holidays."

"That's next week!"

"Not for me. I'm leaving tomorrow."

"Do it tonight, then. Please!"

Starr stared for a moment. Lockman tried to keep a straight face. "All right," Starr said, "I'll do it."

"Thank you." Lockman blinked, as if suppressing tears. If he kept working on him, he could probably push Starr further than Martin Jones. Lockman's wallet was locked in the glove box of his ambulance. He had not seen Sonya since he and Starr had gone with her to that same motel.

December 1985

Boudreau knew he was suffering an attack of cop's paranoia—he couldn't help thinking he was being set up. After months of silence, Kevin Donovan had called at five-thirty on a wet, cold preholiday evening and told him to be at a Chinese restaurant an hour's drive north of the Public Safety Building at seven o'clock, forcing Boudreau to call Diane's answering machine at her apartment in the hope she would retrieve her messages before setting out with Paulie for Boudreau's apartment. "Make it a pizza-and-movie night, if you want," he had said, being vague about what was calling him away, lest her telephone was being tapped—in a deal like this, if it was a deal, ignorance was always the best defense. Sitting in his car across the street from the restaurant, an old two-story building in a ramshackle neighborhood, Boudreau checked the .38 under his arm, the .25-caliber strapped to his ankle. He felt like an idiot. If somebody wanted, he could hit Boudreau as he crossed the street.

Which he proceeded to do. The street was empty. So was the restaurant, which was dimly lit. A middle-aged Chinese man behind the counter perked up.

"Mr. Donovan's table?"

The man smiled. "Room B upstairs."

"Is he here?"

"No, not here. Room B."

"Is he in room B?"

"No, you go room B."

"Let me have a beer. I'll drink it here while I wait."

"What kinda beer you want?"

"Tsing Tao?"

He smiled again. "You got it."

Boudreau took a seat at a front table, facing the door. The window was frosted, making it impossible to see the street. Boudreau was beginning to relax anyway. This was the government's way of doing things. The beer arrived as Donovan walked in, grim-faced, followed by five other guys who looked left, right, and up the stairs, followed by Wayne Spencer, who broke into a big grin when he saw Boudreau. Donovan looked at the beer.

"Figured you'd drink something weird. Come on, I reserved a room upstairs so we won't be disturbed."

At the back of the group, Spencer gave Boudreau a thumbs-up.

Upstairs in room B, Donovan introduced the other five, Robinson, Howells, Snowcroft, Sciscio and Kerr, all special agents, in their thirties, neat and well-groomed, so alike they could exchange clothes or even eyeballs without anybody noticing. They were willing to let Donovan order for them, sweet-and-sour pork, egg foo yung, almond chicken—the kind of Chinese food popular in Wichita, Kansas. Boudreau ordered citrus beef, hot-and-sour soup for everyone, and six more Tsing Taos. He told Donovan, "The Germans built a brewery in Shanghai when it was their protectorate, and the Chinese have never changed the recipe. Tsing Tao is probably the best real German beer you can get in this country."

Spencer was grinning again. "Phil knows food."

Kevin Donovan took a deep breath. "Boudreau, you've been treated badly by everybody on this deal, no question. On behalf of all of us here, I want to apologize."

"All right, let's go on."

"Good, glad to hear it. As you know, Spencer here has been doing some work on your Green River candidate, Garrett Lockman. It looks promising, to tell you the truth. Why didn't you tell us he was a walkaway from King County Jail when you first gave us his name?"

"I didn't know it at the time."

"When did you learn it?"

"Later."

"Why didn't you tell us?"

"I figured you knew—" He stopped. "Are we going to pull each other's chains? You didn't come all the way up here simply to avoid the press." Boudreau saw Sciscio and Howells exchange glances, or was it Robinson and Snowcroft? "We're in Snohomish County. The only guy from the King County Sheriff's Department here is Spencer, and I wouldn't give sixty-seven cents for his loyalty to the sheriff—"

"Hey!" Spencer said, but he was grinning again.

"Wayne, what you know about the King County Sheriff's Department would fit comfortably up a gnat's ass."

Spencer laughed. "Don't be shy, Phil. Speak your mind. Just spit it right out."

"All right," he said, looking at Kevin Donovan. "Assuming for the moment that the Green River killer is Garrett Lockman, you've had the can tied to your tail. This is probably the most visible failure in the history of the FBI, and it's not your fault."

Donovan sat back. "I'm glad you see that. Look, you're from New York and your father was New York PD, so you know what a rabbi is. There are still some guys on the sheriff's department who get stiff when your name is mentioned, mostly because, like Ron Beale, they think you're dirty—or they don't like the women you're involved with."

"Woman," Boudreau corrected. "And I don't give a fuck what they think."

Donovan winced, and Boudreau remembered that he was the one who didn't like dirtymouth. Donovan said, "Anyway, we're going to be your collective rabbi. We're going to get you on the Green River Investigative Team and we'll back you up completely. Let's have your quick take on Lockman."

Boudreau told him about the Eagle Guns and Ammo job and its aftermath. "I have to assume that the sheriff's department got wind of him and decided he'd make a good jailhouse snitch. Given what I know about him, I'd have to say that Lockman sized up the situation pretty quickly, and told people exactly what they wanted to hear. I had a look at his file. He went straight from sentencing to the work-release program. He drove the poor son of a bitch at Holyrood Spring and Axle damned near out of his mind."

"Sheehan," Spencer said. "He really began to wonder why there was so much interest in Lockman after we showed up. 'Hey, there was a guy here

a long time ago.' I knew right away it was you. I told him we were following up."

Donovan glared, but not so Spencer could see it. If Spencer was contemplating a career with the FBI as a consequence of his contributions to
the Green River case, he was wasting his time. He definitely did not fit
the FBI's own profiles. Boudreau said, "Lockman convinced Ron Beale
he was more valuable on the street."

The waiter arrived with the soup and beer. Everyone was quiet as he la-
dled the soup into cups. As Donovan watched, his expression became
more unhappy. Boudreau said, "Everything in the soup is in your
mother's kitchen."

For the first time in Boudreau's experience with him, Donovan smiled.
He was almost unrecognizable. "That's what I'm afraid of. My mother
couldn't cook to save her life."

Now I understand you, you son of a bitch.

"Why are you so difficult to get a handle on, Boudreau?"

"I told you. I'm from New York."

"Tell me about Diane Heidt."

"She's my private business."

"That's what I mean. That's a rocky relationship—please don't start
yelling about us spying on you. We want to let you in, but we can't if
you're going to tell her—"

"What made it seem like a rocky relationship was her discovery, late in
the game, that I had a Green River candidate. She thought I should have
told her. Now she has a little more trust in me." Probably misplaced, he
thought. If the FBI now thought Garrett Lockman was the Green River
killer, he couldn't tell Diane. *No question—FUCK!* He almost yelled the
word aloud.

"Good soup," Wayne Spencer said with his mouth full.

"Let's eat," Donovan said. "We have the rest of the night to talk about
this."

"I have a few questions of my own," Boudreau said.

"Okay, let's hear them."

"How did Beale fix on me as a suspect?"

"Somebody called him before the first body was found. Said the girl's
killer was the strangest cop of all." Donovan smiled again. "Beale thought
that was you."

"That isn't how the FBI got into it so quickly."

"After Ted, we were waiting for a copycat. Actually, this is one of several areas we'd targeted as likely for a new serial killer. As Ron Beale and I

had agreed long ago, he called me as soon as the body was found—well, you saw: we were there when you arrived."

"So that was phony, calling me down there."

"Not exactly. You did identify her, don't forget."

Icing on the cake. "But that still didn't keep Beale from thinking of me as a suspect."

Kevin Donovan stopped spooning up the soup and looked Boudreau in the eye. "Ron Beale is a Bible-thumping moron."

"And Dan Cheong?"

"A no-talent bootlick. Which gets us to the first of our problems. The King County Sheriff's Department is trying to save its own butt on this one. If Garrett Lockman is the boy, the sheriff is going to do everything he can to keep the information that Lockman was an informant from the public. The public doesn't understand police work. We're going to have to build a case against Lockman so tight that the sheriff has no choice but to ride along. It could get complicated." Donovan thumbed his chest and looked around the room. "*We* want to solve this case, is that clear?"

"So much for the first of our problems," Boudreau said. "What are the others?"

"One is that it really seems to be true that Lockman was out of town— all the way to Atlantic City, New Jersey—when the first five girls were killed."

"Two guys, like the Hillside Strangler."

"Okay, we have at least three candidates, guys he talks to on the telephone, but at this stage, that's all we have on them. He talked to them at length on the telephone from Portland. There's two in Seattle and one in Redmond."

"What else?"

Spencer went for more soup, which freed two of the others to do the same.

"Leave some for me," Donovan said. "Let me ask you a question first, Phil. May I call you Phil?"

"No. What's the question?"

Donovan sighed. "Are you in? We have other leads to check, but we feel strongly about this guy. You and Spencer and two of my men exclusively on Lockman. On paper you'll be reporting to somebody from King County, but in fact you'll be our operation. Are you in?"

"As leader of the team, yes."

"That's tough. We're used to a leadership role."

"I'm the most qualified. I have the skills and experience, and I know the turf."

Donovan looked at the ceiling. If Boudreau had to guess what was passing through his mind, it would be, *If this leads to another screwup, I can always blame Boudreau.* "Okay," Donovan said. "It's a deal. There's one other thing. I said this could get complicated—"

The door opened again and the waiter wheeled in a serving cart laden with covered platters. Donovan stayed quiet until the waiter had the platters on the table and was wheeling the cart out again.

"Let's just call it a condition of employment. Maybe 'condition of the playing field' would be a better way to put it. If it's Lockman, and your interviews with him years ago tell the truth about his interest in police work, we can assume that he knows not only what constitutes evidence, but also the importance of developing an evidentiary chain. The telephone logs of the Green River Investigative Team show calls to his address in Portland. He would know that. The FBI can't participate in mishandling evidence. We can't even be close to it. So here it is: Not only do we have to build the case against Lockman so tightly that the sheriff's department can't ignore it, it has to be so tight that it won't be possible for Lockman to drag in the sheriff in the first place. If Lockman is the Green River killer, that makes him one of the most evil human beings ever to draw breath in this country. If he tries to drag the sheriff into it, we have to be able to show that the attempt is just more of his evil—but even better, we have to lock that door before he gets to it. Phil—*Boudreau*—we think Beale and Cheong made cash payments to him for information, and worse, in the absence of anything to suggest otherwise, we have to proceed on the assumption that he recorded some or all of the telephone conversations he had with those two. We have to have every imaginable shred of evidence of his connection to Beale and Cheong beforehand."

Failure would leave the can tied to whose tail? "From what I remember about his apartment, Garrett Lockman never throws anything away." He turned to Spencer. "What do you know about Lockman now as a result of the work you've done?"

"Hours and hours on the telephone with the three guys, one more than the other two, often into the middle of the night. We've begun to match credit-card charges with the dates and times of the disappearances of the victims. One of the cards, issued to Walter Murdoch, puts Lockman close to Sea-Tac within hours of four of the disappearances."

"That won't work. It's the kind of stuff that could put the pope on the grassy knoll."

Donovan moved forward. "Good. It's got to be much more than coincidence. We have to have an overwhelming case. Boudreau, where do you think Lockman is now?"

"Spokane."

"What makes you think so?"

"Spencer here called his foster parents' home and relayed the conversation to me immediately after. The foster mother—his aunt—told Spencer that they hadn't seen Lockman in years and years. What I know about Garrett Lockman is that he's completely manipulative. They're a couple of cornball jive-asses who are definitely not smarter than every other person who has ever dealt with him. And that includes Ron Beale, who saw a careerful of major crime, Dan Cheong, and to some extent, me."

"How do you mean?"

"Lockman never could talk me into anything, but he did leave me feeling dirty just for talking to him."

"What do you think he's doing in Spokane?"

"Going to school, probably."

Spencer grinned: he knew something. Donovan asked, "How do you figure that?"

"He doesn't want to work. He's never had a real job in his life except for a tour as a security guard in the seventies. I don't count the navy because he failed at that. He probably has veterans' benefits he can tap into. Even as a fugitive, he would do that, because, at bottom, he's just another criminal asshole. And finally, that's what you usually do when you live with your parents. My son lives with me now and that's what he does, he goes to school. For Lockman, it's the perfect cover. It gives him the respectability that diverts suspicion from him."

Donovan looked to the agent on Spencer's left. "Tell him, Tom."

Tom Robinson, Boudreau fixed in his mind. Robinson said, "Garrett Lockman has been collecting veterans' checks as a law student at Holy Name University."

"It's beautiful," Spencer said. "We know exactly where he is. It's as good as house arrest."

"Not exactly," Boudreau said. "As long as he's free, he's killing girls. It's how he gets his sexual pleasure."

Donovan reached for the almond chicken. "We're going to be moving on this as quickly as our circumstance allows. We should have this wrapped up in three months."

———

After Christmas Boudreau received a note from Adrienne telling him to stop the child-support payments. He called his lawyer. "Ask her to put it in writing," Sid said. "If she means it, she'll say it so clearly that it will stand up if she changes her mind." Boudreau called her that same night.

"Tell your lawyer to draw up a paper and I'll sign it," Adrienne said. "Look, I don't want you calling me anymore. Work it out so that we don't have to see each other, too." She hung up.

His first thought was that Paulie was going to notice the change and he would ask both of them about it. Boudreau saw he would have to say it was a joint decision, for the good of them all.

JANUARY 1986

Garrett Lockman sat on a stool with his hands on his knees in the center of the one-room basement apartment of Waldo Starr. The disheveled and distraught young Mr. Starr lay supine on an ancient daybed so collapsed it looked hollowed out, like a canoe. The sheets did not look like they had been changed since Starr moved in—eighteen months ago, he had told Lockman. The smell of the place tended to support Lockman's theory about the sheets. Starr sniffled like a schoolboy, and Lockman laughed in his face. He took a swig from his bottle of vodka, eyeing Starr's computer. Starr used the computer for all his schoolwork, he said. The gizmo looked completely out of place in all this chaos and filth. Starr cried, "You've ruined my life!"

"God, you sound like a girl. I haven't ruined anything. I haven't done anything. You're going to be a lawyer. I don't see why the hell you're so upset. After all, you didn't kill anybody. I didn't kill anybody—"

Starr glared, silent—afraid to speak? Perfect.

Lockman said, "What do you want me to do? I didn't know anything was going to happen. You can say you went around to the motel and told the clerk a story I gave you, but given the situation, I'm going to deny having anything to do with a prostitute. I want to be a lawyer as much as you do. You can't prove I had the slightest involvement in the case, and you're the one who can actually be tied to, what's her name? Sondra?"

"You know perfectly well it's Sonya." Starr sat up and wiped his eyes with the heel of his hand like a child.

"*Was* Sonya," Lockman corrected. "If we're going to be precise, let's not mince around the central fact. Da bitch be daid. She was found strangled and naked in an empty lot. But you didn't kill her! I certainly didn't—"

"It's only a matter of time before the clerk recognizes me."

Starr seemed to be trying not to contradict him now. This was real progress. "What are you going to do, send him a class picture? What is he going to recognize you from?"

"Why did you do this?"

A last feeble twitch of rebellion. Lockman's tone grew cold. "I've already said, I didn't do anything. If you want to continue to make vague accusations of criminal activity against me, I'll have to get a real lawyer to write you a letter, copying the president of the university and the dean of instruction. What is that going to get you?"

"We knew her!" Waldo Starr cried. "We saw her in October, November—"

"For blow jobs. For me. But I don't think you'd want it getting around that all you wanted to do was watch. And don't worry, I'll vouch for you on that subject, if you tell me that's what you want, even though that should put us in really good with the dean. *Schmuck! Nobody* saw us!"

"How can you be so sure?"

Lockman gave a tart little smile. "My law-enforcement experience has taught me how to take the proper precautions. Now get smart. Only one person in the world, that clerk, can link you with Sonya. Listen! He thinks you represented a Spokane cop. Do you think he's going to tell that to the Spokane PD? 'A lawyer who said he represented one of you guys was in here before the holidays'?"

"Maybe the police didn't give out everything they had."

Lockman rolled his eyes for effect. "You'd better study human behavior. Even if that clerk didn't think you were for real and absolutely ached to spill his guts, the last thing he's going to do is call the police and say, yes, she was using my motel to turn thirty-dollar tricks. Nobody is going to connect you, and nobody can connect me. Look, I'm telling you, just go to your classes, hit those books, pass the bar exam, and go out there and smash crime. Is that so difficult to take? *Nothing changes!* In fact, if anything, you should be glad I'm not hurt that you didn't give me a chance to prove my loyalty to you—"

"What do you mean, loyalty?"

"Well, if you hadn't been so paranoid from the moment you saw the article in the paper, I would have told you that I was going to stick by you regardless, that I consider us a team, that I believe there's a special synergy between us. You and I could take over the law school if we wanted."

"Are you nuts? What are you talking about?"

"President of the Student Bar Association. We work to elect one of us, then the other. It's strictly ceremonial, but there's a lot of power, if you stop to think about it."

"Nobody would elect me anything."

"Me, then. We campaign for me."

Waldo Starr stared at him. "Let me ask you something. What would you have done if Sonya's body had been discovered while I was still in North Dakota?"

"Oh, I would have saved the clipping for you."

His eyes widened. "Why?"

"It would have been of interest to you, wouldn't it?"

"What do you really want, Lockman?"

"Would I have done wrong if I had shown you the clipping? My God, you were just complaining that the motel clerk can identify you. I could have taken a hike on you. A lot of guys would have, you know. If you'd found out on your own about Sonya's death, you'd be stark, raving crazy that the police were after you. Isn't that true? Look, I'm *trying* to be your friend. You're a difficult guy, and you know it."

Starr studied him silently. Lockman was sure he had the rube in a position where he could not possibly go to the police. The possibility of her body being found while Starr was still in North Dakota? That was just stupid. Lockman had waited until Starr was back from the holidays before going out to look for her.

And she had died spectacularly well. If he had not taken her out into the country, someone would have seen the ambulance shaking with her death throes, they had been so violent. All that had kept Lockman from taking a bite out of her had been the memory of how Ted Bundy had been caught. No forensics, either—Lockman had practiced safe sex, wearing a rubber. All that connected him to her now was the lingering odor of her feces in the ambulance.

The monster was alive and well, in spite of the restriction on its activities. Now Lockman knew he could continue, but carefully, if he traveled great distances. It would be better in the summer, when high-school girls would be out hitchhiking. White high-school girls, sweeter than the world knew. . .

"Look, as your friend, can I make a couple of constructive suggestions?"

Starr's lower lip trembled. "All right," he whispered.

"Clean up this place," Lockman said. "Air it out. Put some food in the refrigerator. Act like it's a home."

"Is this the way it's going to be? You telling me what to do?"

"My God, I'm just trying to give you a little help. It's obvious that you don't know how to live, that you need a little organization."

"Can I be alone now?"

Lockman rose, capping his vodka. "No, I thought we'd go out, celebrate your return to Spokane. I'll pay. Why are you sitting there? Free beer!"

Waldo Starr got to his feet. "What the hell, I didn't kill anybody."

Garrett Lockman clapped him on the back. "There you go! That's the spirit!"

March 1986

Don't talk to the media. If a member of the media attempts to contact you, refer that person to your supervisor or a team press officer.

Boudreau could not help feeling confused. He had learned that his transfer to the Green River Investigative Team was official when he read about it in the newspapers. Reporters called him, but only one had showed any insight: "Why now? After all this time on the sidelines, do you have a special assignment?" Boudreau had felt particularly stupid about following the instructions, telling the reporter to call Sheriff's Lieutenant Lester Lucas, his supervisor-on-paper. Lucas had a genial, country boy's seeming befuddlement about the job that was just too mechanical to be believed. "Gosh, boys, you know we don't discuss the investigation," was Lucas's standard reply to questions. "Hell, if we have anything to announce, you all know it will come from the big boys."

A fiftyish man with leathery skin and wire-rim glasses, Lucas kept himself well clear of Boudreau and his group. There would be no question about the responsibility for another Green River Investigative Team failure. Fair enough—he had not asked for this. He always had a toothy country grin for Boudreau, with a "How're ya doin'?" verbal flourish. Boudreau would nod in return, and Lucas would finish the exchange with a "Good," or sometimes, more flamboyantly, "Awright!" If Boudreau needed pencils or paper clips, he knew better than to involve Lucas in the process. Whatever Boudreau thought he was saying by avoiding Lucas, there was no question that he was also acknowledging that Lucas was doing his own thankless job as well as anyone could ask.

After three months Boudreau's new group was still working through Lockman's credit cards and telephone bills, feeding information to their middle-aged computer operator, Madeleine, who was willing to work late but once took a whole afternoon consulting manuals to customize the program to print two columns, the dates of Lockman's locations on one side, the victims' disappearances on the other. Reverse the columns? No problem, but could it wait until morning? Sure. It had taken Boudreau weeks to assimilate what had been done before his arrival, to come to an understanding of the organizational difficulties he had inherited.

Final blame for the complexity of the problem Boudreau's group faced rested with Lockman himself. His credit-card bills had been sent to mail drops, and the bills had to be cross-checked with the credit-card companies for his other known aliases, which in turn had to be traced to still other mail drops, some of which remained active. Garrett Lockman was Walter Murdoch was Clifford Lloyd was Donald Loving was Charles Griff was Steve Maddox and a dozen others. Bill Alvarez bought gas in Redmond and later that day Sidney Zimmerman ate at a pizza joint in Bellingham. Then there would be a gap of no charges for three or four or five days. Boudreau called American Express for a list of stolen traveler's checks cashed in the Pacific Northwest after 1982. He didn't ask for the serial numbers of the checks stolen in Coronado while Lockman was in the navy because a copy of that list was already part of Lockman's file. If Boudreau's group knew Lockman gassed up in Portland under one name, charged a meal in Tacoma three hours later under another, and cashed a traveler's check under a third name in Vancouver, British Columbia, that night, the gaps in his seemingly endless wandering contracted by just that much. Boudreau's group was connecting a mass of dots, inch by inch. The process was like flipping a stack of early maps of the interstate highway system, the fat green strips of transcontinental highway inching toward each other like worms in heat. Sometimes Lockman's path came tantalizingly close to the last known locations of dead or missing street girls and prostitutes—but that was another incomplete list. Everyone now assumed they would be digging up bodies for years. Clearly it would be argued that Lockman's proximity to his alleged victims was nothing more than serendipity. Anyone traveling through the Pacific Northwest as much as Lockman would inevitably pass within a few miles or a few hours of one or more of the disappearances. A weakness in that argument was that practically no other human being had spent as much time on the road as Garrett Richard Lockman. But the big problem with the time line, as it was coming to be called, pointing to Lockman as the Green River killer was that there was absolutely no other evidence that Lockman had ever so much as swatted a fly.

One of the problems of the process of Boudreau's team was the absolute need to keep away from Lockman's family and friends, lest he hear that the police were asking questions about him. Lockman was still collecting VA benefits through his enrollment at Holy Name's law school. Boudreau couldn't call Jack Murphy in Spokane now. *Someone from the Green River Investigative Team called? What was the name of the man he asked about? Is that person a suspect?* Not only would the investigation of Lockman be hopelessly queried, Boudreau's career might be over. At this stage, the members of the team who had taken the heat for past mistakes wanted more than to just solve the case, they wanted to bask in the glory of the credit for the bust. They wanted to *wallow*.

A necessarily remote running down of Lockman's three known telephone confidants, if that was what they were, was proving mostly futile. Tom Parkinson worked for a hardware store, was married with two children, rented a cheap little house, had one credit card with a line of two hundred and fifty dollars, and never ran up a telephone bill of more than forty dollars a month. Jimmy Dobbs's situation and lifestyle was only slightly better. He had cable and his wife enjoyed a weekly trip to the beauty salon, but the record indicated that neither one had moved a tenth of a mile out of their little orbits in the last three years.

The third guy, the bachelor, Martin Jones, was the interesting fish. His driver's license photograph suggested he could be the tapioca-colored guy mentioned by Uhuru and his bunboy, Marlon. Jones had no record—on paper, he was a perfect straight arrow. He made sixty thousand dollars a year at Boeing, had thirty-seven thousand dollars deposited in the company credit union, and was paying off his mortgage on an interest-saving fifteen-year schedule. His car, a Toyota Corolla, was paid for. He spent three or four weekends a year in Las Vegas and Loughlin. Police in those jurisdictions had no record of him. Hotels in which he stayed had no special notations in their files, meaning he was neither a high roller nor a deadbeat. He signed for breakfast buffets and an occasional steak. For one. The Nevada records said he was always alone. The records that were available for the Seattle area indicated he was always alone here, too. No social life. No family life. No personal life. No sex life.

Just hours and hours on the telephone with Lockman, sometimes for five or six nights in a row.

When he had Kevin Donovan's approval, Boudreau called Walla Walla for an update on Thomas Brownall. Due to be released in August, Brownall was a model prisoner, subdued, a participant in group rehab, a correspondence-course student, a diligent worker in a variety of assignments. Letters every other week and packages three times a year from an aunt in Arizona. Weekly letters and, in the past year, monthly visits, from a Cynthia Hohner of Tacoma. According to a parole-board report, Brownall had advertised in the alternative press for a pen pal, and a relationship had developed. Brownall had told the parole board that he and Hohner were contemplating marriage. No contact with Lockman. Boudreau sent copies of his interviews with Lockman after the Eagle Guns and Ammo bust to Donovan. When Donovan got back to him, Boudreau took Sciscio, Robinson, and Spencer with him downstairs to Donovan's office. Donovan had Lockman's package on his desk in front of him.

"You're saying that what Lockman told you about Brownall manipulating him was exactly the opposite of the truth, and that after Lockman walked away from jail he built a similar relationship with this Martin Jones? That that's at the heart of the Green River killings? I don't get it."

"Lockman needs a male girlfriend, somebody to impress and dominate. We think he and Jones spent all those hours on the telephone being weird together."

"Okay, that was then, this is now. How often does he talk on the telephone with Lockman in Spokane?"

"Once or twice a month."

"Any regular schedule?"

"No."

Donovan tapped the package. "For hours like this?"

"The longest Spokane-Seattle call was three quarters of an hour."

"I don't buy it. First, this Jones guy is a real citizen. He's even got a security clearance. We haven't got a prayer getting something as thin as this past the county guys on the team. A lot of them know about Lockman's walkaway, who he was working for. To some of them Ron Beale is a god. And if I go to a judge to put a tap on Jones's line because I think he has information about a series of interstate kidnappings, for instance, even the friendliest judge is going to ask if we have anything more than this three-cushion psychologizing. I'm not saying you're wrong, but nothing in all the years I've been in the game even remotely suggests that this is more than two fruits sucking each other off. Get something solid. Jones is an engineer. For all we know, he sweeps his own telephone line. To tell you the truth, I see a very disciplined guy here. How far along are you with the time line?"

"We know where Lockman was—where he punched in—about a third of the time. It puts him within driving distance of a dozen disappearances for which we have seven identified bodies. It isn't police work, it's archaeology."

"What about souvenirs?" Donovan asked. "The profiles say these guys can't resist taking souvenirs and reliving the experience. Lockman just moved back into his parents' place. What did he do with all his stuff?"

Boudreau said, "We can't move forward on any of that until we can take this investigation to other agencies. We have to be able to involve Spokane and Portland."

Donovan looked toward the door, where the rest of the team hummed along as smoothly as an insurance company. "Not yet," the look said. "Keep working on the time line."

———

IF DONOVAN WAS concerned with what Boudreau was discussing with Diane, he wasn't saying so. There was nothing Boudreau could tell Diane anyway. Boudreau could see what had been done to him: he had been neutralized through absorption, like a victim in a cheap horror movie. If he made too much fuss, he would be relieved and discredited, struck career-dead. All he could do was watch the paper pile up, waiting for Madeleine to finish diddling the computer, attend meetings as maddening as broken phonograph records, where no one was willing to admit there were no new ideas. It was no comfort to contemplate the fact that the team had been stuck in this same rut not just for as long as he had been on it, but for all the years preceding. In just a matter of months Boudreau had learned what it was like to feel his identity slipping away. Working the streets had been only a little less futile, but at least he had not felt like a fluorescent-colored clerk.

He had Paulie five days a week and every other weekend as Adrienne continued to chase her new personal dragon, the alcoholic, sometimes violent, and apparently matrimonially disinclined Mr. Travers. Adrienne was away more weekends, taking more sick days, and was less interested in her son than ever. Paul was Boudreau's sole source of information about her situation, and only as Paul wanted to talk about himself. He thought he could see Paul acquiring an unpleasant objectivity about his mother, but Diane said Boudreau was trying to anchor his son's life experience to the black cloud of his own guilt. Was he? When she wasn't around, he sometimes watched Paulie while he slept, wishing he could read the boy's thoughts.

Diane had taken advantage of Boudreau's transfer to move off in a new direction of her own, reaching out to people who had passed through San Francisco in the summer of 1967, to see if there was a common experience since then that could fit under the title FLASHBACK. "I've changed," she said. "I don't know if it's the result of barreling through forty or meeting you or whatever, but I just have to get something else done in order to feel worth my salt."

They were planning another trip to Little Bitterroot. They spent the weekends Paulie was with his mother at Diane's apartment on the other side of Lake Washington, taking nights off from each other during the middle of the week. Routine and security elbowed aside spontaneity and adventure. No matter. The intimacy of their friendship required play. What Diane called the note in the lunch pail. Surprise. *Style.*

——

THE CALL EXPECTED since the end of the winter, that more remains had been found, came at the beginning of April. The team had another promising suspect, Duane Hartman, a railroad worker who lived near Sea-Tac and whose schedule left him with a lot of free time. Word had come upstairs from Donovan that it was in the interests of Boudreau and his group not to argue against the candidacy of Mr. Hartman, whose only crime seemed to be an intense interest in sex, probably because he wasn't getting any.

So be it. High-level politics seemed to be at work here, and if Donovan was running scared, he wasn't going to admit it to Boudreau. For all Boudreau knew, his own position depended completely on Donovan's political savvy.

Boudreau had been called to Green River dump sites twice after bodies had been found, and had visited the other locations since he had come on the team simply to familiarize himself with them. Now he was Mr. Inside riding to the scene through the fine spring mist in a black-and-white, lights boiling, sirens howling, discovering again that he was not a cop who could conceal his embarrassment over being at the center of such a stupid fuss. He could only sit in the car's death seat cringing silently, his eyes focused beyond the citizens gawking at all this power and importance speeding purposefully to an empty lot—an otherwise empty lot, for two sets of remains were lying there, being kept from their plastic bags until he, among the many others, could behold them. The first reports had it that a stray dog had sniffed out the shallow graves and had been caught running around with a legbone in his teeth. It was the kind of detail the investigative team's press office was supposed to keep out of the media.

Boudreau's destination was south of the airport again, not far from the South 200th Street site. Television vans were pushing through the thickening traffic. Wayne Spencer stepped out from behind the wheel, arched his back, patted his spreading gut with both hands, and looked at Boudreau. "This was how we met, remember? I got up that day thinking I had to write five tickets or hear it from the chief. Ever since I've been up to my ass in the crime of the century."

"And never close to clearing it."

"Phil, I believe we should have listened to you at the start and surrounded Lockman with a SWAT team."

Boudreau let the others lead the way through the litter and last year's dead, flattened weeds. To the remains. You had to smell death only once. In that certain sense Spencer was right: they had come full circle. Boudreau's memory of the living Hot Lily, the tattoo flashing on the inside of her thigh, was as clear as it had been the day her body had been pulled onto the Green River bank, Hot Lily and Uhuru in that rat's-ass filthy apartment with the teenager parading her pussy in front of a cop who now seemed to himself far too young for the job. Unloved at the time, maybe his whole adult life until then, Boudreau had felt the tattoo working on him somewhere southeast of his watch pocket, a leering Uhuru watching him, looking for a sign, a hint, of the kind of moral collapse that governed Uhuru's entire life.

Raincoated uniformed officers stepped aside to let Boudreau and the others through to the dump site. The smell of death rose up. The earth smelled of death and moist spring. "They were facedown," somebody said. "We turned them over." A half-excavated grave hardly a foot deep appeared before them, the loose dirt the color of unbaked gingerbread, a skeleton on its back, so fresh the ligaments still held the bones together. The rims of the eye sockets shone with silently materializing raindrops.

"At least he left the gold in her teeth," Spencer said.

It took a moment to register, for Boudreau to lower his eyes from her eye sockets to the open jawbone half-buried in the glistening, doughy soil. It took another moment to find the gold Spencer referred to, a glint in the first molar on the lower right side, the styled curve and fold of gleaming yellow metal. Boudreau had heard from athletes of such moments, when time slowed, when the human eye seemed to act like a zoom lens: with time slowed, the focus zooming in, Boudreau saw the tooth anew, and again, again, space and time collapsing not just here but in his whole life, through Shuckers and the sophisticated dress, rouge on her cheeks, that snotty attitude, back further still, on the Ave near the U, then in his apartment, her resistance to his style of lovemaking . . . *blinding*: this mouth, these arms, reaching, closer, surrounding him, her name just out of the reach of his memory at this moment, him reaching for her, pulling himself out of Spencer's grasp, *quickly*, his knee grinding in the mud, his hand plunging down toward her in ultimate violation, his thumb slicing open upon a dead, earth-stained tooth, blood pouring into the earth, all woe, guilt, and horror rising up from deep inside his soul, flooding over him, people turning around:

He had cried out?

What?

The name.

How had Lockman gotten hold of her?

Boudreau *screamed*!

PURSUIT

May 1986

No Bitterroot. No summer, for that matter. Boudreau knew right away. So did everyone around him. When the identity of the body had been confirmed, the morning after its discovery, Les Lucas came around and asked him if he wanted some time off. The gesture confused Boudreau, especially the look that accompanied it, a penetrating gaze, the hillbilly facade erased so completely that he wondered what Lucas was really thinking that he did not want to say. The question came up again later in a conversation with Diane, when Boudreau asked her what had happened between them lately that made her seem so distant. As soon as the words were out he saw the same look in her eyes. And just as quickly she knew he was wondering what she was thinking. "I have a test for you," she said. "How to know when you're crazy. Guaranteed accuracy."

"Okay, when is that?"

"When you think nobody understands you."

"You think I think that?"

"I don't know, but when that idea is running around in your head, you're over the top. As I say, guaranteed."

He didn't answer, because she had revealed something he had been trying to conceal from himself, thinking instead that he was boxed in by the system. The investigation of the disappearance of Betty Antonelli had been out of his hands from the start; all he knew now, what had been passed on to him, was that she had failed to return to her apartment in Tacoma one afternoon three months after she had moved there to take a new job. He had told the guys on the case that one of the first things she had said to him was that she liked cops, but that, he heard back, had led nowhere. Diane asked, "Do you want to see a shrink? A guy. Combat veteran."

Boudreau started to cry silently. But he didn't answer, and Diane took his hand. "Maybe you're not ripe yet. But my colleague will write the letter that will get the downtime that even your hayseed boss can see you need."

The following week Boudreau went into Lucas's office and closed the door and gave him the letter and said he thought he needed some time off after all. Lucas did not let him finish the day. No pep talk, no best wishes, just a matter-of-factness that left Boudreau more intensely puzzled than ever. He was home before the end of the lunch hour, wondering what he was going to do with himself the rest of the day.

He had never thought he had limits, it had never occurred to him, but apparently he had gone through them without even knowing. A seamless, silent slipping into a gray, dreamless, empty place. When Paulie was at school, or with his mother, or Diane was at home on the other side of Lake Washington, Boudreau spent the time in his living room, staring, all but unable to move. Was this a breakdown? One night after Diane asked him what he was thinking about, he told her his life, his parents' lives, Paulie's, and hers, all in the same way, what they meant, where everybody was headed.

"If you're not ready to talk to a professional yet, why don't you take some real time off? Get out of town. Paulie knows something is up. If Adrienne wants him home with her, I'll keep tabs on him. Trust us. Trust us all."

But they couldn't trust him, he thought at once. He told them he was going to drive down to Astoria and the Oregon Dunes, but instead he headed east, over the Cascades and through apple country to the east side of the state. To Spokane.

An ugly place, grim and dark. Until now, Boudreau had only passed through it on the interstate with Diane and Paulie. He had both of his guns, a map of the city, and Lockman's address. He holed up in a sour-smelling furnished room downtown and spent the first day scouting the city and the campus of Holy Name University.

And remembering Lockman. Every interview, every conversation. Everything he had put in his own file about the man, recalling the face, the cunning, the rage. Remembering that the man was a killer, only a killer, nothing but a killer.

That night he found the Lockman family home in a well-groomed patch of suburb on the north side of town. An ambulance, the biggest vehicle on the block, was parked in the Lockman driveway. Boudreau turned around and drove up to the highway, killed a half hour over a cup of coffee, and drove back again. The ambulance had not moved.

Boudreau parked at the far end of the block, three hundred feet away, under a tree. He had to be careful. If some home owner called the cops, he would be in very serious trouble, all the way back to Seattle. *What were you doing there?* He retraced his path back out to the highway and telephoned the Lockmans' number. A woman answered.

"May I speak to Garrett, please?"

"Who's calling?"

Boudreau was ready. "Martin Jones."

"One minute."

Boudreau heard the handset on the other end clatter and then he heard her voice but not her words in the telephone distance. Silence — Boudreau could hear his own blood in his ears. On the other end, somebody approached the telephone. And hung up. Boudreau was disconnected. Not knowing exactly why, he ran back to the car.

He rolled up Lockman's street with the lights out and parked under the tree again. He rolled the window down and shifted in the seat so he could hear. And waited. After an hour a door opened and closed, then a car door slammed. The headlights of the ambulance came on.

Boudreau shuddered with a sudden chill. Had he provoked Lockman? How? As the ambulance backed down the driveway Boudreau started his own little car, let it roll forward again with the lights out.

Up on the highway, Lockman turned toward downtown. The poor rear visibility of the ambulance made following it easy, in spite of the rapid pace Lockman was setting. An asshole had to make only one mistake, Boudreau's father had taught him. From Lockman's point of view, the ambulance was no mistake, in fact the ideal vehicle to transport both the living and the dead. In the gray maze of the aging downtown, Lockman swung east, uncharted territory for Boudreau.

In another few blocks it looked all too familiar, an area of cheap bars and motels, the sidewalks littered with drunks, pimps, dope dealers, and whores, a couple of whom waved at the driver of the ambulance as it rolled by. Then, as if on impulse, the driver pulled over. Boudreau stopped a block back.

He watched Lockman get out of the ambulance and step onto the sidewalk. It was Lockman, too, no doubt about it. A little older and heavier, his hair shorter than it had been at the start of the decade. He was carrying a topless, flask-shaped pint bottle half-filled with clear fluid—Boudreau had found vodka in Lockman's apartment years ago. A drunk, too? He took a swig. Two black girls approached him. The three talked animatedly, with some laughter. After some minutes, a moment of silence. A disagreement? An impasse, probably. Now Lockman touched the tip of his index finger to his lips, then to the nipple of the smaller girl—instantly Boudreau remembered seeing the same gesture in a French movie in a revival house in New York years ago, a minor crook saying good-bye to a girlfriend. *Rififi*. The smaller girl pulled back with a yell Boudreau could hear. Logical: no money, no honey. She cursed Lockman. He yelled back. The taller girl shouted and a third girl came running. Clutching his bottle, Lockman backed up toward the ambulance, turned, and ran around the front to the driver's side. The smaller girl's voice rang out as Lockman closed the door behind him:

"Motherfucker!"

Boudreau almost laughed, but then Lockman stepped on the gas, veering the ambulance up on the curb and down again, long enough to send people scattering. A woman threw her high-heeled shoe at the ambulance, but just that quickly it was out of her reach, turning at the corner.

With Boudreau after it, even as the women saw what he was doing. After a few more blocks, on darker, quieter streets, it became clear to Boudreau that Lockman was headed home again. Keeping well back, Boudreau followed him the rest of the way, rolling past the Lockman house with the ambulance in the driveway as the lamp by the front door went dark.

The next morning, at six-thirty, Boudreau was parked in a lot outside a furniture store on the highway that gave a view of the direct route he had plotted the night before. The ambulance appeared at twenty to nine, Lockman at the wheel, peering into the outside rearview mirror before pulling into traffic. Boudreau let his little Plymouth slip into the traffic four cars behind the ambulance. He had the layout of the parking lot of the Holy Name Law School committed to memory. When Lockman rolled in, Boudreau stopped at the corner. Lockman got out of the ambulance and started away, a book under his arm, the aging schoolboy. A woman called his name. He turned, squinted, peering, until he found her three rows over. He waved, every inch a schlemiel like any other, Boudreau thought, with God-knew-what goofus musings caroming around in his kinky-haired noggin. Out here in the daylight, he was not the same person as last night.

He would have you believe.

Boudreau arrived in Seattle that night before ten. Diane was waiting outside the apartment door at the top of the stairs. When he muscled his suitcase inside, she closed the door and locked it. "That was quick."

"I decided I didn't want to kill anybody."

"Well, I hope you're not surprised. Want a beer?"

He nodded, following her out to the kitchen, where the dishes in the rack told him they had finished the cassoulet he had made at the beginning of the week. He picked up the telephone and dialed Wayne Spencer. There was nothing new, Spencer said.

"I'm coming back to work," Boudreau said. "The paperwork might take a couple of days. In the meantime get hold of the file of Betty Antonelli for me. I knew her and I want to see if they did their usual skin-deep, pure-bullshit job on finding out how she got tagged."

"I'll call you when I have the file."

Boudreau hung up and took the beer from Diane. "I saw him."

"I gathered."

"He's still at it." She was watching him, so he added, "I'm all right."

"But different. I'll ask my friend to write the note for your medical file so you can go back to work."

———

ON THE FACE of it, Betty Antonelli had been treated like any other victim, like Megan Reardan, for instance. The year before Antonelli's disappearance, Megan Reardan had gone out for cigarettes; her boyfriend had not reported her missing because she had been sixteen and he had believed the authorities would arrest him on sex charges. As a result, no one knew Megan Reardan was even a Green River candidate until her body was found, sixteen months after her disappearance. The case was cold; there was nothing investigators could do but make the record.

In the same way, what the team knew about Betty Antonelli was that she had moved to Tacoma three months before her death to take a job in sales at a downtown hotel, that she had joined a health club within walking distance of her new, one-bedroom apartment, and that most of her new neighbors had never even seen her. No boyfriends, no close girlfriends. Her coworkers at the hotel described her as "lively, with a good

sense of humor." As for the night of her disappearance, a Friday—
Boudreau had to consult a calendar for that fact—she had gone from the
hotel to the gym, and had left there at seven-fifteen. Detectives canvassed
bars, restaurants, and shops between the gym and her apartment with a
four-year-old graduation photograph from the U. No one recognized her.
Her parents and siblings were not able to offer much. She had moved
away from home at the age of eighteen. She had brought home a couple
of boyfriends during her college years, but none recently. There was no
mention in the file of her night with Boudreau, or her subsequent experience with Beale and Cheong. It made no sense. The only explanation
Boudreau could accept enraged him. He told Spencer to meet him in
Queen Anne for lunch, and then sat at the table in the restaurant with
only a cup of coffee until Spencer arrived.

"Come on, we're going someplace else."

"What's up?"

"I want to make sure we have privacy."

In Boudreau's car they rolled in silence down the hill to the Space
Needle. In the elevator, Spencer said, "You're paying."

"Oh, yeah."

Spencer grinned. "Everybody hear that?" he asked the tourists. "Take
your time up on top, in case I have to come around for your names for
depositions."

People laughed. At the maître d's station, Boudreau flashed his badge
and told him they would be out in half an hour. The maître d' led them
into the rotating restaurant. In the distance the mountains were shadows
on the haze. "Have them bring today's specials," Boudreau said.

"Baked salmon with lemon butter, thinly sliced Vidalia onions, and ca-
pers. Very good, sir."

"Don't come to Seattle if you don't like salmon," Adrienne had told
him an eon ago. "And coffee," he said.

"I understand," the maître d' said, and backed away.

"All this for privacy?" Spencer asked.

"Absolutely. Did you look at the Antonelli file when I asked you to pull
it for me?"

"Yeah. You're not in it, that stuff you told me about. I wondered. It's got
to be someplace. I mean, it happened."

"After we found her body, I told them that she told me she liked cops.
There's no follow-up."

"Hey."

"Because they already knew. From what she told them that Saturday
years ago. She *really* liked cops."

Spencer grinned again. "I've been meeting women like that. Wow. Beale and Cheong and them know?"

"Beale and Cheong and *Donovan* and them," Boudreau corrected. "What do you know about the rest of the team's attitude toward me?"

"You know that some of the county guys who came up under Beale hate your guts."

"Has anything changed for you since I came on the team?"

"Well, I'm more out of the loop than ever. Like you. Like everybody checking Lockman."

"I want to find out what Betty told them."

"Well, we can't hit them straight on."

Boudreau grinned. "We, eh?"

"What am I doing here?"

"You *were* being interrogated. Now you're getting an assignment."

Boudreau was finished telling him what he wanted when the fish arrived, and while they ate he answered Spencer's questions about why they had come up here to talk. "So we're going around in a circle at eight hundred feet so nobody can aim a directional mike at us. If this is what it takes, it's okay with me. I could have lunch here every day."

"Next time you pay."

"Next time we'll meet at Denny's."

A week later Spencer called from the end of the trail Boudreau had mapped out for him. That he was in Everett was beside the point: he had been looking for one of Betty's old roommates, one in whom she had confided. "She remembers you," Spencer said over the telephone. "You called her that morning?"

"After I saw Betty being followed when she left my place."

"This gal's married now, and she wants to stay out of it. She doesn't want cop cars outside her house."

"Then she knows something."

"She sure as shit does!"

It was midafternoon. Boudreau followed Spencer's directions from the I-5 to a stand-alone steak house outside a mall in well-heeled, all-American suburbia. A shiny new Acura Legend was parked beside Spencer's heap. Inside the restaurant, it took a moment for his eyes to adjust to the darkness, and he heard Spencer call him before the empty red-clothed tables and banquettes emerged from the gloom. Spencer was sitting in the far corner with a brunette in her twenties wearing an expensive dress and a touch too much makeup. She smiled nervously, two crooked teeth showing she could have used orthodontic work fifteen or twenty years ago. A waitress materialized.

"Nothing for me, thanks."

Spencer introduced the brunette as Carol. No last name.

"Thanks for meeting me here," she said. "My neighbors are all my husband's longtime friends and I—"

"Perfectly understandable," Boudreau said smoothly. "We're sorry about Betty, sorry we have to put you through this sort of upset, but if you can shed any light on what happened to her, we'd be grateful—"

"You fucked her, didn't you?" she blurted suddenly. "God, you sound so businesslike!"

"I'm sorry. But my partner will confirm that I needed some time off after I identified her body."

"Oh. Well. Okay. I'll tell you, it made me crazy when I saw it on television. My skin crawled. I've had like nightmares for weeks. I had my reservations about the things Betty would tell me—"

"What things?"

"About picking up cops. She loved picking up cops. When you came into the sports bar that night, she told us you were someone she always wanted to nail."

Betty had said as much to him, but his ego had not allowed him to put it in its true context. "Let's talk about that night and the next day. Did she talk about what happened, what they said to her?"

"She told me the cops told her you were a suspect, but Detective Spencer here says you're actually heading a group inside the Green River Team now. But at the time they asked her all kinds of questions about what you did, how many times she did it with you—"

"You mean dirty-minded stuff."

She gave him a tense, crooked smile. "Yeah. She said they were even creepier than they were saying you were."

Which meant plenty creepy, he thought, considering the way she had spoken to him in Shuckers. "How many times did they interview her?"

"Just the once, I think. But they called a couple of times, and then there were the hang-up calls. We thought they were from you."

"Did you tell the cops?"

"There weren't that many of them, only three or four, right after that Saturday. When I say *we*, I don't mean Betty, I mean her roommates. Betty herself actually thought the calls were from somebody else she saw that day downtown. She was on her way out of the Public Safety Building when a guy she'd seen a couple of times in coffee shops in Pioneer Square came in. He recognized her, too, and let me think, what did he say to her? He was very nervous. He asked her what she was doing there, and she said she could ask him the same question. They got into I'll-tell-you-if-you-tell-me stuff, and finally he said he was an undercover officer. Then he begged her not to say anything to anybody about seeing him in the Public Safety Building. And never to say anything to him if they ever bumped into each other outside."

"What did he look like?"

"She said he was funny looking. That's what made it hard for her to believe what he said, and why she suspected the calls were coming from him. She said he was too funny looking and nervous to be a cop."

"Where was he going?"

"I wouldn't have any idea. She said she was going out when he was coming in."

If he was Lockman, coming in to snitch, to rat somebody out, headed to the office she had just left, he could have read her name and telephone number upside down from paperwork left on somebody's desk. "Did she ever say she saw this man again?"

"No, but she moved out on us not long after that. This was long before she went to Tacoma. I only found out about that from the TV. How did you find me? Detective Spencer won't say."

Spencer wasn't a detective yet, but if allowing her to think so had helped him get this information out of her, he was on his way to a promotion. "You can tell her," Boudreau said.

"Through your old landlord and the girl whose name was on the lease that year."

"She could have told you all this!"

"She didn't want to."

Quickly she looked from one man to the other. "Can I go now?"

"Sure," Boudreau said. "Your husband—is he an older man?"

She slid out of the banquette and stood up. "Yeah, kinda. How did you know?"

I'm getting to be one sour old turd, Boudreau thought. "Thanks for your help," he said pleasantly. She turned on her heel. Spencer was grinning. He waited until she was out of the dining room.

"Fucker! Their wedding picture was on the piano in their living room. He must be sixty! What do we do now?"

"More. Where everybody can see it."

———

AT THE TIME of Betty Antonelli's disappearance, Garrett Lockman had been on the road, using credit cards to buy gas in Vancouver, Washington, across the Columbia River from Portland, north to Bellingham, Washington, and Vancouver, British Columbia, back down to Oregon. When Megan Reardan vanished, the future law-school student had been selling a car through the Seattle *Times*, using Tom Parkinson's telephone number to take calls from would-be customers.

Following up on information about the vehicle in the ad in the *P-I*, Boudreau found the eventual buyer, a restaurant-supply executive named Soo, who said that the seller had told him he worked in a secret capacity for the government—a funny thing to tell a stranger, Soo had thought at the time. Later, at a group weekly update, when Robinson said that Soo's information didn't mean anything, Spencer jumped on him. "It means that the motherfucker is crazy, that's what it means. Here's a guy who couldn't get a job as a substitute school-crossing guard telling people he works as a spy for the government. This is not your ordinary taxpayer." Spencer stopped and looked around. "Jesus, does that mean he thinks he can be a lawyer?"

No one answered.

Without checking with Donovan, Boudreau called Jack Murphy at home in Spokane, and asked him to pull the unsolved murders of girls and women in that city going back to 1982. Murphy was now within months of retirement.

"You know, you guys on Green River ought to talk to each other once in a while. That information was faxed to you by the Spokane County sheriff some time ago. The guy who did the work said he was told not to noise it around. You guys have got some office politics going there. It's no wonder you can't find your way to the men's room."

"Let me have that stuff anyway, will you, Jack?"

"Sure, of course. Hey, maybe they didn't tell you because they don't want you to know. They could be checking you out because of that Antonelli angle. You knew her? Jesus. That makes you a survivor, for Christ's sake. You could go to the meetings."

Boudreau snorted. "That was supposed to be kept secret, too."

"Give me a break," Murphy said. "Why do they think we became cops? We want to know everybody else is as crooked as we are."

"You're retiring not a moment too soon, Jack."

Boudreau was wondering if his own retirement was going to come more quickly than scheduled. He was thinking of the look in Les Lucas's eyes when he had asked if Boudreau wanted time off. Had knowing Betty Antonelli made Boudreau an active suspect again? There had been no problem getting back on duty.

Boudreau called Dorothy Gold and identified himself as a member of the Green River Investigative Team. "I'm following up on some information you gave our Wayne Spencer some months back, about Clifford Lloyd?"

"Is he the Green River killer? My friend actually said it! He swindled me out of a thousand dollars. I gave him money to give to his landlord, and when I tried to move in, the real landlord showed up with new tenants. I'm still out a thousand dollars. Do you have Cliff in jail?"

"You have a friend who said he was the Green River killer? Could you arrange with her for both of you to talk to me? I'll come down there at your convenience when you're willing to talk in detail."

"Give me your number and I'll get back to you. Do you think you can do it on a Saturday afternoon? Then she and I can spend the weekend together."

"Don't talk yourselves out before I get there."

She called back to make the date a week from Saturday, and on Thursday Murphy faxed over a list of Spokane PD's unsolved murders and disappearances going back five years—long enough, if Lockman was the target. Spencer found the old report downstairs, gleaned from newspaper clips. In keeping with his policy of getting as many hands as possible on everything, Boudreau asked Sciscio and Robinson to compare the two files.

On Friday afternoon Boudreau called Spencer into his office and said that he'd just realized they were missing an important piece of evidence.

"What's that?"

"The videotape of Lockman at the Miss America Pageant in Atlantic City. I've never seen it."

"I remember when it came in from the network. We had it at the old office, but I haven't seen it in years. I thought it was here somewhere, but there have been so many staff changes that nobody I would want to talk to, if you get what I mean, would know what I'm talking about."

"Take a look for it. If you can't find it, ask the network for another one. Tell them we moved into a new office. Tell them we left it on a radiator."

"This makes us look really stupid."

"We *are* really stupid. Keep pushing the envelope. Has anybody tried to match Lockman up with murders and disappearances before 1982? He was in the navy and, before that, attended the university. It shouldn't be too much trouble getting those agencies to spit up his old addresses. We'll see what happened in his old neighborhoods. Maybe we'll wind up getting him for double-parking, like Al Capone."

"Tax evasion."

"I know that. I was making a joke."

Sciscio and Robinson reported that Murphy's murder file tallied with the one of fifteen months ago. Since then, Murphy's file showed, there had been no homicides or disappearances of special interest in the city of Spokane.

—

DIANE SAID SHE would drive down to Medford on Friday to visit Lonnie, her old classmate, and would meet him in Portland Saturday night and take him out to dinner. Boudreau wanted to time his own drive to Portland. Dorothy Gold faxed him an excellent map that he matched to his own so he could visualize the route from door to door. His only problem was Adrienne. This was not one of her Paulie weekends, and she wasn't going to inconvenience herself by changing all kinds of plans without letting Boudreau know that this was not something he could think he could get away with whenever it suited him. Boudreau stayed silent. Some guys put up with this their whole lives. They could not argue on the job, they could not argue in their personal life. Postal workers with one tenth his stress reported for work with enough weaponry to shoot up a whole zip code. Maybe it was symptomatic of the vague depression that gripped many policemen that when it came time for them to break down, they simply put the barrels of their revolvers into their mouths and pulled the triggers.

He was on Lockman's street two and three-quarter hours after leaving Seattle, driving no faster than traffic allowed, which in the 'burbs was heavier on Saturdays than in the middle of the week. Heavier in the boonies, too, part of the ancient forest that reached northward across two countries to the arctic circle. Lockman's street was part of the forest, too, with trees as tall as apartment buildings. Dorothy Gold and her friend came out of a house across the street from Lockman's old address. Slightly overweight, Gold had more gray in her hair than Boudreau. Her friend seemed more severe and nervous: she watched Boudreau like a dog on a leash. There was no mistaking the expression on the faces of the two women: "We're glad you're here."

The friend, Myra Goss, was one of those priceless perfect witnesses who could recall not only if she had been drinking, but where she had had three beers, or two beers, and where she had gone next. So she was very clear on seeing Lockman only once, having a buzz on at the time, watching him go to fireball at the slightest provocation, validating conclusions she had come to while listening to the stories Dorothy—Dottie, to her friends—had been telling her about the strange man who lived across the street. And she remembered the stories better than their teller, and when Dottie faltered, Myra would interrupt, "That's not what you told me," and Dottie would remember more clearly, going on to tell other things she had not told her friend previously. Boudreau called Diane at their hotel and said he would meet her at the restaurant. Boudreau had Dottie draw a floor plan of the house across the street. The house had a new owner—it already had a new roof.

He was late getting away for dinner and drove in the dark to downtown Portland. When he came out of the tunnel he was supposed to make a left and go north for about a dozen blocks. The restaurant was at the top of a high-rise office building. Driving through Portland on the interstate, Boudreau had seen only ordinary cityscape, like that of Newark, New Jersey, or Philadelphia. But now he saw he was in the midst of upscale apartments, sophisticated shops, and glass-walled office towers on streets lined with mature trees—the city in the forest, beautiful, even restful. But bizarre, given what Boudreau knew now about the horror that had taken place here.

—

HE GOT OUT of bed after midnight and sat at the hotel-room window and looked at the moonlight on the snow covering Mount Hood, fifty miles to the east. He had told Diane only part of what he had learned today, and that only after dinner, which had been her treat, one of the best meals of his life. Another eerie juxtaposition, a perfect jewel of a restaurant almost within hailing distance of a nightmare so intense it still had him reeling.

Diane had told him to park the car in the garage across the street from the high-rise and take the special elevator up to the restaurant. When the doors opened upstairs, he thought he was in the wrong place until Diane came into focus and waved. She saw right away that something was weighing on him. He kissed her, nuzzling her cheek, inhaling her scent, and got a big smile in return. His confusion about where he was must have been all over his face. This was a private club, she said, open to the public in the evenings. The dining room was wood-paneled and thickly carpeted, the glass outer walls giving a view of the Willamette River. He sat back and tried to enjoy it. Diane told him that Lonnie had looked at the material she had collected for her book, the interviews, completed questionnaires, statistics, and said that it only proved that a lot of people who passed through San Francisco in the late sixties to get high and laid a lot had gone on to do other things, some of them interesting. Diane said she had just stared. No book—at least, not the kind of book she had thought she would write. Now she could see that what she had really wanted to do was tell her own story as it had been repeated in the stories of others ten thousand times over: the breakout from emotional and sexual repression, the unforeseen consequences of going too far in the other direction. She could see now that she had wanted to find an historic validation to her life; and now she could see she had been one of many who had simply zigged and zagged reactively at certain times and places. Worse than her disappointment about the book was her anger over now being able to see her historical self so plainly. Lonnie had told her she was up to her armpits in patients from all over southern Oregon suffering the effects of changing sexual mores. "I'm pissed off," Diane said. "I wanted to count for more than some kind of regional yuppie shithead." Boudreau wanted to console her, but at this moment it seemed that the best thing he could do now was keep his mouth shut.

He ordered rack of lamb. The soup of the day was carrot, made with reduced, flavorful vegetable stock and thickened in the blender with onions and celery sweated down in oil and butter. His mother would have been impressed, he told Diane, and the lamb, carefully removed from the bone and served with a perfect gravy, was only better than the soup. But Boudreau could not clear his mind. The images the women had planted in his head were still too vivid. When he apologized for being quiet, Diane told him she could see that something had happened to him this afternoon.

Only when the table was cleared did he tell Diane that the women he had interviewed this afternoon had given him information that led him to conclude that Garrett Richard Lockman had taken his victims down here to Portland and had killed them in a room in his basement he had built for the purpose. One of the women, Lockman's neighbor, had seen a large bottle of chloroform on a shelf in his garage, and when she'd asked what it was for, Lockman had told her it was for the neighborhood cats, which he hated. Anyone familiar with the behavior of cats would know that Lockman's story was nonsense. The neighbor confirmed Boudreau's group's paper trail of evidence that Lockman always owned a vehicle—a van, an ambulance, a station wagon—large enough to transport bodies, and that he was often gone for days at a time.

And when Lockman returned, Dorothy Gold had said, he would be unusually exhausted. *Spent* was more accurate. His interest in the Green River case had been intense and enduring. He told people he was working for the government on the case in a special, secret capacity. Neither of the women could recall specific dates for his comings and goings, so nothing they had told Boudreau amounted to much as legal evidence. But it was the kind of independent confirmation of several key points that had to be made about a real suspect in the series of killings. . . .

Hours ago. Looking at Mount Hood, he couldn't help thinking about how he could put it into play. He heard Diane roll over in the bed behind him, and turned around. She sat up, uncovered. "Phil?"

"I'm fine. Just awake."

"Me, too." She looked at her watch. "Too late for a nightcap, too early for breakfast. Do you want to go home?"

He moved to her side. "I'm feeling that murderous rage again."

"You're a classic case. You didn't have a single gray hair before you found Betty Antonelli."

"There's more. I couldn't tell you at dinner." He shuddered as he drew a breath. "Through it all, I've tried not to think of what he was doing to the girls. Finding Betty Antonelli pushed my nose in it, but as I found out yesterday afternoon, I was still not really focused—" Why did he want to tell her? Was he a little boy crying to his mommy? He said, "Dorothy Gold told me that Garrett Lockman regularly woke her up in the middle of the night with the smell of backyard barbecuing."

"She smelled it? Oh, Jesus!"

"She asked him about it." He was thinking of his own weakness and perversity, telling her something so disgusting. "He said he got hungry at odd hours because of his schedule working on the Green River case. He couldn't help when he got hungry, he said."

"He got defensive, in other words."

"Then he giggled. I know that giggle. He thinks he's put one over on you. The evidence of what he did in that house is gone now. Lockman was clever enough to beat us when it came to harvesting his victims, so it's an even bet that he was just as skillful covering up that he cooked them and ate them. Why did he do that? Cannibalism, I mean?"

"It goes with the territory, according to the literature. It's supposed to be an original move, but it's just another step of a well-charted progressive mental disease. Deep down, he knows he's the most inadequate thing that has ever walked the earth. Cannibalism is the ultimate way of proving it to himself."

" 'In for a penny, in for a pound.' He said that to me once, saying he was quoting his mother."

"Come on, let's get out of here. You'll be ravenous by the time we get to Seattle."

If she was making a joke, even inadvertently, he felt too fragile to want to pick up on it.

———

SPENCER CALLED BOUDREAU twenty hours later. Diane had gone home in the early evening, and Paulie was sound asleep in his room. "Sorry to bother you at this hour, Phil, but it's important. Let me come up there."

"I'll unlock the front door. Be quiet on the stairs."

An hour and a half later, in Boudreau's living room, Spencer was holding up a videocassette. "I found this today in the press office with the news videos."

"You went in on Sunday?"

He shrugged. "To search the press office."

Boudreau grabbed the cassette. "You may amount to something yet."

Spencer helped himself to coffee while Boudreau got the tape going. First, a familiar network logo. Then a glossy, gossamer-curtained stage. The camera pulled back to reveal a runway and an audience on both sides. In a few minutes watching the pageant became almost impossible. The manic gesturing of the host, the glued-on smiles of the contestants, the silliness of a waxen beauty playing a xylophone, the dated commercials, especially for movies and cars. . .

Spencer said, "I watched this four times already."

Boudreau took a moment. "Four? Then you're sure?"

Paulie's door opened and he stuck his head out. "Oh. Hiya, Wayne."

"Hey, kid. You're gettin' big."

"Yeah, right. Keep it down, will you?"

Spencer looked to Boudreau with an overacted expression of surprise at the boy's audacity. Boudreau said, "Paulie, can you dupe this tape?"

"Sure, but it will look lousy. What is it?"

"The 1982 Miss America Pageant. It's important."

"Okay, if you don't mind furry." He closed the door.

Boudreau said, "He and his pals make movies with a camcorder. Now he wants a computer."

"Give it to him."

"I can't afford the one he wants. He says it will be obsolete next year anyway." He turned to the television set. "Tell me about this."

"The last time, I slow-mo'd through every audience shot. Lockman's not in it. I met him, I know what he looks like. He's not in it."

"That's not what Beale told me."

"And everybody else. Dan Cheong was standing right there, nodding on every word."

Boudreau was thinking of what he had just learned in Portland. He reached for the telephone.

"Who are you calling at this hour?"

"Everybody."

———

BOUDREAU HIT THE remote button that stopped the tape. Robinson reached for the wall switch and turned the lights on. Les Lucas asked, "Are you absolutely sure that Lockman isn't in that audience somewhere?"

Spencer said, "I can tell you exactly when the blonde hits the clam on the violin."

"What about those gas charges that put him back east?"

Sciscio said, "It was his card that was used, that's what we know. Anybody could have signed the slips."

"And they're disposed of when the gas bill is paid," Robinson said.

"You should have told me about this Dorothy Gold," Donovan said. "It could be trouble with Portland."

"I've already told you," Boudreau said mildly, working toward the necessary lie, "she said when she called that she was leaving the area. We had a time problem. Besides, we have Portland people on the team now."

"But it took everything we had to talk them into it. This is the one thing Portland is afraid of, that the killings took place down there."

"Fuck Portland," Les Lucas said as Donovan looked pained. "And fuck Ron Beale and Dan Cheong. I don't give a shit if he was their snitch. I am not going to have this filthy bastard eating girls' gizzards on my beat. There's no doubt about that?"

"None," Boudreau said. "It's in the literature. Eventually they all sink to it."

Lucas sighed. "Well, it boils the snot out of my okra. Some days it don't pay to get out of bed." He got up and headed for the door. "Good work, Boudreau."

"Wayne gets the credit. He put in the hours."

Lucas gave Spencer that noncountry stare. "Kevin, let's meet in your office and see how quickly we can get this up to speed."

Donovan remained seated, glaring at Boudreau. He waited until Lucas was down the hall. "You other guys get out. I want to have a word with Boudreau in private."

Robinson and Sciscio moved out. Spencer wanted Boudreau to see him grinning, but Boudreau kept his eyes on Donovan as Spencer followed the others. He closed the door behind him. Donovan hissed, "You sandbagged me."

"What are you talking about?"

"When I got you on the Green River Investigative Team, I told you that this, this right here, was an FBI operation. You were to clear everything through me. I should have seen this tape before anybody else. Is this our only copy?"

"No."

"How many others are there?"

"I don't know, a lot. The network can make all we want anyway."

"Are you wearing a wire?"

"Don't be stupid. All I want is Lockman. When this is over, I'm going back to Seattle PD to finish my twenty. Then maybe I'll become a caterer."

"As long as you understand that you're not a major player in this game. Don't try to make yourself one."

"Donovan, I don't give a flying fuck about generating career capital. What for, to hang out with guys like you? You were with Beale and Cheong when they hauled Betty Antonelli down to the Public Safety Building, where she may have crossed paths with Lockman. Did you see him that day? She saw somebody who fits his description. If it was him, he recognized her later. If you want to shuffle the fact that you believed Beale's bullshit about Lockman to the bottom of the deck, fine. If you want the collar, take it. Become the next J. Edgar Asshole, for all I care. But stay the fuck out of my way until I finish the job I could have done years ago!"

Suddenly Donovan let out a barking laugh and clapped his hands. "You changed the game!"

Boudreau got up. "And you'll adapt. How quickly you adapt amazes me. After we found Betty Antonelli, you let them toss my name back into the suspect bin. Lucas coming around to see if I wanted time off when he never asked me the time of day before? This is an FBI operation, you said. He wouldn't have done squat without your knowledge."

Donovan looked at the ceiling, obviously thinking it over. "You still don't have a clue. You've *always* been a suspect, as far as Beale and Cheong and their people are concerned. Betty Antonelli's body almost clinched it for you. There's always been another team behind yours, checking everything you've done."

"Checking on Lockman, you mean. Like running down the murders in Spokane."

"That, and many, many other things." Suddenly Donovan grinned. "We had him under surveillance, couldn't get anything. When we heard him on the telephone calling somebody Felix, identifying himself as Oscar, some people were ready to shoot you like a dog."

"The Odd Couple? Didn't anybody get that? It was a play. It was on tele-vision for years."

Donovan held out his thumb and forefinger a fraction of an inch apart. "You came this close. Cooler heads prevailed."

Boudreau stared at him.

"Cooler heads prevailed, I said." Donovan was looking him in the eye. "You'll get what you want. Now just get out of here."

JUNE 1987

Anton Charles's annual spring outdoor cocktail party was just beginning to roar when Garrett Lockman arrived wearing his old navy dress whites. Perfectly appropriate, since it was after Memorial Day. Conversation stopped. Men and women alike turned to look. Anton Charles swept up to him, removed his sunglasses, winced, and put the glasses back on.

"My God, you glare. You look like the third lead in a John Wayne navy movie. Are you insane?"

Lockman laughed. "Take a guess."

"What's the idea?"

"According to the law of the land and a tradition that's even older, I have every right to wear this uniform." He smiled brightly. "I served my country, which is more than I can say for most of the people here, including you."

"You will do absolutely anything to get attention, Garrett. You're up to something. What is it now?"

"Campaigning. I'm running for reelection."

"I told you not to do that."

Lockman waved to a priest across the garden. "That's because you're a small-minded old tart."

"Stop that," Charles said through his teeth. "The reason I don't want you to do it, as I very carefully explained to you, is that no one in the history of the United States has ever been president of his student bar for two terms. It is just not done."

Flashing a big grin, Lockman waved to a pretty female student who did not like him. "All the more reason for me to do it. Who then? Aren't I the most remarkable person who ever let you suck his dick?"

"I want you to leave," Anton Charles said icily.

"Hey! Lighten up! I'm just having a good time at your party. We're going to see each other later, aren't we?"

"We'll see how you behave. And try to stay sober, will you? People were talking about you two weeks ago."

Lockman couldn't remember the occasion Charles was talking about. "I can pass out my cards, can't I?"

Charles looked alarmed. "What kind of cards? You can't solicit votes in my home."

"My business cards."

"These people know who you are and how to reach you."

"So?" He pretended to look around. "Ah, now I see where you set up the bar. I'll get my own drink."

"I told you, go easy."

At the bar Lockman glanced behind him to see that Charles was turned away, then got a double scotch and started to circulate. Fifty people crowded Charles's well-tended little postage stamp of a rear garden, priests, nuns, lay faculty from other schools of the university, lawyers from downtown, some people from the Spokane District Attorney's Office. As president of the Student Bar Association, Garrett Lockman was a very small fish, but he was the only man wearing navy dress whites, which had heads turning. At last he came upon Waldo Starr, tieless, uncombed, badly shaved, looking like he needed a bath, standing with Bill Slade, and Slade's wife, a mousy brunette whose name Lockman could not remember. Starr eyed him up and down while Slade just broke out in a big, stupid grin.

"Not a costume party, Lockman," Starr said.

"I'm entitled to wear this uniform. If you'd ever worked for this country, as I have, in a variety of capacities, you'd have more respect for it, its institutions, and its symbols."

"I didn't know you ever worked for the government," Mrs. Slade said.

"Don't believe him," Slade said.

"I used the past tense," Lockman growled. "Be careful how you express yourself."

Slade thought about this. He was rock-hard, with short blond hair. "What are you going to do, sue me?"

"You know what I can do." Lockman had seen him in a car with another woman. "Let's just put it this way: I'm counting on your vote for reelection to the presidency of the Student Bar Association."

"That sounds like a threat. What are you hinting around? Spit it out, or you might be spitting teeth."

Lockman grinned. "Now that is a threat. And if you make good on it, you'll never be a lawyer, of course."

Waldo Starr said, "You're absolutely wild, Lockman."

"Who's going to New York for the ABA convention?"

"Who's scared to death of New York?" Starr asked. "Who wants me to sell him a gun to take to New York?"

Slade laughed. "A gun to New York? How?"

"United Parcel. No big deal."

Mrs. Slade asked, "You sell guns?"

"Absolutely not. You have to have a federal license to sell guns. The one thing we can't do is violate the law."

Lockman laughed out loud and patted Starr on the shoulder. "The last thing we want to do, that's for sure. Thank you for your support." He drifted away, draining his glass, and headed back to the bar for a refill.

When the air cooled, half the party moved indoors, while the rest left for the law school's hangout near the campus. Lockman did not want to be under Anton Charles's scrutiny, so he slipped away to join the second group. In the bar, because the drinks were no longer free, he switched to vodka. He was on his fourth double vodka, sitting with a dozen other students, including Charlie Taylor, Ed Mills, Heidi Lawrence, Courtenay Woods, and Waldo Starr, when Joanie Singer arrived. Lockman was so stiff drunk he knew he could sit perfectly still and be taken for sober. Heidi and Courtenay were real beauties, long-legged and slim, the kind of women he had never had, had never even talked to for long without being brushed off. He could not help being nervous around women like these, and being secretly drunk did not calm him. From time to time he stared at Waldo Starr, who always avoided making eye contact with Lockman when they were with others, as if the others did not know that Starr was Lockman's gofer. In a school where the faculty was packed with pansies, Starr's public distancing of himself from Lockman was probably good social strategy, but Lockman knew that it really was Starr's way of prancing around in front of his master, like a dog that slipped its leash.

"You're unusually quiet tonight," Joanie Singer said to Lockman when she was settled. She was from Chicago, pudgy and unkempt—and a little blurry-eyed herself tonight, it seemed. She made Lockman think of an unattractive Dottie Gold, but she was open and friendly, even helplessly so.

"Oh," he said, looking at his ice cubes, thinking that he had to speak very slowly, "I'm just listening. Wearing the uniform reminded me of too many unhappy memories. I guess it was a mistake. Can I get you another drink?"

"No, thanks. I'm all right. What unhappy memories?"

"Work the navy trained me to do. I was so good at it that the government kept me on after my discharge for special assignments. I'm looking at you women and trying not to think of something that happened. Let me buy."

She handed him her glass. "Vodka and Sprite. Thanks."

Lockman was at the bar when the Slades walked in. He watched them in the mirror behind the bar. They headed toward the table where Joanie Singer and the others were sitting. The bartender arrived with Lockman's order, causing him to look in the other direction—good thing: when he looked back again, Slade was turning his head away. They had been talking about him. When Lockman returned to the table, the Slades were moving chairs up next to Waldo Starr. He gave Joanie Singer her terrible potion.

"What did Bill Slade say about me?"

"Oh, he asked what I thought of your uniform."

"And?"

"You were in the navy, you're entitled. Besides, you look good in it. And it's nice to have a change in the routine. I'm one of the few people who likes Spokane, but even I'm willing to admit that things get pretty repetitive."

"What else did Slade say?"

"I think he's a little drunk."

"You don't have to protect him."

"I'm not! Really, he didn't say anything!"

"I'm sorry. The things I've been through have left me permanently, oh, scarred, I guess. I don't sleep well."

"You were on special assignments?"

"I shouldn't have mentioned it. Eastern Europe. I had to kill somebody. It wasn't supposed to happen, but there was no choice. I had to follow orders."

"Well, it's over. Don't think about it."

"I realize that it wasn't just the uniform that evoked the memory, it's all you women. That's who I had to kill, you see. A woman."

Her eyes were wide. "You killed—"

"It was a case of her being in the wrong place at the wrong time. I shouldn't have mentioned it. I'm sorry."

"How did you do it?"

Holding his right wrist with his left hand, he brought his right forearm up to his chest. "Like this. She never made a sound. Look, don't mention this to other people, please. What I wanted to talk to you about, what I should have been talking about, is my campaign for reelection. It's an awful juxtaposition, I know, but—"

"Don't worry." She patted his hand.

"Hey, Lockman!" It was Slade. "What kind of bullshit are you shoveling now?"

He didn't look at Slade, but put his drink down, got up, and headed for the door. Joanie Singer said something. Slade answered her, and people laughed, including, Lockman heard, Waldo Starr—that worm! All Lockman had to do was make a telephone call, and Starr's life was finished. Slade didn't know how easy it would be for Lockman to kill Slade's little woman, that twerpette, even get away with it—but for all Lockman knew, Slade wanted to get rid of her as much as Lockman wanted to hurt Slade. Next year, in the spring semester, Lockman would fix Slade's record in the university computer. With everybody eager to get out of town, Slade would find himself twenty credits short of his degree.

Outside the bar, Lockman couldn't remember where he had parked the ambulance. How drunk was he? If he waited for long, and Joanie Singer didn't follow him out, he would be even more hurt than he was now. The last thing he wanted was to enter into a "normal" relationship with a Joanie Singer, a woman other men wouldn't go near—he might wind up stuck with her. The ambulance was around the corner. Except for consequences to the dress whites, it would make sense for him to sleep it off in the back. And being seen there by a Bill Slade. Did he want to cruise? No. Too drunk. No plan. He stumbled toward the corner, drunker than he had imagined, drunker than he might have ever been before. Now Lockman remembered Anton Charles. Couldn't go back to Charles's place, either. Had to remember not to grope in his pocket for the key to the ambulance until he was at the driver's door, in case he dropped the key. It wouldn't go far. Couldn't get on his hands and knees the way he was dressed. If he had to walk home, at least he would know that the key was under the ambulance, safe.

———

He woke up at dawn in Hazel and Al's driveway, the ambulance at an odd angle to Al's Buick—and much too close! Halfway between drunk and hungover, head splitting, eyes burning, Lockman got out, almost losing his balance, and saw that the heavy chrome bumper of the ambulance was pressed deeply into the right tail lamp of the Buick. The Buick's fender was compressed and pushed forward, the paint wrinkled like cellophane. Lockman turned. A track through the lawn led back to one of Hazel's curbside azaleas, crushed like roadkill. Lockman got back in the ambulance.

The gear lever was still in drive, the ignition key switched on. The lights were off—he must have pushed in the switch. He couldn't remember. He couldn't remember anything after leaving Anton Charles's party, just that he had gone with some others. He moved the ambulance out to the curb and locked the doors.

The rest of Sunday started to come back to him. Joanie Singer. He could remember talking to Joanie Singer and leaving because of Bill Slade. Had he done anything to call attention to himself besides smacking Al's pride and joy? Lockman couldn't remember.

He flopped onto his bed in the uniform. He wanted unconsciousness to fall on him like Al's Buick. But he was still awake when he heard someone moving around in the other bedroom. As quietly as he could, he tiptoed to his door and turned the little lock.

In a few minutes more there was a knock on the door. Al called him. As secure as he was, Lockman kept his eyes closed and pretended he was asleep. He forced himself to think of Deeah Anne Johanssen's firm, fat ass, which was always enough to give him an erection—or at least the belief he would get one if he had not drunk himself limp.

———

"Is he gone?"

"Who?"

"Al. Is he gone?"

"Yes. Come out now, Garrett, please."

"I hate to hear him yelling at you like that, Hazel. It just tears me up."

"It doesn't mean anything. He's going to be at his office all day. It's hard for me to hear through the door. You know I don't hear so good anymore. Come out, Garrett."

Lockman opened the door a crack. He wanted Hazel to beg a little more than usual. It would work in his favor for days to come. Hazel would remember how hard it had been to calm him the next time Al tried to get on his case. Lockman knew Hazel was deaf. She was getting old, curling over like a boiled shrimp. Her skin was so dry it looked like he could pinch off a handful. She stepped back.

"Oh, you look like you've been sick!"

"That's what I said. Al always wants to jump to the conclusion that I've been doing something wrong. The food at Anton's party must have been put out in the sun too early. My cramps were so bad, it was all I could do to get home. By the time I came around the corner here, I felt like I had a knife in my belly."

"You should have awakened us."

"What was the point? I knew it would pass. If it didn't, there was nothing you or anybody else could do about it. I'm sorry about his precious car, but I'll pay for it. He'll have it back as good as new by the end of the week."

"How are you going to pay for it? All you have is your little benefits check. We have comprehensive. We're completely covered, except for the deductible."

This is what he wanted to do for the rest of eternity, he thought: discuss the nuances of automobile insurance with this quivering old bag. "I'll write a check for that right now. You can call him and tell him that I'll take his car to the body shop of his choice."

"You don't have to do that. Please don't worry about it. We're both so proud of you."

"I wish I could believe that about Al."

"I'll talk to him."

"Don't. I don't want to put you to any trouble."

She moved closer, to hug him, but he stepped back. She was incontinent now and smelled like an oppressively scented diaper pail. He wasn't going to have to pay Al anything. Hazel would cover it out of her sugar-bowl money. As far as she was concerned, if Lockman said he had been abducted by aliens, she would not let anyone, even Al, say another word.

———

LOCKMAN ASCENDED THE cellar stairs and closed the door behind him. "Spotless, as near as I can tell," he called as he trooped toward the glow of the television set. "If all else fails, you can clean houses for a living. It will give you a chance to wear women's clothes outside, too."

Martin Jones pushed back on his recliner and glowered. He was wearing a scarlet silk robe with a feathery collar, black patent-leather pumps, and full makeup. He had taken to painting his toenails purple. A prostitute so ugly would owe her clients money. "I'm wondering why you're calling me again, Lockman. Are you figuring you can flop here whenever you're passing through town?"

"I didn't have to let you know I was going to be in Seattle at all, my faithful Indian companion. You would have never known I was going to New York. I could have just changed planes at Sea-Tac. But I thought it would be nice to get together and celebrate the good old days."

"Get drunk on my booze, you mean."

"I'm not drinking as much as I used to. I think it was a phase I was going through. No, actually, I have some things for you. To add to your collection. Souvenirs."

Martin Jones sat up, interested, then settled back into his leather-covered womb, seeming to deflate a little. "I don't know. You're such a trickster. What are you up to? How do I know you're not trying to frame me with something?"

Garrett Lockman clapped his hands. "That's wonderful! In these walls you've got the evidence of—what? Sixty, seventy murders? Don't you get it? At the least you're an accessory, a coconspirator. Some prosecutors might say you're as guilty as I am. And you're worried about me framing you. If a tornado ever hit this house, your next best move would be to stick your tongue in a light socket."

"We don't have tornadoes in Seattle, Lockman."

"Come on, let's go out."

"Where? There's nobody on the street these days except the chicken hawks and diseased kids."

"We can mosey. It's not like we can't give a good account of ourselves. You've always been a solid citizen, I'm a solid citizen now—"

"What shit. If cops run a check on you and find you're in law school, they'll split their sides laughing."

"Are you coming out?"

"Where did you get money? How about paying me back?"

"Hazel gave me a couple of bucks for New York. Some isn't going to make much of a difference to you."

"Against what you owe me, you mean."

"If you must."

Martin Jones used his remote control to channel-surf, stopping at

Showtime, where the latest Emmanuelle chewed the nipple of a writhing blonde. "No, Garrett, tonight I think I'll stay in."

Lockman laughed. "For a little soft-core porn?"

"I can go around the corner and rent all the hard-core I could ever hope to watch. If you want to crash in the guest room, you're welcome— that's as much as I want to celebrate the good old days—but the bar is most definitely closed." Martin Jones turned his head to gaze on Lockman. "No problem for you, of course, since you've cut down on your drinking."

"You don't want to go out."

"In fact, I don't want to do anything."

"Am I supposed to read a larger meaning into this behavior? If so, Martin, I'd just as soon you say what's on your mind directly, without all this affectation."

Martin Jones raised himself a little, perhaps a sign of rising emotion. "Affectation? You called me from Spokane, all sweetness and light, telling me about your trip, saying you wanted to stop over before going on to New York. I said I'd pick you up at the airport, which I did, and as soon as we were out of the terminal you started in on cruising the old haunts even though I told you over the phone that I didn't want to do that, that nothing was happening—thanks to you—but no, you just had to keep right on campaigning like a kid who wants a toy. You're like a little kid, Lockman. You have to have a toy. That's the reason you stopped in Seattle. You're looking for action. You want to drag me into something, and I just don't want to do it."

"You got yellow."

"On the contrary. As it turns out, my period of remorse was only temporary. Our experience actually whetted my appetite. But I'm smarter than you. If I ever get back into it, I'm going to vary my MO. And I know when it's time to lay off. This is that time. Maybe that's what made me roll back originally, something I realized."

"What's that?"

"You're going to get caught."

"Bullshit. If they haven't caught me by now, they're never going to catch me. I'm not doing it anymore."

"Oh, no? You said you brought me souvenirs. You can't stop lying. Is that clear enough? You have no idea what I went through over the years, taking your abuse, listening to your mad schemes. As soon as things got a little hot for you—never mind me—you lit out like a cat being chased by a dog. Did it ever occur to you how that was perceived?"

Lockman grinned. "By whom?"

"By me!"

"Oh, for God's sake."

Martin Jones sat up straighter, so his pumps almost touched the floor. "See? See? Let me ask you one question, Lockman—"

He grinned. He felt like a spectator in the upper deck, watching the two of them. Cochise thought he was going for the knockout, but in fact he was losing on points faster and faster. "Okay, but I don't know if I'm going to answer it."

That stopped him. He looked away, but only for a moment, coming back with surprising swiftness. "What did you feel for me?"

"What?" He knew exactly what Jones was talking about.

"What did you feel for me? All those years. Putting me through all that emotional turmoil."

Lockman shrugged. "We were friends."

"No, that's not an answer. What did you feel?"

"I liked you. I still like you. Jesus Christ, I hope you're not hoping for me to say that you made me hot."

"Don't start that stuff again."

"Me? I'm not starting anything. Look, I thought we could have a good time tonight. Talk over the old days. Let me get the souvenirs." His suitcase was in the hall. He got it and opened it on the bar. The goodies were in a plastic bag. He tossed it into Martin Jones's lap. Jones held the package under the light of the floor lamp beside him, a pink brassiere and a pair of lime-green panties.

"Are you going to tell me how you got these?"

"A girl in school. She was short on money, so I talked her into taking off her clothes and doing stuff for me."

Actually, they were Sonya's. Jones opened the bag, looked in, and made a face. He sealed the bag again and flipped it onto the couch. "Law-school students bathe once in a while, especially if they're going to put on a show for someone who can talk about them. You got this stuff off a dead whore. A whore you killed. Did you strangle her?"

Lockman decided that Jones didn't deserve to know. "You're just spoiled, my wee friend. Whenever I brought you underwear in the past, they were washed clean. Tell me how I'm supposed to hang up a woman's underwear to dry with Hazel on the premises."

"Okay, now—"

"Aren't you going to say thanks?"

"Okay, thanks. I'll probably have to get rid of them, though, figuring how you really got them. If you can't wash milady's underwear, then you can't take your other usual precautions, either. Have they found her body? Now, if you don't mind, answer my first question."

"Which question is that?"

Martin Jones rolled his eyes. "Let me make it simple so that even a law-school student can understand it. What. Did. You. Feel. About. Me?"

"I told you. I liked you. We're friends. We shared adventures together."

Martin Jones looked away. After a moment Lockman saw his face reddening, turning blotchy. The little geek was crying, and it was all Lockman could do to keep from laughing. "Come on, let's go out."

"Back to that again," Jones whispered. On the television screen, Emmanuelle gawked at a limp penis. Jones aimed the remote and zapped to a blurry black-and-white Robert Donat. He looked over at Lockman again, making no effort to conceal his distress. "I don't know. Back when you were living in Portland, when we saw a lot of each other, when we were on the phone so much, I felt a real bond between us. I felt you looked forward to the next adventure as much as I did, but I allowed myself to be deceived, because whatever it was that I was feeling—it wasn't sexual, I assure you, because, as I've told you, I am absolutely not interested in having sex—whatever I felt, as much as I wanted to believe you were feeling it, too, the plain and simple fact of the matter was that you weren't."

"Make sense. I'm not following you."

"You weren't feeling anything inside. You weren't feeling anything at all. It was always another one of your tricks. I don't know, you have an inability to stay in one emotional place for any length of time."

"What the hell are you talking about?"

"I'm talking about the way you constantly choose pleasure."

"So?"

"When the choice is between pleasure and anything else, anything, you always choose pleasure at the expense of everything. And everyone. I don't know, I kept hoping you'd break through, that the fun and games would stop and there would be some peace—" He sat up. "I can see that you don't have any idea what I'm talking about."

"That's what I'm saying. I don't know what the fuck you're talking about. I doubt that you know yourself." Lockman considered making another crack about the time Jones had gotten so drunk, or even telling him it had never happened, just to see what Jones believed this time. "Are you pissed off because I hung up on you that time?"

"What time?"

"Last year. You called me in Spokane and I hung up on you without speaking."

Martin Jones grinned. "You've done a lot of things to me, Lockman, but you've never hung up. You're losing your mind—or are you trying to pull something new?"

Lockman thought of needling him about what he meant, swallowing Lockman's sword, but he had pushed Anton Charles too far. The same with Waldo Starr. For all Lockman knew, Hazel had gotten the name of the caller wrong—Lockman had thought that in the days after, when Jones hadn't called back. Lockman walked around behind the bar, opened the little refrigerator, and pulled out a tray of ice cubes. "Do you want anything?" he asked, keeping his eyes below the bar so he couldn't see Jones. "I'm going to have a drink. Let me fix one for you, too, killer "

"No." It was like a moan. "Nothing." He heard Jones push the recliner back again. "Have whatever you like. I'll set the alarm so you get to the airport on time, no matter what shape you're in."

———

WHEN HE REACHED the corner of Eighth Avenue and Forty-second Street, Garrett Lockman realized he was more frightened than he had ever been in his life, so frightened he did not want to take another step. New York was worse than Tijuana. Day and night, it was noisier, more crowded, faster—horrible: if you didn't get out of people's way, you were going to get cursed and trampled. Russian and Arab taxi drivers seemed so ready to drive over your toes that you dared not step off the curb. The sidewalks were occupied by a secret army of the insane, because no one really seemed to notice them: shuffling panhandlers hustling spare change, crack-crazed young bums crashed in doorways, strangely dressed women with skin like old leather pushing shopping carts in all directions. The whole place smelled like a garbage can on a hot summer's day. And worst of all, it never stopped: last night, lying in bed, Lockman had listened to the screaming sirens, and as soon as he had been able to fall asleep, garbage trucks had come snarling up the street. Lawyers' convention? Lockman couldn't concentrate on anything, much less the dreary stuff lawyers loved so much. This was only the second night and he didn't know how he was going to get to the end of the convention.

He had come this far from his hotel in the hope of having a little fun without being seen by other conventioneers. Fun, his kind of fun, seemed to be available everywhere: if he had just wanted a hooker, he could have found one outside the hotel entrance. But Lockman didn't want stories getting back to Spokane, didn't want suspicions being raised. Martin Jones thought that changing the MO would confuse the cops even more. Changing the MO meant that you were inexperienced each and every time you tried to do the thing. A geek like Jones had no chance anyway. He was too afraid, and sooner or later he would run into a woman tough enough to beat the shit out of him.

Lockman carefully regarded the gaudily dressed women silhouetted against the lighted store windows. A couple of black women stirred indolently, but he looked away to discourage them. In another moment a little teenager with badly dyed blond hair stepped up, eyed him, and smiled. She wore tight black shorts, a red tank top, and pendant earrings. Her makeup looked caked on, muddy with sweat around her dark hairline. "Looking to party?" she shouted over the roar.

"Could be. How much does it cost in the big town?"

"You ain't a cop, are you?"

"Do I look like a cop?"

She let her eyes shift left and right. "Who knows what a cop looks like? They gotta hire everybody these days."

He laughed. "How about you, then? You could be a cop."

"Yeah, right. You gotta car?"

"No."

"Tell you what. You go across the street to that tenement over the Irish bar there, go up to the third floor, and I'll meet you. For fifty bucks, you'll get the best lovin' you ever had in your life."

"I go up there and your pimp follows and mugs me."

"This is Noo Yawk, Bebo. You could get mugged right here on the sidewalk." She started away.

"Wait a minute." She came back. Lockman said, "Let's go to a real hotel and I'll pay you a hundred."

"Yeah, right. I just do the one thing, see what I'm sayin'? Oral. And you gotta wear a rubbah. I ain't gettin' AIDS. Fifty bucks, take it or leave it."

"Don't give me that. I checked the prices down on Thirty-sixth Street. It's thirty bucks down there."

"Then get your ass back down to Thirty-sixth and get yourself a slab of the dark meat. That's what you're talking about. Get a pair of those big, thick lips wrapped around your joint, shut your eyes, dream of me, and save yourself twenty dead presidents. Hell of a deal. Tell you what. You make up your fuckin' mind now or get the fuck off my corner. We're talkin' real lovin' here."

"I want to pay you a hundred because I want to take pictures of you."

She frowned. "What kinda pictures?"

"With your clothes off. Doing things to yourself. How tough is that?"

"Okay, but you don't get nothin' else. Touchin' me is extra. And we gotta use my room."

"You got a deal. And we go up to the room together."

"Yeah, right, what the fuck."

He wanted her help getting across Eighth Avenue, but suddenly, quick as a sparrow, she darted in front of a bounding wave of taxicabs. On the other side she looked back at him with her mouth open in surprise. He had to wait for the next green light. When he got across, she was a few feet up from the corner, under the marquee of an adult theater. Three triple-X features. "What happened to you? I coulda made anuddah fifty bucks while I was waitin'."

IN HIS HOTEL room later Lockman found his message light blinking, but he was so eager to see what was in the little hooker's purse that he sat on one of the beds with his back to the telephone and emptied the contents onto the bedspread. No paper money, which figured: she had hidden his hundred when she undressed. A nickel and two pennies. A pink rat-tail comb. A single-edged razor blade, the whore's weapon of choice. If she had been able to use it, she would have gone for his eyes. Blind him with his own blood. He counted four large bobby pins. A blue nylon wallet with a Velcro closure, which he set aside for last. The ring of keys, a few of which were for the kind of padlocks he had seen on the other doors in the tenement. Two coins he had to look at carefully to identify: subway tokens. He pocketed them.

He opened the wallet. No credit cards, of course. The little plastic envelopes into which she would have put them were filled instead with color pictures of girls her own age, one signed, *Luv ya, Angie. Marie,* black-and-white pictures of two middle-aged couples squinting in the sun, one outside an aluminum-sided house, the other beside a '59 Olds, an ugly car with none of the classic grace of the models of the early fifties. In the envelope facing the identification-card window was a professional color photograph of a toddler, a girl holding a ball and laughing at someone next to the camera. Angie a mom? Lockman went on to the identification. *If found please return to: Angela Ruiz, 37-68 64th Street, Woodside, New York 11377. DOB: 3/17/68.* It took Lockman a moment to realize that her birthday was Saint Patrick's Day. No luck for her. There was a telephone number, but it was crossed out. Lockman slipped the card out of the window and looked at the other side. Another telephone number, this one with a 718 area code. Around here? He would have to check before calling.

He left the purse on the bed, turned on the television set, and operated the control box on top until he had the adult entertainment channel. Soft-core from Germany, starring a girl with a Pekingese face and bad plastic implants. Lockman turned off the sound and undressed and filled a glass with vodka. He put his penis in Angela Ruiz's purse. He had some good pictures of her. Now he was getting hot, just as he had told her.

He picked up the telephone handset and dialed for his messages. The woman on the other end said she couldn't find any. He told her his light had been on and there ought to be at least one message. She would look again, she said. Silence. On the screen, the second female lead, bare to the waist, with even lousier breasts than the star, brushed the star's hair. Lockman still had his penis in Angela Ruiz's purse. Now he was thinking that he would turn off the television set as soon as he was done with the telephone. The operator came on again.

"Mr. Lockman? I have your message. Call Al."

"Anything else?"

"That's it. Call Al."

He hit the disconnect button and turned out the light and looked at the movie, which was only getting worse. The two women were in a bubble bath together, giggling and splashing water on each other. With the handset tucked between his shoulder and the side of his head, he dialed an outside line and then 509 and then home. On the third ring Al, sounding very small and far away, said hello.

"Al, it's Garrett. You called?"

Al made a sound like a growling hum, moaning with his mouth closed. *"She's gone!"*

"What?"

"Hazel! She's gone!"

"She left you?"

"No, you stupid—" He stopped. "She's dead. Hazel is dead. She died this morning. In the kitchen—"

"How?" Lockman didn't feel anything, not even shock. What was he supposed to feel? It was like being on a bad television series, going through the motions, the laugh track turned up when things weren't funny. "What happened?"

"A hemorrhage. I found her on the floor when I came downstairs." It was clear he had been saying the words all day. On the screen was a middle-aged actor, a cheap toupee skewed on his head, his potbelly well girdled. He was talking and his mouth did not match the soundtrack.

"You called the doctor," Lockman said.

"Of course I called the doctor. But I know a corpse when I see one. She went downstairs to make breakfast while I got ready to go to the office, and when I came down, she had been there too long for anyone to do her any good."

"What do you mean, too long?" Lockman yelled. "How do you make decisions like that?"

"Well, sonny, her eyes were open and they couldn't see the pink froth that had come out of her nose and mouth. Hazel would never lay on the kitchen floor facedown in a pink froth that had come from her nose if she were alive, would she, you stupid son of a bitch? Now, her funeral is Friday at ten o'clock here in Spokane, which gives you plenty of time to make the arrangements to get home." Al hung up, and with cruel suddenness, the dial tone sounded.

Lockman dropped the handset as if it had hurt him. The buzz continued as the handset hit the night table and spun around on the end of its cord. Lockman couldn't help laughing. Some news to hear while watching crummy German porn, stroking your boner in the purse of Angie Ruiz. He hung up the telephone and cranked the television sound. The leading lady was with her leading man, who had a bulbous nose and glaring eyes—in these epics, grossness epitomized manhood. Lockman finished the vodka in the glass and poured some more. Chapter Seven: Al plays a practical joke. No, this was real. Would he now have to kiss Al's ass to maintain his situation? Would Al's own secrets come out at last? Was he porking some ugly widow on the west side of town?

The room began to whirl. Lockman laughed as Fräulein Implants told Herr Grosser Aktor she was saving herself for true love. In her league, true love meant being willing to accept a credit card. Lockman turned the sound up louder still, and yelled without emotion. He closed his eyes and tried to call up the image of Deeah Anne Johanssen, as if she could save him one more time, but instead of her strength and health and beauty, he saw nothing. He heard the sickening thump of her body hitting the bottom of the cellar stairs a continent away. He had chased that particular dragon one too many times, and now he had the sudden thought that his own life really had ended then, so far away. Lockman felt empty and limp in the lurid New York night. He turned the television sound to the maximum and screamed, hoping that someone would come to pound on the door.

—

IN THE MORNING he found himself sitting on the floor, silent, his back against the wall. He had blacked out again—he couldn't imagine how long. One eerie thing seemed to be staying with him: in the middle of the night, for a very long period, he had not known what city he was in.

SEPTEMBER 1988

Boudreau worked his way through the forty-seven-page, single-spaced draft document at exactly the same pace he had set at home last night. Today, instead of an audience of one, Diane, his listeners, grouped around a long folding table in the investigative team's conference room, were Kevin Donovan, Les Lucas, Captain Randall Murray of the King County Sheriff's Department, who was the new head of the Green River Investigative Team, his new assistants, Lieutenants Frank Moray of the Portland Police Department and Alec Dobson of the Seattle PD, two detectives from the Royal Canadian Mounted Police, the three other members of Boudreau's group, three more FBI agents, two additional members of the King County Sheriff's Department, another Seattle detective, a Snohomish Sheriff's Department detective, a stenographer, and a clerk overseeing a reel-to-reel tape recorder. None of these people had been part of the Beale-Cheong network. After Donovan had told Boudreau so long ago that people had talked about killing him, he had gone on to Les Lucas's office to hear Lucas tell him that nothing would work until they could proceed without having to look over their shoulders. Changes would have to be made, rules about silence—especially in the presence of the press—would have to be hammered out and enforced. "We're going to get you some people you can count on," Lucas had said. Then silence and the stare. Boudreau had stared back. If the exchange had not signified trust, it had been meant to elicit belief: here they were, many, many fresh faces. The sheriff's department had to be protected, of course, because law enforcement itself had to be protected. A public that did not understand that detectives relied almost completely on snitches to solve crimes would go beyond calling for the heads of detectives who had been duped by a snitch; it might go so far as to impose changes in procedure on all of law enforcement that would ensure that no crime would ever be solved again.

The first seven pages of the report backgrounded the Green River murders, the thirty-seven cases identified so far, what the disappearances had in common, where the bodies had been found, a discussion of the evidence or the commonalities in the lack of it.

Boudreau continued through *Part Two: Background of Garrett Richard Lockman*, a biographical sketch beginning with the circumstances of his birth in Medford, his placement with his aunt and uncle in Spokane, the little that was known of his early life, his careers at the University of Washington and the navy, and finally, a carefully censored account of his life in the Pacific Northwest since 1980. Omitted from this last section was any connection Lockman may have had to the King County Sheriff's Department—as an integral part of their process, no one was permitted to say even in unofficial, behind-closed-doors conversation that a connection had ever existed. And law-enforcement bureaucracy was not an empty fist. The penalty for not falling into line would be as severe here as in the New York PD. Only a fool would give the matter another thought.

Boudreau read quickly, skipping sentences. According to this expurgated account, from the time of Lockman's escape from jail to his relocation in Spokane, he had been engaged in criminal enterprises, including fencing stolen property, smuggling, forgery, fraud, use of the mails to defraud, and a dozen other offenses, down to giving false information in order to obtain state licenses.

On to Part Three, a detailed account of the Green River murder victims, their ages, occupations. Here the emphasis was on numbers, the ages of the victims, heights, weights, their own criminal records, and socioeconomic origins. An end user of this document—presumably, a judge contemplating the issuance of a search warrant—could make whatever inferences from the data that he or she wished.

Kevin Donovan led the group through the fourth part, which placed

Garrett Richard Lockman in relation to the times and locations of the disappearances of all but the first five victims, the twenty-third, and the thirty-first. Next Donovan located Lockman in relation to other unsolveds in the Pacific Northwest, going back to his college days, starting with the murder of Deeah Anne Johanssen, whose body was found two blocks from Lockman's residence at the time, a student's studio apartment. Boudreau still had a vivid impression of the sudden hot rush he'd felt remembering being in Lockman's presence so many years later. Could Lockman have known that Boudreau had been first on scene in the Johanssen case? Boudreau's name had not appeared in any of the newspaper accounts back in the seventies, but he had been told that a television station had given his name on one eleven o'clock broadcast. It didn't matter either way, Boudreau knew. A murderer sitting in a coffee shop with a cop was going to think of the murder. He wouldn't be able to resist focusing gleefully on the notion that the cop had no idea of what he had in front of him.

Lockman had been within two hours' drive of more than a dozen strangulation murders of girls and young women in Idaho, Montana, eastern Washington, and the Portland area in the last fifteen years. But so had a whole bunch of guys who had already been convicted of murdering women. Boudreau had checked San Diego for the years Lockman had been there. Over thirty murders of women under similar circumstances, more than half of them cleared, two of the killers having killed five of the women between them. Boudreau didn't think Lockman could have committed more than one or two of the unsolveds, given the restrictions the navy had put on him. That meant that in just those three years a lot of men in the San Diego area had killed women for the fun of it.

Boudreau resumed, working the group through synopses of interviews with Lockman's Portland neighbor, Dorothy Gold, her friend Myra Goss, and Lockman's onetime crime partner, Thomas Brownall. Gold in particular had witnessed Lockman's strange behavior, his late-night comings and goings, his middle-of-the-night barbecues, heard his claims of being a member of a federal law-enforcement unit working on the Green River murders, his assertion that his Portland basement contained a "secret room" used in the Green River case.

Brownall, on parole from Walla Walla for his role in a series of burglaries with Lockman in the early eighties, had told them that he had been approached in San Diego in 1977 by Lockman with a scheme to buy and resell certain navy electronics equipment useful to criminals and spies: listening devices, radar detectors, sonar, and the like. While Brownall insisted that he did not go into business with Lockman, records furnished by the navy showed a steady stream of goods disappearing over the two years Lockman had had access to them. Lockman's proximity to the devices and his suspicious behavior led to the navy's decision to cut him loose. Brownall's denials of evident criminal activity and the probability of a desire for revenge made him an unreliable witness, but it was to be noted that Lockman often talked to Brownall about cutting up prostitutes, and Ted Bundy's cleverness and/or stupidity.

None of the people interviewed so far had ever seen Lockman on a date, heard him talk about women in his past, praise or admire one. On the other hand, Brownall said Lockman was intensely interested in pornography, often talking of trying to obtain "snuff" films, in which women were supposedly murdered.

Donovan's turn again, carrying the group quickly through the appended research papers and psychological profiles so precious to his career. Boudreau had brought home copies months ago for Diane to review, articles that had appeared in such arcane publications as the *Journal of Interpersonal Violence* and *Behavioral Sciences and the Law*. Her desk was covered with pages of her own manuscript, which Boudreau had not read. What had started as an experiment for her had become another dimension of her life. "I've grown another head," she said about her writing, "and it's thinking constantly about the little world it lives in. How's that for sane? Got any extra heads of your own that need shrinking?"

About the FBI's Behavioral Science Unit and its criminal profile-generating process, she said, "An evolutionary step. Certainly not the great breakthrough Donovan wants you to believe. Psychological profiling is only as good as the person using it. And once you know what kind of person you're looking for, you're still faced with the problem of knowing where to look for him. The FBI had an excellent profile of George Metesky, the Mad Bomber of New York City, years ago, but Metesky went on for years. Someone with all the disorders in the book may not be able to hold a job, but in our society that doesn't necessarily mean he's going to be poor. If a serial killer owns his home, he has a built-in means of body disposal. If he's smart enough to get his victims outside his own jurisdiction, you may never know what he's up to. The salient point in the Green River case is that the killer knew he could not leave forensic evidence that could be used against him. And the one piece of luck in the case, that a detective knew him and suspected what he was capable of, was ignored because Lockman positioned himself behind people who had reason to protect him. All the science in the world can't overcome that.

"Being able to protect himself in all these ways, not incidentally, shows a sure grasp of reality. Some will argue that anybody who stoops to cannibalism must be crazy, but this is evidence that Lockman doesn't disassociate when he doesn't want to. Is he in the grip of his appetites or merely indulging them? He knows they're criminal, that's the important thing."

Boudreau and Diane were going through other changes. Adrienne had pressed Travers for a wedding date. Travers's response had been to take a hike. Adrienne was sober and trying to stay that way, attending A.A. meetings almost every night. Paulie, who was twelve now, felt his mother's pain. The result was that Paulie was spending more time with Adrienne than with Boudreau, and Boudreau, in spite of everything, including his ability to reason, was feeling a sense of loss. Diane had caught him sitting in the living room one night when Paulie was with Adrienne.

"He's making a good choice for himself, old man," she said, rubbing his back. "You gotta let go. He wants to be there for his mother. What's not to like?"

"No more dinosaurs."

She bit his ear. "We've always got you."

Boudreau knew he was not the same guy anymore. He supposed that at this time of his life he should have been willing anyway to give up the last brashness of youth, but something ugly wanted to take root in him. Kevin Donovan had told him Ron Beale had bared his teeth and thrown his former colleagues out of his house when they had said they now accepted Boudreau's suspicions about Garrett Lockman. Donovan had waited for Boudreau's reaction, but none had come.

"Don't you care?"

"What am I supposed to care about?"

Donovan finished the presentation and Randall Murray made a note and closed his folder. Murray was a big man of fifty-five with an attitude of command. "There's still no evidence tying Lockman to the murders."

"He's studied police work," Donovan said.

"That's the point I'm making," Randall Murray said. "He knows enough to squirrel away the souvenirs. We never found his share of the traveler's checks, and he's been passing them ever since." Murray looked to Les Lucas. "He's still in Spokane?"

"That's right."

"And we can hold him for the time he owes plus a year for the walkaway less good behavior. That's how much time we would have to find those souvenirs—and everything else. Anybody who fucks up might as well shoot himself in the head."

Murray was on his feet and headed toward the door, his entourage trailing in his wake. Donovan signaled to the clerk to turn off the recording machine. "You're done," he said to the stenographer. Donovan folded his hands and waited until the two were out of the room.

"When do we move?" Wayne Spencer asked.

Les Lucas answered, "Ah, we're going to go on television and ask the public if it has any information on the case."

The expression on Wayne Spencer's face, as fleeting as it was, saying, "What the fuck?" was so perfect that Boudreau had to look away to keep from laughing. The idea had come from on high. At first, going on television had made no sense to Boudreau, either, until he looked at how the case would unfold before the public. If the team kept things moving, no one would doubt that the public's participation had cracked the case.

And if Garrett Lockman ever got out the message that he had been a police informant, people would dismiss it as a madman's attempt to save himself.

Unless, of course, he produced a journal.

Or a tape recording.

Two nights later Boudreau lasted until nine o'clock before he turned out the lights, went down the stairs, and drove across Lake Washington to let himself into Diane's apartment. She was already in bed, silent as he got in beside her, against her back, and wrapped his arms around her. She wriggled against him to signal she didn't need much foreplay to be ready for a doggie-style, sleeping-pill quickie.

Later he was in her living room, unable to sleep again, when the telephone rang. In the bedroom Diane picked up, listened a moment, then called, "Himself!"

Boudreau picked up the living-room telephone as Diane appeared in the doorway. "Yeah, Wayne."

"Seattle Homicide wants to talk to you. Fred Lam. He called me because he knows we work together. I got him holding for a three-way call. Here we go." Boudreau heard a click. Spencer asked, "Can you hear us, Fred?"

"Yes. Phil, are you there?"

"Yeah, Fred."

"You know Lionel Franklin, goes by the name Uhuru?"

"I thought Uhuru was his name. Yeah, I know him."

"Did you know David Ackley, who was murdered in 1984?"

"Describe him."

"You knew him, Phil," Spencer said. "Skinny kid. I was in the doughnut shop when he told you Uhuru was coming in."

"I just wanted to be sure we weren't thinking of two different people. He was murdered by a transient who got out of town. You got him?"

"They got him in Springfield, Missouri, where he was doing ninety days and told a jailhouse snitch that he did a kid in Seattle for a black pimp named Uhuru. Uhuru thought the kid was ratting on him. In return for a life sentence instead of the rope, the guy will identify Uhuru as the guy who gave him ninety bucks to do the job. The guy has a witness, too. Do you know where this Uhuru hangs out?"

"I know where he lives," Boudreau said through his teeth. He'd seen Uhuru a couple of months ago in a Chrysler LeBaron convertible, and he'd run the license plate. The address recorded was that of the sparsely furnished apartment with the big-screen TV.

"I'd like to get him ASAP," Fred Lam said.

Boudreau was on his feet. "Let's do it now. Fred, let Wayne ride along. Uhuru is a big guy and he's got a bodyguard with a weight lifter's build."

Boudreau thought he understood the reason for the conference call. Spencer's heart would have broken if he had not been asked. Boudreau was thinking he would have to keep a close watch on him. Spencer had gone from radio patrol in a sleepy suburb to a desk job in a paper-pushing boondoggle with practically no time on the street. And he was going to be in on the arrest of the century?

Diane was holding Boudreau's clothes. "I felt you get out of bed hours ago. Are you all right?"

He told her quickly about Uhuru and David. "I'd stop in midfuck to get this piece of shit."

"Remember you said that when one of my patients calls."

"Pussy."

"Asshole."

The shorthand they had evolved to express their mutual esteem. She knew he thought she was the wisest person he had ever known, and when all else was stripped away, he knew to respect the ways she was vulnerable to him, even if the vulnerability itself baffled him. He dressed quickly. "All they care about is making sure nobody ever knows the truth."

"I was wondering when you were going to say that. The important thing is what you care about."

"I care about squashing Garrett Lockman like the fucking bug he is."

"Do it with your bare feet. Whatever it takes."

By four-thirty Uhuru's apartment was under surveillance by six detectives, Lam and his partner, a Native American named Crowfoot, and the lobster shift's only available detective team, two white guys whose names Boudreau couldn't remember. They were in the garage, with Lam and his partner. Boudreau and Spencer were on the street in a plain-wrap, checking every ten minutes by radio with the guys inside. Uhuru came along at five-fifteen as the night was beginning to pale. Boudreau gave the signal over the radio. He and Spencer, their guns drawn, hurried on foot to follow the little convertible into the garage before the heavy, electrically operated gate swung down again. The inside guys had gotten the building manager to identify Uhuru's parking space, on the first level down. Boudreau and Spencer got in under the gate as the LeBaron turned into the downhill ramp, tires squealing. The detectives ran faster. They heard a screech of brakes and a horn blowing. Fenders crunched, followed by the clatter of breaking glass. Somebody shouted. Another guy—Uhuru?— cursed. Somebody yelled, "Stop him!" Boudreau turned the corner as Uhuru rolled into view, running smoothly for a big man. He saw Boudreau and raised his hand as if to wave him off, keep him from getting hurt, but Boudreau picked up speed, moving to intersect Uhuru's angle, and then hit him as hard as he could, kicking at his legs to tangle them up, sidestepping as Uhuru went headfirst into the headlight of a brand-new Oldsmobile. He bounced, corpselike, skidding on his face. Boudreau couldn't help thinking of the ninety bucks. Uhuru had haggled. Shifting his gun to his left hand, Boudreau kicked him twice in the ribs, once in the neck, and once behind the ear. Boudreau knew he was taking his rage over the top, but he didn't care. Spencer was over Uhuru with the barrel of his gun pointing up his nose. Boudreau hurried down the ramp. The other four detectives had Marlon surrounded. He was shirtless and had his fists up.

"Give it up, Marlon!" Boudreau called. "You're out of this!"

Marlon regarded him suspiciously as Boudreau pushed into the circle of detectives. "Uhuru is upstairs in custody for murder. You weren't in town when it happened. Don't buy into it."

Marlon looked confused, a little panicky, and when his eyes moved away from Boudreau's, Boudreau came up with his right fist to clip Marlon heavily on the point of the jaw. Marlon rocked back, his legs twitching in an imitation of the Ali shuffle. Lam's partner hit Marlon in the kidney with his fist. When Marlon straightened up, Lam hit him in the belly, just under the ribs. Marlon doubled over. Lam's partner hit him in the kidney again and Marlon went down, writhing. One of the white guys was on him with handcuffs.

"Uhuru fell," Boudreau said.

Lam shrugged. "He was fleeing. I'll call an ambulance. Better tell the kid up there what happened so we're all rowing in the same direction."

Putting his gun away, Boudreau headed back up the ramp. Spencer was getting cuffs on a still-unconscious Uhuru. Boudreau said, "He fell."

Boudreau's knuckle was skinned: he had hit Marlon harder than he had thought.

"Sounds right to me," Spencer said. "Tripped over his own feet."

Bits of glass stuck out of Uhuru's bloody scalp and forehead. Boudreau hoped one was embedded in Uhuru's brain, turning him into a giant broccoli. One of the white guys appeared at the bottom of the ramp. "The ambulance is rolling."

"How do you feel?" Spencer asked. "I mean, this guy had that kid hit for talking to you."

"No, for talking to a cop. The worst thing you can do is take this shit personally." He dared not reflect on how he bore witness to the statement with his own life. "You think I didn't tell David to get the hell out? He had no place to go, and we had no place to put him."

"Okay, take it easy."

Boudreau wasn't going to ask if he had been yelling. He was shaking when the ambulance rolled up, and the attendant looked into his eyes. "Want a Valium?"

"No, they make me feel like shit."

"Maybe you want to get a ride home."

Boudreau's little car was in the lot downtown. Uhuru was on a gurney, being rolled to the ambulance. Damned lucky—Boudreau still wanted to hurt him. Fred Lam looked up to Boudreau and motioned him over. "The suspect stumbled over his own feet and fell into that car over there?"

"Yeah."

Lam studied him. "You want a half a Demerol?" Boudreau shook his head no. "You look like you're going to puke your brains out or something. Can the other guy take you home?" He waved Spencer over. "Come on, get the old guy home." He patted Boudreau on the shoulder. "Fast hands."

Spencer grinned. "The other guys told me. Good footwork, too. That big tub of shit fell *hard*."

Boudreau was walking up toward the garage entrance, where bright daylight poured in. "Fuck him. A guy like him doesn't care enough about anything to get hurt over it. You have to set the agenda, let them know it hurts. It pays to be a little nuts."

"Well, you can take it easy now. Do you want to go to your place or back to Diane's?"

"Mine. Jesus Christ, just don't offer me a pill."

"Huh?"

"Forget it. Wait a minute." Boudreau walked over to a parked Mercedes and urinated on it, working the stream the length of the car. He was still trembling and overheated, twanging like a guitar string. He knew he had overdone it, even if none of the others had the courage to say so. "My father would approve of my choice of targets."

Spencer didn't answer, which surprised Boudreau. Did Spencer know him well enough to have been able to guess that he was going to mention his father during a deal like this? Spencer was not a guy who could keep his mouth shut when he believed he had an original thought. He said nothing as they crossed the street to the plain-wrap, and they rode uptown in silence. Boudreau closed his eyes. Maybe he was more tired of police work than he thought.

Spencer stopped the car outside Boudreau's building. Old Man Gunter was out on the stoop picking up his newspaper. He eyed Boudreau disagreeably as he turned to go inside. Boudreau opened the car door. "Thanks. I'll call in as soon as I get upstairs."

"Phil?" He waited for Boudreau to look around. He was glaring. His teeth were clenched. "You got a funny-looking dick. Did anybody ever tell you that?"

Piper. Those were Piper's exact words. "They all do," Boudreau said as he got out. "But that don't stop 'em." He kept going up the walk. It wasn't as if Spencer didn't already know what Piper was. If Spencer ever brought up the subject again, Boudreau would tell him to go fuck himself. That would be the end of it, unless Spencer wanted to mix it up. Then Boudreau would have to hit him with a chair.

———

THE TELEVISION CREW showed up the following week. The press room became the show's production office. The wall outside was decorated with mug shots of the victims, telling the world that the real police needed cheap and obvious visual aids to inspire them to do their jobs properly. Boudreau stayed as far from the bright lights and the people huddled around them as he could, and as a result he was the last to hear the story of what happened after a particularly flamboyant homosexual production assistant yelled, "Quiet on the set!" The grumbling suddenly grew louder, and someone in a corner shouted, *"BOOM!"* People jumped as if a real gun had been fired, and the laughter didn't stop even when the director called a ten-minute break.

Boudreau's scarcity caused no shortage of actors for the show. The hams materialized as if by magic, including one fundamentalist who let it be known that, if required, he could cry on cue. Boudreau was inclined to keep a closer eye on the politics of the situation. That some Bible-

boosting bonehead saw himself as the new Brando meant that the investigative team was going to churn its way through this charade that much
more quickly.

If Spencer was keeping away from Boudreau, Boudreau's own distance
from the office hoopla made it difficult for him to tell. He had said nothing to Diane. She really didn't like Spencer and didn't need to hear
Piper's name again. For that matter, Boudreau hadn't been able to answer
her question about his skinned knuckle completely. "They resisted," he'd
said in a voice so dead it had stopped further conversation. Uhuru and
Marlon had wound up in the hospital prison ward, Uhuru with a concus-
sion, Marlon with blood in his urine. How did Boudreau tell the woman
who loved him that he didn't give a fuck about the damage done them?
That he couldn't open himself to the emotion that arose from the con-
templation of David's last moments? A stabbing victim who was bleeding
to death had time to think about what was happening to him. Months and
years later fat Uhuru sat on his throne sucking up his drugs and watching
big-screen TV and being waited on by his punk. What was Boudreau supposed to make of that? Being anywhere near the emotions evoked was not
healthy to the human spirit.

Boudreau was looking at his list of Lockman's friends and acquain-
tances, matching them to the telephone bills. A little mystery had
emerged. Until the fall of 1985, Lockman and someone in the home of
Tom and Sheila Parkinson had talked on the telephone almost weekly,
and more frequently at the end, when all calls had suddenly stopped.
Something had happened.

Boudreau had already called the Parkinsons, representing himself as a
surveyor for the city Department of Human Services, which was contemplating opening a neighborhood day-care center. Just a few questions,
Mrs. Parkinson. It is Mrs. Parkinson, isn't it? Yes, the first of two or three
dozen answers—Boudreau now had a statistical rundown on all four
members of the household, ages, places of birth, parents' names. Tom
Parkinson was from Spokane, a graduate of the high school Garrett Lockman had attended. Okay, but why had the calls stopped?

———

BY DESIGN, BOUDREAU did not see the television show. That afternoon,
Paulie arrived at his father's apartment with Diane as the two of them had
done for years. While they dialed up pizza and Cokes Boudreau went
down to the Pike Place Market for a bowl of cioppino, a green salad with
oil and vinegar, sourdough bread, and an icy bottle of Sierra Nevada Pale
Ale. He was waiting for his food, looking out the window at the huge

shadow of an incoming container ship, when Kevin Donovan sat down opposite him.

"Your girlfriend told me where to find you. No television for you tonight?"

"You know I can't discuss official police business," Boudreau said.

"That's a great answer. I wish I'd thought of it before they made me watch the tape."

"A special showing for the bigwigs?"

"With champagne and hors d'oeuvres. They had to get our approval anyway, but they put on the dog so they'd have the inside track later. It's going to be a big story when we get this guy."

"The television people don't know anything, do they?"

"No. Absolutely not." The waiter arrived with the cioppino. Donovan looked at it with a pained expression. He sat back until the waiter was out of earshot again and waggled a finger at the food. "What is that stuff?"

"Seafood stew with tomatoes, green peppers, onions, garlic, oregano—"

"I don't know how you do it."

"How do *you* do it? You eat the same bland crap day in, day out. If I had a parrot, she'd eat better than you."

"All right, all right. Something's happened. One of our guys was involved in a shooting a couple of hours ago and took a bullet. Wayne Spencer. He's in no danger, but it's why I'm here. I figured you'd want to know. Spencer was having dinner at a Denny's near his apartment when two guys with guns hit the register. They must have been loaded on crack or something. Spencer followed them out to the parking lot—"

Oh, Jesus, Boudreau thought.

"He got one. The other got him. In the shoulder. I just came from the hospital. He's in a lot of pain and he's scared, but he's going to be all right. It's bad enough as it is, but he was very lucky. When I was in the emergency ward with him, his arm kept wanting to flop off the gurney. He had to hold on to it with his other hand. It will take him years to get back, if ever. He got a look at the car and they've identified the dead guy, so they'll get the other one. Look, is there anything going on between you guys? I thought you and Spencer were tight. I asked if he wanted to see you, and he just turned his head away."

Boudreau was looking out the window at the black, mysterious water. Had he done anything involving Wayne Spencer that had not hurt the big dope? "Nothing's going on, if that's what you want to know. My father shot a couple of guys in a parking lot. I told Wayne the story. Maybe he was wishing he'd never heard it." *Wayne Spencer, meet Betty Antonelli...*

Suddenly Boudreau sat back. What was he doing? He didn't kill Betty Antonelli, he didn't tell Wayne Spencer to be a hero.

"I'm sorry about Spencer. My father was almost fifty years old when he had to shoot those two guys. If Spencer didn't have my father's experience, he didn't have his old NYPD training, either. Which, as you may know, was the best available in the country at that time." Boudreau drew a deep breath. "Now let's get something straight. You and I have had years to figure out how to work with each other. But even at this stage of the game, I still don't even know your wife's name—"

"Maureen. I've known her since grammar school."

"The point is, we've done it. I need my space from you. I can't enjoy my dinner in front of a guy who just made a face over it."

"I'm sorry."

"You didn't come here just to tell me that Wayne Spencer was shot. You wanted to find out if anything was happening that could rock your boat."

"That clears the air."

"You bet it does. To hell with Spencer, the newspapers are going to call him a hero. His press clippings will set him up in some dumbshit rent-a-cop job for life. In Vegas, for Christ's sake. Showgirls giving him freebies. And he'll have a disability pension besides. That's the worst-case scenario. You're set for life, too. You know it. The FBI record is going to say that in spite of all the local incompetence, you carried the ball for the FBI and solved the Green River case. The president of the United States is going to want to have his picture taken standing next to you. But while you and Spencer are getting your balls licked by people who really know how to do it, we'll still have kids who live in abandoned cars, work the Pike, and lose their lives for ninety bucks. You know and I know it's happening right now, while the team makes the country sit through a show-and-tell charade so it can tiptoe around the mistakes that kept us from hanging Lockman years ago. Now *please* let me enjoy my dinner. Just get out of here. Go back to your Maureen and your lumpy mashed potatoes and leave me the fuck alone."

JANUARY 1989

"Batman, call Robin," the answering machine whispered. "Batman, call Robin ASAP."

Schmuck, Garrett Lockman thought as he dialed the number of Martin Jones. They hadn't spoken in months. What was so urgent to the little fool now? Jones picked up on the second ring and said hello in a brusque, manly way.

"You dumb shit," Lockman said. "Who are you trying to impress? Is there anyone anywhere on the planet who is going to call you? You have no friends or social life."

"Neither will you, soon enough," Martin Jones said. "Take down this number and call it from a pay phone. I need ten minutes to get there."

"I've got no time for games—"

"Do this my way. It's important."

While Lockman waited the ten minutes he found a pen and a spiral notebook. Important? He was ready. He drove out to the highway to an available telephone at a Wienerschnitzel hot-dog stand. "All right, smegma breath, what's on your mind?"

"Did you see *America's Master Criminals* on TV tonight?"

"They can't teach me anything."

"That's just about what they said on the show. The whole hour was about the Green River killings. It's just a matter of time before they're onto you, Lockman. You're going to wind up in jail. Or worse."

Lockman got out the pen and notebook. "All right, what did you see that makes you say that?"

"They did the whole story, where the girls had been seen last and when, where their bodies had been found. They interviewed an FBI agent who said they were looking for someone who lived on the I-5 corridor anywhere between Seattle and Portland, someone who knows the roads east. He said they're using new techniques that give them a picture of the killer. He said they're looking for someone with some police experience or interest in police work, somebody who has studied police work, somebody who knows how to imitate a policeman, a big man. Let's see, what else? Someone who has poor relationships with women, who drives a van or panel truck or similar vehicle. Someone who drinks a lot, maybe doesn't work, who lives in disorder."

"What bullshit! I live right. I don't drink much. The women students at Holy Name have no complaints with me. If I've driven any of those vehicles, it's because I've driven everything ever made. A lot of people are interested in cops, that's why they're so popular on television. This was on tonight? Why didn't you call me beforehand?"

"I didn't know it was on until I looked in the *TV Guide*. They gave out an eight-hundred number for people to call if they thought they knew something. I'm telling you, just for starters, those neighbors of yours down in Portland—"

"Hello? Those folks don't even know my name!"

"They had a lot of interviews—"

"Who with?"

"Parents of the victims, their boyfriends."

"That's because they didn't have an hour's worth of program. Long-suffering moms? Give me a fucking break! 'My Betty Ann was such a good girl, especially when it came to sucking cock in the trailer park.' You're a cunt, Martin. You cry over empty matchbooks."

"I've got the name and number of that lawyer who got Uhuru out on bail on that murder charge. Take them down."

"Give them to me."

Martin Jones repeated them twice. Jones had sent Lockman a newspaper clipping about Uhuru's case: the lawyer had gotten Uhuru's bail reduced to fifty thousand dollars, which he had been able to cover with the bail bondsman with the title to his condo. "I have to tell you now, Lockman, if you've got any stuff that ties you to the victims, you'd better get rid of it!"

"I already took care of that! Nice talking to you, noble savage! It's cold out here! Keep 'em flying!" Lockman hung up and got back in the ambulance. A television show was the last possible act of desperation for the police. It was a good thing it was winter and Lockman was here in Spokane. In Portland, hanging around Seattle, Lockman would be tempted to go out and drop a corpse in the middle of the Sea-Tac Strip. Silly little Martin Jones cautioning him about souvenirs still didn't understand that he had them all. Or did he? Had Jones done something else with them? It didn't matter, as long as he kept quiet. What could he say anyway about those long, long-distance late-night telephone calls? Why would he want to say anything, when it implicated him in murder? His word against Lockman's. The only murders that could have yielded any evidence were those Jones himself had committed, alone, and if he didn't know it, there was no statute of limitations on murder. In fact, if the police couldn't unravel any of the other killings, they would blame them all—*more!*—on Martin Jones.

Lockman got out of the ambulance again and called Anton Charles. Charles said hello as if he were standing under a street lamp in San Francisco.

"Anton, it's Garrett."

A silence. "Do you know what time it is?"

"A quarter to ten. I was just wondering—"

"Ah, you're looking for adventure and you thought I might be available. How sweet. Where are you, Garrett?"

"Not far from home."

"But you don't want to go there. You don't want to be alone. Always a problem with you. If I let you come over, you'll be here until daybreak, and I'm much too old for that. So nothing doing, Garrett. Be a good boy. The best thing you can do is go home, turn out the lights, get into bed, and jump-start a sweet dream."

"Actually, I was thinking—"

"Save your thinking for the law. Go home. Whatever you do, don't come here. Am I clear?"

Without another word, Garrett Lockman hung up. He called Waldo Starr. Starr had passed his bar exam and was working for the Spokane

County Prosecutor's Office. According to Lockman's informants, Starr was a joke in court, often so incompetent he had judges screaming at him.

By the sound of his voice, Waldo Starr had been asleep. "Funny, you calling. Boy, that clinches it. Did you see that show on TV tonight?"

"What show? What are you talking about?"

"The Green River killings. Made me think of you."

"I don't know what you're talking about."

"Show on TV about the Green River killings. It did everything but give your name as the killer. You're the guy who's obsessed with sex, prostitutes, and the Green River killings. Why did you call me, Lockman?"

"I thought you might want to go out for a few beers."

"At this hour? Who do you think you're kidding? Pray for your soul, Lockman. Go to confession and ask for forgiveness. Do you have any idea what you've done to me?"

"You have an overactive imagination, Waldo—"

"I told you not to call me!"

"What? I don't know what you're talking about."

"You don't remember, do you?" Starr asked.

"When was this?"

"Stop drinking, Lockman. Talk to a priest."

"What a dud! No fun to be had with a putz who goes to bed at nine o'clock—"

Starr hung up. Lockman stared at the telephone. Starr had told him not to call? When? Lockman had no memory of any conversation with Starr recently. A party? One night at the bar? For all Lockman knew, he had also had some kind of blowout with Anton Charles. That didn't matter. He was through with Charles anyway.

And just that quickly, Lockman was thinking that this might be a night to let the monster out again. Blackouts and the idea, however fanciful, of the police moving in only added to the thrill. He returned to the ambulance and got the motor and heater going. As cold as it was, if he decided to cruise, he'd have no trouble finding an appropriate subject. He was getting an erection without even really thinking about doing anything. He turned on the radio and found the news, something about Gorbachev pleading with members of the Supreme Soviet.

Lockman rolled, his eyes working left and right, then in the mirrors, searching for black-and-whites. He knew this drill—he was the old hand, the retired gunslinger back for one more shoot-out. Lockman could feel his blood pumping through his veins, the monster coming alive. How long had it been since the last killing, last summer in Idaho, that thirteen-year-old? He had lost all count of how many he had done over all the years. Images of tonight's possibilities rose up before his eyes, of again being inside a woman as he strangled her, of her fighting and heaving against him, of those little squeezes that would be her very last gifts to him. Cops combing the countryside? Moms on the airwaves moaning over their lost trollops? More treats for Lockman to think about at the right time. . .

Al was asleep sitting up on the plastic-covered couch in the living room when Lockman entered from the garage four hours later. The television set was showing an old circus movie, the sound off. Lockman tried to tiptoe past him, but suddenly Al sprang to life. "Huh? That you, Garrett?"

"Yeah, Al. Go to bed."

"What time is it?"

No point in lying. "Almost two."

"Where were you?"

"Out."

Al jabbed the remote and pushed himself to his feet. "What do you mean, out? What kind of answer is that to a civil question? Where were you?"

"All right, if you must know, I was visiting friends."

"Until two? What kind of people stay up until two o'clock on a weekday night?"

"College students, Al. I go to college, remember? I'm in law school."

The old man hobbled closer. He was always stiff when he woke up. "Don't talk to me like that."

Lockman smiled. "What's the matter, Al? You wake up from a sound sleep and start yelling at me."

"I wish—"

"I know what you wish. You wish you had gone before Hazel. But figuring what you think of me, that really isn't very selfless of you. Look, I've had a tough night. It wasn't strictly social. I'm very, very tired. Exhausted. I had to help somebody prepare for her final."

"That wasn't what I was going to say, Garrett. I know you think you can get away with anything you want. Hazel did that by spoiling you rotten. What I was going to say was that I wish I could get to the bottom of you. One second you're here, then I don't know who you are. A long time ago your mother made me promise to take care of you if she died first, and I'm trying—"

"You mean Hazel."

"Why do you do that?"

"What do you mean?"

"Hazel fed you and took you to the doctor when you were sick. Why can't you call her your mother?"

Lockman grinned. "Because she wasn't." He wasn't going to say she had always called him her "nephew and foster son." The last thing he wanted at this point was to be understood. "Is there anything else, Al?"

"Yes. There will be a memorial Mass for her on Sunday at four o'clock—"

"What did that cost you?"

"You make me sick."

"Hey, if one of your cronies at the K of C asked you the same question, you would have answered it proudly."

Al was already headed to the bedroom. With Hazel's death, it was as if the whole Catholic nightmare had floated out of her head and into his, or he had come to believe that she was in the next world waiting for him with a rolling pin. Al even complained that Lockman never went to visit her grave. He had gone once soon after her death without telling Al, at night, and had relieved himself. The opportunity to call her mom had entered his mind then and there, but it had slipped away just as quickly. Instead, across the fresh, mounded squares of sod, in the largest possible letters, he had written his name.

—

LOCKMAN WENT TO the memorial Mass, and arranged to stay busy otherwise by going to student and faculty parties, receptions, and dinners. No further word from Martin Jones, and nothing in the Spokane and Seattle papers about the Green River television program. Winter was the season of no body discoveries, which naturally tended to push the Green River story off the front pages, if not out of the newspapers altogether, and Lockman was more confident than ever that his first call on the television show had been correct: an act of desperation.

With the start of the first thaw he thought of making the jump over the mountains to Seattle, but even the interstates could be shut down if the weather turned bad enough. Martin Jones didn't call him. Lockman thought of calling Jimmy Dobbs, but they had not talked in over a year. Lockman's latest trophy was still lying undiscovered in the woods just across the Idaho state line. He had nothing to do but wait for classes to start again, to try to keep his drinking under control. Al stored his liquor in a cabinet in the dining room, but Lockman kept his own stash of vodka under a moth-eaten SS uniform in the bottom drawer of the dresser in his bedroom. When Al was home Lockman stayed in his room, the vodka bottle on the night table less than two feet from his pillow. He put on the uniform, watched porn videos, especially *Cocksuckers' Christmas*, his all-time favorite, and masturbated, careful not to stain the astonishingly heavy trousers. When he awoke he was still fully dressed but freezing cold, his bladder bursting, the television screen churning silent snow.

———

Pounding on his door jolted him awake. "Garrett Lockman! Open up! Garrett Lockman?"

He was in his underwear. He swung his feet around to the floor. "What?" Through his booziness he realized the voice wasn't Al's. "Who is it?"

"Police! Open up!"

"Just a fucking minute," Lockman muttered as the door burst open, a piece of the doorframe flying over his head. Overcoated men filled the room, two grabbing his arms, and the muzzle of an automatic was pressed forcefully to his forehead. Garrett Lockman focused his eyes down the length of the man's arm, to the eyes looking back into his. Lockman recognized them, but his brain would not give up a name. Behind the man, out in the hall, bony old Al stood in his baggy underwear, his toothless mouth hanging open haplessly, his eyes fixed on Lockman. No, on the gun at Lockman's head. Lockman's bladder opened, the piddle rushing through his underwear to hammer the carpet. Around him, men looked to each other and smiled. All except the man on the other end of the gun. The name floated up and came into focus: *Boudreau.*

Lockman was looking at Phil Boudreau. Boudreau's hair had turned so gray Lockman had not recognized him. Boudreau looked disheveled—wild.

"*I told you,*" Boudreau growled.

Lockman's sphincter loosened. He emptied his bowels noisily.

"Jackpot," said one of the cops.

"I win the pool," announced another, almost as matter-of-factly.

January 1989

Keeping his eyes on Lockman's, Boudreau put the gun away. "Garrett Lockman, you are under arrest for escaping from the King County Jail on January twelfth, 1982. Who would like to read him his rights?"

"Let me clean myself!" Lockman cried.

"Read this fuck his rights!" Boudreau shouted. "Before another fucking thing!"

"Don't ushe that language in thish houshe!" Al yelled.

"Get the mummy out of here," somebody said. Sciscio pulled a Miranda card from his breast pocket and began to read from it. The smell of feces filled the room. One of the Spokane detectives opened the window. Lockman rubbed his arms and stamped his feet, but then stopped.

"You don't want to jiggle that biscuit in your drawers too much," said Robinson gleefully.

"Cut it out," Donovan said.

"Do you understand these rights as I have read them to you?" Sciscio asked.

Lockman was looking at Boudreau. "All this for walking away from jail?"

"Do you understand these rights as I have read them to you?"

"Let me clean up!"

"Do you understand these rights as he's read them to you?" Boudreau asked.

"You're in charge? My, aren't you getting up in the world!"

"Look, everything stops until you respond to the question. If we have to ask you again, we'll all go out to the living room and have a seat, you included, while you figure things out. Now, for the last time, do you understand these rights as they have been read to you?"

"All right, I understand these rights! You guys sure are making a big deal over a walkaway!"

Boudreau pulled the search warrant from his coat pocket. "This gives us the authority to search the premises, including the shed outside." Lockman's eyes got wider. Boudreau said, "Where will we find fresh underwear?"

"I'll get it."

"No, Garrett, from now on you're going to be treated as an extremely dangerous man. Get used to it."

"Mind telling me why?"

"Are you going to tell us where to find the underwear or do we have to look for it?"

"Second drawer. Get me fresh socks, too. A clean shirt hanging in the closet. The blue one. Make sure the socks match, will you?"

Boudreau saw Robinson and Sciscio exchanging glances, and Donovan trying to hide a smile. The first search warrant had been shelved when the comment had come back through channels that a federal warrant would be granted if the police claimed to have received information that the fugitive possessed a firearm. A federal judge had been trying to be helpful. *Save your ammunition*, had been the message. The gossip had spread quickly through the law-enforcement community: they had the guy. Then they found out that there was a large metal shed on the back of the lot and the search warrant had to go back for a third redo. Everybody wanted to see error-free execution in the process of sending Garrett Lockman to his reward, but nobody wanted to do the job. Everybody wanted to play poker with Jesus, but nobody wanted to die. To Lockman, Boudreau said, "These other guys will watch you wipe your ass."

Lockman said, "Really. Watch your language. It freaks the old guy out."

"Tell us how you killed Deeah Anne Johanssen and we'll see what we can do."

Lockman paused before he said, "Who?" Too long. Diane had helped Boudreau prepare for this moment. Lockman, she had said, would be under terrible stress and his performance would be less than seamless. In the doorway, Les Lucas motioned to Boudreau.

"Don't worry about your socks, Garrett. Nobody's going to see them."

"I'm not going to be on television?"

Heads snapped up. "Why would you be on television?" Donovan asked.

"I'm making a joke."

"I don't get it."

"That's your problem. You guys are all crazy. I'd like to clean up now."

Boudreau moved to the door. "We have to deal with the old man," Les Lucas said quietly. He stepped aside to let Boudreau lead them back to the living room. Les Lucas was now Boudreau's great, good friend, and so was Randall Murray. Passing the evidence through Boudreau reduced the number of people officially handling it to an absolute minimum, they said. By being his friends, shielding and protecting him from the politics and power struggles higher up, Lucas and Murray could keep Boudreau out of the power loop, too, while they advanced their own causes. Boudreau had his focus elsewhere. In a few more minutes, according to Diane, Lockman was going to think he was up to speed inside when in fact he would be falling apart.

Al Lockman was sitting on the couch, still in his underwear, still toothless. He glared at the approaching cops. Boudreau gave him his card.

"I don't have my glasses," the old man snapped.

"It might be a good idea if you got dressed. Some of us are going to be here awhile."

Al Lockman stood up. "What's the big idea? You guys barge in here like Nazis—"

Donovan produced his ID. "Special Agent Kevin Donovan of the Federal Bureau of Investigation—"

"I don't care! I'm a taxpayer! I was in the war! If you wanted something, all you had to do was phone me—"

"That's not the way it works, sir—"

"Maybe you ought to get dressed," Boudreau said to him.

"Why?"

"We have a warrant. We're going to search the premises."

"What for?"

"It's in the warrant. Does your son own a firearm?"

"I don't know. You have to come in the middle of the night like storm troopers for that?"

"Under the circumstances, yes."

"What are the circumstances?"

"Garrett Lockman is a fugitive from justice who we have reason to believe is in possession of a firearm. That's what the warrant says." He leaned in, close enough to whisper. Trying to focus, the old man already looked startled. Boudreau said, "We think Garrett is the Green River killer."

The old man's eyes widened and, for a split second, looked away. He believed it, or believed it was possible. Lockman had thought he was going to be on television. Now the fight went out of the stepfather with the mention of Green River. The innocent as well as the guilty soiled their clothing, but these were specific, positive signs, no matter how the two Lockmans might protest later.

Al Lockman was not creating unexpected problems. In most jurisdictions the law presumed the unreliability of a suspect's immediate family, and some jurisdictions even held them blameless for hiding him or aiding in his escape. The unexpected problems here had come from certain Spokane area detectives. The locals wanted in on the case, unashamedly admitting that the limelight might mean a ticket out. One of the detectives, Tom Logan, had all but demanded to be the arresting officer until Les Lucas had taken him aside. Everybody on state and federal levels wanted this done quickly and cleanly, Lucas had lectured patiently but firmly. Everybody wanted a clear line of evidence. The FBI was looking to get out from behind its biggest failure in the field. Did Logan want that responsibility falling on him? He backed off, but a couple of members of the investigative team who had worked with him in the past still thought him unreliable. One more reason why Randall Murray, who had stayed behind in Seattle, had approved this commando strike and the still-unannounced decision that Boudreau, Les Lucas, and the three FBI agents were going to escort Lockman to Seattle immediately. It wouldn't take days for the local press to learn that the Green River Investigative Team had arrested a man in Spokane. More like hours: someone in the Spokane County Sheriff's Office might have tipped his friends at the local newspaper already. The Green River Investigative Team was going to control the flow of information—at least, public-relations announcements were going to be made in Seattle. As it was, there would be more than enough misinformation, gossip, and outright bullshit about this case.

Robinson stepped out of the bathroom and motioned to Donovan and

Boudreau. Les Lucas turned to Al Lockman and said, "You want to put on some clothes, old-timer. You'll feel better."

Robinson spoke quietly to Donovan and Boudreau. "He wants to call a lawyer now, this minute."

"What's the problem?"

"At this time of night?"

"Let him call as soon as he's ready."

"Shackles first," Boudreau said. Something they had discussed at length. From here on Garrett Lockman was not going to move from one room to the next without shackles.

Boudreau returned to Lockman's bedroom, where four men were emptying the closet and the dresser. On the bed were several police uniforms and a box full of police badges. One of the Spokane detectives was stacking videocassettes. Another tossed Boudreau a purse. "Bingo."

Boudreau opened the purse and took out a wallet. It was, or had been, the property of Angela Ruiz, of Queens, New York. Boudreau recognized the address: in high school he had gone to a wedding reception at a catering hall on Roosevelt Avenue only a few blocks away. Lockman had been in New York? The investigative team knew nothing about it.

The telephone number on the ID card was scratched out. Boudreau slid the card out of the window and turned it over. Another number. He picked up Lockman's telephone and dialed it. Disconnected. As he hung up Lockman shuffled into the bedroom, bent over by the weight of the chain that bound his wrists to his ankles. He glowered at Boudreau. "You can't use my telephone. I can sue you."

"Sue and go fuck yourself."

Lockman glanced behind him. "Don't you have any respect? That old man is mourning the death of his wife."

"People are mourning the deaths of a lot of women, Garrett. Want to tell us about Angela Ruiz?"

He stared. This was the second mention of women: it established the agenda. Everybody in the room was listening. People had discussed this moment endlessly. Boudreau and Diane had gone over it for weeks. Lockman said, "I'm not talking to you until I have a lawyer."

Boudreau was ready. He tossed the purse back to the Spokane detective. "He'll have to catch up with us."

"Where are you taking me?"

"King County Jail."

Lockman reared back. "You can't put me in with the GP. Everybody knows that. Ask Ron Beale."

"Retired. He's touring Canada in a motor home."

"At this time of year? Who do you think you're kidding? Where's Dan Cheong?"

"Relocated to Santa Rosa, California." Stan Pfeiffer had taken him on, making sure everyone knew he had burned no bridges behind him. "He doesn't remember your name."

Lockman shook until his chains jingled. "This is your doing, isn't it, Frenchy? Because of what you told me? Trying to cover your tracks?"

"Speak up. What do you think I told you?"

"The whores on your beat, how you really hate them."

He didn't see the detectives behind him exchanging glances. Boudreau said, "No, that was your analysis of the job I had at the time. I still have my notes of that conversation, and I've reread them many, many times over the years. So have the rest of these gentlemen. You've got hard choices to make here, Garrett. You and I have been over this course before. Make your call—unless, of course, you want to tell us about Andrea Witter."

"Who?"

"Sixteen years old. Disappeared in May of 1983, found in March of 1986."

Lockman's eyes widened again. This was the first mention of Green River victims. "Oh, no! You're not doing that to me! I didn't kill anybody!"

"How about Betty Antonelli? In her twenties, full-figured. Gold tooth right here?" Boudreau hooked his lower lip with his little finger. "She had a dog. We never found the dog, Garrett. A brown-and-white mutt. What did you do with the dog?"

"Do you think I ate it?"

"Maybe."

Lockman stared at Boudreau a moment, then stretched to his full height and smiled. His next question was like a slap in the mouth. "Was she someone important to you?"

Boudreau caught himself. "We think you killed her."

The smile lingered a moment, then Lockman suddenly backed up. "Oh, no! This is your personal revenge, Frenchy! You're doing it because of what I know about you!"

Boudreau was ready. "What do you know about me?"

"Your ex-wife is a whore! She's fucked so many guys you can't be sure whose kid your son is!"

No one moved. Diane had told Boudreau that Lockman would go on the attack, and because of that Boudreau had convinced the team's consulting psychologists to submit scenarios of Lockman's behavior when he was arrested. Going on the attack had been high on their list of possibilities, too. Boudreau had pushed until the consultants said that since Boudreau was the only cop Lockman knew well enough to attack, he was the most likely target. Les Lucas had called for scenarios, but this was worse than any of them had imagined. Boudreau held his ground.

Lockman gave Boudreau a big smile. "Hey, babe, we know Adrienne's cunt is busier than Pioneer Square! The little kid in the next room? What's his name?"

Eight years ago? Lockman had stalked him? And Paulie and Adrienne? Lockman was watching to see if Boudreau would rise to the bait. Silence. Boudreau was reeling, but he wasn't going to answer, not until he had caught his breath, until he knew he had his wits about him.

"You're not going to hang Green River on me!"

"Nobody mentioned Green River, Garrett."

"I recognized the victims' names!"

"Deeah Anne Johanssen wasn't a Green River victim. Angela Ruiz wasn't a Green River victim."

Lockman looked from Sciscio to Robinson to Boudreau.

"Somebody call Wayne Spencer to relay the news to Captain Murray," somebody said. "We got the right guy."

Spencer was on light duty in the office while he built up strength in his arm. He was a hero to the media donkeys, none of whom had seen the notch he had carved in the handle of his gun. "Yeah," said somebody else. "We got him, all right."

"It doesn't mean a thing!" Lockman screamed.

DELIVERANCE

January 1989

Lockman was right, Boudreau recognized at once. Lockman could argue that he had followed the Green River case—the investigative team even had testimony to that effect—and the naming of two of the known Green River victims had caused him to assume their interest was in Green River. The lawyer Lockman called had a beeper, and he called Lockman back in ten minutes. In another few minutes Lockman hung up.

"Sorry, boys, my lawyer tells me to keep my mouth shut until he sees me tomorrow at King County. That is where you said you were taking me, isn't it?"

More from Diane's playbook: the window of opportunity closing as soon as Lockman talked to a lawyer, not because the lawyer told him to be quiet, but because Lockman saw he now had an ally. "Tell the locals to warm up the car," Les Lucas said to Boudreau. "Call the charter pilot."

"Don't I get a chance to talk to my father? We have a household to run."

"You can say good-bye to him at the door. Tomorrow he can see you in Seattle or you can telephone him collect."

Lockman didn't answer, and he didn't start talking again until the Spokane cruiser was near the airport, when he wanted to pump them for useless information about their flight arrangements. What kind of plane? Which charter service? How long was the flight time? They kept quiet. According to Diane, if someone told him to shut up, he would step up the barrage tenfold.

He had wanted socks to match the shirt. Diane had told Boudreau that Lockman would try to control his turf no matter how small it became. And he would make the adjustment effortlessly. He would feel no sense of loss as his horizons contracted.

The little turboprop had eight seats and an overhead so low that two of the FBI agents and Lockman banged their heads as they moved down the narrow center aisle. Boudreau never liked flying anyway, and this flight was noisy and rough in the black winter night. They descended out of the metallic sunrise into Sea-Tac, where the runway lights twinkled out of the shadow yielding to the brightening sky. Lockman was looking out the window, just as Diane said he would. It was just another adventure to him.

But a tiring one. Lockman was out of energy when he was turned over to the jailers. Boudreau was grateful when he finished before noon the paperwork on what was still, by design, a routine case. He called Diane and told her she would find him asleep in her bed, but not that he was feeling queasy over what Lockman had told him, absolutely establishing that he had stalked Boudreau, Adrienne, and Paulie for weeks, if not months.

And that at the time Boudreau had thought of the possibility of Lockman stalking them only once.

The media circus began while he was asleep, and by the time he woke up, Diane was in the living room using the remote to flip around the television dial, the local anchors herding catch-up remotes from the jail, the investigative team offices, and Spokane. *Law-school student. Walked away from King County Jail.* The Spokane cops were describing the late-night arrest as if they had done it alone. *Convicted felon. Nazi paraphernalia. Pornographic videotapes.* The frenzy was as sensational as anything Boudreau could remember ever happening in New York.

"They're not mentioning your name," Diane said.

"Thank you, Jesus."

"How are you doing?"

"He spied on Adrienne years ago. Made certain representations."

"From his point of view, he might be telling the truth."

He eyed her. "You know something. What do you know?"

"She's doing all right. Let Paulie handle it."

Handle what? "He's a kid!"

"Her kid as much as yours, and nobody knows it better than him. That's the person he is. Don't worry."

Don't worry? When? While thinking of what must have been going on in Lockman's mind when he'd stalked Adrienne? What had scared him off, getting caught? The fear that Boudreau would have seen him for the puke he was?

Don't worry. Maybe while trying to avoid center stage downtown the next day during the media-choreographed Dance of the Shitheads. Or that evening, while seeing a TV crew outside his apartment before the crew saw him, and scooting over to Diane's apartment again.

In the next days the whole case was dragged through the newspapers again and again, sidebars and features repeatedly detailing how and when the victims disappeared, when and where their remains had been discovered. Descending on Seattle were television crews from Australia and Germany, the American tabloid television shows, the newsmagazine programs on all three networks. You ran a gauntlet to get into the office. You answered no questions. You were careful with strangers. If you had business with someone you didn't know, you made sure he identified himself.

Under all the glare, the detectives were going through the trailer loads of stuff Lockman had saved since grade school. The consulting psychologists wanted to move in with it, they were so fascinated. But no evidence so far of any of the Green River killings. No evidence of a connection to Beale and Cheong. And no evidence of any other killings, either, thanks to the New York Police Department.

Boudreau couldn't get anybody on the other side of the country to pay attention to him. "Look, all you gotta do is see if Angela Ruiz died, for Christ's sake!"

"You sound like a New Yorker."

"I am."

"What the hell ya doin' out there? Doesn't it rain there alla time?"

"Nah, that's a gag," Boudreau answered, and slammed down the receiver.

It was another month before Boudreau called Tom and Sheila Parkinson again. They didn't recognize his voice as the one belonging to the surveyor from the Department of Human Services. They agreed to see him that same evening. Boudreau told Les Lucas, who smiled. "Sounds like they were waiting for the cops to call. Are we going to get a break?"

Boudreau kept his mouth shut, lest he jinx his luck. Lockman had done everything else so carefully, maybe he had chosen his friends the same way.

The Parkinsons' little house was overheated and smelled of small children. They had three, the most recent born two years ago. Tom Parkinson was an assistant manager at a hardware store. Sheila Parkinson was a rail-thin, exhausted-looking woman of thirty with badly dyed blond hair and small, quick eyes that stayed on Boudreau from the moment her husband opened the door. The older kids were awake in the back of the house — noisy about it, too. Every wall in the pastel-green living room bore their fingermarks, and the furniture was threadbare, the cushions collapsed.

"What happens with what we tell you?" Sheila Parkinson asked.

"It depends on what it is. If you tell me about a murder, then it's a big deal. Not so much for jaywalking."

For the first time since Boudreau's arrival, she looked at her husband. "I'm going to tell him. I don't care."

"All we know is what he told us."

"I know that. That's what I'm going to tell."

Somehow Boudreau had passed some secret test she had given him. The message communicated subliminally to her husband, because he suddenly looked from Boudreau to her and back again. He asked, "Uh, you want some coffee?"

"No, thanks."

They lived hand-to-mouth. So did he, but it was bigger hand, bigger mouth. The precariousness of the Parkinsons' existence reminded him of his uneasiness with his own situation. He had spent most of his professional career focused on this case. At the start he had been a young man with a spring in his step, and now he was too old for basketball.

Lockman used to visit them, Sheila Parkinson said. He would stay for three or four days at a time, during a period that coincided almost exactly with the two and a half years of the Green River murders. He would arrive at this house bone-tired from what he said were secret government assignments. He would always be drunk by the end of the night. Sometimes he rambled about what he was doing for the government, but his speech was so slurred and his attention span so short that nothing he said ever made sense. Sometimes, drunk themselves, they'd get a little crazy with him. Nothing serious, Tom Parkinson assured Boudreau; sometimes the guys would get down to their underwear, Sheila to her bra and panties.

She saw Boudreau's eyes narrow, and she said, "It didn't get really sick until Disneyland."

"He took us to Disneyland," Tom Parkinson said. "It was his favorite place when he was in the navy, he said. He said he felt guilty for all the times he wound up on the couch, eating us out of house and home. It wasn't true, he always brought Chinese food. I never even *tried* Chinese food before he showed up. Geez, I don't know for sure how he found me. He said he was driving through the neighborhood, looking up the names of old friends in the local telephone book. He said he did it everywhere he went. He told me he had reconnected with a lot of old friends that way.

"He talked about the Disneyland trip for months, then all of a sudden he disappeared. Then he showed up again and it was all hurry up, we gotta go this weekend. So we got Sheila's folks to baby-sit and we went."

"I was never in an airplane before," Sheila Parkinson said quickly.

"Garrett was very tense," Tom Parkinson said. "The closer we got to John Wayne Airport, the more nervous he got. Finally he like pulled into himself and just looked out the window."

"He made us wait outside while he rented the car," Sheila Parkinson said.

Lockman probably had not wanted them to see that he was using a phony credit card and driver's license. Boudreau didn't want to listen to their personal complaints. "What kind of sick stuff happened? Let's get to that."

"Well, there was a whole lot of stuff that happened that led up to it," Tom Parkinson said.

"We got to Orange County Friday afternoon," Sheila Parkinson said. "With all the big, modern hotels around there, he made us stay in this stinky little rathole motel. He got drunk that night. This was after he took us to this like fake Chinese restaurant across the road from Disneyland. He always acted like he knew so much about food, but he really didn't—"

Boudreau stifled a smile. "What's a 'fake' Chinese restaurant?"

"The waitresses were these frumpy white women. Anyway, they had a bar, and he started drinking there. To tell you the truth, that's when I started worrying about him."

"What do you mean, worrying about him?"

"You know, what he'd do, get loud or throw up. But when we got back to the rooms, he passed out pretty quick."

"He got us adjoining rooms," Tom Parkinson said.

"He had it all arranged in advance," Sheila Parkinson said. "I wondered about that, too. I mean, we were going to be together all day Saturday and Sunday. How close did we have to get? The next day he had this like humungous hangover and acted like he was too sick to go to Disneyland. I thought, okay, fine, we'll go by ourselves, except we didn't have the money for the tickets."

"I had to tell him to shape up," Tom Parkinson said.

"I told you to tell him!"

He turned to her. "You didn't have to say that."

"It's true. I had to tell you, 'Either he stops the crap or I'm going back to the airport if I have to walk.' "

"The crap being emotional blackmail," Boudreau said.

"Yeah," Sheila Parkinson said. "Like, 'What do you want to go to Disneyland for? It's for kids. We can spend the day right here in the rooms.' That's when I put my foot down. I didn't go all the way to Orange County, California, for that. When we actually got inside the park, he cheered up and apologized to me, which I thought was cool. I mean, he had zoned out, but we had seen him zone out before. We were used to it. So we went from Pirates of the Caribbean to Space Mountain and had dinner at the New Orleans place. It could have been a better time, but it wasn't bad. I wanted to stay until the park closed. You know, get all I could. When it got dark, he started to lose it again. He wanted to get out bad. The night does something to him, I think."

Tom Parkinson said, "If you're wondering why we didn't tell him to go back to the rooms by himself, you don't know what kind of a person he is. He can be very persuasive—"

"*Unstoppable* is more like it," Sheila Parkinson said. "If he wants something, he's not going to stop working on you until he gets it. Anyway, he started campaigning for us to get out of there, and finally, when it was after nine o'clock, I gave in. Getting him to nine o'clock was important to me. I mean, he was driving me crazy. I knew what he wanted, he was dying for a drink. There's no alcohol at Disneyland, not even beer. He wanted to get back to the rooms, like there was nothing else to do at the park. It was making me nervous, and I said so. That's when he got in a sulk. 'All right, if you're going to be a baby about it, I know another place to go.' "

"He took us to a Mexican place, a dump."

"He was disappointed when he got there, as if it had changed since he had been there last. Anyway, even though it was a Mexican place, he insisted that we drink Long Island iced teas. I can't handle even one, but he wanted to knock back the first round real fast and get to the second. He was very nervous, looking at me."

"Looking at you."

"He has this way of staring. You can see his wheels working, but you can't figure out what he's got on his mind. I've asked him, and whatever he said, I didn't believe. I mean, there was something about the way he answered me that made me think he was lying. After a while he says, in a very low tone, as if he was talking only to me, not to Tom, 'I had to kill somebody once, you know. On assignment. I can't tell you where or when. I had to kill a woman.'" She gestured to her husband. "This one says, 'Oh yeah? How?' And Garrett goes like this." She brought her arm up to her chest in an awkward imitation of the bar-arm choke hold.

Parkinson said, "And then I said, 'You're full of shit.' I thought he was. Now I'm not so sure. I mean, things sort of fit together."

She looked away from him disdainfully. "The point is, Garrett shut up. If he was going to say more, that was the end of it."

"Why do you think he said it in the first place?"

"I told you, he was looking at me, talking to me. He insisted I have a second Long Island iced tea. That was it for me. I don't even remember the ride back to the motel."

"I had to put her to bed," Tom Parkinson said.

"And then the two of you really started drinking," she said.

"Not really," he said blandly. They had been over this incident many times, Boudreau decided, and Lockman's arrest and the attendant publicity had reawakened ugly feelings in her. Hubby was in denial, hoping the passage of time would carry the subject downwind again. To Boudreau, he said, "He and I had a few more drinks in his room, and then I turned in. He was sitting up watching TV when I closed the door to our room. I thought I locked it, but I guess I didn't."

Sheila Parkinson's lower lip trembled as she looked from her husband to Boudreau. She said, "I still don't know what woke me up. It was dark in the room. It took me a moment to realize what was wrong with me—I mean, I was still drunk. It wasn't any fun. I just felt lousy. I was lying on my side, looking at him—this one, on the other bed—when I sensed that somebody was standing over me. At first I thought it was Tom, even though I was looking at him. Have you ever woke up drunk?"

"I understand what you're saying."

"Okay. But I figured it out, that it wasn't Tom. And I froze. I wasn't thinking of Garrett at all, but that some guy had broken into the room. Then I heard this quick little snick-snick-snick sound—I knew what it meant, what he was doing. I couldn't believe it! I was too scared to move. I didn't know who it was. Then I had his semen on my face. He came on me. I could smell it! I freaked! I started screaming."

"I was on my feet looking him eye to eye before I realized I was awake," Tom Parkinson said amiably. "Even in the dark I could see the guilty look in his eyes. She's screaming at the top of her lungs, he's yelling that he was drunk and didn't mean it, he's backing toward his room, and I'm trying to shout over both of them."

"Then I turned on the light."

"Right, she turned on the light, and I could see. I'm telling you, I have never been so sick in my life. He's backing toward the door, she's yelling. He closes the door and locks it, still yelling that he was drunk. She's in the bathroom washing, yelling at me now, that it was all my fault, and then the telephone rings. They want us out of there or they're going to call the police. What we didn't know was that somebody in the motel had already complained about the noise from his television set."

"I had to get out of there anyway," said Sheila Parkinson. "I had his stink on me and I was trying to scrub it off. Did you ever get a smell up your nose and not be able to get rid of it?"

Boudreau nodded, thinking of rotting corpses. Right now Garrett Lockman was sitting in his cell in front of a thirteen-inch color television set provided by his uncle Al, watching *Family Ties* and *Cheers*. Just as Diane had predicted, Lockman was docile now, even pleasant and polite. You could see through to his cunning, as Sheila Parkinson had just said: in his eyes you could see him weighing and measuring every gesture and nuance as he looked for weakness in you and advantage for himself.

Boudreau didn't believe every word of Sheila Parkinson's account of what had happened in southern California. Lockman had made her nervous? He had looked at her? What Boudreau had difficulty believing was what she had not said but wanted him to accept, that she had been completely innocent of the processes at work among the three of them. Drunk and down to their underwear? The debate taking place in the psychiatric community about the participation of the victim in the crime had some informational value here, but not in terms of law enforcement. Being a tease was not a crime—and not because the dreariness of the rest of her life made her pathetic. Her husband was a dunce who was proud of it, but even he must have realized he was sharing her with his friend rather more than society condoned, but his failings and oversights were not crimes, either. But what Lockman had done was defined by statute as sexual assault. Boudreau said, "So you left the motel in the middle of the night."

"I wanted to go straight to the airport," Sheila Parkinson said. "He was all apologetic, saying he had been drunk, he was going to make it right, all that stuff. I just wanted to get away from him. I didn't want to ride in a taxi with him to the airport. Tom asked him for a loan so we could travel by ourselves, but he said he didn't have any money. Finally we had to drag our suitcases to an automatic teller machine so we could get fifty dollars. We changed to another flight later. When he tried to approach us in the airport, I started yelling again. Then he said he wanted the purse back."

"What purse?"

"He had given me a purse the year before, some kind of beige cloth thing, with flowers printed on it. I knew it wasn't new when he gave it to me. It was dirty and had brown stains on it. I couldn't believe him! He wanted it back? I told him I'd already thrown it away even though I hadn't and to leave us alone or I'd call the police."

Now Boudreau asked, "Do you have the purse?"

"I threw it away as soon as I got home."

"In the garbage," Boudreau said. "The truck took it away. To the dump." *Where it was buried under twenty thousand tons of garbage.*

She smiled nervously. "It was important, wasn't it?"

"I have no way of knowing." The stale, pissy smell of the little house closed in on him. He got up. "Thanks for your help," he recited. "If you think of anything else, be sure to give us a call."

———

WAYNE SPENCER'S COLLAR was open and his tie pulled down to the third shirt button. The warehouse wasn't warm—in April, far from it—but because of the quantity and age of its contents, the air was motionless, heavy with the dust and mold of decades, and hard to breathe. And Spencer's job wasn't all that arduous: he was to push the buttons on the tape recorder that was immortalizing the proceedings. In the center of the building was a clear space perhaps thirty feet across. Twenty undertaker's folding chairs had been arrayed in a circle in the center. The detectives occupying the chairs were surrounded by labeled cartons of homework assignments a quarter of a century old, report cards, yellowed newspapers, books, toys, oversized paper-covered model planes in various stages of decay, women's clothing, women's underwear, women's purses, photographs of women, videotapes of women, reels of eight-, sixteen-, and thirty-five-millimeter pornographic film, pinup-queen gas station calendars, dirty comic books, girlie magazines, envelopes and boxes full of bills, check stubs, and receipts, new-car brochures, car owners' manuals, and junk: plastic boxes of screws, nails, nuts and bolts, balls of twine, wire, cable, thread, string; electrical sockets, plugs, extension cords, switches, and fuses; radios, scanners, radar guns, television tubes and parts, auto parts, including a dozen different carburetors, and the entire dashboard of a Cessna 172 airplane.

The cops were using their laps and the floor in front of them as temporary desks, tending piles of folders, envelopes, clipboards, and loose-leaf and spiral notebooks. To Boudreau the rest of the crowd looked as uncomfortable as he was. Occasionally someone pulled or pushed his chair on the concrete floor, and the scraping sound reverberated so loudly against the cinder-block walls and corrugated steel roof of the warehouse that it hurt the ears.

Next to Spencer, Randall Murray called upon the leader of the search warrant evidence evaluation group, Detective Roy Collins of the King County Sheriff's Department, for the first report. Collins was in his thirties, a fitness and martial-arts enthusiast, and his tapered shirt looked like it was going to explode. He swallowed and then gestured to the piles of stuff surrounding them.

"What we have here is at least six hundred thousand separate pieces of evidence that have to be evaluated. We have to catalog and classify every single item. As everybody knows, we've found nothing so far that ties the suspect to any of the Green River victims." He looked around. "A lot of this stuff doesn't even belong to him. Our best guess is that it was taken out of other people's garbage, other people's homes. And as far as tracking stuff down, we could take the numbers off the back of the instruments on the airplane dashboard, for example, but what are we going to learn, that a plane was trashed in Montana?"

Three Spokane detectives, including Tom Logan, had come to Seattle for this. Logan, an overweight, pink-faced man of forty-five, did the talking. "Holy Name has headed for the mattresses. As far as the university administration is concerned, Garrett Lockman is a nonperson. A couple of vehicles he owned that were parked in Holy Name lots have been towed. Since he lied on his application to the law school, all of his credits have been withdrawn. One professor, a fruit named Anton Charles, is very nervous, but he is talking a little more than some others, who look like they want to run when they see us coming. Maybe Charles thinks talking is the way to cover his own trail. Our guess is that something very private transpired between Lockman and Charles. According to him, Lockman would get drunk and talk about a secret career he had with the federal law enforcement. Charles said he always assumed the talk was just drunken BS. We tracked down one female former student, name of Joan Singer. People in the school said that she told them that once when he was very drunk, Lockman said he had to kill a woman as part of a secret mission, but when we asked Singer about it, she denied he ever said anything to her about secret missions or federal service, much less killing anyone. She's a lawyer now, and she looked us straight in the eye when she told us this, so the message was clear. She doesn't want to get involved, and if we force the issue, she's going to be one lousy witness."

Reports followed from the coroner on the two bodies found most recently—numbers forty-two and forty-three—and from the RCMP on

Lockman's Canadian activities. The coroner told the same story they had heard more than thirty-five times before, the remains had been so old and badly decomposed that all that could be learned, from dental records only, was the victim's identification. No cause of death, no evidence of sexual contact. No nothin', Boudreau thought. Years ago the Mounties had matched Lockman's 1983 itinerary to three killings in Vancouver, BC, and Victoria, but now they felt obliged to concede that they could not make any substantive connection between the killings and the suspect.

Boudreau distributed updates on the time line. With the credit-card trail enhanced by hotel and motel records, speeding tickets, Lockman's own checking-account records, Boudreau's group had been able to place Lockman closer to twenty-three of the disappearances. That was the good news. The bad news was that the paper trail seemed more than ever to clear him of the first five killings.

"What about that Indian friend of his?" somebody asked.

"He was in town," Les Lucas said, "but in every other way, he's absolutely clean."

"He doesn't fit the profile anyway," said Kevin Donovan.

"What do you mean?"

"He's not white!"

"This guy isn't going to get away, is he?" Randall Murray asked.

"Who are you talking about?"

"Lockman, for Christ's sake! Does anybody here think he's innocent? What about journals? Tapes? Photographs, for Christ's sake? With all this shit here is somebody going to tell me he *didn't* keep a record of what he was doing? Who he was talking to? Who he was meeting in a goddamned supermarket parking lot?"

Suddenly two loose-leaf notebooks and a stack of papers flew across the concrete floor. A chair crashed. Boudreau looked up as Les Lucas stomped toward the door. "Goddamn!" he yelled. "*Goddamn!*"

———

THE BODY COUNT climbed to forty-seven, perilously close to the ceiling, which was fifty. The word had come down perhaps from the governor himself: under no circumstances was anyone to admit that more than fifty women had been murdered by one man in this jurisdiction in the modern era. No one was ever supposed to say even privately, to members of his family, that the death toll was much higher than the official number.

———

"Is THIS, AH, Detective Phil Boudreau, of the Seattle Police Department?"

"Who's calling?"

"Angela Ruiz. Are you Boudreau? A cop here in New York told me to call you."

Heah in Noo Yawk. "Yes, I'm Boudreau. It's good to hear your voice."

"Oh, yeah?"

"It means you're not dead—"

"You got that goofy perv who stole my purse?"

"Yes, but I'm going to have to keep the purse for a while longer in case I need it for evidence. I have a few questions to ask you, if you don't mind."

"You're a cop, all right. Look, I'm calling long distance, and it ain't cheap."

"I'll call you right back—"

She was silent a moment. "What the fuck, you guys can probably trace the number with them computers anyway." She gave him her telephone number and hung up. He dialed and she picked up again immediately. "You're in Seattle, right? I seen it in a movie one time. Let me tell you something, asshole. That purse was stolen in New York, which is a real city, not some pile of shit lousy excuse for a dump like Seattle, and New York is the only place your fuckin' evidence should be. Even I know that much 'n I didn't finish seventh grade!"

"Would you mind telling me how it was stolen?"

"Fuck you, mind. I want my purse, man. That hillbilly dickhead stole it when he was supposed to be takin' pictures of me. It took me like about one fuckin' second to figure out that what he wanted was my real name. Like he wanted me to tell him, and I told him to go fuck himself."

"Did he do anything with it? Did you ever hear from him again?"

"I saw him that same night! The fruit told me he was hangin' around Thirty-sixth Street, so I walked down there, and sure enough, after a while he comes out of the hotel there so fuckin' drunk he could hardly stand up, laughin' and singin'. When the cops came by I told them that he stole my purse. They ast him about it, and it was like he was stone sober. He whips out this ID that says he's the president of some kind of lawyer association and there I am lookin' like a whore, so guess who they believe? And as soon as they're gone he's dancin' around me and the other girls, laughin' and singin'. I ast him what he was singin' about, and he had like this giggle, right? He goes, 'The wicked witch is dead,' and giggles and sings some more. He like dances around me and gets up real close and says, 'Do you know how many women I've killed?' "

"He said that?"

"Those exact words. That's when I decided to get the fuck out of there, man, 'cause like this guy is some kind of a nut. And *stoned*, man, I never seen anybody packin' such a load and able to act sober like that when the cops came."

"Give me your address, I'll send you your wallet."

"How come you're changin' your tune?"

"I just realized how much I missed hearing the familiar voice of home—"

"What kinda shit is this? You tryin' to tell me you're from New York?"

"That's right, I—"

"Well, motherfucker, you took the biggest wrong turn in the history of the world. You forgot how much you're missin'. Did that chickenshit kill somebody?"

"Maybe."

"Beauty. Send him back here, I'll kick his ass. Let me give you my sister's address, 'cause I move around a lot."

August 1989

Somewhere Inside the Death Star
Skywalker!
Your old buddy Solo is handling the worst the Vader can dish out, including the dreaded gamma pulsator ray. . . .

Garrett Lockman stopped rereading his letter to Martin Jones as he heard the door at the end of the corridor slam with a heavy metallic sound and the guard approach with his chains rattling. Lockman folded the letter and slipped it into his pants pocket. He had initiated the correspondence with Jones to vex the cops who were reading his mail. Jones had been only too eager to respond. Perhaps Jones believed their "romance" was on again. For Lockman it was something to pass the time between visits from Al, his lawyer, and the clamor of daytime television. Lockman's little window gave him a view of a bit of the roof of the Kingdome and, to the left, the I-5 and a planting of trees above, which had gone from bare dark brown to jade to a green so dark from today's rain that it looked like a vast forest. Sometimes Lockman closed his eyes and forced himself to dream he was walking in that forest, making new discoveries at every turn. He had not talked with the police in months, having nothing to say to them, but thanks to old Al, who himself was still enraged over being treated by the police like a criminal, Lockman now had a bombshell. While Lockman was flashing it to the cops, old Al would be giving it to the Seattle press—not the Spokane *Spokesman-Review*, which had betrayed them all, including Hazel, by not printing the complete truth about their family, which to Al meant the Lockmans' contribution to the community for three generations. After all of that, the *Spokesman-Review* had printed only that the investigative team had called Garrett Lockman "a likely suspect" in the Green River killings. For Al the family name was forever sullied by the police attempt to try his nephew/foster son in the media, and the media's eagerness, in Al's phrase, to "spread its cheeks." Now that the chips were down, old Al, in his impotent, thrashing little way, had turned out to be a pistol.

"All right, sunshine," the guard said, "it's time to dress you for company."

"You're right on time. How dutiful you all become when you think you're going to get something." Lockman stood up in his cell and extended his wrists for cuffing. He was long past complaining about being shackled to move from one floor to another only to have the shackles removed again when he reached his destination. It was all Frenchy Boudreau's idea. As Lockman had just written to Martin Jones:

> . . . The Vader is omnipotent in his ability to numb all the microgalactic corners of the subject mind. Inside the Death Star the Emperor's bionic prototroops obey the Vader's dicta down to the last subatomic. . . .

"Fink!"

"Rat! You're gonna die, rat!"

"Shut up!" the guard barked as he led Lockman back to the elevators. In these five cells were the only other prisoners Lockman had seen since his arrival last winter. Isolation was part of the softening-up process, he knew, and it was not an accident that the other prisoners in this little block thought they knew Lockman's "history" as a police informer. The morons never stopped to think that they were dealing with a super criminal, one for whom crime was the true revolution. What was he doing in isolation, if he was not so dangerous to the status quo?

Lockman and the guard stood facing the elevator and the television camera until another guard at a monitor somewhere in the bowels of the jail took notice of them. An elevator arrived and the door opened. The two men stepped inside. "Where to?" asked a voice from a speaker.

"Four," the guard said. "Police interrogation."

"Don't tell me that the prick is finally going to talk," the voice said.

"Don't count on it," Lockman answered with a laugh.

The door opened again. Lockman knew exactly the number of steps to the next steel door, the number of steps to the left to the visitors' booths, including the so-called untapped lawyer's booth. He had only a fair idea of the number of steps to the right to the police interrogation room. He had written to Martin Jones:

> Later in this current temporal sector I will be escorted to the Intergalactic Turboencabulator, where I will be subjected to deconstructionism forty ways to the ace, seven days to Sunday, anally, orally, and on a red pepper coulis all the way to the river, and chances are that I will wake up on the other side of the known stanportis, my faithful emissary from the planet Ringo, more chemotherapy than Kimosabe. All contributions tax deductible, consult your local physician, professional driver on a closed course, do not attempt.

Let the cops figure that out.

Another guard waited at the door to the interrogation room, and watched dully as Lockman's guard removed the shackles. Lockman put on his usual little show of rubbing his wrists before stepping into the dingy, fluorescent-lit room where the Vader himself, Frenchy Boudreau, and two others were sitting at the table. The older one looked familiar. Now Lockman remembered seeing him at the time of his arrest. Lockman took the single chair opposite the three and smiled to them all. Their wet coats on a chair in the corner smelled of the rain. On the table was a telephone and, in front of the younger, blond man, a portable tape recorder.

"I recognize you," Lockman said to the older man, "but I've forgotten your name. If I ever knew it."

"Captain Les Lucas, of the King County Sheriff's Department." The man had the deep, rolling baritone of a country boy. "This fella on my right is Officer Wayne Spencer, and on the left—"

"I know Frenchy. How're you doin', Frenchy? Gettin' much lately?"

Boudreau didn't answer, barely holding Lockman's gaze. Lockman had to keep himself from smiling. Boudreau had a manila folder in front of him. The young cop pushed the portable tape recorder to the center of the table. Lockman looked him straight in the eye, "No tape recorders."

"Just routine, Garrett," Les Lucas said. "This way there's no danger of us misquoting you."

Lockman laughed. "Don't be silly. With the right engineering, you could make a tape sound like I'm singing 'The Star-Spangled Banner.' In French."

Nobody laughed. "Come on, Garrett, be sensible," Les Lucas said.

"Not me. You know I'm crazy. No taping. I'll go back to my cell and watch *The Young and the Restless*. Do you know what they do on that show when they get too restless?"

"No, what?"

"They go to bed!"

The blond guy shook his head, smiling. On a nod from Lucas, he stood up to retrieve the tape recorder, reaching around with his right hand. Now Lockman saw that his left arm hung limply at his side. Lockman saw that he had the opportunity to multiply his advantage. "What's the matter with your arm?"

The blond guy slowly raised his eyes. "I got shot."

Lockman was startled. Carefully he offered a smile. "What happened to the guy who shot you?"

The blond guy's eyes never wavered. "I killed him."

Lockman was silent. The cops didn't miss it. Lockman turned to Lucas. "Did you bring my food?"

The cops looked at each other.

"I told you I'd talk if you brought me two pastrami on rye. I wasn't kidding."

Boudreau picked up the telephone and touched zero. "Al Holobaugh, please."

"Be sure to tell him hand-sliced," Lockman said.

While Boudreau gave the lunch order, Les Lucas said, "All right, Garrett, you see you have a done deal. Now what is it that you wanted to tell us?"

"Let me have my lunch first." He had written of this moment to Martin Jones, describing it perfectly. The realization that the words were in his pocket, so close to them, wriggled through him thrillingly. Did they have any idea they were so transparent? No, of course not.

The Vader is in fact a shape-shifter who speaks in a variety of guises, but it is possible for this entity to see through them all to the nasty scorpion ol' Vade really is. . . .

Boudreau leaned forward. "Let's get to it, Garrett. Stop the crap."

"No, you stop the crap! You look terrible, Frenchy. What the hell have you been doing to yourself? Maybe you ought to think about a new career. I don't think police work agrees with you. Or are you just eating diseased cunt?"

"Whatever you say, Garrett," Boudreau said with an unexpected smoothness. "We'll wait until your lunch gets here. In the meantime, let us ask you a few questions."

Lockman turned his palms up. "Ask all the questions you want. I probably won't want to answer any one of them."

Boudreau opened the folder and read from the top sheet. "How did you support yourself from the time of your walkaway to your enrollment in Holy Name Law School?"

Lockman grinned until Boudreau was forced to look up. Lockman shook his head slowly, noting in the process that the young blond killer was glaring at him. Boudreau nodded, clicked a ballpoint, and made a check mark on the left side of the sheet next to the question, then wrote NA on the right. He cleared his throat. "Do you still have in your possession any of the traveler's checks stolen from the American Express office in Coronado, California, in October of 1978?"

Lockman turned his palms up again. As before, Boudreau wrote on both sides of the typewritten question. It was some kind of paper-pushing variant on the Chinese water torture. Boudreau asked, "Do you own any firearms?"

"No."

Boudreau wrote again, taking much more time than necessary to record Lockman's one-word answer. Yes, it was the water torture. Boudreau coughed. "Garrett, in your effects we found evidence that you have used many aliases. Would you like to tell us why you have used many aliases?"

Lockman stayed silent. He wanted to wave to the blond guy, who was glaring at him as if he had been rehearsed.

"You answered the previous question," Boudreau said. "Would you like to answer this one?"

"No."

"Take a stab at it," the blond guy said.

"It not only kills, it speaks!"

"That makes two of us. Now answer the question."

"No."

"All right, then," Boudreau resumed in the same smooth tone he had affected from the start, "let me ask you about the many thousands of miles you drove throughout the Northwest in the years between your walkaway and your enrollment in law school. Why did you do so much driving?"

Lockman laughed. "I like to drive. I even sleep on the driver's side." The blond guy was staring at him. "Of the bed. The driver's side of the bed."

Boudreau began to write again. He turned the sheet over and kept writing. Lockman looked to Lucas, who was looking back at him, staring into his eyes. Lockman was beginning to dislike this intensely. It was part of a plan, of course, but what plan? Why? Boudreau suddenly stopped writing. "Would you like to expand on that?"

"Expand on what?"

"How much you like to drive. You said you like to drive. Why do you like to drive?"

"What is this?"

"Some questions. We said we'd like to ask you some questions while we're waiting for the sandwiches, after which you said you were going to make a statement. Among your effects we found papers and identification saying that you were mayor and emergency-services director of a town called Dingle, Washington. Do you hold those positions?"

Lockman stayed silent. This was really funny, but it was beginning to bug the hell out of him. Did they take *Dingle* seriously? He had had those documents printed in case he was ever stopped in his ambulance, and so long ago he had forgotten about them. He shrugged, all the answer they were going to get out of him.

"We haven't been able to find the town of Dingle, Washington, on the maps or in any of the gazetteers, Garrett. Is there a Dingle, Washington?"

"What are you doing, Frenchy? Just what the fuck do you think you're doing?"

"Be careful with your language, Garrett. I meant to caution you before. This is a public building. We're just trying to make the best use of the time while we're waiting for your sandwiches. Is there a Dingle, Washington?"

"You know as much about it as I do! Dingle, dingle dingle! What do you think you're doing?"

"Just a few questions, that's all. Let me try another. When you were using the bar-arm choke hold on those girls, did you fuck them up the ass or in the pussy?"

"I don't have to put up with this!"

"You wanted the sandwiches, Garrett. You don't want to make your statement until you have your sandwiches, so we're just trying to fill the time. Do you want me to repeat the question?"

Les Lucas said, "It's really very simple, Garrett. When you were using the bar-arm choke hold on those girls, did you fuck them up the ass or in the pussy?"

"The reason we ask, Garrett," Boudreau said, "is that we've just learned that a homosexual named William Bonin down in Los Angeles confessed to garroting his victims while he fucked them up the ass so that their death throes would give him a more intense sexual thrill. Now, we know you're not a homosexual, Garrett, in spite of your close association with certain professors at Holy Name. All we want to know is how you fucked those girls when you killed them. Up the ass or in the pussy? People should know exactly what a crime like this really is. Nothing complicated about it. All that shaking juiced the killer's fruit."

"Tell us how you fucked them, Garrett," Les Lucas said.

"I'm not talking anymore. I'm going to wait for the sandwiches and then I'll make my statement."

The blond guy said, "Three people have told us that you told them that you killed women. What about it, Garrett?"

"You're lying. Or they are. Give me their names. I have the right to confront my accusers. I'm going to sue them."

Boudreau said, "Sheila Parkinson says you sexually assaulted her in California."

"That woman is crazy. She is completely crazy. I'm going to sue her, too, along with the Seattle newspapers and the *Spokesman-Review*."

The blond guy said, "Tell us about the gun, Garrett."

"I don't know anything about any guns."

Boudreau said, "According to an affidavit sworn to by Mr. Waldo Starr, now an ADA in Spokane County, when you were both students at Holy Name, you talked him into selling you a nine-millimeter automatic. Mr. Starr swears that he sold you this gun in the spring of 1986."

"Mr. Starr is a liar."

"Mr. Starr is a sworn officer of the court and made this statement under oath. You're a convicted felon who won't answer even nonincriminating questions. In this world of worlds, who do you think is going to be believed?"

"You should do a background check on Mr. Starr! At Holy Name the women called him the 'Janitor Rapist'. He is a very shady guy. For all you know, he's your Green River killer—it's a perfect cover!"

They stared at him, silent.

"It is!"

They still stared. Were they trying to panic him? Lockman spoke slowly. "I'm not worried about him, at least not about any so-called testimony. What a howl!"

Les Lucas stood up. "That's it. We don't need this. We'll eat the sandwiches ourselves."

"Are the big brave police going to welsh on their deal? Right now in Spokane my uncle Al Lockman is holding a press conference, showing the proof that I had nothing to do with the killings. Al has my signature on credit-card slips that show that I was on the other side of the country when the first five girls disappeared. It's all over! In six months I'll have served my time, and then it's adios! So let's have the sandwiches before I tell my lawyer you're trying to bribe me with food to violate my civil rights!"

Les Lucas reached for the telephone.

"What are you doing?"

"Sending you back."

"What about my sandwiches?"

Lucas spoke into the handset. Boudreau closed his folder and got to his feet. The blond guy grinned again as he stood up. Why was he grinning? Was this part of their plan, too? Lockman could feel his lower lip quivering.

"Thanks for all the help," Boudreau said as he tended to his papers. What had he written? He looked up again. "Garrett, this may be the last chance I'll have to tell you: you're the worst thing that ever happened to me."

Last chance? What did that mean? "My ass! When I get out of here I'm going to sue you from one end of the state to the other. You especially. My regards to your wife! Excuse me, *ex*! X marks the spot—"

Boudreau shook his head. "Garrett, she and I have been divorced for years. You're shooting blanks."

"When am I going to get my property back? All that stuff you seized last January? If you guys take so much as one *National Geographic*—"

Boudreau eyed him carefully. "We're taking good care of your *National Geographics*, Garrett."

"You'd better. It's a complete set, hard to come by. Am I going to get my sandwiches now?"

Les Lucas said, "The sandwiches have nothing to do with these questions, Garrett. We told you, just a few questions while we waited for the sandwiches, after which you were going to make a statement. You're the one who said we were trying to bribe you with food. We have to keep the record clean of intimidation, bargains, or threats. You said you didn't mind if we asked you some questions. What did you do to those girls when you used the bar-arm choke hold on them? Did you fuck them up the ass or in the pussy?"

"You practiced this! You rehearsed it! Wait until my lawyer hears you've been harassing me!"

The blond guy opened his jacket to reveal another tape recorder strapped to his ample gut. "It's all on tape, Garrett."

"I told you no tape! I told you no tape! Now take me back to my cell!"

"You got it," Boudreau said, his voice absolutely flat. Lockman stared at him. The young guy was smiling again, to himself. Lucas looked at him with a confused, questioning expression. The young guy gave Lucas a thumbs-up. Only Boudreau's face was grim. Lockman could feel his lower lip trembling again. Something had happened—what? Boudreau didn't want to look at him.

"You're a dickhead, Frenchy."

"That's right."

"You want to tell me what's going on?"

"No."

"Oh, that's original! What were you writing?"

"None of your business," Boudreau muttered as he reached for his coat. Lockman looked at the other two: now Les Lucas was grinning, too. The young guy looked like he wanted to laugh out loud.

"I'll want to see those notes. Let's get that on the tape recorder, too. You made notes and we'll subpoena them if and when the time comes."

"Whatever you say," Boudreau whispered. "You had it right the first time. I'm a dickhead." His eyes met Lockman's: he looked like an old, old man. Lockman looked at the others again. They were still grinning like apes, and now, without knowing why, Lockman felt nauseous. Then he remembered: Waldo Starr. He was the problem!

Not for long, Lockman thought.

If he was going to kill a man at last, this was the way to do it, from the confines of prison, at a great distance. *Let somebody try to top it for a virtuoso performance.*

August 1989

"No *National Geographics*," Boudreau said from the backseat of the car. Raindrops ran down the nape of his neck.

"What?" Lucas asked.

"You heard him," Spencer said with a grin. "No *National Geographics*. We don't have any *National Geographics* in evidence. We didn't take any *National Geographics* out of Lockman's house or the shed in back."

"We've been looking for most of a year for self-storage receipts," Lucas said.

"They aren't hidden in a self-storage yard," Boudreau said. "They're where Lockman had easy access to them. He just forgot exactly where."

Lucas used the car's hands-free cellular telephone to reach out to Randall Murray to tell him that Lockman had inadvertently tipped them to the existence of other caches of evidence. "Did we ever check to see if Al Lockman owned other properties in Spokane?"

Murray's voice came out of the dashboard. "Of course we did."

"How about under other names?" Spencer asked. "Al is a dentist. He's incorporated to limit his liability in case he gets sued. It's what all the medical assholes do. He'd do the same thing with his real estate."

"You're goddamned right, kid," Murray said. "Good thinking."

Good *cop* thinking, Boudreau told himself. Someone first meeting Spencer wouldn't be able to imagine him as anything but the tough-hided, nasty old bull he had become. Boudreau almost laughed aloud: was he sitting in judgment?

The next morning the secretary of state of the state of Washington backtracked Albert Lockman as the sole officer of three different corporations with Spokane addresses giving "real estate" as their principal businesses. Spokane PD and the Spokane Sheriff's Department quickly searched the city and county computerized tax rolls to confirm the locations of Al's three rental properties, all single-family residences on the city's north side. Late in the afternoon Boudreau and Spencer flew to Spokane to swear to a judge that they had heard Garrett Lockman claim ownership to collectibles not recovered in the search of the Lockman residence earlier this year, and to present the affidavit of Waldo Starr concerning the sale of the automatic. Looking over the affidavit, the judge couldn't help sighing. As a prosecutor, Boudreau and Spencer already had been told, Starr had acquired a countywide reputation for fumbling incompetence. People thought he was strange. Boudreau, for one, had known it ever since Starr had come forward with the information about selling the gun to Lockman. Any other civil servant would have seen the connection to a suspected serial killer as a career destroyer. But Starr had thought he was doing his duty. A born schmuck, Boudreau had thought, just the kind of guy Lockman always sought out.

Tom Logan had already drafted a plan to pounce on all three houses in the early hours of the following morning. In the meantime a fat-cat friend of local law enforcement arranged for Boudreau, Spencer, Logan, and three other Spokane detectives to have dinner at the Spokane Club.

The place had the plush, moderne ambience of a nightspot in an old Warner Brothers gangster movie, and the dubious menu of a hotel dining room near a quiet airport. The first thing Spokane cops wanted to hear was the story of Spencer's shoot-out. Being a hero agreed with Spencer; as the center of attention, he happily forgave all priors. He jabbed a fork toward Boudreau. "His father gets an assist. Of course, the old man didn't fuck it up so he was dragging his arm around like that guy in the Frankenstein movies."

"Don't let him kid you," Boudreau said to Spencer's audience. "His arm is coming back. But one bad guy's gone for good. And the other one will be wearing a garter belt and stockings in Walla Walla for the next ten years."

"The warden made sure he was introduced to all the right people," Spencer finished.

"He could get AIDS that way," somebody deadpanned, and people laughed.

One of the Spokane cops told an old, bad, gay joke. As a test, Boudreau told his father's joke about Harry who was bored with life. The joke was at least thirty-five years old. It got screams. Another of the Spokane guys commented on how close Boudreau and Spencer were. Spencer said, "Yeah, right. For a while we were even fucking the same dame." Pause. "Of course, I didn't know it at the time." Over the laughter, he said, "Boudreau is all heart. Maybe not all." He held up his thumb and forefinger an inch apart. "That much ain't heart."

"That don't get you even, even if you're telling the truth," somebody said to Spencer over the laughter.

"Tell them what I call your girlfriend, Phil."

"Not me. And *you* watch yourself."

"Hitler." He raised his hand in an abbreviated version of the Nazi salute. "I call her Hitler."

"She's a shrink, and a lot better than the dumb bastards collecting our consultation fees," Boudreau said. "Thanks to her, we back up before Lockman knows he's going to fart."

"That part is true, I will admit," Spencer said. "If we hadn't rattled the motherfucker, he might have thought twice about mentioning the *National Geographics*."

"All from her playbook," Boudreau said. "It's the same stuff the FBI is using. Let's just say she explains it better. She has more common sense. More life experience."

"What the hell, she's older than J. Edgar Hoover," Spencer said. "But I'll tell you, now that I've seen them at work, I don't think the FBI could find Darryl Strawberry at a Ku Klux Klan clusterfuck."

"But DEA is worse," a Spokane cop said, "and ATF is worse than the other two. The only big rep worth a damn is the one belonging to the Texas Rangers. And all they have is about a hundred old guys. Old *tough* guys. Listen, if you can twist a guy like Lockman around so easily, how are you going to fight an insanity defense?'"

Boudreau started, "It isn't that easy to twist—"

Logan said, "Concealing his crimes so he could commit more is all you need to know about whether he could tell right from wrong. I've got a copy of the tapes Lawrence Bittaker made of the girls screaming as he pulled out their clits with a pair of pliers. He made the tapes so he could pull his pork and reminisce—"

"I don't want to hear about it," Boudreau said.

"Why not?"

"What for?"

"What is Bittaker doing now?" the guy sitting next to Logan asked.

"Watching TV in his cell," said Spencer. "Granting interviews. If he's suing California because his morning coffee isn't hot enough, I wouldn't be surprised. And women write to him saying how much they want to chomp his gland."

The waiter tapped Logan on the shoulder, and he pushed away from the table and followed the waiter into the hall.

Spencer said to Boudreau, "Piper called me, you know. She was back from New York to visit her parents and I guess she decided she needed a workout. I told her to meet me in a bar near the U. A biker-bitch joint. I didn't show up. She never called back to complain. Maybe I started her on a whole new career."

Logan reentered. "Well, we don't have Waldo Starr to kick around anymore. He blew his head off with a shotgun this morning. His landlady just found him. She said she was wondering why he was so quiet today."

"Dead will do that to you."

"Next time the old bag might not be so quick to snoop in her tenant's digs."

Spencer turned in his seat. "Do you think this place will give us body bags?"

Everybody laughed. "*Doggie* bags!" somebody shouted.

"What did I say? Oh, Jesus."

———

THE GUN STARR sold Lockman was found the next day, and Starr's suicide note surfaced two days after that, arriving at the home of somebody who hardly knew him, a three-page cry of despair. The only satisfaction he could take from his time on this terrible planet, Starr wrote, was in the knowledge that the Green River killer was already in jail. But no name. He did not point to any evidence. Simply, *The Green River killer is already in jail.* The letter was passed to the newspapers, and they printed that line, and the information that Garrett Richard Lockman, in jail, had been called by the Green River Investigative Team "a likely suspect" in the Green River killings. No digging to find the connection between the two men beyond the sale of the gun, for which Lockman was being charged under a catchall federal statute. Similarly, the television news anchors read the important line aloud, repeating the information that Lockman was being charged with possessing a firearm while a fugitive from justice, raising an eyebrow while turning the page. No comment from Lockman or his lawyer, no comment from the Green River Investigative Team. To the law-enforcement community Waldo Starr was as much an embarrassment dead as alive, and Lockman's side was only too pleased not to press the issue.

One of the members of the law-school faculty called the investigative team to ask about Starr's computer. Everyone knew that Starr had owned a computer. He had told many people he kept a journal in it. Publicly— and for the faculty member—the investigative team had no comment.

One night weeks later Boudreau told Paulie what had happened to the damned thing. Except to say that the man had lived like a pig, Boudreau passed over the condition of Starr's basement apartment, not mentioning the brains and skull fragments embedded in the ceiling and two walls, or the condition of the body, headless except for a bloody piece of jawbone. Boudreau and the others had arrived from the Spokane Club as Spokane PD detectives were finishing their videotaping and before the coroner had cleared the body. No problem with the cause of death: Starr's big toe was still wedged tightly in the shotgun trigger guard. The computer squatted on Starr's desk surrounded by a three-inch layer of gritty papers and books. Logan turned the computer on. On the screen appeared the prompt:

ENTER PASSWORD

"Hey, look at this!"

Boudreau had learned a little about computers from Paulie. "Don't touch it!"

Too late. Logan pressed the enter key. On the screen appeared:

INCORRECT PASSWORD!!!
You Have 30 Seconds To Enter Correct Password

On the screen appeared the image of a clock, black on amber, one large hand ticking from six up toward twelve.

"Turn it off!"

"I want to see what happens."

Boudreau tried to reach around to get at the power switch. Logan elbowed him. "You're out of your jurisdiction, Boudreau."

The clock ticked up to twelve, then disappeared.

ALL FILES HAVE BEEN ERASED

And finally:

PHUCK KEW, KOPPAHS!!

"The asshole," Paulie said. "The files are gone. He had the computer encrypted so you wouldn't get at them."

"Encrypted," Boudreau said, savoring a new word. "Okay. Don't tell anybody about this."

"You think I'm like you?" He smiled. Thirteen now, he was almost as tall as his father, gawky thin, with the beginnings of a mustache darkening the corners of his upper lip. "You don't need what he wrote anyway. That gun he sold Lockman that you found is going to do it, won't it?"

Yes, but Boudreau couldn't tell Paulie how. Paul was the last person on the face of the earth Boudreau would want to know how the gun charge was going to do it. Instead, Boudreau told him about the *National Geographics*. One of the local cops remembered them on a list of items taken in a burglary years and years ago. As the victim had said at the time, *National Geographics* were worth money—which was exactly the kind of thing a certain kind of cop would remember. Paul was beginning to develop a taste for cop stories, and he liked that one. Boudreau asked, "How's your friend's book?"

Paulie had told his mother he wanted to spend a week with his father to talk about personal things—she was supposed to believe he meant the facts of life—when in fact he wanted to read the typescript of Diane's book, which she was passing around among her friends while she thought more about it. She had not let Boudreau read it during the writing, and now he wanted to wait until they were at Little Bitterroot again before settling down with it. Diane had been telling Paulie for years that knowing her story would help him understand his mother's better. Now he told Boudreau, "She lists the things she did that hurt her before she had to reinvent herself. Mom's getting to that point."

"She is?"

"*She* says she learned it from me. Looking at me trying to help her made her realize she had hit bottom. I don't really think she got that far, but that's what she says."

The telephone rang. "You answer it," Boudreau said. He knew that for too many years he had focused on Lockman to the exclusion of the rest of his life like a hypnotized chicken staring at a spot on the ground. It wasn't going to do him any good to tell himself that he would catch up with his kid next summer at Little Bitterroot. Paulie and his mother were already making plans to drive to San Antonio, New Orleans, and Florida.

"We were just talking about you," Paulie said into the telephone. "No, no, I'm not spoiling it for him. What's interesting is like with some of these guys, I'm going, 'No, no, don't do that, you're only going to piss her off.' Also, I didn't know it was going to be so *raunchy*. I mean, I'm just a kid. You could have warned me. He's sitting right here, where the light is shining on his bald spot. Hang on." To his father, he said, "It's your squeeze."

Boudreau took the handset. "Did you hear that?"

"It's nothing compared to what I'm going to do to you," Diane said. "I'm going to report you for un-American behavior. You don't have your television set on. Tomorrow's *Spokesman-Review* will be printing a copyrighted story to the effect that Waldo Starr showed up at a motel in December 1985, saying he was a lawyer representing a Spokane policeman—"

"He wasn't a lawyer then. He was still in law school."

"If you were watching the news, you'd know I know that. Listen. The story he told the motel clerk was that a prostitute named Sonya Moore stole his client's wallet, and that he wanted to find Moore to get the wallet back. The client, he said, was a Spokane policeman. She was found in a field less than a month later, strangled—"

Paulie kissed him on the top of the head. "*Bonne nuit, papa.*"

"I heard that," Diane said. "He asked his French teacher for help with his accent."

Boudreau waited until Paulie closed the bedroom door, and then found he couldn't talk. He didn't want to talk about Waldo Starr anyway.

"Are you all right?"

It took him a moment to say, "No."

"Well, I'm not coming over. I'm in my bathrobe and I just colored my hair."

"I'll watch the news. How long—"

"My hair? Years, sleuth."

———

IN THE SPRING, upon completion of his fourteen months in King County, Garrett Lockman was transferred to Spokane County Jail to be held without bail awaiting the disposition of the federal charge of possessing a firearm while a fugitive from justice. Out of the glare of the big-time media, he was declared by the Green River Investigative Team as "no longer a likely suspect" in the killings. Interest in him evaporated. He was calling the newspapers and television stations, Boudreau was told, to complain about the execution of the second search warrant, the publication of Waldo Starr's letter, and jailhouse food. The food was awful, terrible, it smelled funny, tasted funny. He had lost twenty pounds, he was telling anyone willing to listen.

Of course he still continued to refuse to talk to the police. Reporters called the investigative team to ask about Lockman's situation, and were told that Lockman was a manipulative sociopath looking for any way to attract attention, but he was not the Green River killer. The press was also told by the investigative team that Lockman didn't realize, in his effort to get some ink, that the community now perceived him as a petty crook who had allowed his friend to go to prison in the traveler's checks case instead of giving up the checks and taking his share of the punishment. And he was the man who had disgraced one of the state's great institutions of learning with his deceptions. The message was clear enough: if you wanted to write something sympathetic toward Lockman for having been falsely accused, this was how the investigative team would respond. No one printed a word about Lockman's complaints. And no one questioned what had happened to make him no longer a "likely suspect" in the Green River killings.

Lockman was sentenced to thirty-three months on the gun charge. Two months later Al Lockman died in his sleep. His nephew/foster son was already in a federal facility in Oregon, and since the connection between them was not that strong in law, Al was buried by members of the Catholic community and his friends in the Liars' Club. By then the Lockmans merited no more than a paragraph in one of the three Puget Sound papers, and an inside article, Detective Logan of the Spokane PD reported to Boudreau, in the *Spokesman-Review*. One of the guys on the team visiting the federal pen in Oregon to interview another prisoner came back with the prison scuttlebutt that Lockman had lost almost thirty pounds. And looked horrible.

Kevin Donovan was packing. The Green River Investigative Team was being reduced in force. No new television programs calling for the public's help in solving the Green River killings were being contemplated, now or in the future.

May 1990

The altimeter indicated twelve thousand feet as the little jet finally slipped through the clouds to give a view of the rising sun. The clouds were dark, and ahead in the distance the Rockies poked through the gray fluff as hard as glaziers' points, edges gleaming gold. Garrett Lockman watched the pilot trim the plane to a more gradual ascent. They were going to cruise at thirty-eight thousand, the pilot had said. Inside, the plane was very like an *Enterprise* shuttlecraft, though smaller, and someday in the future people would look back on planes like this as the forerunners of things probably exactly like shuttlecraft tobogganing down to planets' surfaces. All this for Lockman and two guards from the Bureau of Prisons. "Bureau of Prisms," he called it. He was being taken to Marion, Illinois, where the BOP had a hospital facility. He wasn't feeling any worse, but he wasn't feeling any better, either, thank you very much. The only thing about the plane that wasn't like a shuttlecraft was the noise. With the engines aft, the passenger compartment hissed through the thin air loudly, as if gaseous molecules were ripping at the skin of the fuselage. The engineers had to get this right, if shuttlecraft were going to achieve speeds many times faster than the Mach .8 of this primitive device.

Even in exile the Mighty One contemplates the distant future.

Space Rider to Altair Four:
Some notes on the new airsled. We are en route over a lost planet. . . .

Lockman had to move again in the narrow seat to find a comfortable position. Whatever was making him ill was now a hot dull ache in his belly. What had started as a little indigestion developed into a cramp, then a bellyache, a *big* bellyache. For months he could not get anyone to take his requests to see a doctor seriously, or refer his complaints up the chain of command. When Lockman told one guard he had a bellyache, the guard had replied, "You all do." Lockman did not see a guard for a week while the bellyache grew. He could feel it. Now there was an occasional stabbing pain in his lower back. He wasn't kidding himself about what the upset stomach and the pain meant; he was, after all, the sort-of son of a dentist. But he was waiting for the results of the tests they were going to run in Marion before he came to any hard conclusions. He wasn't going to panic.

His other problem was that he didn't exactly remember when all these things started happening. He had become positively lousy at dates, probably because he was so lousy at doing time, spending his days planning how he would use the hour out of his cell, which was really his hour on the telephone. He had to plot every minute. He was doing business over the telephone with Al's lawyer in Spokane, the cost of every collect call being applied to the expenses of executing Al's estate, which turned out to be less than three hundred thousand—much less than Lockman had expected. That would hit a fellow in the belly, he had thought—when? When had he thought it? And now that he was sometimes puking up little strings of blood, the prison authorities refused to address the question of when he had first complained about his stomach hurting. He had been in three jails and prisons so far and didn't know which one to blame first. For what? Uncle Al's lawyer and Lockman's lawyer in Seattle were sympathetic, but told him to get his health back before thinking about somebody else to sue. When he got out, Lockman planned to sue all the governments involved in his arrest and damage to his reputation, all the law-enforcement agencies, all the media, around the world, and especially Phil Boudreau, whose vendetta this was. The Green River

Investigative Team had never produced a particle of evidence connecting him with the Green River murders.

The chains on his wrists and ankles started weighing on him again, and he had to find a new position on the narrow airplane seat to carry him through the next few minutes. They were advancing into rough weather, nothing dangerous, but the commercial airlines always flew around such systems. The fear Lockman felt over the plane crashing made him forget the real reason why he was glad there was no lunch on board. He did not have the appetite to eat anything, and in the attempt to reduce his mounting terror over what was happening to him, he would have tried to force himself to eat to satisfy the others aboard that he was not that sick. He had planned to send Frenchy Boudreau a wish-you-were-here postcard from Illinois until someone told him that anything he wanted to mail out would have to be rerouted from the prison in which he was serving his time, making the gag a complete exercise in futility. He felt like one of those protesters being hosed down the street, the force against him too powerful to resist. He had nothing to grab onto, no handholds. . . .

A hole opened in the cloud cover over the eastern Oregon desert and Lockman looked down at the dark land beneath. With time off for good behavior, which could not be denied, he could be out as early as next January—sooner, if the tests showed he needed special care. It might take a court order, but Al's money would pay for it. The special treatment he needed, too, if that was the case.

———

AS IF TO remind him of the power they had over him, in the evenings after the tests the authorities moved him in a wheelchair across the road from the hospital to the ultra-maximum security facility behind the great steel fences topped with rolls of shiny razor-sharp concertina wire. His cell was five by eight feet, a concrete sleeping pad, toilet, and sink. No radio or TV. He was at the end of the block with no one in the adjoining cell, a long way from the open sky that had brought him here. Nothing to eat. He could think about food, but he dared not imagine it intensely, or it would make him sick. He couldn't call Martin Jones. Jones had already told him he would not accept interstate collect calls without written assurance from Al's lawyer that the calls would be paid for out of the estate. Al's lawyer told Lockman he could not possibly get such an expense past a probate judge mindful of criticism because the executor was a notorious person. "I know you're sick, Garrett, but the law won't cut you a break because of it. Even if people took you to be a good guy, but as it is, all they can see is your record, as you know."

Lockman wound up thinking of that. He spent the night sick with the chemicals the doctors had given him for the tests during the day, and in the absence of anything else in the world to do, he thought of the people who were aware of his criminal record, and wondered what they made of it. His essence was becoming part of their landscape, his spirit a part of the spirit of their world.

More tests the next day, exactly the same tests, in fact, because the doctors wanted to be sure, they said. The results would be in on Monday, meaning Lockman would have to spend the weekend in the little concrete tomb, staring at a wall. He was thinking he would pass the time constructing a fantasy that would plunge him deeper into the problem of doing time, time slowed down, time turned gray. . . .

But on Saturday night he was awakened by the sensation of a fiery sword being pushed through his belly, and he sat up screaming, the act of sitting up making his agony only worse. He yelled and yelled again into the silence. As if his cell wasn't bugged, it took them minutes to respond, then return with a gurney for a hurry-up, bounding ride back across the road. Different doctors, new shots, sweet dreams, all the way back to Deeah Anne Johanssen, alive again, strong and firm in him again, smiling, loving him. The seducer was really Demerol—from the depths of his unconsciousness he recognized its effects from very private experiments with dear, departed Uncle Al's professional stash. Lockman fought the images, telling himself he wanted the truth . . . and then he was back in the barren gravel yard, where he was watched, pursued, by an evil freak with pink-and-yellow eyes. . . .

When he awakened again the nightmare was in hot pursuit. Was there nobody on duty on the floor? Finally somebody came in. It was Tuesday afternoon, and the doctor who could discuss his case with him wouldn't be back until Thursday. Lockman was chained by the ankle to the foot of the bed and his arm was numb from the IVs. No TV here, either. He heard no one pass in the hall. And his stomach hurt in spite of the drugs they were pumping in him. What the hell was he supposed to do with his time?

Lockman spent the time on his back, finding pictures in the paint on the ceiling.

Some of them were even dirty.

———

THE DOCTOR PUT the X rays up for viewing as Lockman waited in his wheelchair. This had taken a week? Shoe stores used to X-ray your feet instantly. *Look down through the eye slot and wiggle your toes.* The doctor turned out the ceiling light so they could see the pretty pictures. With a pencil he outlined an oval in the center of the first film. "See this dark mass? It's a cancer. It's in your pancreas and liver. We can't operate on it, and in the opinion of the relevant personnel in the Bureau of Prisons, nobody else can, either." He turned the light on again and began to take down the pictures. "You've got six to eight months. If you've got anything you have to get in order, now is the time. This is an extremely painful cancer and there isn't going to be much left of you at the end. Just so's you know." He was winding the string on the flap of the manila envelope that now contained the X rays.

"I'm fucked," Lockman said.

The doctor made the knot complete. "Big time."

Lockman decided that how he handled himself through this would be another part of his legend. He was going to show grace under pressure. He was drawing a line in the sand.

Something to tell Martin Jones. Jones would want to pay closer attention now.

Scottie:
We enter a new sector, destination unknown. Word has come down from Fleet Command that I am to be the next Grebothian sacrifice. . . .

That night the Demerol wore off and depression rolled in over the desolate lowland of his soul and later he was told that the whole prison had heard him screaming. Bellowing. The same phrase, over and over.

"*I told you! I told you!*"

———

AFTER A FEW days back in Oregon Lockman felt better. He was able to contemplate his situation. His story was complete. It would be told as long as there were men who wanted to kill women. He called Phil Boudreau person-to-person at the Green River office. Boudreau wasn't there.

"Is this police business?" a cop called past the operator. "Operator, you're talking to King County Detective Wayne Spencer. Ask him if it's police business."

"Is this police business?" she chirruped.

"Ask Phil Boudreau to call me."

"Is it something I can help you with, Garrett?"

Now Lockman placed the voice and the name. This was the young killer, his comrade-in-arms. "Can you get Boudreau to call me back?"

"I can leave him a message. Do you want me to leave him a message, Garrett?"

Lockman hung up and asked to be put back in his cell.

—

BOUDREAU NEVER CALLED back. Lockman had to reconstruct the telephone conversation with Spencer to understand what must have happened: Spencer had not given Boudreau the message because he thought he saw a career opportunity for himself. He thought he could manipulate Lockman into calling back and being connected to him again.

Maybe young Dirty Harry thought he had a way of attracting Lockman's attention in spite of himself? It was almost funny, it was so presumptuous.

Lockman had three months to go on his sentence when he wound up in the prison hospital again. He asked for Demerol. They gave him something else that did not work as well.

December 1990

Phil Boudreau was on the island of Kauai, in the Hawaiian chain, the day Garrett Lockman was rolled out of prison on a gurney to be driven in a commercial ambulance in an all-day snowstorm from southwestern Oregon to the eastern edge of the state of Washington. Boudreau was in the town of Hanalei, in a bungalow Diane had rented for the month. She had finished the second revision of *Flashback* and was sure she was cured of book writing forever. Hanalei received more rain every year than Seattle, coming in brief, warm downpours. This was the town mentioned in the sixties' magic-dragon anthem, and the local population remained larded with potbellied, shirtless old hippies, some of whom had been here for twenty-five years. Boudreau had been aware that Lockman's release date was coming, and now he regarded as a personal step in the right direction the fact that he did not fix on it as a reality until some days after its actual occurrence. Three months ago he had heard immediately that Lockman had called, lost heart, and hung up. Boudreau had listened to the tape recording of the call three dozen times in the hope of hearing—what? A hint of change? A willingness to talk?

Bunk.

When he finally remembered Lockman's release, Boudreau was sitting at a bar in the center of town with a view of a mountainside of waterfalls. He felt better than he had in years. What got him around to Lockman that afternoon was his own musings on the quality of the eavesdropping equipment one of the other agencies had wanted to install in Lockman's house. It was the best stuff that confiscated dope money could buy: with the volume cranked up, a dropping pin sounded like a ship collision. But at this point practically no one was interested in bugging Lockman any-more. All evidence of a connection between Lockman and the law-enforcement community had been destroyed with the same distraction with which a cat covered its mess. For that matter, Boudreau couldn't get any interest in taking another look at Martin Jones, arguing vigorously for it. Where was the money going to come for it, now that their budget was gone? Some were arguing that Martin Jones was too much an invert, a ha-bitual masturbator, to misbehave overtly often. If ever. For all Boudreau knew, maybe so. But the lack of enthusiasm worked both ways: Boudreau thought a Lockman surveillance was a waste of time. Even dying of can-cer, Lockman would not change his act. He knew too much about police work not to suspect a bug.

All Lockman had to do to convince himself he was the winner, Boudreau knew, was to keep his mouth shut until death shut his mouth for him. Nobody wanted even one last Q&A, because allowing Lockman to make a game of his silence would keep the focus on him until the very last. Lockman would die knowing there never would be a trial, so he could never be convicted—and if there wasn't any evidence now, there never would be, just ever-mounting conjecture—*perhaps*. The Green River killings remained unsolved, and that would be enough victory for him. He would be the object of study as long as crimes were committed. Maybe he would even become an immortal, the Elvis of serial killers.

His status in the Serial Killer Hall of Fame was passing through Lock-man's mind all the time. Phil Boudreau was sure he had murdered more than a hundred women in the fifteen years since Deeah Anne Johanssen had had the bad luck to cross his path. She had done that at a critical mo-ment in the development of a personality that defined itself first, accord-ing to the texts, with animal torture, bedwetting, and fire starting, and was hardened in an environment that was itself psychopathic, or at least bor-derline. Johanssen's possibly accidental death had shown Lockman that committing murder gave him an overwhelming sexual pleasure. And here was the personality's final self-definition, moments before its own death, itself fitting the statistical pattern of these guys dying sooner than later, and often violently. Far from being an original, in an eerie way Lockman had spent his whole life on a well-charted route to oblivion. A wonderful career for the born loser who wanted to be remembered exactly as he was. The complete narcissist, Lockman loved himself for a life he had fashioned as if evil could be made into art. How do you stop a boy from becoming a puke when he's so low in self-esteem that the idea intoxicates him?

Lockman had always chosen evil. He had wallowed in its process.

Boudreau caught his own process later in the afternoon. Under it all, he was thinking of himself as the one who had been defeated. The idea failed the reality test. Lockman was the one who was dying.

The next afternoon during a typical Kauai tropical shower Diane won a round of Stump the Bartender. She ordered a Negroni. The bartender, who was in his twenties, had never seen a Negroni except in books. At that moment he could not remember any of the ingredients. "Like taking candy from a baby," she whispered so only Boudreau could hear as she scooped the wad of paper money out of the brandy snifter. "I'm going to blow you to dinner. Or whatever."

MARCH 1991

The black rental sedan rolled noisily into Lockman's snow-covered drive-way, rousing him from a groggy, heavily drugged unconsciousness. Even in his stupor he immediately felt apprehensive and angry, for he had asked his visitor yesterday to call from the airport when he arrived in Spokane. Lockman couldn't be sure if he remembered hearing the telephone ring a little while ago or not. With difficulty he turned in the bed to push the button signaling Jessie, the live-in nurse. Outside, the automobile engine kept running. Lockman could imagine his guest behind the wheel, trying to get himself together, taking deep breaths, noting his sweaty palms.

All of Lockman's joints hurt. His ankles were swollen to twice their natural size. Jessie was not responding, as usual. In addition to her sloth and inattention, Jessie added still another burden to Lockman's travails. Jessie was a politically alert *Negress*. Now the floor creaked. She was at the kitchen door.

"What do you want?"

"Would you come around so I can see who I'm talking to? Just a little courtesy."

She appeared over him, her huge round head floating like a furry dirigible against the dusty gray ceiling. "All right, how's this? Now, what do you want?"

The place stank of disinfectant, urine, and feces. "Did the telephone ring about a half an hour ago?"

"Yeah." All old Hazel would need to start spinning in her grave was to know that the last woman to keep this house while it was in the Lockman name was someone of the African persuasion. Probably carrying off the world's own load of trophies, too. Lockman was going to be buried with Hazel. And Al. Lockman wished he had had the courage to bury Hazel facedown, her waffled old ass on *receive. Never in her life.* Jessie said, "Gentleman told me he was on his way from the airport."

"Why didn't you tell me?"

"You were sleepin'. What are you gonna do about it anyway? Come on, boy, get real. What in the world are you gonna do about it?"

"I've wet myself again, I know I have."

"No, you haven't, I cleaned you up an hour ago. Why don't you stop all this stuff and enjoy the time you got left?"

She turned to leave. Two of the three most important black women in history were Aunt Jemima and Mother Fucker. Lockman couldn't remember the third. The engine outside stopped, a car door opened and closed, and a shadow swept darkly across the ceiling as the visitor passed the window as he headed toward the front door. The bell rang. Jessie stopped. "Who is this guy?"

Lockman pulled his atrophied facial muscles into a smile. "A friend. It's okay."

"I don't want you to have no coughing fit. One too many of them is going to kill your sorry ass."

"I appreciate your concern."

She opened the door. Phil Boudreau stepped in, his raincoat over his arm. The gray in his thinning hair surprised Lockman all over again. Boudreau looked around until he saw Lockman in the hospital bed in the far end of the living room. Lockman watched Boudreau's eyes widen momentarily. Lockman got it all the time now, from Al's lawyer, from the head of the agency that had supplied Jessie. Lockman just had to look at his hands to know his appearance was horrible.

"All right, the place smells of piss," he said genially. "At least it's mine. Come on in. Do you want anything to drink? Jessie will get you a cup of coffee."

"Who might you be?" Jessie demanded.

Boudreau pulled his badge from the inside pocket of his jacket. "I'd like you to go into the family room, close the door, and turn on the TV. I'll get you when I'm done."

"He has no jurisdiction here," Lockman croaked.

"Everywhere in the state, Garrett," Boudreau said, looking him in the eye.

"I'm gonna believe him," Jessie said to Lockman. "You look comfortable enough." She turned to Boudreau. "Now, do you want somethin' to drink?"

"No, thanks."

"I'm incontinent now," Lockman said as she exited. "What we all have to look forward to."

"Some of us."

Lockman pulled himself up to a sitting position. "You, too. You'll die in bed. Like this. An inch at a time. I wish it on you. You deserve it. You have no idea what the pain is like. Sit over here so I can breathe my cancer on you. For all we know, it really is contagious. You keep reading of cancer researchers dying of it. Who knows?"

Boudreau sat down in the wooden chair facing the bed. With the window behind him, Lockman could see a lot of Boudreau's scalp. Close up, Boudreau appeared to have aged twenty years in the nine Lockman had known him. Boudreau was looking into his eyes. "What do you weigh now?"

"How long do I have to live, you mean? Right now I weigh about a hundred and ten. How do I look? We have all the mirrors covered. It's like an episode from *The Twilight Zone*. I promised myself I'd live until spring. According to the calendar, it's here, but it's still winter outside. One last twist of the knife."

"It's a sunny day. The runoff is pouring into sewers downtown. Hang on for a week."

"How do I look? Tell me."

"What do friends like Martin Jones say?"

Boudreau wanted to play the Martin Jones game again? He had forgotten how many times over the months and years he had mentioned Jones, that he had made it a red flag. But Lockman gave Boudreau points for patience.

The mass under Lockman's ribs that pressed painfully on his lungs and heart now made him reach for his oxygen mask. He took three deep inhalations, paused, and then took a fourth. He waited until he had his breath again. "I haven't seen Jones since I got out of jail. He says he doesn't want to spend the money to fly over, but in fact he's scared. Are you wearing a wire?"

"No."

"Is this place bugged? I've been wondering."

"Not by the investigative team. But that isn't to say that some other interested party isn't listening."

"Who?"

Boudreau shrugged. "The tabloids. Television."

Lockman laughed. "But I'm not a suspect. They believe whatever you tell them. How can I believe you about anything?" He half gestured toward the family room. "How do I know *she* isn't a cop?" He didn't have the strength to walk to the family room and back without being held up, without forgetting where he was going before he was halfway across the room.

"It doesn't make any difference, Garrett. There's nothing you can do about it anyway."

"Christ, you even sound like her. She *is* a cop!"

Boudreau shrugged again.

"What do you want? You look like you hope I'm going to tell you that some monster grew inside of me and took control. Oh, wait, I can get to the bottom of this. Who paid for your airline ticket?"

"I did. I put it on a credit card."

"Did you come here in the hope I'd confess? A single word, yes, no, to put your little heart at peace? If I have to die young, you can live your long life not knowing." He stopped to get his breath. "If you didn't come to hear me confess, then you came to gloat, no matter what you tell yourself, and somehow, Frenchy, I expected better of you." He had to catch his breath again. "You didn't come to gloat, did you? If you did, why are you beating a dead horse, if you don't mind my saying?"

"Let's back up. You're the one who originally called me."

Lockman groped for the oxygen. His lungs were burning. This time he took seven pulls on the mask. He pushed himself up again. "You're not pulling that one on me. I called you months and months ago while I was still in the federal joint in Oregon. Let's assume for the moment that it really does take you five months to return a call. I don't remember what I wanted to talk about. Ah, you're *not* gloating. So then you really did fly all the way over here because you think I'm going to confess. Very funny."

"Nothing like that, Garrett. We know you did it. You don't have to say anything. I'm just here to wrap up a few loose ends. First, Waldo Starr. The tape of your collect call to Starr about Sonya Moore—"

"What do you mean? You can't just tape calls from a prison pay phone. Where is this tape?"

"The FBI has the original. I don't know how many copies there are now. A lot, believe me. I wasn't as impressed with your performance as some of the other guys, because you worked me over the same way. Or tried. Remember? Before I put you in jail. The guys who were impressed with the tape said listening to you work on Starr was worse than watching a cat bite the head off a bird."

Lockman clapped his hands. "This is great! I'm on my deathbed and you come here to harass me! If it wasn't for this happening, I'd be free— out there! I'd be out buying and selling my cars and zooming over all the interstates. And the hell with you."

Boudreau smiled. "No, I don't think so. You came close to dying a long time ago—"

"When was this?"

"While you were in law school here. After we found the body of Betty Antonelli. I was a hundred feet behind you. I was thinking about shooting you in the back of the head, but I couldn't take the next step."

"Did you know her?"

"Did you?"

Lockman was silent. Antonelli was the one who had looked vaguely familiar to him. After a couple of days on the obstretician's table she had been able to help him realize why: he had seen her coming out of the Public Safety Building years before. At the end of her life she wouldn't tell him what she had been doing there. She had fought him to the very end. She had been . . . *unsatisfactory*. After the arrest he had wondered why Boudreau had mentioned her. Now Lockman knew. She had been in the Public Safety Building seeing Boudreau. On personal business.

Delicious!

"If, as you say, you failed at murder, why did you say you didn't think I'd be zooming around the interstates now? Tell me about it."

"We had a meeting about you."

"What meeting? Oh, tell me. Tell me about this meeting."

"Hmm?" He was acting as if he hadn't been paying attention. Lockman tried to push himself up again.

"Don't fuck with me, Boudreau. You said there was a meeting."

"Let's see. We decided not to cooperate with the media when they call for help with your obituary. One of the reasons you murdered all those girls was to make yourself famous. As much as we can, we're going to keep that from happening."

Lockman moved to offset the pain under his ribs. "Who was at this meeting?"

"People who have been with the case from beginning to end. A few invited others. We wanted to add up what we had on you. The fact that the disappearances stopped when you left the Seattle area, that what you told Beale and Cheong you were doing when the record always shows you were doing something else, that everything you ever said to them was a lie to keep your run going. We called the meeting because we wanted to find out what kind of consensus we had on you. We agreed unanimously that you were guilty. Thanks to your knowledge of police procedure and the rules of evidence, we didn't have evidence to convict in court, just our own judgment based on years of experience. We had to figure out what to do about you. That's what the meeting was about."

"And you decided to keep me from being famous. What are you, Froggo, some kind of clown? You expect me to believe this tall tale?"

"In the end we figured we had the responsibility to kill you. As I say, we drew strength from each other."

Lockman was up on one elbow. The pain in his abdomen was awful. "Kill me?" He began to cough loudly. He was reaching for the oxygen as Jessie came rushing from the family room. She took the mask and pressed it firmly to his face as she cranked up the valve. He wanted to keep coughing, but she lifted him up as she continued to press the oxygen mask to his face. The cancer was in his lungs now, and if he did not have the painkillers, he would be screaming in agony. His arms hurt, his ankles, even his toes. In his abdomen was a solid, growing mass of pain. He had not gotten an erection in a year, had not had a clear thought of Deeah Anne Johanssen in all that time. Had her soul lived in his dick all these years? Instead he had bedsores. Shit was dried on his ass no matter what Jessie said about keeping him clean. He would be buried with shit stuck to him.

"Get out," he said to her.

She looked to Boudreau, who nodded.

"She is a cop!"

"No, Garrett, her son works for the Spokane Sheriff's Department. She came to work here only when you were too debilitated to cause anyone trouble. The house is not bugged. At this point, a lot of people don't want evidence of your guilt in Green River in existence."

"Bullshit! You still have your hopes up! You want vindication! What's this crap about killing me?"

"We also figured we had the right to tell you. The right to rub it in. Make sure you knew you hadn't gotten away with it. That we got you." Boudreau reached into his coat pocket and withdrew a little amber bottle capped with an eyedropper, which he unscrewed. "You complained about the food in jail?"

"What?"

"You complained that it smelled funny. You complained that it tasted funny." Boudreau stood up and waved the open bottle under Lockman's nose. "Did your food smell like this?"

Boudreau gave him another whiff. Lockman stared at the vial. His heart was pounding in his chest as he hadn't felt it in months. In prison, after a certain point, his whole life had taken on that smell. He looked up. He had seen Boudreau's expression before. His eyes were hooded, deadly. "What is that?"

"A steroid. Like cortisone. Very liver-toxic. Massive, steady oral doses *always* cause cancer. Does that sound like a tall tale to you? A *joke*?"

March 1991

"You're a liar!"

"Face it, Garrett, if we had allowed you to walk out of jail, you would have killed another teenager before you got around the first corner. Ted Bundy proved that. You gave us no choice. Believe it, just as sure as you're lying there dying."

Boudreau capped the bottle and put it back in his coat pocket. He could barely look at Lockman, there was so little left of him. Diane had gotten descriptions of what Lockman's appearance would be like from her medical friends, but they had not prepared Boudreau for this horror. Lockman's eyes had lost their definition, dark holes in a waxen skull. His wrist seemed as thin and frail as a bundle of twigs wrapped in a gray rag. Boudreau could see death all over him. *An inch at a time* described it. Lockman wasn't just dying, he was becoming death. From the inside out.

"You *murdered* me?"

"Did you really think we were going to let you get away with murdering all those girls for your sexual pleasure because of *some fucking rules?*"

In fact only six people had attended the meeting, which had been called by Randall Murray. Les Lucas had sat on the edge of his chair, ashen. He had known what was coming. Beale had broken down and sobbed. He and Cheong had lied about Atlantic City to protect the best informant they had ever had. That was the least of it. He and Lockman had discussed the Green River killings almost every time they had talked, as often as once a week over a period of two and a half years. Lockman had had Beale's home telephone number when the first anonymous call had come in, but Beale was certain that the voice had not been Lockman's and the call not long-distance. But people higher up the political totem pole than the investigative team were ready to believe that the evidence that Lockman had been out of town for the first five killings had been faked. No one doubted that Garrett Richard Lockman had been the principal perpetrator in the Green River killings. If Lockman had had a partner, some were thinking, he could have killed him before returning to Spokane. Boudreau was still thinking Jones, but he had no interest, no support, no budget. Now that Lockman was dying, most people wanted the case behind them, exactly on the terms Boudreau had just described.

"You murdered me!"

Boudreau stood up. "Now you know what you did to those girls. I owed this trip to myself. I had to see." Boudreau was still willing to believe that thinking about what Lockman had done and why he had done it had almost driven him insane. He knew Lockman would never confess to having stalked Adrienne, as clearly as his statements pointed to the fact.

Without a word of direct conversation on the subject, Diane knew what was happening. She said Boudreau's grimness reminded her of her uncle who had been on strike for a year. Part of her book had been about her rediscovery of her blue-collar roots and how proud she was of them. "Who does the dirty work?" she had asked him, not expecting an answer. "Whatever it takes," she had said.

Paulie wasn't so intuitive. He was thinking his old man had to recover. A child, even one as old as Paul, didn't know enough about the real world to be able to imagine this, that someone might be changed forever. Newly minted Detective Wayne Spencer was long past childhood: changes in people's behavior had allowed him to grasp what kind of decision had been reached and now he wanted to hear every word from Lockman's mouth this afternoon, every detail. On the other hand, Les Lucas never wanted to discuss the case again.

Lockman reached for him with a withered arm. "Your lives are so perfect you could decide whether I could have one at all?"

"We're going to live comfortably with this. You might have lived another thirty or forty years. Think about that in the time you have left. Who took your life. And why."

Lockman blinked. "You'll never know if I was one of them."

"One of who?"

"Those guys with your first wife. With your kid in the next room. What she talked about, that she still loved you, how she couldn't understand why you had left her—"

"Why didn't you kill her when you had the chance?"

Lockman smiled softly. "I would have been caught. See? Now you're wondering. Was I one of them?"

"You're going to die an asshole, Lockman. Good-bye. Your last moments are going to be particularly horrible. The painkillers don't work at all at the end. You'll beg for death. Beg for hell. And go knowing we've done everything but put a tag on your toe to see that you get there."

Without looking again at Lockman, Boudreau buttoned his coat. He crossed to the family room and rapped on the door and turned away before it opened. He had to get out. He had seen enough smelly pasteboard suburban tombs to last him a lifetime.

"I didn't do anything!" Lockman rasped. "You've killed an innocent man!"

Boudreau did not look back. Outside, he tried to expel the air in his lungs before he took a new, deep breath. In the car he looked back at the living-room windows, thinking of Lockman inside. Was he complaining to the nurse? Or did he really know that it was too late for that? That Boudreau had held off from this visit until Lockman was too weak to operate a telephone? According to Diane's medical friends, Lockman had only hours before the onset of the final coma. For all Boudreau knew, Lockman was beginning to die at this moment.

Everything here in Spokane was much smaller than Boudreau had remembered, and he had allotted himself more time than he had needed for his business. He wasn't hungry; it might be days before he would want to eat again. He would be getting to the airport more than an hour ahead of schedule.

On the other hand, he was thinking, if he hurried, he might be able to catch an earlier flight back to Seattle. The weather was clear, and by day the trip was really quite beautiful. If he caught a jet, he would be in Seattle in an hour.

June 1991

The girl waited in the rain for the driver of the car to power the passenger window down. She leaned into the quiet dry darkness inside. "Want to party? You want to have a good time?"

"How much?"

"How much do you wanna spend? A hundred bucks gets you a real good time."

Martin Jones released the electric door lock. "Get in the car," he said. "I have a place not far from here. You don't mind posing for pictures, do you? I'll pay you extra."

POLICE CONFIRM SERIAL MURDERER
APPEARS TO BE AT WORK IN AREA

The disappearances of 12 women and the murders of 29 others in King, Pierce, and Snohomish counties since 1985 are being tracked as possible serial killings, some most likely linked, King County police are now saying. . . .

No one is saying any of the murders since 1985 are the work of the Green River serial killer, but whoever is doing the killing shares some habits with the notorious murderer: he abducts mostly prostitutes, kills them, and leaves their bodies in rural areas . . .

—the Seattle *Times*
January 22, 1993